U0066662

瑞蘭國際

瑞蘭國際

瑞蘭國際

瑞蘭國際

領隊導遊英文一本搞定！

陳若慈 著

最實用的「領隊導遊英文」應考用書

相信讀者們從小到大、從國中到高中，求學路上所唸的英文和生活可能都沒有太大的關連，只是為了考試而唸，背完就忘，且英文考題中的冷僻單字、硬梆梆的文法，和自己想像中唸完就可以開口說一些簡單的會話似乎也有落差。然而，身為領隊、導遊，最重要的職責就是溝通，也因此領隊導遊英文考試，都以實務上常見的單字、議題為主，其中包含了交通、住宿、觀光景點等等，都是實際旅途中真正會用到的英文！

正由於領隊導遊英文考試和其他一般的學校、公職考試相較之下不那麼的死板，所以學習方法當然也不必死K硬記。建議除了考古題之外，只要平時多瀏覽相關的旅遊英文資訊，或是國外的旅遊網站（詳見附錄），那麼在賞心悅目、吸收新知之餘，一定還能練習到英文，不失為實用又輕鬆的準備領隊導遊英文考試的方法。

在準備考試時，多看與旅遊相關的英文資訊也會有諸多幫助，但相信大部分的考生，若是沒有一本正式的領隊導遊英文參考書籍在手，還是心有不安。然而目前市面上有關此類的應考書籍，只是單純地將所有單字未經消化、分類地一昧列出，考古題的解析也只是將題目翻譯出來。如此一來，對於需要快速入門、吸收內容的考生來說並沒有太多的幫助，太多資訊反而會導致統整上的混亂。有鑑於此，《領隊導遊英文一本搞定！》有別於其他參考書籍，特別於Part 1就先將最常考的重點依情境整理出來，讓沒有頭緒的考生可以迅速了解命題方向；而在Part 2和Part 3實際練習考古題後，也有非常詳盡的解析可供參考。本書不只希望考生及格而已，更重要的是希望讀者能快速地了解、吸收領隊導遊英文，縮短考前衝刺的寶貴時間，一舉金榜題名，順利成為一名出色的領隊、導遊！

有任何問題，也歡迎上Facebook https://www.facebook.com/tourguideEnglish一同討論。

陳若慈

關於專門職業及技術人員普通考試導遊人員、領隊人員考試

簡單來說，本項考試就是為了取得導遊、領隊證照的考試。然而領隊、導遊考的科目各有不同，唯一相同的是兩者都會考「外語」這科。而《領隊導遊英文一本搞定！》，就是為了這兩種應試類別中的科目——外語（英語）所撰寫的。

應考資格：

凡中華民國國民，具有下列資格之一者，即可應考：

一、公立或立案之私立高級中學或高級職業學校以上學校畢業，領有畢業證書或學位證書者。（同等學力者，須附教育部核發之同等學力及格證書）

二、初等考試或相當等級之特種考試及格，並曾任有關職務滿四年，有證明文件者。

三、高等或普通檢定考試及格者。

應試科目：

導遊人員考試分成「筆試」與「口試」二試，第一試「筆試」錄取者，才可以參加第二試「口試」。領隊人員考試則僅有「筆試」。

<table>
<tr><th colspan="2" rowspan="2">應試類別</th><th colspan="2">應試科目</th></tr>
<tr><th>第一試（筆試）</th><th>第二試（口試）</th></tr>
<tr><td>導遊人員</td><td>外語導遊人員</td><td>1、導遊實務（一）：包括導覽解說、旅遊安全與緊急事件處理、觀光心理與行為、航空票務、急救常識、國際禮儀。
2、導遊實務（二）：包括觀光行政與法規、台灣地區與大陸地區人民關係條例、兩岸現況認識。
3、觀光資源概要：包括台灣歷史、台灣地理、觀光資源維護。
4、外國語：分英語、日語、法語、德語、西班牙語、韓語、泰語、阿拉伯語、俄語、義大利語、越南語、印尼語、馬來語等十三種，由應考人任選一種應試。</td><td>採外語個別口試，就應考人選考之外國語舉行個別口試，並依外語口試規則規定辦理。</td></tr>
<tr><td>領隊人員</td><td>外語領隊人員</td><td>1、領隊實務（一）：包括領隊技巧、航空票務、急救常識、旅遊安全與緊急事件處理、國際禮儀。
2、領隊實務（二）：包括觀光法規、入出境相關法規、外匯常識、民法債編旅遊專節與國外定型化旅遊契約、台灣地區與大陸地區人民關係條例、兩岸現況認識。
3、觀光資源概要：包括世界歷史、世界地理、觀光資源維護。
4、外國語：分英語、日語、法語、德語、西班牙語等五種，由應考人任選一種應試。</td><td>不需口試。</td></tr>
</table>

※注意！應試科目均採測驗式試題，因此英語考試也都是四選一的選擇題，共計80題。

及格標準與成績計算方式：

一、外語導遊人員考試，筆試+口試平均加總成績滿60分為及格。

筆試：即為第一試，成績占75%（如上方表格外語導遊人員4科：導遊實務（一）＋導遊實務（二）＋觀光資源概要＋外語）。筆試成績滿60分為及格標準，依以上4科成績平均計算。但若筆試有一科為0分（缺考亦以0分計算），或外國語科目成績未滿50分，都不算及格，也不能參加口試。

口試：即為第二試，成績占25%。首先筆試（第一試）平均成績須達60分，才有資格參加口試。口試成績則須滿60分才及格。

簡單來說，也就是筆試成績須及格（滿60分），才有口試資格，口試也須滿60分，才會錄取。而其中任一科均不得缺考、或是0分，且外語筆試至少須達50分，整體才算及格。

二、外語領隊人員考試，筆試平均加總成績滿60分為及格。

以4科筆試成績平均計算（如上方表格外語領隊人員4科：領隊實務（一）＋領隊實務（二）＋觀光資源概要＋外語）。筆試成績平均滿60分為及格標準，但若筆試有一科為0分（缺考亦以0分計算），或外國語科目成績未滿50分，都不算及格。

※注意！導遊、領隊考試平均考試成績須滿60分才算及格，但單就英語筆試這科，若未滿50分，即便其他科目再高分、平均成績有達60分，也不算及格！

資格取得：

一、考試及格人員，由考選部報請考試院發給考試及格證書，並函交通部觀光局查照。但外語導遊人員、外語領隊人員考試及格人員，應註明選試外國語言別。

二、前項考試及格人員，經交通部觀光局訓練合格，得申領執業證。

相關考試訊息：

測驗名稱：專門職業及技術人員普通考試導遊人員、領隊人員考試

測驗日期：每年3月（筆試）及5月（口試）

放榜日期：當年4月（筆試）及6月（口試）

等　　級：專技普考

測驗地點：分台北、桃園、新竹、台中、嘉義、台南、高雄、花蓮、台東、澎湖、金門、馬祖十二考區舉行。

報名時間：前一年11月開放報名

實施機構：考選部專技考試司

更多相關資料，請上考選部網站查詢。

http://wwwc.moex.gov.tw

考前準備要領

準備考試，特別是英文這科，除了需要時間、精力之外，其實很大一部分是心理仗。相信很多準備領隊導遊英文的考生，可能很久沒有碰英文了，或者即便陸陸續續有使用英文，但是看到密密麻麻每份有80題的英文試題，還是會頭皮發麻。雖然網路上許多過來人的建議都是「把考古題做完一遍就對了！」但如此苦幹實幹的硬道理，可能只適用於本身英文程度就不錯的考生，對於那些老早就把英文忘光光的考生，若不是意志堅強、耐力十足，相信很難乖乖把一篇篇的考古題做完。

然而準備領隊導遊英文是有訣竅和方法的，因此，依照不同的程度，閱讀本書的順序也有所不同。《領隊導遊英文一本搞定！》特別替不同程度的考生分別打造最適合的準備要領，讓考生能以最少的時間掌握考試精髓，才有剩下的時間可以安心準備其它科目！

首先，先來看看自己符合以下哪一項：

初階　自認英文程度不佳，自從脫離學生時代，就幾乎再也沒有碰過英文，程度停留在高中英文，甚至程度需要打7折，屬於只要看到英文就頭痛的考生。

中階　自認英文程度還可以，看到英文不害怕，即便無法完全了解，也能猜出大概的意思，工作或生活上也不算是與英文脫節的考生。

高階　不論是工作、生活，或多或少都會用到英文，雖然不算頂尖，但基本的聽說讀寫幾乎都沒問題的考生。（這裡的高階其實算是自已與周遭英文程度的比較級，絕非專業程度的高級。相信專業人士也不需要閱讀此書，即可直接應試。）

本書為了以上3種程度的考生，特別設計3種不同的使用要領，幫助考生以最輕鬆的方式準備考試！

在開始之前，先了解本書的架構：

Part 1　本書將歷屆考題去蕪存菁，嚴選最常考的16大命題，挑出16大類相關的必考關鍵字群組，有別於單字未經統合整理的參考用書，以情境方式分類，將相關字組一網打盡，好閱讀、好記，最能事半功倍。

Part 2 + Part 3　本書收錄98-102領隊、導遊英文考古題共10回，並且為這10回做了解析。特別要注意的是，這部分的解析不單只是單純的答案以及翻譯。解析已將考題整理成完整的句子，所以不會有填空的問題。此外重點字也特別做了標注，所以可以說是最詳盡的考題解析。總之，這是一份挑出重點、統整必考單字、列出其它屆類似考題，並分析其中差異的完全解析，每一篇都是歷屆考題精華集錦！每看完一篇，都像做完兩篇試題一樣功力倍增！重點保證不漏接！

Part 4　領隊、導遊各有一篇最常考的精選考古題，以及答案解析。

使用要領：

初階　由於大部分的考生程度都屬於初階，初階當中又有一部分是相當害怕英文、不知從何開始的考生，故將初階再分為「從零開始」以及「入門」兩個使用說明，讀者可選擇適合自己的方式。

	Part 1 ➡	Part 4 ➡	Part 2 + 3
從零開始	先將Part 1看完一遍，熟悉關鍵單字。	直接從精選考古題的解析看起，將解析當成重點整理來研讀，看完一篇之後再試做該篇的精選考題。	先挑看完其中幾篇解析，而後才做考題。熟悉考試模式後，再挑從未看過解析的考古題小試身手。
入門	先將Part 1看完一遍，熟悉關鍵單字。	直接試做精選考題（多半已出現在Part 1中），再比對答案以及閱讀解析。	評估自己在Part 4的表現，若覺得需要再加強，則先挑幾篇看完解析，再做考古題。

中階 自認英文程度還可以，建議先做精選考題，測驗一下自己的程度，而後再看Part 1，都熟悉之後，可直接進入歷屆考題。

	Part 4 ➡	Part 1 ➡	Part 2 + 3
中階	先將Part 4做完一遍，並看解析，了解自己的不足的地方。	再看Part 1的重點整理，了解考試方向及重點。	直接做考題，而後比對解析。若途中覺得過難，建議挑幾篇先看解析，再回頭做題目。

高階 英文程度不錯的考生則可直接練習歷屆考古題，而後再翻閱Part 1複習重點，於考前再做一遍Part 4精選考古題即可。

	Part 2 + 3 ➡	Part 1 ➡	Part 4
高階	直接做考題，而後比對解析。	確保重點不漏接。	考前再做精選考題，溫習考題以及解析重點。

目　錄

Part 1 領隊導遊英文必考重點

1 航空

作者私囊

和機場、飛機等等相關的主題、句子，保證是一考再考。所延伸的飛安、轉機等情境主題，也請務必熟記相關用法。而這篇也依序整理出，一到達機場，一路到飛機上的相關考古題。

抵達機場 / 辦理登機手續

關鍵單字

the check-in desk 辦理登機手續的櫃台

arrival desk 入境櫃台

claim baggage 認領行李

baggage claim tag 行李存根

confirm 確認

reconfirm 再次確認

present 出席的

land 著陸、抵達

loyalty points 會員點數

departure lounge 候機室

customs 海關

weigh luggage 秤重行李

baggage allowance 行李限額

confirm flight 確認班機

confirm reservation 確認預約

depart、take off 起飛

baggage carousel 行李轉盤

points 點數

baggage claim office / counter / center 行李領取中心

必考佳句

- When you arrive at the airport, the first thing you do is go to the check-in desk.
  當你到達機場時，第一件事就是要去辦理登機手續的櫃台。 100導遊

- When we get to the airport, we first go to the check-in desk where the airline representatives weigh our luggage.
  當我們到達機場，首先我們到櫃台辦理登機手續，此處的航空公司工作人員會將我們的行李秤重。 98導遊

- We arrived at the airport in good time, so we had plenty of time for checking in and boarding.

  我們及時抵達機場，所以還有很多時間可以辦理登機。99領隊

- Even though you have confirmed your flight with the airline, you must still be present at the check-in desk on time.

  即便你已經和航空公司確認班機，你還是必須準時到辦理登機手續的櫃台報到。99導遊

- The flight is scheduled to depart at eleven o'clock tomorrow. You will have to get to the airport two hours before the takeoff.

  班機預定於明天11點起飛，你必須在起飛前2個小時抵達機場。99導遊

- Though most airlines ask their passengers to check in at the airport counter two hours before the flight, some international flights require their passengers to be at the airport three hours before departure.

  雖然多數的航空公司要求乘客於班機起飛前2個小時到機場的櫃台登記，有些國際線班機還是需要乘客在起飛3小時前到達機場。102導遊

- I was overjoyed to learn that I had accumulated enough loyalty points to upgrade myself from coach to business class.

  我感到超級開心，因為我已經累積足夠會員點數讓我從普通艙升級到商務艙。101領隊

- Tourist: What is the baggage allowance?

  Airline clerk: It is 20 kilograms per person.

  旅客：行李的限額是多少？

  航空公司職員：每個人20公斤。

- As a general rule, checked baggage such as golf clubs in golf bags, serfboards, baby strollers, and child car seats are not placed on a baggage carousel.

  一般來説，託運行李像是高爾夫球俱樂部的高爾夫球袋、衝浪板、嬰兒推車以及兒童安全座椅不會被放在行李轉盤上。100導遊

證件

關鍵單字

pick up 領取

passport 護照

get on / get off airplane 上 / 下飛機

entry permit 入境許可證

boarding pass 登機證

identification 證件

expiry date 到期日

visa 簽證（申請passport或是visa都是用「apply 申請」）

必考佳句

- Now you can purchase a seat and pick up your boarding pass at the airport on the day of departure by simply showing appropriate identification.
  現在你可以買票（購買座位），並且於出發當天於機場出示適當證件來領取登機證。
  101領隊

- A boarding pass is a necessary document for the passenger to get on the airplane.
  登機證是乘客登機的重要文件。 99導遊

- You will get a boarding pass after completing the check-in.
  在完成登機報到手續之後，你將會拿到一張登機證。

- People traveling to a foreign country may need to apply for a visa.
  人們到國外旅行可能需要申請簽證。 98領隊

- You must check the expiry date of your passport. You may need to apply for a new one.
  你必須檢查您的護照的到期日。你也許需要重新申請一本新的。 100領隊

- If you're travelling to the United States, you may need a visa.
  如果你到美國旅行，你可能需要簽證。 100領隊

❂ He got his visa at the eleventh hour.

他在最後一刻拿到簽證。98領隊

❂ When traveling in a foreign country, we need to carry with us several important documents at all times. One of them is our passport together with the entry permit if that has been so required.

當在外國旅遊，我們需要隨身攜帶幾份重要的文件。如果被要求的話，其中一項就是我們的護照和入境許可證。102導遊

安全檢查 / 飛安相關

關鍵單字

leave the ground 起飛

flight safety 飛行安全

airport security rules 機場安全規定

search 搜查

carry-on bags 隨身行李

ban 禁止

on board、in flight 飛機上

security check 安全檢查

result in 導致

carry 攜帶

prohibited items 違禁品

examine、inspect 檢查，兩者都為檢查之意，但inspect更有「權力」。

必考佳句

❂ Before the plane leaves the ground, we must watch a video related to flight safety.

在飛機起飛前，我們必須觀看和飛安有關的影片。100領隊

❂ Disobeying the airport security rules will result in a civil penalty.

違反機場安全規定會導致民法的刑責。101領隊

❂ Please examine your luggage carefully before leaving. At the security counter, every item in the luggage has to go through inspection.

在出發前請仔細檢查你的行李。在安檢櫃台時，行李內的每一項物品都會被檢查。

99導遊

❁ In the interests of safety, passengers should carry neither dangerous items nor matches while on board.

為了安全考量，乘客不能帶危險物品或是火柴登機。101領隊

▲ 重點：in the interests of 因為……的考量。

❁ For safety reasons, radios, CD players, and mobile phones are banned on board, and they must remain switched off until the aircraft has landed.

由於飛安的因素，收音機、CD播放器、手機都禁止在飛機上使用，且必須保持關機的狀態直到飛機降落。101領隊

❁ If you carry keys, knives, aerosol cans, etc., in your pocket when you pass through the security at the airport, you may set off the alarm, and then the airport personnel will come to search you.

如果你帶著鑰匙、小刀、噴霧罐等東西在你的口袋，當你通過機場的安檢區時，你可能會引發警報器，接著機場的人員會來搜查你。101領隊

❁ Prohibited items in carry-on bags will be confiscated at the checkpoints, and no compensation will be given for them.

隨身行李中的違禁品將會於檢查站被沒收，且沒有任何的補償。101領隊

❁ All passengers shall go through security check before boarding.

上機前所有旅客都應該通過安全檢查。98領隊

❁ Beware of strangers at the airport and do not leave your luggage unattended.

小心機場的陌生人，不要讓你的行李無人看管（在視線之外）。98領隊

▲ 重點：國外常見告示牌寫Please do not leave personal belongings unattended.。

海關 / 移民局

關鍵單字

immigration officer 移民官

customs 海關

aliens 外國人

passport control 護照審查管理處

hesitate 猶豫

customs officers 海關官員

deport 驅逐出境

clear customs 結關、清關或者通關，指進口貨物、出口貨物和轉運貨物時，進入一國海關關境或國境必須向海關申報，辦理海關規定的各項手續

必考佳句

- When answering questions of the immigration officer, it is advisable to be straight forward and not hesitating.
  當回答移民官的問題時，建議實話實說，並且不要猶豫。102導遊

- Customs officers usually have a stern-looking face and they have the right to ask us to open our baggage for searching.
  海關官員通常看起很嚴肅，而且他們有權利為了搜查的目的而要求我們打開行李。102導遊

- The man at the passport control did not seem to like the photo in my passport, but in the end he let me through.
  在護照審查管理處的人似乎不喜歡我的護照照片，但最後還是讓我通過了。101導遊

- It took us no time to clear customs at the border.
  於邊界通關沒有花我們什麼時間。102領隊

- Aliens who overstay their visas would be deported back to their country of birth.
  超過簽證時間的外國人會被驅逐出境送回他們的出生國家。102領隊

- Each country has its own regulations regarding fruit and vegetable imports.
  關於水果與蔬菜的進口，每個國家都有其規定。101領隊

登機前廣播

關鍵單字

require 需要

boarding gate 登機門

final boarding call、last call for boarding、final call announcement、final call
最後登機廣播

必考佳句

- "Good evening, ladies and gentlemen. This is the pre-boarding announcement for flight 67B to Vancouver. We are now inviting those passengers with small children, and any passenger requiring special assistance, to begin boarding at this time. Please have your boarding pass and identification ready. Regular boarding will begin in approximately ten minutes. Thank you."

  大家晚安，各位先生女士們。這是飛往溫哥華的67B班機的登機前廣播。我們現在先請帶小孩、或是需要特別協助的旅客，準備現在登機。請準備好您的登機證以及證件。一般旅客約將於10分鐘後登機，謝謝。98導遊

- This is the final boarding call for China Airline Flight 009 to Hong Kong at Gate C2.

  這是中華航空飛往香港的009班機於C2登機門的最後登機廣播。102導遊

- In some airports, there is the final call announcement, but in others, they only have blinking signals on the sign board. Passengers are responsible for their own arriving at the boarding gate in time.

  某些機場有最後登機的宣告，但有些沒有，只有告示牌上一閃一閃的訊號。乘客必須自行負責及時到達登機門。102導遊

- Didn't you hear the final call? Come on, we need to go now or we'll miss our flight.

  你沒有聽到登機前的最後廣播嗎？快點！我們要現在過去不然就會錯過班機了。100導遊

機組人員

關鍵單字

flight attendant 空服員

steward 空少

captain 機長

stewardess 空姐

cabin crew 機組人員

必考佳句

- On my flight to Tokyo, I asked a flight attendant to bring me an extra pillow.
  在前往東京的班機，我要求空服員給我額外的枕頭。101導遊

- Flight attendants help passengers find their seats and stow their carry-on luggage safely in the overhead compartments.
  空服員幫忙乘客找到座位，並且幫助他們將隨身行李安全地放於頭頂上的置物箱內。99導遊

座位相關

關鍵單字

window seat 靠窗的座位

middle seat 中間的座位

aisle seat 靠走道的座位

必考佳句

- Please check your ticket and make sure that you are sitting in the correct seat.
  請檢查你的票並確認你坐在正確的座位上。100導遊

  ⚠ 重點：make sure 確定。

- When I take a flight, I always ask for an aisle seat, so it is easier for me to get up and walk around.
  當我搭飛機時，我總是要求靠走道的座位，這讓我比較容易起身走動。98導遊

飛行中

關鍵單字

cruise 飛行、航行

fasten 繫緊

on board 在飛機上

taxi in 飛機在航道上滑行

turbulence 亂流

seat belt 安全帶

touch down 著陸

get off an airplane / a bus / a train 下飛機 / 巴士 / 火車

get on an airplane / a bus / a train 上飛機 / 巴士 / 火車

必考佳句

- The airplane is cruising at an altitude of 30,000 feet at 700 kilometers per hour.
  飛機目前以每小時700公里的速度，航行於30,000英呎的海拔上。 98領隊

- Airliners now cruise the ocean at great speed.
  飛機目前以高速來越洋飛行。 98領隊

- I was very scared when our flight was passing through turbulence from the nearby storm.
  當飛機通過來自附近暴風的亂流時我真是嚇壞了。 101導遊

★ 機上遇到亂流時，經常會廣播以下注意事項：

例句 "We are approaching some turbulence. For your safety, please keep your belts fastened until the 'seat belt' sign goes off."
「我們正接近某個亂流，為了你的安全，請繫緊安全帶直到座位安全帶的指示燈熄滅。」 101領隊

例句 Please keep your seat belt fastened during the flight for safety.
為了安全，飛行途中請束緊您的安全帶。 98領隊

★ 補充：buckle up 繫好安全帶

例句 My father always asks everyone in the car to buckle up for safety, no matter how short the ride is.

不管路程多短，為了安全著想，我爸爸總是要求車上每個人都繫好安全帶。 101領隊

⚠ 重點：buckle up = fasten seatbelt 繫好安全帶。

- Please remain seated while the plane takes off.

  當飛機起飛時，請保持就坐。 99領隊

- I found myself on board an airplane.

  我發現我自己在飛機上。 100領隊

- After the plane touches down, we have to remain in our seats until we taxi in to the gate.

  飛機降落後，我們必須待在座位上，直到滑入機坪入口。 100領隊

- When you are ready to get off an airplane, you will be told not to forget your personal belongings.

  當你已經準備下飛機時，你將會被告知別忘了帶走你的隨身物品。 99導遊

- During take-off and landing, carry-on baggage must be placed in the overhead compartments or underneath the seat in front of you.

  在飛機起飛和降落其間，隨身行李都必須放置於頭頂上的行李隔間內，或是在你的座位底下。 101領隊

轉機

關鍵單字

direct flight 直飛班機

connecting flight 轉機班機

transfer 轉機

stopover 中途停留

必考佳句

- Passengers transferring to other airlines should report to the information desk on the second floor.
  要轉搭其他班機的旅客請到2樓的櫃台報到。101領隊

- Client: Are there any direct flights to Paris?
  Clerk: No, you would have to transfer in Amsterdam.
  客人：有到巴黎的直飛班機嗎？
  服務員：沒有，你必須到阿姆斯特丹轉機。102領隊

- The flight will make a stopover in Paris for two hours.
  飛機將短暫停留巴黎2個小時。101領隊

- Due to the delay, we are not able to catch up with our connecting flight.
  因為延遲，我們無法趕上我們的轉機班機。102領隊

班機延誤／取消

關鍵單字

delay 延誤

stormy weather 暴風天氣

impending 即將發生的、逼近的

due to 因為

divert 轉向

inclement weather 惡劣天氣

disaster 災害、災難

必考佳句

- There was a slight departure delay at the airport due to inclement weather outside.
  因為外面惡劣的天氣，機場班機起飛有些延誤。100領隊

- Our flight was diverted to Los Angeles due to the stormy weather in Long Beach.
  因為長灘的大風暴，我們的航班被迫轉向到洛杉磯。101領隊

⚠ 重點：diverted 被轉向。stormy weather = inclement weather 天氣惡劣。

✽ The airlines could have explained to us about the long flight delay, but they just kept us waiting and did not say anything.

航空公司大可以和我們解釋班機嚴重延誤的原因，但他們只是讓我們等，什麼也不說。 102導遊

✽ "Flight AB123 to Tokyo has been delayed. Please check the monitor for further information about your departure time."

飛往東京的AB123班機已延誤了，請查看螢幕上進一步關於起飛時間的訊息。 98導遊

⚠ 重點：check有各類的用法，考生請務必牢記，此處的check為查看、確認，check亦可作為帳單。check-in則為登機手續。

✽ As the flight to the Bahamas was delayed for eight hours, all passengers were going bananas.

飛往巴拿馬的班機延誤8小時，所有乘客都快氣瘋了。 98領隊

✽ Due to the impending disaster, we have to cancel our flight to Bangkok.

因為即將到來的災害，我們必須取消到曼谷的航班。 100領隊

✽ Due to the delay, we are not able to catch up with our connecting flight.

因為延遲，我們無法趕上我們的轉機班機。 102領隊

★補充：delay和postpone的不同

① postpone 延期

例句 If the rain doesn't stop soon, we should consider postponing Joe's farewell party.

如果雨再不停，我們應該考慮延期喬的歡送派對。 100導遊

例句 The meeting has been postponed to next Monday.

會議延到下星期一舉行。

postpone一般指有安排的延遲，常說明延到什麼時候。

② delay 延遲

常表示由於外界的原因而拖延，如：

例句 The storm delayed the flight. 班機因風暴延遲。

準備降落 / 下飛機

❁ After disembarking the flight, I went directly to the baggage claim to pick up my bags and trunks.

下飛機後，我直接走向行李認領處拿我的包包和行李箱。101領隊

⚠ 重點：常考單字為baggage claim 行李認領。

2 交通

作者私囊

不論是帶團，或是自助旅行，在旅途中一定會遇到各類型的交通英文，只要了解基本的單字，便能輕鬆了解題意。而這些單字除了考試之外，實際旅遊上也非常實用，快納入自己的口袋吧！

關鍵單字

transportation vehicles 交通工具

leave for / head to 前往某處

express 快的、直達的、快車

itinerary 旅程、路線

charter bus 遊覽車

zone 地帶、地區

guarantee 保證

get on 上車

maintain 維護

leave 離開

set route 固定的路線

destination 目的地

shuttle service 接駁巴士服務

instruction 命令、指示

insert into 插入

get off 下車

必考佳句

- All transportation vehicles should be well-maintained and kept in good running condition.
  所有的交通工具都該有完善的維護，且保持良好的運作狀態。98領隊

- This express train leaves at 9:30 am every day. You can plan a short walk before that in the itinerary.
  這班快車每天9點半出發。在那行程之前，你可以計劃散個步。99領隊

- When a train arrives, the first thing you need to do is to check if its destination matches with where you want to go before you step in.
  當火車到站，在你踏進車廂前，你需要做的第一件事就是確認目的地是否相符。

❂ A bus used for public transportation runs a set route; however, a charter bus travels at the direction of the person or organization that hires it.

用來當大眾運輸工具的巴士有固定的路線，然而，承租的巴士（遊覽車）依照租車的人或團體來行駛。101領隊

❂ I called to ask about the schedule of the buses heading to Kaoshiung.

我打電話過來問關於開往高雄的巴士時刻表。101領隊

❂ Some cities do not have passenger loading zones. It is advisable to follow the instruction of the tourist guide to get off or get on the tour bus to guarantee safety and comfort.

有些城市沒有乘客上下車的指定地方。因此建議遵照遊客指南來上下車來確保安全以及舒適。102導遊

❂ Our hotel provides free shuttle service to the airport every day.

我們飯店每天免費提供到機場的接駁巴士服務。99領隊

⚠ 重點：THSR Shuttle Bus 台灣高鐵接駁巴士，如從車站至機場兩點固定來回的，即稱shuttle bus。

❂ To use a TravelPass, you have to insert it into the automatic stamping machine when you get off.

要用旅遊通，當你下車時，你必須將票插入自動剪票機。99領隊

❂ The driver has made a request that you throw all your garbage in the bin at the front on your way out.

這位駕駛要求你們下車時將垃圾丟入前方的桶子內。98導遊

⚠ 重點：made a request也可作為ask，都為要求別人。

❂ A: "Excuse me. Can I take this seat?"

B: "Sorry, it is occupied."

A：「抱歉。我可以坐這個位子嗎？」

B：「抱歉，這座位有人坐。」101導遊

⚠ 重點：位子有人坐有2種常見說法，The seat is occupied / taken.而詢問位子是否有人坐，則可以說：Is this seat taken?

3 金錢

作者私囊

不可否認的，出門在外就是需要金錢！而此單元除了旅人常見到的換匯、退款等花費議題外，也包含經濟概況，甚至是個人理財、花費等，都是常見考題。請務必把握這大類的單字！

個人花費 / 購物

關鍵單字

cash 現金

traveler's check 旅行支票

foreign currencies 外幣

deposit 存入

surcharge 附加費用

refrain from 避免，有忍住、抑制之意

necessary 需要的

budget 動詞為控制預算，名詞為預算

A bargain is a bargain. 説話要算數

credit card 信用卡

exchange rate 匯率

withdraw 提領

savings account 儲蓄存款戶頭

transaction 交易

unnecessary 不需要的

stuff 物品、東西

bargain 好價錢

bargain-hunting 四處覓購便宜貨

currency exchange / money changing / exchange money 換匯

denominations 面額，In what denominations? 要什麼面額的？

charge 名詞為費用，動詞為收費，把帳掛在⋯⋯

budget airline / low-cost airline 廉價航空

必考佳句

- You can get cash from another country at the currency exchange at the airport.
  你可以在機場的換匯櫃台拿到其他國家的現金。（100導遊）

❁ Money changing can be complicated. When in doubt, always ask someone who is knowledgeable .

換匯可以是非常複雜的。當有疑慮時，請問了解的人。102導遊

❁ We don't recommend exchanging your money at the hotel because you won't get fair rate.

我們不建議你在飯店兌換你的錢，因為你不會有公平的匯率。99領隊

❁ May I have two hundred U.S. dollars in small denominations?

我可以兌換美金200美元的小額鈔票嗎？98領隊

❁ Client: I would like to change 500 US dollars into NT dollars.

Bank clerk: Certainly, sir. Please complete this form and make sure you put the full name in capitals.

客戶：我想要將500美元換成新台幣。

銀行行員：沒問題，請填此表格並且確保用大寫寫全名。100領隊

❁ I would like to withdraw $500 from my savings account.

我想從我的儲蓄帳戶內提500美元。98領隊

❁ This traveler's check is not good because it should require two signatures by the user.

旅行支票不好用因為它需要持有者的2份簽名。102領隊

❁ I would like to charge this to my American Express card, please.

我希望可以用我的美國運通卡付費，麻煩了。102領隊

❁ I'm afraid your credit card has already expired. Would you like to pay in cash instead?

恐怕你的信用卡已經過期了。你希望改以付現代替嗎？99領隊

❁ When you charge a foreign purchase to a bank credit card, such as MasterCard or Visa, all you lose with most cards is the 1 percent the issuer charges for the actual exchange.

當你用信用卡支付國外購物，像是MasterCard卡或是Visa卡，簽帳購物的損失是多收實際消費的1%附加費用。98領隊

- Other banks, however , add a surcharge of 2 to 3 percent on transactions in foreign currencies. Even with a surcharge, you generally lose less with a credit card than with currency or traveler's checks.

  其他銀行於外幣交易時則加收2-3%的附加費用。即便有附加費用，相較於付現或是旅行支票的損失還是比較少。98領隊

- Therefore, don't use traveler's checks as your primary means of foreign payment. But do take along a few $20 checks or bills to exchange at retail for those last minute or unexpected needs.

  所以不要以旅行支票當成國外付款的主要工具。但還是要準備幾張20美元面額的支票或鈔票，以便最後一刻或是臨時購物之需。98領隊

- The easiest way to look for the shop that you want to visit in a shopping center is to go to the directory or information desk when you fail to find out the answer from passers-by.

  要在購物中心找到想要逛的店家，當你問路人得不到答案時，最簡單的方式就是走到導覽區或是櫃台。102導遊

- A boutique is simply another name for a small specialty shop.

  精品店也表示是賣特殊紀念品的小商店。102導遊

- Sara bought a beautiful dress in a in a fashionable boutique district in Milan.

  莎拉在米蘭的流行時尚區的一間精品店買了一件漂亮的洋裝。101導遊

- To save money, buy just what you need and refrain from buying unnecessary stuff.

  為了省錢，只買你需要的東西，且克制不買不需要的東西。99導遊

- Parents should teach their children to budget their money at an early age. Otherwise, when they grow up, they will not know how to manage their money.

  父母應該在孩子還小時就教導他們如何控制花費，否則當小孩長大時，將不知如何理財。98導遊

- If you want to find the cheapest airplane ticket, bargains can usually be found through the Internet.

  如果你想要找最便宜的機票，通常可以在網路上找到好價錢。99導遊

❁ All drinks served on the airplane are complimentary.

所有在飛機上所供應的飲料都是免費的。98領隊

費用 / 退款

關鍵單字

complimentary 免費

fare （大眾運輸）票價

refund 退款

tax rebate 退稅

fee 費用

toll-free service line 免付費服務專線

compensation 補償

entitle 有……權力

必考佳句

❁ A complimentary breakfast of coffee and rolls is served in the lobby between 7 and 10 am.

免費的早餐有咖啡和捲餅於早上7點到10點在大廳供應。102領隊

❁ You will have to pay extra fees for overweight baggage.

你必須替超重的行李支付額外的費用。98領隊

❁ The museum charges adults a small fee, but children can go in for free.

博物館向成人收取少許入場費，但小孩則可以免費參觀。98導遊

❁ You will pay a fare of fifty dollars for your ferry ride.

你要付50元的費用來搭乘渡輪。98領隊

★補充：fee和fare的差別

① fee 服務費

pay the lawyer's fees 付律師費

a bill for school fees 學費帳單

② fare （大眾運輸）票價

例句 What is the bus fare to London? 到倫敦的公共汽車費是多少？

例句 travel at half / full / reduced fare 半價 / 全價 / 減價

例句 Most taxi drivers in Kinmen prefer to ask for a flat fare rather than use the meter.

大部分金門的計程車司機喜歡使用單一費率而非使用計程表。100導遊

❸ If you have any problems or questions about our new products, you are welcome to use our toll-free service line.

如果你對於我們的新產品有任何的困難或是疑問，歡迎撥打我們的免付費服務專線。98領隊

❸ If the tapes do not meet your satisfaction, you can return them within thirty days for a full refund.

如果這些膠帶不能讓你滿意，你可以在30天內退還並獲得全額退款。101領隊

❸ If I cancel the trip, will I be refunded?

如果我取消行程，我可以退費嗎？100領隊

★補充

人之於refund（退費）為被動，refund此處為動詞，亦可為名詞，如：

例句 The guest is given a refund after he makes a complaint to the restaurant.

這名客人在他和餐廳抱怨之後拿到退款。99領隊

❸ Am I entitled to compensation if my ferry is canceled?

如果我的遊輪行程被取消了，我有權力要求補償嗎？102領隊

❸ If you have the receipts for the goods you have purchased, you can claim a tax rebate at the airport upon departure.

如果你有購物收據，離境時可於機場要求退稅。98領隊

經濟 / 貿易

關鍵單字

overlook 忽略

inflation 通貨膨脹

economic prosperity 經濟繁榮

booming growth 蓬勃成長

economic recession 經濟蕭條

economic trauma 經濟創傷

bail out 保釋、紓困

surge 激增

fine 處以……罰金

spur domestic consumption 刺激消費

impact 衝擊

economic slowdown 經濟趨緩

economic uncertainty 經濟不確定性

boost the economy 振興經濟

revenue 稅收

economic recession 經濟蕭條

international trade 國際貿易

decline、decrease 下降、減少

litter 亂扔廢棄物

必考佳句

- Because of its inexpensive yet high-quality medical services, medical tourism is booming in Taiwan.

  因為價格不貴又高品質的醫療服務，台灣的醫療觀光正蓬勃發展中。98導遊

  ⚠ 重點：booming為景氣好的，而另一常見的blooming（開花），常用於興榮興盛之意，如 a blooming business 興隆的事業。

- Government officials have overlooked the impact of inflation on the economy.

  政府官員忽略了通貨膨脹對經濟的影響。98領隊

- There is no denying that much of the world is still mired in an economic slowdown, but some of the brightest examples of significant and lasting opportunity are right under our nose.

  不可否認的世界大部分都深陷於經濟趨緩的狀況下，但其實有一些最棒以及持續的機會正在我們的眼前。102導遊

- Thanks to India's economic prosperity and the booming growth of its airline industry, more Indians are flying today than ever before.

  歸功於印度的經濟繁榮與大幅成長，以及該國航空業的成長，如今有更多印度人搭飛機。

- Tourism has helped boost the economy for many countries, and brought in considerable revenues.

  旅遊業在許多國家已經幫忙振興經濟，且帶來許多可觀的收入。99領隊

- The $3,600 shopping voucher program was designed to spur domestic consumption, and for most people, these vouchers are really "gifts from heaven."

  每人$3,600的消費券是設計來刺激國內消費的方案，對於大多數的人來說，這些消費券真的是天上掉下來的禮物。98導遊

- The depth of the current economic trauma is one that the ordinary Irish man or woman has found hard to accept, let alone fully comprenend.

  目前經濟創傷的深度，達到一般愛爾蘭人難以接受的程度，更別說要充分瞭解了。100導遊

- In time of economic recession, many small companies will downsize their operation.

  在經濟不景氣時期，很多小公司都會縮減他們的經營。98領隊

- The American government has decided to provide financial assistance to bail out the automobile industry. Car makers are relieved at the news.

  美國政府決定提供財務援助來紓困汽車工業。汽車業者對此新聞感到欣慰。98領隊

- International trade allows countries to buy what they need from other countries.

  國際貿易讓各個國家可以向其他國家購買所需的東西。99導遊

- Many emerging countries are facing economic uncertainty after the breaking up with former union.

  很多新興國家自從與前聯盟瓦解後，都面對經濟的不確定性。102領隊

★補充：

關於break的片語如下：break 打破，以下許多片語請牢記：break up 打碎、分手、瓦解；break down 停止運轉；break into 破門而入；break through 突破。

❂ Since the economy is improving, many people are hoping for a raise in salary in the coming year.

既然經濟已經好轉，許多人希望明年能加薪。 99領隊

★補充：文法小教室

rise、raise、arise都有升起的意思，但各有不同：

① rise（rose, risen）是非及物動詞，其後不可有受詞。

例句 The sun always rises in the east. 太陽從東方升起。

② raise（raised, raised）是及物動詞，必須接受詞。

例句 Please raise your hand if you know the answer. 如果你知道答案，請舉手。

例句 The company will raise salaries by 5%. 公司將加薪 5 %。

例句 Many concerns were raised about South Africa hosting the World Cup in 2010, but in the end South Africa pulled it off and did an excellent job.

對於南非舉辦2010世界盃的疑慮升高，但最後南非消除了這些疑慮且表現出色。 101導遊

③ arise是非及物動詞，其後不可有受詞，常指事情的發生。Arise from / out of...即「由……造成」。

例句 Accidents always arise from the carelessness.

許多事故都源於粗心。 99領隊

❂ Although the unemployment rate reached an all-time high in mid-2009, it has fallen for four consecutive months by December.

雖然失業率於2009年年中一直都很高，但到12月時已經連續下降4個月。 99領隊

⚠ 重點：unemployment 失業；reach 抵達、伸手及到、達到，在此指達到。

其他

必考佳句

- By 2050, Africa's population, both northern and sub-Saharan, is expected to surge from 900 million to almost two billion.

  到了2050年，非洲的人口，包含北非和撒哈拉沙漠，預計會從9億激增至20億。 100導遊

- We have seen a marked increase in the number of visitors to the theme park, but cannot understand why the total income indicates a decline.

  我們看到主題樂園的遊客數已有顯著的增加，但卻不懂為何總收入卻下滑。 102領隊

  ⚠ 重點：decline、decrease都是下降、減少的意思。

- Our company has been on a very tight budget since 2008.

  自從2008年，我們公司的預算就很緊縮。 99領隊

- You will be fined for littering in public places.

  在公共場所亂丟垃圾會被罰錢。 98領隊

  ⚠ 重點：fine 處以……罰金；litter 亂扔廢棄物。國外路邊常見的標示Do not litter、No littering都是不要隨意丟棄的意思。

  ---

4 旅程／旅行

作者私囊

此分類包含各式各樣旅遊相關的情境以及詞彙，非常生活化，除了考試之外，旅行時也很實用！以下精選的考古題例句都相當簡單，請務必把握得分關鍵！

旅遊趨勢

關鍵單字

view as 把……當作是（= regard ... as）
development 發展
luxury 奢侈品
exotic 異國情調
rewarding 有價值的
domestic flight 國內航班
international flight 國際航班
infrastructure 公共建設
affordable 提供得起的、買得起的
necessity 必需品
ecotourism 生態旅遊
reward 獎賞
domestic 國內的
international 國外的
prosperity 興旺、繁榮
impact 影響

必考佳句

- For many, vacations and travel are increasingly being viewed as a rather necessity than a luxury and this is reflected in tourist numbers.
  對許多人來說，度假和旅行漸漸被視為一種必需品而非奢侈品，由增加的旅遊人數可看得出來。 101導遊

- The developments of technology and transport infrastructure have made many types of tourism more affordable.
  科技以及交通建設的發達，讓許多型態的旅遊更使人能夠負擔得起。 101導遊

* Ecotourism is not only entertaining and exotic; it is also highly educational and rewarding.

  生態旅遊不只富有娛樂性和具有異國情調，更有高度教育性和有價值的。101領隊

* The prosperity of domestic tourism is related to the policy of our government.

  國內旅遊業的興盛與我們政府的政策有關。100領隊

* Increasing tourism infrastructure to meet domestic and international demands has raised concerns about the impact on Taiwan's natural environment.

  增加旅遊業的公共建設來滿足國內外的需求，對於台灣的天然環境而言已經有所影響。102導遊

* The number of independent travelers has risen steadily since the new policy was announced.

  因為新政策的頒布，有越來越多的自助旅行者。

實用知識

關鍵單字

step out 踏出

accommodation 住宿

a train / bus route 火車 / 公車路線

brochure 小冊子

chart 圖表

unavailable 不可得的

draw attention to 引起對……的注意

plunge into 跳入、投入

inquire 詢問

route 路線、路程

map 地圖

wireless internet access 無線網路

available 可得到的

appreciate 欣賞

take caution 注意

ravine 溝壑、深谷

familiarize with 熟悉，常見的用法也有get familiar with

必考佳句

* Before you step out for a foreign trip, you should inquire about the accommodations, climate, and culture of the country you are visiting.
  在你踏出國外旅程之前，你應該先詢問有關納國家的住宿、天氣和文化。101領隊

* Before taking a bus, it is advisable to check out its route on a computer or read carefully the route chart at the bus stop.
  在搭公車之前，建議先在電腦上查明路線，或是在公車站時仔細閱讀路線圖。102導遊

* All the routes on the city rail map are color-coded so that a traveler knows which direction she/he should take.
  城市鐵路地圖的所有路線用顏色區分，這樣旅人才知道他們要搭哪個方向。99領隊

* Don't over pack when you travel because you can always acquire new goods along the way.
  旅行時不用打包太多東西，因為你總是可以在旅途中取得新物品。101導遊

* As a general rule, it's best to avoid wearing white clothing and accessories when traveling. Go with darker colors that hide dirt well.
  一般而言，外出旅行時最好避免穿白色衣服，深色服裝比較能夠隱藏汙漬。101導遊

* At the Welcome Center, you will find plenty of resources, including maps, brochures, and wireless internet access.
  在迎賓中心，你可以發現很多資源，包含地圖、小冊子，以及無線網路。101導遊

* Go to the office at the Tourist Information Center and they will give you a brochure about sightseeing.
  去旅遊中心他們會給你一本觀光手冊。99領隊

* City maps are always available at the local tourist information center.
  城市地圖可在當地旅遊中心取得。98領隊

* In order to appreciate the architecture of the building, you really need to get off the bus and get closer to it.
  為了欣賞建築物的結構，你真的需要下車，並靠它近一點。

- Travelers should familiarize themselves with their destinations, both to get the most enjoyment out of the visit and to avoid known dangers.

  旅客應熟悉所前往的目的地，可以享受觀光外也能避免已知的危險。98導遊

- Watch out for your own safety! Don't be a target of thieves while you are traveling.

  注意你的安全！當旅遊時別成為小偷的目標！99導遊

- Do not draw attention to yourself by displaying large amounts of cash or expensive jewelry.

  不要藉由展示大量的錢和貴重首飾，引起別人對自己的注意力。100領隊

- The heavy rain in the valley often affects my sight, so I sometimes have to pull my car over to the side of the road and wait until the rain stops.

  山谷內的大雨經常影響我的視線，所以有時候我必須停在路邊等雨停。101導遊

- Motorists are strongly advised to take caution when they drive along windy mountainous roads to avoid plunging into a ravine.

  強烈告誡摩托車騎士當行經風很大的深山時，要特別注意避免墜入深谷。100導遊

- Be sure to dress warmly when hiking in the mountains. It gets cold in the afternoon.

  當在山中健行時記得穿得保暖。下午會變冷。99導遊

計劃假期

關鍵單字

package holiday 套裝行程

journey 旅程

excursion 遠足

in advance 事先

high season 旺季

itinerary 行程（具有詳細計劃的含意）

tour 旅遊

ahead 事先

nail down dates 敲定日期

equator 赤道

contingency plan 備案 | pricey 貴的

It is high time 正是應該……的時候、是……的時候了

必考佳句

- If you take a package holiday, all your transport, accommodation, and even meals and excursions will be taken care of.
  如果你選擇套裝行程，你所有的交通、住宿和餐食、旅遊都會被打點好。99領隊

- Some tourists like to make plans and reservations for local tours after they have arrived. They prefer not to have every day of their vacation planned ahead.
  有些觀光客喜歡在抵達目的地時，才安排當地的旅遊計劃以及預約相關事宜。他們不喜歡事先安排好。98導遊

- Cindy and her husband are so busy that it is difficult for them to nail down dates for a vacation.
  辛蒂與她的丈夫是如此的忙碌以至於很難敲定去度假的日期。100導遊

- It is high time to talk about travel as the holiday season is now beginning in most countries north of the equator.
  隨著北半球國家的假期到來，差不多是該討論旅行的時候了。100導遊

- The manager gave a copy of his itinerary to his secretary and asked her to arrange some business meetings for him during his stay in Sydney.
  經理交給他的祕書一份旅行計畫（行程），並且要求她幫他在雪梨安排一些業務會議。101領隊

- Your detailed itinerary is as follows： leaving Taipei on the 14th of June and arriving at Tokyo on the same day at noon.
  你詳細的行程如下：6月14日離開台北，當天中午抵達東京。102領隊

- Do they have a contingency plan if it rains tomorrow and they can't go hiking?
  如果明天下雨他們不能健行的話，他們有緊急備案嗎？102領隊

- The downside of touring in this city is that it's very pricey.
  這座城市觀光的缺點就是物價昂貴。102領隊

旅遊活動

關鍵單字

leisurely 悠閒地

take [have, go for] a stroll 散步、漫步

adventure 冒險

uninhabited 無人居住的、杳無人跡的

hiking 健行

wander 漫遊、閒逛

safari 狩獵遠征

cruise ship 載客長途航行的遊輪

guided tour 有導遊的遊覽

savor 細細回味

必考佳句

- Susan Manning's trip to Buffalo was a/an leisurely one. She took her time.

  蘇珊．曼寧去水牛城的旅程是悠閒的。她從容不迫地度過她的時間。99導遊

- I just spent a relaxing afternoon taking a stroll along the river-walk.

  我剛剛沿著河邊散步，度過了一個悠閒的下午。101導遊

- I love to go wandering; often I take my bicycle to tour around the countryside on weekends.

  我喜歡閒逛，我週末常常騎腳踏車到鄉間旅行。102導遊

- His one ambition in life was to go on safari to Kenya to photograph lions and tigers.

  他畢生的雄心之一就是到非洲狩獵遠征，拍攝獅子和老虎。100導遊

- Exploring the culture and history of Africa sounds like a great adventure. It will be a lot of fun!

  探索非洲的文化和歷史聽起來是個很偉大的冒險。這將會很有意思！99導遊

- They cruised all around the Mediterranean for eight weeks last summer and stopped off at a number of uninhabited islands.

  他們去年夏天航遊地中海8週，並在一些無人島上停留。100導遊

- Our guided tour around the farm lasted for two and a half hours.

  我們的農場導覽共持續2個半小時。99領隊

- The hiking route of the Shitoushan Trail is not steep and so is suitable for most people, including the elderly and young children.

  獅頭山步道的健行路線不太陡峭，所以適合大多數的人，包含老人和小孩。100導遊

- Whenever there is a holiday, we always go hiking.

  無論何時有假，我們總是去健行。100領隊

- Even though John has returned from Bali for two weeks, he is still savoring the memories of his holidays.

  即便約翰已經從峇里島回來2個星期了，他仍然對他的假期回憶念念不忘。102領隊

5 旅遊景點

作者私囊

領隊的職責之一，便是介紹國外觀光景點。因此博物館、歷史遺跡、壯麗風景等相關的英文，絕對得熟記！除了書本之外，建議也可經常瀏覽國外各大旅遊網站，如TripAdvisor等旅遊評論網站（詳見附錄），可得知國外各大城市以及景點名稱。在準備考試期間，不但能欣賞吸引人的旅遊相片，還能藉此學習相關英文，對於旅遊景點這類的考題，絕對大有幫助！

關鍵單字

exotic 異國風情的

foreigner 外國人

historic site 歷史遺址

tourist 觀光客

resort 名勝

island 島嶼

temple 廟宇

National Palace Museum 故宮

museum 博物館

scenic waterfall 美景瀑布

capital 首都

contrast 對比

visually impaired 視障

auction 拍賣

headquarters 總部、總公司

established （被）建立

foreign 國外的、陌生的

site 地點、場所、網站

tourism 觀光業

tourist destination 觀光景點

The Statue of Liberty 自由女神像

casino 賭場

palace 皇宮

concert hall 音樂廳

secluded beache 隱密性海灘

peak 山頂

cuisine 美食

bursting with 充滿

physically impaired 殘障的

compete with 比得上

demand 需要、要求

operate 運作、運轉

secluded 隱蔽的、僻靜的

be steeped in 充滿著、沉浸於

enigmatic 謎樣的

cascade 疊層成瀑布落下

amazing 令人驚豔的

spectacular 壯觀的、壯麗的

path 小徑、小路

wonders of the world 世界奇景

photogenic 上相的

fascinate 使神魂顛倒

enigma 謎

breath-taking 令人屏息的

thrilling 令人興奮的

landscape 風景、景色

meander 蜿蜒而流

charming 迷人的

known for = famous for = well know for 知名

remarkably 引人注目地、明顯地、非常地

必考佳句

- Thailand is a pleasure for the senses. Tourists come from around the world to visit the nation's gold-adorned temples and sample its delicious cuisine.

  泰國是個讓人感官感到愉悅的地方。來自世界各地的觀光客來拜訪此國家以黃金裝飾的廟宇，以及品嚐美食。102導遊

- The Philippines is a country with more than 7,000 islands and it has dozens of native languages. What is even more amazing is the contrast between the north and the south, particularly their people's religious belief and political conviction.

  菲律賓是一個有著超過7,000座島嶼，且有幾十種方言的國家。更令人驚訝的是南北方的對比，特別是人們的宗教信仰和政治理念都不一樣。102導遊

- Paris' Cultural Calendar may be bursting with fairs, salons and auctions, but nothing can quite compete with the Biennale des Antiquaires.

  巴黎的文化節目可能有展覽、講座和拍賣會，但沒有一個可以和巴黎古董雙年展相比。102導遊

- Macau, a small city west of Hong Kong, has turned itself into a casino headquarters in the East. Its economy now depends very much on tourists and visitors whose number is more than double that of the local population.

澳門，位於香港西邊的小城市，現在已成為東方的賭場總部。其經濟仰賴比當地人口多上兩倍的觀光客。102導遊

- Strictly speaking, Venice is now more of a tourism city than a maritime business city.

  嚴格來說，威尼斯比較像觀光城市而不是海洋的商業城市。102導遊

- I like Rome very much because it has many historic sites and it is friendly to visitors.

  我非常喜歡羅馬，因為它有很多歷史遺跡，對遊客也很友善。102導遊

- Kyoto is my favorite city because I prefer traditional Japanese culture to electronic culture.

  京都是我最喜歡的城市，因為我喜歡傳統的日本文化更勝電子文化。102導遊

- A single visit to Rome is not enough. The city's layered complexity demands time.

  只去一次羅馬是不夠的。這座城市具有各種面向的複雜度需要時間瞭解。101導遊

- Established in 1730, Lancaster's Central Market is the oldest continuously operating farmers market in the United States.

  設立於1730年，蘭卡斯特中央市場是美國一直持續營運最老的農夫市場。101導遊

- High in the mountains of Chiapas, San Cristóbal del la Casas is one of the most photogenic spots in Mexico: colorful, historic, and remarkably complex.

  聖克裏斯多佛古堡位於契亞帕斯山上，是墨西哥最適於拍照的旅遊景點之一，多采多姿，有歷史意義，並且非常複雜。101導遊

- With its palaces, sculptured parks, concert halls, and museums, Vienna is a steeped city in cultures.

  維也納有皇宮、用雕刻裝飾的公園、音樂廳和博物館，維也納是一座充滿文化的城市。101導遊

- The oldest of all the main Hawaiian islands, Kauai is known for its secluded beaches, scenic waterfalls, and jungle hikes.

  身為夏威夷群島最古老的島嶼， 考艾島以隱密性海灘、美景瀑布與叢林健走 聞名。101導遊

- The Statue of Liberty, a gift from France, is erected in New York Harbor.

  自由女神像，是來自法國的禮物，豎立在紐約港。100領隊

- Although there is more than one Paris in the world, there's really only one Paris in the world. It is the capital of France.

  雖然全世界有一個以上名叫巴黎的地方，但是世界上其實只有一個巴黎，那就是法國的首都。100領隊

- For centuries, artists, historians, and tourists have been fascinated by Mona Lisa's enigmatic smile.

  數個世紀以來，藝術家、歷史學家，以及觀光客都對蒙娜麗莎謎樣般的微笑深深著迷。99導遊

- Hong Kong is one of the world's most thrilling Chinese New Year travel destinations. The highlight is the spectacular fireworks display on the second day of the New Year.

  香港是世界上最令人興奮的中國新年旅遊景點之一。最精彩的部分是大年初二壯觀的煙火表演。100導遊

- The amusement park is a famous tourist attraction in Japan. Tourists of all ages love to go there.

  這座遊樂園是日本很有名的觀光景點。各年齡層的觀光客都喜歡去那邊。99導遊

- This monument honors the men and women who died during the war.

  此紀念碑是為了榮耀在戰爭期間陣亡的男男女女。98導遊

- The results of the New Seven Wonders of the World campaign were announced on July 7th, 2007, and the Great Wall of China is one of the winners.

  新世界七大奇景的結果於2007年7月7日公布，中國的萬里長城為優勝者之一。98導遊

- A canal meanders along a leafy bike pass, through green parks, and pass the city's four remaining windmills.

  一條運河沿著葉子覆蓋著的單車道蜿蜒而行，穿過綠色公園和城市剩下4座的風車。101導遊

- Spectacular fireworks shows lit up the sky of cities around the world as people celebrated the start of 2012.
  壯觀的煙火照亮了世界上許多城市的天空，來慶祝2012年的開始。101導遊

- The temple was really colorful. It had blue and red tiles all over it and there were statues of different gods on the walls and on the roof.
  寺廟非常的色彩繽紛。鋪滿藍色和紅色的磁磚，且在牆上以及屋頂上有許多不同的神明雕像。100導遊

- I'll pay a visit to the Wolfsonian, an extraordinary museum in Miami. I love its collection of decorative artifacts and propaganda materials from 1885 to 1945.
  我會參觀沃爾夫索尼亞博物館，這間位於邁阿密的博物館很特別。我喜歡他的裝飾性藝術品以及1885年到1945年的宣傳資料收藏。102導遊

- The landscape of this natural park is best seen on bike or foot, and there are numerous trails in the area. All paths offer breath-taking sceneries.
  騎單車或是步行最能看出這個自然公園的景色，園內也有許多步道，都能看到令人屏息的 風景。101導遊

- The view of cascading waterfalls in the rainforest is spectacular.
  雨林中觀賞階梯狀的瀑布是很壯觀的。101導遊

- People let off fireworks to celebrate New Year.
  人們點燃煙火來慶祝新年。99領隊

- Costa Brava is a popular tourist destination in northeastern Spain, thanks to its moderate climate, beautiful beaches, and charming towns.
  西班牙東北部的布拉瓦海岸是很受歡迎的觀光景點，多虧了它溫和的氣候、美麗海灘和迷人小鎮。101導遊

- My most memorable trip is climbing Mount Fuji. Getting to the peak and seeing the sunrise from the top of the clouds was amazing.
  最令我念念不忘的旅行就是爬富士山，登頂在雲層上看日落真是太棒了。101導遊

- A good place to end a tour of Rome is the Trevi Fountain. Legend has it that if you toss a single coin into the Trevi, you are guaranteed a return to Rome.

  特雷維噴泉是結束羅馬之旅的好地方，傳說只要投一枚硬幣到噴泉內，就保證可以再訪羅馬。100導遊

- Visitors to New York often talk about the feeling of excitement there. It is a city full of energy and hope.

  拜訪紐約的遊客總是討論來此的興奮感，這是個充滿活力以及希望的城市。99導遊

- Claire loves to buy exotic foods: vegetables and herbs from China, spices from India, olives from Greece, and cheeses from France.

  克萊兒喜歡買異國風情的食物，來自中國的蔬菜和草藥、印度來的香料、希臘來的橄欖，以及法國來的起司。99導遊

- Barcelona is beautiful but it's always packed with tourists in the summer.

  巴塞隆納很漂亮但夏天總是塞滿遊客。98導遊

- The Louvre's Tactitle Gallery, specifically designed for the blind and visually impaired, is the only museum in France where visitors can touch the sculptures.

  羅浮宮的觸感畫廊，專門替盲人以及視障所設計，這是法國唯一可以觸摸雕塑的博物館。98導遊

- Mount Fuji is considered sacred; therefore, many people pay special visits to it, wishing to bring good luck to themselves and their loved ones.

  富士山被視為神聖的，因此許多人會特別拜訪，希望可以替自己以及所愛的人帶來好運。101領隊

- Palm Beach is a coastline resort where thousands of tourists from all over the world spend their summer vacation.

  棕櫚灘是海岸度假勝地，來自世界各地的上千名遊客都到此來度過暑假。101領隊

6 飯店住宿

作者私囊

提到於飯店下榻，除了價錢之外，設施以及服務則是一般人最大的考量。而到了旺季，訂房的順利與否也是很大的決定因素，因此與飯店住宿相關的實用單字，便是領隊導遊英文最重要的命題之一，在歷屆考題中幾乎都有出現，請務必熟讀！

關鍵單字

accommodation 住宿

bed down 下榻

reservation 預定

vacancy 空房、空位

in advance 事先

luxurious 奢華的

be ranked 被排名

be categorized 被分類

panoramic 全景的

facilities 設施

parlor 休息室、接待室

file a complaint 投訴

satisfactory 令人滿意的、符合要求的

cater 迎合，或承辦伙食

front desk 櫃台

hotel clerk 飯店服務員

valet parking service 代客泊車

feature 特色

lodging 住宿

reserved （被）保留的

vacant 空的

room rate 房價

high season 旺季

luxury 奢華

be graded 被評分

delivery service 寄件服務

complimentary 免費

amenities 設施

boutique 流行女裝商店、精品店

alternative 其他的選擇

unsatisfactory 不令人滿意的

reception 接待處

concierge 旅館服務台人員 / 門房

guest service 客戶服務

concierge service 管家服務

leave message 留話給……

take message 幫……留話

fill out registration form 填寫登記表格

airport limousine service 機場禮車接送服務

必考佳句

- If you plan and time it right, some swapping home can let you stay somewhere for free.

  如果你計劃且時機合適，有些交換住家可讓你免費入住。101導遊

- A reserved room or seat is being kept for someone rather than given or sold to someone else.

  被保留的房間或是座位是替某些人保留，不能提供或出售給他人。100導遊

- You don't have to worry about where to stay tonight. My friend in downtown area will find you a night's lodging.

  你不需要去擔心今晚在哪過夜。我在市區的朋友會幫你找到過夜的地方。99導遊

- It is the high season, and I'm not sure whether the hotel could provide enough accommodations for the whole group.

  現在是旺季，我不確定飯店是否可以提供足夠的住宿給整個旅行團。102領隊

- During the holidays, most major hotels will be fully booked. An alternative is to try and find a guest house near your desired destination.

  假期期間，大部分的主要飯店都被訂滿了。其他的選擇只得試著找看看接近你目的地附近的民宿。98導遊

- Jessica's customers complained because they had to pay twice for their accommodation.

  潔西卡的客人有抱怨，因為他們必須支付兩次住宿費用。100領隊

- Reservations for hotel accommodation should be made in advance to make sure rooms are available.

  旅館的訂房應提早訂，才能確保有房間。98領隊

- The hotels in the resort areas are fully booked in the summer. It would be very difficult to find any vacancies then.

  度假勝地的飯店在夏天時被訂滿了，很難找到空房。102領隊

- Either the reception or the cashier's desk of the hotel can help us figure out the exact amount of money and other details we need to join a local tour.

  不是飯店的接待處就是收銀台，可以幫我們釐清正確的金額以及其他我們想參加當地旅遊的細節。102導遊

- Tourists have a wide range of budget and tastes, and a wide variety of resorts and hotels have developed to cater for them.

  觀光客有不同的預算以及品味，因此也有各式各樣的度假村和飯店來符合他們的需求。101導遊

- Quick and friendly service at the front desk is important to the satisfaction of tourists.

  櫃台的快速以及友善服務對於觀光客的滿意度很重要。99導遊

- Hotels are ranked internationally from one to five stars, depending on the services they offer and the prices of rooms.

  國際上飯店被分級成一至五星級，是根據飯店所提供的服務以及房價所分類。98領隊

- The "Ambassador" is centrally located in Hsinchu, a few minutes by car from the station. It offers a panoramic view of the metro Hsinchu area.

  國賓飯店位於新竹的正中央，距離車站開車只要幾分鐘。它提供了新竹市區的全景。102領隊

- Guest: I have made a reservation for a suite overnight.

  Clerk: Yes, we have your reservation right here. Would you please fill out this registration form and show me your ID?

  客人：我已經訂了今晚的套房。

  服務生：是的，我們這邊已經有你的訂房紀錄。麻煩您填上這個登記表格並出示您的證件。102領隊

❂ A complimentary breakfast of coffee and rolls is served in the lobby between 7 and 10 am.

免費的早餐有咖啡和捲餅於早上7點到10點在大廳供應。102領隊

❂ As for the delivery service of our hotel, FedEx and UPS can make pickups at the front desk Monday through Friday, excluding holidays.

關於我們飯店的寄件服務，聯邦快遞公司以及聯合包裹速遞公司會於週一至週五於櫃台取件，假日除外。101領隊

❂ Working as a hotel concierge means that your focus is to ensure that the needs and requests of hotel guests are met, and that each guest has a memorable stay.

作為飯店的門房表示你的重點是要確保客戶的需求與要求被滿足，讓每位房客有個難忘的停留回憶。101領隊

❂ If you have to extend your stay at the hotel room, you should inform the front desk at least one day prior to your original departure time.

如果你必須延長在飯店房間的時間，你至少應該在原訂離開時間前一天告知櫃台。101領隊

❂ The hotel that he selected for the conference featured a nine-hole golf course.

他為這次記者會所選的旅館以九洞的高爾夫球場為特色。101領隊

❂ Client: What are this hotel's amenities?

Agent: It includes a great restaurant, a fitness center, an outdoor pool, and much more, such as in-room Internet access, 24-hour room service, and trustworthy babysitting, etc.

客戶：這間飯店有什麼設施？

代理商：有一間很棒的餐廳、健身房、戶外游泳池和其他設施，像是室內網路、24小時客房服務，和值得信賴的保母服務。101領隊

❂ Is there any problem with my reservation?

我的預約有任何問題嗎？100領隊

❀ Guest: You have answered my questions thoroughly. Thank you very much.
Hotel clerk: You are welcome. It's been my pleasure.

客人：你很詳細地回答我的問題，非常謝謝你。
飯店服務員：不客氣。這是我的榮幸。 100領隊

❀ This group of people would like to stay in luxurious hotels. They need to be five star hotels.

這群人想要住在豪華飯店。這些飯店必須要是五星級的。 100領隊

❀ The hotel services are far from satisfactory. I need to file a complaint with the manager.

旅館的服務完全稱不上滿意。我需要向經理客訴。 99領隊

❀ Guest: What facilities do you have in your hotel?
Hotel clerk: We have a fitness center, a swimming pool, two restaurants, a beauty parlor, and a boutique.

客人：你們飯店有什麼設施？
飯店服務員：我們有健身中心、游泳池、兩間餐廳、一間美容室和女裝店。 99領隊

❀ Guest: What is your room rate?
Hotel clerk: Our standard room costs NT$3,500 per night.

客人：你們的房價是多少？
飯店人員：我們的標準房每晚要價3,500元。 99領隊

❀ It's difficult to find a hotel with a/an vacant room in high season.

在旺季時很難找到有空房的飯店。 99領隊

❀ The caller: Can I speak to Ms. Taylor in room 612, please?
The operator: Please wait a minute. (pause) I'm sorry. There's no answer. May I take a message?

來電者：我可以和612號房的泰勒女士說話嗎？
接線生：請等一分鐘。（停頓）我很抱歉。沒有人應答。我可以幫你留話嗎？ 99領隊

❁ The concierge at the information desk in a hotel provides traveling information to guests.

旅館服務台人員提供旅遊資訊給客人。 99領隊

❁ The waiters will show you where to bed down.

服務生將告訴你今晚你會下榻在哪裡。 100領隊

❁ When you stay in a hotel, what basic facilities do you think are necessary?

當你住在飯店時，你認為哪些基本的設備是必須的？ 102領隊

❁ Airport limousine service, valet parking service, and concierge service are some of the most poplar items among our guest services.

機場禮車接送服務、代客泊車、管家服務是我們最受歡迎的客戶服務項目之一。 102領隊

7 餐廳／飲食

作者私囊

民以食為天，現代人除了重視日常生活的三餐之外，出外旅遊時品嚐美食也是一大重點，因此和吃有關，以及餐廳、點餐等相關英文，也不免俗地經常出現於考題中。

關鍵單字

reserve 預約、預訂

reserve a table 訂桌

set meal 套餐

bowl 碗

authentic 道地的

delicacies 佳餚

fresh 新鮮的

catch on 流行起來

make reservation 預約

specialty 招牌菜

plate 盤子

source 來源

sample 品嚐

stale 不新鮮的

staple 主食

tolerance 容忍度

必考佳句

- If I had called to reserve a table at Royal House one week earlier, we would have had a gourmet reunion dinner last night.
  如果我早一個星期打電話去皇家餐廳訂桌，我們昨晚可能就有美味的團圓飯。101領隊

- This is a non-smoking restaurant. Please put out your cigarette at once.
  這裡是非吸菸餐廳。請立刻熄滅你的香菸。

- Waiter: Are you ready to order, sir?
  Guest: I think so. But what is your specialty?
  服務生：你準備好要點了嗎，先生？
  客人：應該是。你們的招牌菜是什麼？99領隊

- Our client wants to reserve a table for dinner tomorrow.

  我們的客人想要為明天晚餐預先訂桌。100領隊

- Would you like to order a/an set meal or refer to the à la carte menu?

  你想要點套餐，還是參考菜單？100領隊

- Sweets aren't an intrinsic part of a meal, but their presence on the dining table is often a great source of happiness.

  甜點本來不是正餐中的一部分，但它在餐桌上的出現成為快樂的來源。102領隊

  重點：intrinsic 內部的、本體內的；source 來源。

- Three meals a day means that normally one will have breakfast, lunch and dinner each day.

  一天三餐表示，通常表示每天只會有早餐、午餐和晚餐。102領隊

- This restaurant features authentic Northern Italian dishes that reflect the true flavors of Italy.

  這間餐廳的特色為反映義大利口味的道地北義大利菜。101導遊

- At the annual food festival, you can a sample wide variety of delicacies.

  在一年一度的美食節，你可以品嚐各類佳餚。101領隊

- Some people refuse to eat shark fin soup because it is made with parts of protected animals.

  有些人拒絕食用魚翅湯，因為它是以受保護動物的某一部分所製成。100導遊

- The cake was stale, and tasted bad.

  這個蛋糕不新鮮了，且嚐起來不好吃。99導遊

- Baked goods are not a staple of a traditional Chinese diet, but they have been quickly catching on among China's urban middle classes over the last 10 years.

  烘培食品並非傳統中國菜的主菜，但過去10年，這些已經在中國城市的中產階級之間流行。100導遊

❸ People with a low tolerance for spicy food should not try the "Hot and Spicy Chicken Soup" served by this restaurant: it brings tears to my eyes.

對於辛辣食物容忍度低的人不應該試此餐廳的麻辣雞湯，它讓我眼淚直流。99導遊

❸ Many restaurants in Paris offer a plate of snails for guests to taste.

巴黎的許多餐廳提供一整盤的蝸牛給客戶吃。99領隊

❸ Slices of lamb are grilled or fried in butter and served with mushrooms, onions, and chips.

一片片的烤羊肉或是用奶油炸的羊肉，佐上蘑菇、洋蔥和薯片。99領隊

重點：grill 烤，通常熱源只有單面，像是中秋烤肉。

8 社交禮儀

作者私囊

不論是出國帶團（領隊），或是向外國人介紹台灣（導遊），都會和不同文化的人交流，因此適當的社交禮儀便成為非常重要的課題。然而以此社交禮儀的文化命題下，以華人社會來説，婚姻乃是人生大事，因此看似和旅遊無關聯的考題分類，卻也經常出現於考題中。

禮儀準則

關鍵單字

greet 問候

custom 風俗

customs 海關

dress code 穿衣法則

personnel 人員

character 內在的特質

greetings 問候語

customary 約定俗成的

social manner 社交禮儀

occasion 場合

personality 外在的性格

table manner 餐桌禮儀

dos and don'ts 可做與不可做的（注意事項）

appropriate / inappropriate 合宜的 / 不合宜的

polite / impolite 禮貌的 / 不禮貌的

When in Rome, do as the Romans do 入境隨俗。

必考佳句

❁ When Latin Americans and Middle Easterners greet each other, they tend to stand closer together when talking than Americans do.

當拉丁美洲人和中東人彼此打招呼時，他們傾向站得比美國人交談時更近。98導遊

- In most western countries, it's customary for you to bring a bottle of wine or a box of candy as a gift when you are invited for dinner at someone's home.

  在大多數的西方國家中，當你去其他人家作客時，帶一瓶紅酒或是一箱糖果當作伴手禮是種基本禮儀（約定俗成的事）。98導遊

- Dress codes are basically some dos and don'ts about what people wear in an organization or on a particular occasion.

  穿衣法則基本上有些行為準則，關於人們在哪個組織或是特殊場合應該穿什麼樣的衣服。102導遊

- If we remember our social manners, particularly in a big crowd, we shall win people's admiration though we may not feel it.

  如果我們記得我們的社交禮儀，特別是在群眾中，即便我們沒有感覺到，我們應該會贏得人們的尊敬。

- When Americans shake hands, they do so firmly, not loosely. In the American culture, a weak handshake is a sign of weak character.

  當美國人握手時，會握得較為強而有力，在美國人的文化中，蜻蜓點水的握手方式則為軟弱特質的象徵。98導遊

- In many Western cultures, it is rude to ask about a person's age, weight, or salary. However, these topics may not be as sensitive in East Asia.

  在許多西方國家，問他人的年齡、體重，或是薪水是很無禮的。然而這些話題在東亞可能就不是如此敏感。99導遊

- Table manners differ from culture to culture. In Italy, it is considered inappropriate for a woman to pour her neighbor a glass of wine.

  每個文化的餐桌禮儀都不同。在義大利，女士幫鄰座倒酒就被視為不恰當的行為。98導遊

- Do not be afraid to eat with your hands here. When in Rome, do as the Romans do.

  在這裡不要害怕用手吃飯。要入境隨俗。100領隊

婚姻大事

關鍵單字

newlywed 新婚夫婦

tie the knot 結婚

bride 新娘

wedding anniversary 結婚周年

file for divorce 提出離婚訴訟

available 可獲得的

phenomenon 現象

bachelor 單身漢

groom 新郎

bridal tour = honeymoon 蜜月旅行

divorce 離婚

have an affair with 與……有染

significant 有意義的、重要的

必考佳句

- Because son preference has been a significant phenomenon in Asia for centuries, the Chinese actually have a term for such bachelors: "bare branches" – branches of the family tree that will never bear fruit.

  幾個世紀以來，由於重男輕女在亞洲都是很重要的現象，中國甚至稱單身漢為「光棍」──光棍不能為家庭開花結果。100導遊

- The wedding anniversary is worth celebrating.

  結婚周年很值得慶祝。100領隊

  重點：「worth of + 動名詞」與「worth + 動名詞」兩者形式不同，但意思相同。worth of + 動名詞－被動式的動名詞；而worth後面接主動式的動名詞，雖然在形式上是主動的，但其意義仍然是被動的。如 The wedding anniversary is worth of being celebrating. = The wedding anniversary is worth celebrating.

- It is said that there are only a few lucky days available for getting married in 2010.

  據說2010年只有幾天好日子可以結婚。99領隊

❂ Mary is filing for divorce because her husband is having an affair with his secretary.

瑪莉提出離婚訴訟，因為她的丈夫與其祕書有染。 99領隊

⚠ **重點：file除了當名詞「檔案」外，當動詞有提出的意思。例句：The hotel services are far from satisfactory. I need to file a complaint with the manager. 飯店的服務讓人無法滿意。我需要向經理客訴。** 99領隊

❂ The newlyweds are on their bridal tour.

新婚夫婦正在蜜月旅行。 100領隊

⚠ **重點：newlyweds 新婚夫婦；bridal tour = honeymoon 蜜月旅行。**

❂ While many couples opt for a church wedding and wedding party, a Japanese groom and a Taiwanese bride tied the knot in a traditional Confucian wedding in Taipei.

當許多情侶選擇教堂婚禮以及婚宴時，一對日本新郎以及台灣新娘在台北選擇傳統的儒家婚禮互訂終身。 101領隊

9 領隊導遊職責

作者私囊

領隊、導遊實際上帶團的作業項目，也經常出現於考題中。這些不外乎是工作上的挑戰、與旅行社的配合（訂房事宜），或是交通工具的安排、景點介紹等等。這部分除了筆試之外，也是英語導遊口試時可能出現的考題。這部分所列的嚴選佳句相對簡單，建議一句句大聲念出來，亦可練習語感。

關鍵單字

tour guide 導遊

travel agent 旅行社

in peak seasons 旺季

responsible for 對……有責任

mingle 使混合、使相混

deposit 訂金

secure reservation 確保訂位 / 房

broaden horizons 開拓視野

sunny 陽光性格的

shy 害羞的

first impression 第一印象

tour manager 領隊

Tourism Bureau 觀光旅遊局

committed 致力於

challenge 挑戰

shuttle bus 接駁車

make reservation 訂位

re-confirmation 再確認

manner 態度、禮貌

outgoing 外向的

humble、modest 謙虛的

sit back 放鬆休息

courteous、well-mannered、polite 禮貌的

discourteous、ill-mannered、impolite 沒禮貌的

seniors 長者，也可當作前輩、資深人士

rely on = depend on = count on 依靠、信賴

必考佳句

- A good tour guide has to be committed to the people in his group.
一名好的導遊必須致力於照顧他的團員。101導遊

- A tour guide is responsible for informing tourists about the culture and the beautiful sites of a city or town.
導遊應負責告知遊客該城鎮的文化和美麗的景點。101領隊

- As a tour guide, you will face new challenges every day. One of the hardest parts of your job may be answering questions.
身為導遊，每天會面臨到新的挑戰。工作上最困難的工作之一也許就是回答問題。98導遊

- Mingling with tourists from different backgrounds helps tour guides broaden their horizons and learn new things in answering curious visitors' various questions.
與不同背景的觀光客打交道讓導遊開拓視野，也學習回答好奇的旅客不同的新問題。102導遊

- The tour guide is a courteous man; he is very polite and always speaks in a kind manner.
導遊是一個有教養的男生，他非常禮貌，談吐也得宜。101導遊

- The local tour guide has a sunny personality. Everybody likes him.
這位當地的導遊有著陽光開朗的性格。每個人都喜歡他。101導遊

- Before we left the hotel, our tour guide gave us a thirty-minute presentation on the local culture.
在我們離開旅館之前，我們的導遊做了30分鐘當地文化的簡報介紹。101導遊

- Being a tour guide is a very important job. In many cases, the tour guide is the traveler's first impression of our country.
當一個導遊是一份很重要的工作。在許多情形下，導遊是遊客對我們國家的第一印象。98導遊

- Mr. Jones has got the hang of being a tour guide.
Mr. Jones has learned the skills of being a tour guide.
瓊斯先生已經學習到當一位導遊的技巧。100領隊

❋ The tour guide persuaded him into buying some expensive souvenirs.

這名導遊說服他買昂貴的紀念品。100領隊

❋ We were asked by our tour guide on the shuttle bus to remain seated until we reached our destination.

導遊要求我們在接駁車上維持坐姿，直到抵達目的地。98導遊

❋ We're going to be driving through farmland for the next twenty minutes or so, so just sit back and relax until we're closer to the city.

接下來的20分鐘車程我們會駛經農田，所以在接近市區之前，請輕鬆就坐。98導遊

❋ If you want to become a successful tour manager, you have to work hard and learn from the seniors.

如果你想成為一名成功的領隊，你必須很努力地工作並向前輩學習。98領隊

❋ In order to make traveling easier, especially for those who rely on public transportation, the Tourism Bureau worked with local governments to initiate the Taiwan Tourist Shuttle Service in 2010.

為了讓旅遊更容易，特別是針對那些仰賴大眾運輸的人，觀光旅遊局與當地政府一起於2010年開始實施台灣旅遊巴士。102導遊

❋ In case you need to get in touch with me, you can reach me at 224338654 at my travel agency.

萬一你需要和我聯繫，你可以打224338654到我的旅行社和我聯絡。100導遊

❋ For tours in peak seasons, travel agents sometimes have to make reservations a year or more in advance.

對於旺季的出遊，旅行社有時必須早在一年之前、甚至更早就事先預定好行程。99導遊

❋ The travel agent says that we have to pay a deposit of $2,000 in advance in order to secure the reservation for our hotel room.

旅行社說我們必須事先支付$2,000訂金，來確保飯店訂房。98導遊

❋ The travel agent apologized for the delay.

旅行社因為行程延誤而道歉。100領隊

10 國家大事

作者私囊

國家的政策、法律等政治相關嚴肅議題，也會因時事而不時成為考題，像是全球化的移民問題等等。乍看之下似乎考題偏難，其實只要掌握重點單字，即可跨越障礙，輕鬆解題。

關鍵單字

legalize 合法化

bill 法案

congress 立法機關

court 法院

immigration 移民

imminent 逼近的、即將發生的

impose 徵（稅）

cross-strait relations 兩岸關係

metropolitan / urban area 都會區

telephone fraud 電話詐欺

eliminate 消滅

income 收入、所得

caution 警告

outbreak 暴動

difference 不同之處

approval 同意

momentum 勢力

custody 監護權

agreement 協議

immigrant 移民者

financial crisis 金融危機

cripple 嚴重毀壞或損害

census 人口普查

rural areas 鄉村、郊區

fraud 欺騙（行為）、詭計、騙局

welfare 福利的一種

precaution 預防

urge 催促、力勸

indifference 漠不關心

democratic 民主的

必考佳句

❋ A bill to legalize gay marriage in Washington State has won final legislative approval and taken effect starting 2012.

華盛頓州同性婚姻合法化的法案已經通過了最後立法同意，並於2012年生效。

❂ The support for suspending death penalty has gained momentum, and it is very likely that someday the congress of the country will pass its suspension.

支持廢死已越來越有勢力，很有可能某天國會會通過廢死。102導遊

❂ While courts in the U.S. generally favor the mother in the event of a divorce, Taiwan family and divorce laws will grant custody to the father, unless some other agreement is reached.

美國法院通常於夫妻離婚時會偏向女方，但台灣的親屬法則是偏判給父親監護權，除非事先有達成協議。100導遊

❂ Despite facing an imminent labor shortage as its population ages, Japan has done little to open itself up to immigration.

即便隨著人口高齡化，勞工短缺的問題近在眼前，日本開放移民方面還是做得很少。100導遊

❂ According to a new study, the continuing arrival of immigrants to American shores is encouraging business activity and producing more jobs with the supply of abundant labors.

根據新的研究，美國海岸持續到來的移民者會讓商業發展更佳，也會產生更多的工作機會。102導遊

❂ The financial crisis that started in the U.S. and swept the globe was further proof that—for better and for worse—we can't escape one another.

金融危機始於美國，且橫掃全球，更佳證明了——不管是好是壞，我們誰都逃不過。102導遊

❂ Taiwan government said yesterday it will not give up restrictions it imposes on imported beef, after a warning by U.S. lawmakers that the issue could cripple free trade talks.

台灣政府昨天表示不會放棄對於進口牛肉課税的限制，在經過美國立法單位警告之後，這項議題會破壞自由貿易。102導遊

❂ Taiwan's premier said 2010 was a boom year for tourism in Taiwan and he attributed the success to the improvements in cross-strait relations.

台灣的行政院長説2010年是台灣旅遊業大幅成長的一年，他將此成功歸因於兩岸關係的改善。100導遊

- Most countries take a census every ten years or so in order to count the people and to know where they are living.

  大部分的國家每10年做一次人口普查，以計算人口以及其居住地。100導遊

- The Taiwan High Prosecutors Office vowed to harshly crack down on anyone caught hoarding food staples as part of the government's efforts to stabilize food prices amid a string of price hikes following the Lunar New Year.

  隨著農曆新年的到來，台灣高等法院檢察署嚴厲地打擊任何囤積大宗食物的行為，並依此作為政府穩定物價上漲的一連串措施。100導遊

- The Ministry of the Interior has decided to eliminate telephone fraud.

  內政部長決定消滅電話詐騙。99領隊

- People who earn little or no income can receive public assistance, often called welfare.

  賺很少或沒賺錢的人可以有大眾救助，常常稱為福利。100導遊

- The Department of Health urged the public to receive H1N1 flu shot as a precaution against potential outbreaks.

  衛生處勸導大眾接受H1N1流感疫苗作為預防，以對抗潛在的爆發。99領隊

- Public indifference to voting is a problem in many democratic countries with low turnouts in elections.

  大眾對於投票的漠不關心且投票率低是許多民主國家的問題。98領隊

- Martial law was lifted from Matsu in 1992, a number of years later than "mainland" Taiwan. Matsu residents are now allowed to travel freely to and from Taiwan.

  馬祖在1992年解除戒嚴，比起台灣本島慢了幾年。現在馬祖居民可以自由往返台灣。100導遊

⚠ **重點：此處考lift，除了舉起，還有取消之意。**

---

11 社會現象

作者私囊

與國家大事不同，此分類著重於目前世界的走向、趨勢，以及目前台灣社會的概況。而由於網路的興起所造成的各類社會現象，也是近年來熱門的考題。

關鍵單字

cellphone / mobile phone 手機

flourish 蓬勃發展

handy 方便

lift oneself out of poverty 讓某人脫貧

social isolation 社會隔離

ethics 道德

compulsory 義務的

outdated / obsolete 過時的

modern 現代的

take place 舉行、發生

metropolitan 大都市的

rural 鄉村的

decline 下降、減少

heavy user 重度使用者

smother 阻擋、阻礙

poverty 貧窮、貧困

fosters equality 促進平等

population 人口

within the law 合法

environmentally friendly 環境友善的

old-fashioned 舊式的

notion 概念、想法

replace 取代

urban 都會的

demographers 人口統計學家

national treasure 國家寶藏，也就是我們常說的「台灣之光」

必考佳句

- Simply put, no society can truly flourish if it smothers the dreams and productivity of half its population, women.

簡單來說，沒有一個社會可以真正的蓬勃發展，如果它阻擋了一半的人口——女性的夢想以及生產力。102導遊

- The cellphone is very handy because it connects us with the world at large and even provides us with the necessary information on crucial moments.

  手機非常的方便，因為它讓我們充分和世界溝通，甚至在重要時刻提供我們所需的資訊。102導遊

- Technology, such as cellphones, often fosters equality and helps lift people out of poverty.

  科技，像是手機，常常促進平等並且幫助人們脫貧。102導遊

- Many users of mobile phones would get heavy anxious and panic once the phone is missing.

  一旦手機不見時，許多手機的使用者都會重度焦慮或慌張。102領隊

- The Internet is creating social isolation as people are spending more time on computers.

  網路正造成社會隔離，因為人們花更多的時間在電腦上。101領隊

- Seeing the rise of new media technology, many people predict newspapers will soon be obsolete.

  看見了新媒體科技的崛起，很多人預測報紙很快就會過時。102領隊

- The notion that fashionable shopping takes place only in cities is outdated, thanks to the Internet.

  歸功於網路，去大城市購物才時髦這樣的觀念已經過時了。101導遊

- The Industrial Revolution, which began in the nineteenth century, caused widespread unemployment as machines replaced workers.

  工業革命，始於19世紀，由於機器取代勞工，導致普遍的失業。100導遊

- Metropolitan areas are more densely populated than rural areas. That is, they have more people per square mile.

  大都市區的人口密度比鄉村來得高。也就是每平方英里有比較多的人。100導遊

✲ Demographers study population growth or decline and things like urbanization, which means the movement of populations into cities.

人口統計學家研究人口的成長或是削減，像是都市化表示人口往城市移動。100導遊

✲ In 2060, people over 65 will account for more than 41 percent of the population in Taiwan.

2060年，65歲以上的人口將會超過台灣人口總數的41%。102領隊

⚠ **重點：**account for有「說明（原因、理由等）」、「導致、引起」、「（在數量、比例上）占」、「對……負責」之意。例句：How do you account for the company's alarmingly high staff turnover? 你怎麼解釋這家公司高得令人憂心的人員流動率？

✲ Many couples live together even though they are not married. The ethics of their behavior are highly suspect, but technically they are within the law.

許多情侶在還沒結婚前同居。他們的道德行為被高度質疑，但技術上來說他們是合法的。100導遊

✲ As introductory English now begins in elementary, rather than secondary school, and classes have begun to focus more on the spoken language, travelers to Taiwan can get by without having to attempt any Mandarin or Taiwanese.

英語入門始於小學而非國中，且課程也著重在口語，到台灣的旅客可以勉強用英文溝通，而不用講中文或是台語。100導遊

✲ The public education in Taiwan has been compulsory from primary school through junior high school since 1968.

台灣的大眾教育自從1968年來，從小學到國中都是義務教育。100導遊

✲ Living in a highly competitive society, some Taiwanese children are forced by their parents to learn many skills at a very young age.

生活在高度競爭的社會，有些台灣小孩從小就被逼著學很多技能。99領隊

✲ Violent video games have been blamed for school shootings, increases in bullying, and violence towards women.

暴力的遊戲被歸咎於導致校園槍械，增加霸凌，以及對於女性的暴力。102領隊

❸ More and more Taiwanese have come to view cycling not only as a form of recreation but as a way of being environmentally friendly.

越來越多台灣人不只將單車視為一項休閒活動，也是友善環境的一項作法。 98導遊

▲ 重點：environmentally friendly 環境友善，常見的還有user friendly 使用者友善，通常用來形容軟硬體的操作介面。

❸ The birth rate in Taiwan was at a/an record low last year.

台灣的出生率和去年比起來達到紀錄低點。 99領隊

▲ 重點：看到birth rate可知道是record 紀錄的比較。

❸ Baseball is the number one team sport here in Taiwan. The most accomplished player, New York Yankees' Wang Chien-ming, is frequently referred to as a national treasure.

棒球在台灣是第一名的團體運動，最有成就的球員——紐約洋基的王建民，常常被稱為台灣之光。 98導遊

12 介紹台灣

作者私囊

關於台灣的點點滴滴，考題總是五花八門。此處與其它分類不同，會有許多共同單字，因此一併整理成一單字列表。此分類除了筆試外，也常出現於口試中，故其重要性不言而喻。

關鍵單字

spectacle 奇觀

urban 城市的

rural 農村的、田園的

import 進口

ecology 生態環境

take in 欣賞、參觀

serene 寧靜的

Mandarin 中文

a must-see for visitors 必遊景點

derived from 衍生出

National Palace Museum 故宮博物院

rural folk culture 民俗文化

firecrackers 鞭炮

symbolize 象徵

customs 海關

souvenir 紀念品

local snack 當地小吃

throng 人群

fascinate 迷住、強烈地吸引

marvelous scenery 絕美風光

rustic 鄉下的

export 出口

retreat 僻靜之處

spring 溫泉

indigenous 本地的、土生土長的

peak 山峰、高峰

demonstrate 論證、證明

calligraphy 書法

perform 表演

collection 收藏品

fireworks 煙火

symbol 符號

custom 風俗

customary 約定俗成的

indigenous 土生土長的

authentic 道地的

highlight 亮點

tourist destinations、tourist spots、tourist attractions 觀光景點

tourist spots、tourist attractions、scenic spots 風景景點

well known、famous、 renowned 有名的

second to none 不亞於任何人、首屈一指

城市風情

必考佳句

- Bopiliao, located in Wanhua District, Taipei, and serving as the setting for the film, Monga, is a popular tourist spot.

  剝皮寮位於台北萬華區，曾是電影《艋舺》拍片的場景，是個受歡迎的觀光景點。

  101導遊

- Chichi is a town in Central Taiwan that is accessible by rail.

  集集是中台灣有鐵路到達的城鎮。101導遊

  ▲ 重點：形容某處的交通時，經常用accessible by car / rail來形容（是否能開車、搭火車到達）。

- One of Hualien's long-standing traditions is stone carving, which is not surprising considering the city's main export is marble.

  花蓮屹立不搖的傳統之一就是石雕，因此此城市的主要出口為大理石也就不足為奇了。

  100導遊

- Pingxi District in New Taipei City of Taiwan holds an annual Lantern Festival in which releasing sky lanterns has become a tradition. Legend has it that sky lanterns were the invention of an ancient Chinese politician and military leader "Kong Ming."

  台灣新北市的平溪區舉辦一年一度的燈籠節，放天燈已經變成是一種傳統。據說天燈是古代中國政治家，也是軍事領導者孔明的發明。102導遊

自然風景

必考佳句

- Wulai is a famous hot-spring resort.

  烏來是著名的溫泉度假勝地。100領隊

- Taroko National Park features high mountains and steep canyons. Many of its peaks tower above 3,000 meters in elevation.

  太魯閣國家公園以高山以及陡峭的峽谷為特色。許多高峰海拔超過3,000公尺。101導遊

- Many tourists are fascinated by the natural spectacles of Taroko Gorge.

  許多觀光客為太魯閣的自然奇觀所著迷。98領隊

- Many people consider Yangmingshan National Park a pleasant retreat from the bustle of the city.

  許多人認為陽明山國家公園是個遠離城市喧囂的僻靜之處。100導遊

- Besides participating in local cultural activities, people who desire to explore the ecology of Kenting can observe plenty of wildlife and plants.

  除了參與當地文化活動外，想在墾丁探訪生態環境的人也可以觀察豐富的野生動物與植物。99導遊

- Unlike other springs locations, Taian Hot Springs is relatively serene, with no more than six large-scale resorts in the area, so the place is not as congested as Wulai and Beitou.

  不像其他地區，泰安溫泉相對安靜，這區域的大型渡假村不超過6個，所以不像烏來和北投一樣擁擠。100導遊

- Wind and sunshine are very important assets for Penghu, attracting a large number of tourists each year.

  風和陽光是澎湖很重要的資產，每年吸引了大批觀光客到來。99導遊

✿ With crystal clear water, emerald green mountains and various outdoor activities to offer, it's not surprising that Sun Moon Lake is one of the most visited spots in Taiwan.

有著清澈的水、翠綠的山脈，以及多種戶外活動可選，日月潭是台灣遊客最多的景點之一並不讓人驚訝。101導遊

✿ Taiwan is well known for its mountain scenic spots and urban landmarks such as the National Palace Museum and the Taipei 101 skyscraper.

台灣以其高山風景景點聞名，以及城市的地標，像是故宮博物院和台北101摩天大樓。101導遊

✿ Ku-Kuan, east of Tai-Chung City, with its steep cliffs, has become a paradise for rock climbers here in Taiwan.

谷關，位於台中市東部，有著陡峭的懸崖，已經成為台灣登山者的天堂。98導遊

▲ 重點：paradise 天堂，亦常用heaven替代。兩者雖在口語上經常相互使用，但paradise這個字其實是人間仙境的意思；而heaven則是另一個世界的天堂。

✿ When visiting Alishan, one of the most popular tourist destinations in Taiwan, it's worth spending a few days to learn about the indigenous people living in mountain villages and take in the marvelous scenery.

當去最受歡迎的台灣景點——阿里山旅遊時，很值得花幾天去學習原住民的高山生活方式，和欣賞 絕美風光。102導遊

✿ At 3,952 meters, Yushan is not only Taiwan's tallest peak; it is also the tallest mountain in Northeast Asia.

高3,952公尺，玉山不只是台灣的最高峰，也是東北亞的最高峰。102導遊

✿ Taiwan has plentiful annual rainfall but unfortunately its rivers are too short and too close to the sea.

台灣有很豐沛的降雨，但很不幸的河流太短且太靠近海。102導遊

藝術文化

必考佳句

- With 49 shops around the island, Eslite Bookstore was selected by Time magazine in 2004 as a must-see for visitors to Taiwan.

  在台灣島上有49間營業據點，誠品書店於2004年被時代雜誌選為台灣的必遊景點。 98導遊

- Opened in May 2008, the Children's Gallery of the National Palace Museum is aimed at children between the ages of 7 and 12.

  2008年5月開幕，故宮博物院的兒童畫廊是以7-12歲的兒童為對象。 98導遊

- There are around 7,000 convenience stores in Taiwan, the highest concentration in the world. The ubiquitous 7-Eleven chain offers a great range of services, from faxing and copying to bill payments for customers.

  台灣大約有7,000間便利商店，是全世界密度最高的。到處都有的7-11連鎖店則是提供各類型的服務，從傳真、影印到付款。 100導遊

- Cloud Gate, an internationally renowned dance group from Taiwan, demonstrated that the quality of modern dance in Asia could be comparable to that of modern dance in Europe and North America.

  雲門，來自台灣的國際知名舞蹈團體，證明亞洲現代舞水準，可和歐洲以及北美的現代舞媲美。 101導遊

- Cursive II is a recent work of Taiwan's master choreographer Lin Hwai-min. He created Cursive, with its title derived from Chinese calligraphy.

  《行草貳》是台灣編舞家林懷民最近的作品，他創造行草名稱來源則是來自中國書法。 100導遊

- Formed in 1991 and having toured internationally in Europe and Asia, the Formosa Aboriginal Dance Troupe is a group that performs Taiwanese folk music.

  成立於1992年，也曾於歐洲以及亞洲巡迴過，福爾摩沙原住民舞蹈團演奏台灣民俗音樂。 98導遊

- For a lot of foreigners, the hardest thing about learning Mandarin is its tones. If you use the wrong one, you end up saying the wrong word.

  對大多數的外國人來說，學習中文最難的就是音調。如果你的音調發錯，最後發出來的字也是錯的。98導遊

- Taiwan has more than 400 museums. The most famous of these is the National Palace Museum, which holds the world's largest collection of Chinese art treasures.

  台灣有400間以上的博物館。其中最有名的為故宮博物院，它擁有世界上最多的中華文物收藏品。98導遊

  ⚠ 重點：hold除了手握，亦可為舉辦，此處則為擁有。

- The National Palace Museum opens daily from 9 a.m. to 5 p.m.. However, for Saturdays, the hours are extended to 8:30 p.m..

  故宮博物院每天從早上9點開放至下午5點。但每個星期六開放時間則延長到晚上8點半。98導遊

- The Presidential Office in Taiwan is a classic mix of European renaissance and baroque style architecture, combining ornate with simple features.

  台灣總統府是典型的歐洲文藝復興與巴洛克建築的組合，結合華麗與簡約的特色。100導遊

風俗民情

必考佳句

- In southern Taiwan, people's ties to rural folk culture are strongest. Local gods are more fervently worshipped. Tainan, for instance, has a temple heritage second to none.

  南台灣人與民俗文化的連結是最強的，當地的神明被熱烈崇拜。例如台南，寺廟的文化首屈一指。100導遊

- Fireworks and firecrackers are often used in Chinese communities to symbolize greeting good fortunes and scaring away evils.

  煙火和鞭炮常用於華人社會中，來象徵迎接好運以及將晦氣嚇跑。99導遊

❸ It is a custom for some Taiwanese to eat a bowl of long noodles on New Year's Eve. They feel that doing so will increase their chances of living long lives.

在台灣除夕吃碗長壽麵是項習俗。台灣人覺得如此一來能夠延年益壽。98導遊

夜市 / 小吃 / 特產

必 考 佳 句

❸ Pineapple cakes and local teas are some of the most popular souvenirs of Taiwan.

鳳梨酥和當地的茶葉是台灣最受歡迎的紀念品。102領隊

❸ Taiwan Mountain Tea and Red Sprout Mountain Tea are indigenous subspecies of the island. They were discovered in Taiwan in the 17th century.

台灣高山茶和紅芽高山茶是島上土生土長的品種。他們於17世紀時被發現。102領隊

❸ Tourists enjoy visiting night markets around the island to taste authentic local snacks.

遊客喜歡在島上到處參訪夜市，嚐嚐真正道地的 當地小吃。99導遊

❸ Many foreigners who had visited Taiwan remembered the throngs of people packed into night markets and aromas floating through the air.

許多拜訪台灣的外國人都記得人群湧進夜市，以及香氣飄在空中。100導遊

❸ The highlight of our trip to Southern Taiwan was A Taste of Tainan where we had a lot of delicious food.

南台灣之旅的亮點就是台南小吃，我們在那吃了很多美食。101導遊

❸ Night markets in Taiwan have become popular tourist destinations. They are great places to shop for bargains and eat typical Taiwanese food.

台灣的夜市已經成為受歡迎的 觀光景點。他們是買便宜貨和吃傳統台灣料理的好地方。

101導遊

13 活動盛事

作者私囊

舉辦活動，像是舉辦遊行、運動會、各類展覽等等，可以說是最常出現的考題之一，hold / host兩個單字的用法絕對不能忘記！

關鍵單字

host 主辦（帶有主辦人的意思）

take place = be held 發生、被舉辦

popular 受歡迎的

Olympics 奧運

Paralympic 殘障奧運

hold 舉行、舉辦

participate in 參加

popularity 歡迎

Deaflympics 聽障奧運

promote 行銷推廣

必考佳句

- An open-minded city, Taipei hosted Asia's first Gay Pride parade which has now become an annual autumn event.

  身為一座心胸開放的都市，台北主辦亞洲第一屆同志遊行，並且成為每年於秋天所舉辦的活動。100導遊

★補充：舉辦活動的兩個常見單字

① host 主辦（帶有主辦人的意思）

例句 Rio will host the 2016 Summer Olympic Games.

里約將主辦2016年夏季奧運。

② hold 舉行、舉辦

例句 The Olympic Games are held every four years.

奧運每4年（被）舉辦一次。

例句 The first Taipei Lantern Festival was held in 1990. Due to the event's huge popularity, the festival has been expanded every year.

第一屆的台北燈籠節於1990年舉行。而因為這場活動受到極大的歡迎，慶祝活動一年比一年盛大。98導遊

⚠ 重點：hold an event 舉辦活動，而此處活動名稱當主詞，故為被動式，was held 過去被舉辦；has been expanded 每年一直被擴張。

❁ The World Games of 2009 will take place in Kaohsiung, Taiwan, from July 16th to July 26th, 2009. The games will feature sports that are not contested in the Olympic Games.

2009年的世界運動大會將從7月16日至7月26日於台灣高雄舉辦。是以奧運未舉辦的比賽項目為特色。98導遊

⚠ 重點：某事件take place = be held 發生、被舉辦，若是主辦單位為主詞，則可換成 Kaohsiung will host the World Games of 2009。

❁ A total of 3,965 athletes from 81 countries will compete in the 21st Summer Deaflympics to be hosted by Taipei City from September 5 to September 15 this year.

來自81個國家，總共3,965位運動員將於第21屆夏日聽障奧林匹克運動會一同競技，此次將由台北市政府於今年9月5日至9月15日舉辦。98導遊

❁ Expo 2010 will be held in Shanghai, China from May 1 to October 31, 2010.

2010年的世界博覽會將在5月1日到10月31日於中國上海舉行。99領隊

❁ Millions of people are expected to participate in the 2010 Taipei International Flora Expo.

數百萬人期待參加2010年的台北國際花卉博覽會。99領隊

❁ Starting in 2005, the Taipei City Government began holding its annual international Beef Noodle Soup Festival to promote the local favorite to visitors.

從2005年開始，台北市政府開始舉辦年度國際牛肉麵節以推廣本地的美食給觀光客。98導遊

★補充：promote 推銷（動詞）為必考單字

例句 The company is promoting the new products now, so you can buy one and get the second one free.

公司現在正在推廣新產品，所以你可享買一送一的優惠。98領隊

例句 To increase sales of products, many companies spend huge sums of money on promotion campaigns.

為了增加商品的銷售，很多公司花了大筆的金錢在促銷活動上。98導遊

14 人格／個性

作者私囊

乍看之下，可能會覺得此分類和領隊導遊考題似乎沒有關係，但形容人的個性、行為等等的各類形容詞，經常出現於考題中。

關鍵單字

sunny 陽光性格的

shy 害羞的

down-to-earth 樸實的

childish 幼稚的

considerate 體貼的

sensitive 敏感的

reluctant 不願意的

witty 機智的

eccentric 怪異的

outgoing 外向的

humble、modest 謙虛的

mature 成熟的

disciplined 有紀律的

thoughtful 細心的

blunt 遲鈍的

open-minded 開放心胸的

appreciation 鑑賞力

clumsy 笨手笨腳的

courteous、well-mannered、polite 禮貌的

discourteous、ill-mannered、impolite 沒禮貌的

必考佳句

- People love to socialize, and Facebook makes it easier. The shy become more outgoing online.

  人們喜歡社交，而臉書讓此更容易。害羞的人在網路上變得更外向。101導遊

- The local tour guide has a sunny personality. Everybody likes him.

  這位當地的導遊有著陽光開朗的 性格。每個人都喜歡他。101導遊

★補充：描述天氣的形容詞

windy 大風的；stormy 暴風雨的；sunny 陽光的；cloudy 陰天的。

* As children grow and mature, they will leave behind childish pursuits, and no longer be so selfish and undisciplined as they used to be.

  當小孩長大變成熟，他們將會把幼稚的行為拋下，且不再和以前一樣自私且沒有紀律。 99導遊

* Considerate people are sensitive to others' wants and feelings.

  體貼的人通常容易察覺他人的需求以及感覺。 99導遊

* Kenneth is reluctant to confide in others, because he fears that the information he reveals will be used maliciously against him.

  肯尼斯不願意向他人敞開心胸，因為他怕他所吐露的心聲會被惡意地用來對付他自己。 99導遊

* People who have a great sense of humor are often very popular, because they are usually intelligent, open-minded, and witty.

  非常有幽默感的人通常很受歡迎，因為他們通常是聰明、開放心胸以及機智的。 99導遊

* A humble person is usually welcomed by everyone, because he never irritates people.

  一個謙虛的人通常受到每個人的歡迎，因為這樣的人從不激怒其他人。 99導遊

* Elaine Hadley has many hobbies, such as horse-back riding, dancing, and playing with animals.

  依蓮・海德力有許多嗜好，像是騎馬、跳舞以及與動物們一起玩。 99導遊

* Sarah, who often attends symphony concerts, has a great appreciation for music.

  那位常常參加交響樂會的莎拉，對於音樂有極高的鑑賞力。 99導遊

* The book is about a very clumsy boy who always breaks things.

  這本書是關於一名笨手笨腳的男生，他總是打破東西。 99導遊

* Professor Nelson, who is rather strange, displays some eccentric behavior from time to time.

  尼爾森教授是一個奇怪的人，有時會表現出怪異的行為。 99導遊

15 健康

作者私囊

時差、減重、維持身體健康是最常考的三大健康命題。此類別比較不會出現艱澀難懂的單字，多半能以前後文推出答案，但首先要掌握相關單字。

關鍵單字

gain weight、put on weight 增重

fitness 體態

exercise 運動

overweight 過胖

jet lag 時差

contagious disease 接觸傳染病

paralyzed 癱瘓的

conscious 有意識的

miracle 奇蹟

blood sugar 血糖

maintain 維持

diet 節食

obesity 肥胖

body clock 生理時鐘

develop a new symptom 出現新症狀

cure 治療

unconscious 無意識的（昏迷）

subconscious 潛意識的

hazardous 有害的

diabetes 糖尿病

getting in shape、lose weight、lost pounds 減重

chronic health condition 慢性疾病的情形

必考佳句

- Many people have put on some pounds during the New Year vacation.
  於新年假期期間，許多人體重增加不少磅。98領隊

- Please don't order so much food! I have been putting on weight for the last two months.
  拜託別點太多食物！這兩個月我已經開始變胖了。100領隊

- Some families have children in chronic health conditions. At times, the pressure may be overwhelming to every individual in the family and the challenges can affect the quality of family life.

  有些家庭的孩子有慢性疾病的情形。有時候壓力對於每一個家庭份子來說，有如排山倒海而來，而挑戰也會影響家庭生活的品質。99導遊

- Christopher Reeve was paralyzed from the neck down and confined to a wheelchair, after the tragic accident.

  在一場悲劇性的意外之後，克里斯多福・李維從頸部以下都癱瘓了，並且得坐在輪椅上。99導遊

- Shelly has adhered to a low-fat diet for over two months and succeeded in losing 12 pounds.

  雪莉已經遵循低卡飲食兩個多月，並且成功瘦下12磅。102領隊

- Diabetes is a chronic disease which is difficult to cure. Management concentrates on keeping blood sugar levels as close to normal as possible without presenting undue patient danger.

  糖尿病是一種慢性疾病且難以治癒。日常管理上需注意血糖高低需接近正常值，不要讓病人有過度危險的狀況發生。100導遊

- Caused by the disruption of our "body clock," jet lag can be a big problem for most travelers in the first few days after they have arrived at their destination.

  由於生理時鐘的混亂，時差對於大多數的旅遊者而言，在抵達目的地的前幾天會是一大問題。98導遊

- I seem to have a fever. May I have a thermometer to take my temperature?

  我好像發燒了。可以給我溫度計來量溫度嗎？

- Obesity has become a very serious problem in the modern world. It's estimated that there are more than 1 billion overweight adults globally.

  肥胖已經成為現代世界很嚴重的問題。預估全球有超過10億成人過重。99領隊

- Many people have made "getting in shape" one of their new year resolutions.

  很多人的新年新願望都希望可以減肥。102領隊

❁ The chemicals in these cleaning products can be hazardous to our health.

清潔用品中的化學物質對我們的健康可能是有害的。102領隊

❁ The doctor thought she could never walk. But now she can not only walk but run as well. It is really a miracle.

醫生原本以為她不可能再走路了。但是她現在不但可以走，還能跑。這真是奇蹟。98導遊

❁ As a result of the accident, Shirley was unconscious for three weeks before gradually recovered.

這次意外的結果，雪麗在逐漸恢復之前昏迷了3個星期。99導遊

❁ Scientists have found a cure for the rare contagious disease, and some patients now have the hope of recovery.

科學家已經發現罕見接觸性疾病的療法，現在一些病人對於治癒懷抱希望。99導遊

❁ Scarlet fever is a/an contagious disease, which is transferable from one person to another.

猩紅熱是一種接觸傳染性的疾病，是經由人與人接觸傳染。99導遊

❁ Middle-aged smokers are far more likely than nonsmokers to develop dementia later in life, and heavy smokers are at more than double the risk, according to a new study.

根據一項新研究，中年吸菸的人比不吸菸的人在往後的日子裡更容易得到失智症，且有菸癮的人有超過2倍以上的風險。100導遊

❁ To maintain health and fitness, we need proper diet and exercise.

為了維持健康和體態，我們需要適量的節食和運動。101導遊

16 職場／學校

作者私囊

人與人最常互動的場合，莫過於學校與職場，因此領隊導遊英文經常著墨於職場、學校上的點點滴滴，包含面試、加薪、升遷等等，都是相當生活化且實用的考題。

關鍵單字

agenda 議程

personnel manager 人事主管

absent 缺席

salesperson 業務

on behalf of 代表

unemployed 失業

clock in 打卡

assign 分配、分派

applicant 申請者

submit a plan 提出一項計劃

coordination 協調

embarrassing 使人尷尬的，指事物

work as a team 團體工作

survey 調查

prestigious 有名氣的

requirement 需求

expel 開除

faculty 教職員

remind 提醒

return 還

mock interview 模擬的面試

preside over 主持

present 出席

qualified 資格

filed a protest 發起抗議

employee 員工

demanding 苛求的

consider 考慮

submit 提交

disjointed 脫節鬆散的、支離破碎的

crew 工作人員

embarrassed 感到尷尬的

work independently 獨立工作

jeopardize 危害

competitive 競爭的

initiative 倡議

sign up 報名登記

in the dark 一無所知

borrow from 從某處借來

highlight 重點

必考佳句

- According to the meeting agenda, three more topics are to be discussed this afternoon.

  根據會議議程，這個下午還有3個議題要被討論。101導遊

- Beatrix's friend had given her a mock interview before she actually went to meet the personnel manager of the company she was applying to.

  貝翠絲的朋友給她一個模擬的面試，在她真的要和所申請工作公司的人事主管面試之前。100導遊

- It has been my honor and pleasure to work with him for more than 10 years. His insight and analysis are always impressive.

  能與他共事超過10年以上是我的榮幸。他的洞見和分析總是令人印象深刻。101導遊

- Since the president of the company is absent, the general manager will preside over the meeting.

  既然公司總裁缺席，總經理將會主持這場會議。99導遊

- Cathy is an outgoing and successful salesperson, but her background is in web design.

  凱西是很活潑成功的業務，但她的出身背景是網頁設計。99導遊

- Upon agreeing to the plan, the organizers are to set out the procedures.

  一旦同意計劃，負責人員就開始設定步驟。102領隊

- As Tim has no experience at all, I doubt he is qualified for this job.

  因為提姆沒有任何經驗，我懷疑他是否有資格勝任這份工作。102領隊

- The Union has filed a protest on behalf of the terminated workers.

  公會已經代表被資遣的員工發起抗議。102領隊

- The manager lacked coordination and communication skills; likewise, his crew was altogether disjointed.

  這名經理缺乏統整以及溝通技巧，同樣的，他的人員也都很散亂。102領隊

❸ Having been unemployed for almost one year, Henry has little chance of getting a job.

因為亨利已經失業幾乎一年了，他找到工作的機會很小。101領隊

❸ All the employees have to use an electronic card to clock in when they arrive for work.

所有的員工都必須使用電子卡來打卡，當抵達辦公室時。101領隊

❸ The non-smoking policy will apply to any person working for the company regardless of their status or position.

禁菸政策將適用於任何在公司工作的人，不管其地位或職位。101領隊

⚠ **重點**：regardless 無論如何；regarding 關於某事的3種用法："Regarding something"、"With regard to something"、"As regards something"。

❸ I would like to express our gratitude to you on behalf of my company.

我想要代表我的公司向你表達感謝之意。101領隊

❸ Those wishing to be considered for paid leave should put their requests in as soon as possible.

想要考慮有薪假的人應該盡快提出申請。101領隊

❸ Whoever is first to arrive in the office is responsible for checking the voice mail.

不論是誰第一個進到辦公室，要負責檢查語音信箱。101領隊

❸ My boss is very demanding; he keeps asking us to complete assigned tasks within the limited time span.

我的老闆很嚴苛，他一直要求我們在有限的時間內完成指定任務。98導遊

❸ We all felt embarrassed when the manager got drunk.

當經理喝醉時，我們都感到很不好意思。100領隊

❸ If you want to work in tourism, you need to know how to work as part of a team. But sometimes, you also need to know how to work independently.

如果你想要在旅遊業工作，你需要知道如何和團體工作。但有時候你也需要知道如何獨立作業。99領隊

❂ John has to submit the annual report to the manager before this Friday; otherwise, he will be in trouble.

約翰必須在這週五之前提交年度報告給經理，不然他就完蛋了。99領隊

❂ Due to his lack of experience, the applicant was not considered for the job.

由於他的經驗不足，這名申請者不被考慮錄取這份工作。101領隊

❂ The company had the market surveyed by a nationally-known research firm.

這間公司請了全國知名的研究公司來做市場調查。101領隊

❂ Before the applicant left, the interviewer asked him for a current contact number so that he could be reached if he was given the job.

在應徵者離開之前，面試人員向他要他的聯絡電話，若是錄取便得以聯絡。101領隊

❂ May I remind you not to jeopardize your success on an important test by watching a movie instead of studying hard.

讓我提醒你不要因為看電影而沒有用功念書，危害了你的重要考試。100導遊

❂ Most prestigious private schools are highly competitive – that is, they have stiffer admissions requirements.

大部分有名氣的私立學校都很競爭，也就是他們有比較嚴格的入學條件。100導遊

❂ Katherine was reminded to return the book by next Monday, which she borrowed from the school library three months ago.

凱薩琳被提醒下週一還書，她3個月前從學校圖書館借的。99導遊

❂ The students were completely in the dark about their graduation trip because the school wanted it to be a surprise.

學生對於畢業旅行一無所知，因為學校希望這是一個驚喜。100導遊

⚠ 重點：用直譯來看in the dark為在黑暗中，也就是什麼都看不到、不清楚的意思。

另外have no clue也可代表一無所知的意思。

❂ One of the most important parts of these activities is for students to share the highlights of a group discussion with the rest of the class.

這些活動最重要的部分之一就是讓學生和班上分享團體討論的重點。102領隊

- A group of young students has taken the initiative through social media to organize a rally against the austerity plans.

  一群年輕學生透過社群媒體提出倡議以組織策畫來對抗撙節計劃。102領隊

- Stay calm and clear-minded. I'm sure you'll have no problem passing the exam.

  保持冷靜和清晰的思路。我敢保證你可以沒有問題的通過考試。102領隊

  重點：have no problem + V-ing 做某事沒有問題；have problems + V-ing 做某事有問題 / 困難 = have trouble / difficulty + V-ing。

- The school boys stopped bullying the stray dog when their teacher went up to them.

  當他們的老師走向他們時，這些男學生停止欺負流浪狗。101領隊

  重點：stop + V-ing表示停止做某事；stop to V表示停下手邊之事，去做某事。

- Tom was expelled from his school for stealing and cheating on the exams.

  湯姆被學校開除是因為偷竊以及考試作弊。99領隊

- He runs away with the idea, and the other faculty members do not agree.

  他倉促地說出想法，而其他教職員不同意。100領隊

- Bonnie signed up for dancing classes in the Extension Program.

  邦妮報名登記了推廣教育的舞蹈課。100領隊

歷屆外語領隊
英文試題＋中譯與解析

98 年外語領隊英文試題＋標準答案

★98年專門職業及技術人員普通考試導遊人員、領隊人員考試試題

類科：外語領隊人員（英語）

科 目：外國語（英語）

考試時間：1 小時 20 分

※注意：（一）本試題為單一選擇題，請選出一個正確或最適當的答案，複選作答者，該題不予計分。
（二）本科目共80題，每題1.25分，須用2Ｂ鉛筆在試卡上依題號清楚劃記，於本試題上作答者，不予計分。
（三）本試題禁止使用電子計算器。

I. Vocabulary and Grammar. Choose the best answer for each test item.
單字與文法：替每個測驗項目選出最適合的答案。

(　　)1. The plane leaving for Tokyo from Hong Kong will ______ at seven p.m..
(A) depart　(B) departing　(C) departure　(D) departed

(　　)2. You will have to pay extra ______ for overweight baggage.
(A) tags　(B) badges　(C) fees　(D) credits

(　　)3. If you want to become a successful tour manager, you have to work ______ and learn from the seniors.
(A) hard　(B) hardly　(C) harshly　(D) easily

(　　)4. You will get a boarding ______ after completing the check-in.
(A) pass　(B) post　(C) plan　(D) past

(　　)5. May I have two hundred U.S. dollars in small ______?
(A) accounts　(B) balance　(C) numbers　(D) denominations

(　　)6. I would like to ______ $500 from my savings account.
(A) give in　(B) put out　(C) withdraw　(D) reject

(　　)7. The flight to Chicago has been ______ due to heavy snow.
(A) concealed　(B) cancelled　(C) compared　(D) consoled

(　　)8. Please keep your seat belt ______ during the flight for safety.

(A) fasten　(B) fastened　(C) fastening　(D) fastener

(　　)9. You will need to take a ______ flight from Taoyuan to Kaohsiung.

(A) contacting　(B) connecting　(C) competing　(D) computing

(　　)10. Many tourists are fascinated by the natural ______ of Taroko Gorge.

(A) sparkles　(B) spectacles　(C) spectators　(D) sprinklers

(　　)11. City ______ are always available at the local tourist information center.

(A) floors　(B) streets　(C) maps　(D) tickets

(　　)12. The American government has decided to provide financial assistance to ______ the automobile industry. Car makers are relieved at the news.

(A) accommodate　(B) bail out　(C) cash in on　(D) detect

(　　)13. Tourists are advised to ______ traveling to areas with landslides.

(A) avoid　(B) assume　(C) assist　(D) accompany

(　　)14. All transportation vehicles should be well-______ and kept in good running condition.

(A) retrained　(B) maintained　(C) entertained　(D) suspended

(　　)15. ______ birds are suspected to be major carriers of avian flu.

(A) Immigrating　(B) Migratory　(C) Seasoning　(D) Motivating

(　　)16. My boss is very ______; he keeps asking us to complete assigned tasks within the limited time span.

(A) luxurious　(B) demanding　(C) obvious　(D) relaxing

(　　)17. I missed the early morning train because I ______.

(A) overbooked　(B) overcooked　(C) overtook　(D) overslept

(　　)18. In time of economic ______, many small companies will downsize their operation.

(A) appreciation　(B) progression　(C) recession　(D) reduction

(　　)19. You will be ______ for littering in public places.

(A) fined　(B) found　(C) founded　(D) funded

(　　)20. The police officer needs to ______ the traffic during the rush hours.

(A) assign　(B) break　(C) compete　(D) direct

(　　)21. We look forward to ______ from you soon.

(A) seeing　(B) hear　(C) hearing　(D) listen

(　　)22. Reservations for hotel accommodation should be made in ______ to make sure rooms are available.

(A) advance　(B) advanced　(C) advances　(D) advancing

(　　)23. People traveling to a foreign country may need to apply ______ a visa.

(A) for　(B) of　(C) on　(D) to

(　　)24. He likes to travel. He is very ______ in learning foreign languages and cultures.

(A) interest　(B) interested　(C) interesting　(D) interestingly

(　　)25. This is a non-smoking restaurant. Please ______ your cigarette at once.

(A) put in　(B) put on　(C) put out　(D) put up

(　　)26. The hotel services are far from satisfactory. I need to ______ a complaint with the manager.

(A) pay　(B) claim　(C) file　(D) add

(　　)27. The company is ______ the new products now, so you can buy one and get the second one free.

(A) forwarding　(B) progressing　(C) promoting　(D) pretending

(　　)28. Beware of strangers at the airport and do not leave your luggage ______.

(A) unanswered　(B) uninterested　(C) unimportant　(D) unattended

(　　)29. If you have the receipts for the goods you have purchased, you can claim a tax ______ at the airport upon departure.

(A) relief　(B) rebate　(C) involve　(D) reply

(　　)30. We are sorry. All lines are currently busy. Please ______ on for the next available agent.

(A) keep　(B) hold　(C) call　(D) take

( )31. All passengers shall go through ______ check before boarding.

(A) security (B) activity (C) insurance (D) deficiency

( )32. The time ______ is thirteen hours between Taipei and New York.

(A) decision (B) division (C) diligence (D) difference

( )33. This artist's ______ are on exhibition at the museum.

(A) workouts (B) presences (C) masterminds (D) masterpieces

( )34. You will pay a ______ of fifty dollars for your ferry ride.

(A) fan (B) fate (C) fair (D) fare

( )35. People have to learn to ______ their problems.

(A) find fault with (B) cope with (C) come up with (D) end up with

( )36. Public ______ to voting is a problem in many democratic countries with low turnouts in elections.

(A) interpretation (B) intervention (C) contribution (D) indifference

( )37. The news was ______ good ______ true.

(A) to.....is (B) two.....to be (C) too.....to be (D) so.....that is

( )38. The ______ cake appears so ______.

(A) flash.....inviting (B) flesh.....invited

(C) fresh.....inviting (D) flush.....invited

( )39. ______ a fire, the heritage building ______.

(A) It is because.....burned down (B) Because.....burned down

(C) Because of.....was burned down (D) That because of.....had burned down

( )40. Jumbo jet had made ______ for people ______ for a long distance comfortably.

(A) possible.....to travel (B) possible it.....travel

(C) it possible.....to travel (D) it is possible.....travel

( )41. Those who ______ a quake ______ life more.

(A) survives.....cherishes (B) have survived.....will cherish

(C) are surviving.....are cherished (D) are survivals of .....had cherished

II. Word meaning. Choose the best answer for the underlined word or phrase in each sentence. 詞意測驗：請選出詞意與每題以底線標示之字詞最接近的答案。

(　　)42. Government officials have overlooked the impact of inflation on the economy.

(A) highly expected　　(B) failed to notice
(C) found ways of　　(D) forgave

(　　)43. I came across my high school classmate when I traveled to Los Angeles.

(A) met by chance　　(B) planned to visit
(C) moved to see　　(D) was glad to find

(　　)44. John's families moved to the United States. They intended to live there for good.

(A) comfortably　(B) permanently　(C) mostly　(D) temporarily

(　　)45. All drinks served on the airplane are complimentary.

(A) for extra cost　　(B) of self service
(C) free of charge　　(D) first come, first served

(　　)46. The airplane is cruising at an altitude of 30,000 feet at 700 kilometers per hour.

(A) detecting　(B) moving　(C) showing　(D) speeding

(　　)47. Many people have put on some pounds during the New Year vacation.

(A) dressed up　(B) gained　(C) gambled　(D) turned into

(　　)48. I think you are paying too much for the bells and whistles of this new car.

(A) important equipment　　(B) basic ingredients
(C) unnecessary features　　(D) visual differences

(　　)49. After three years, the most wanted criminal is still at large.

(A) is finally kept in prison　　(B) is living miserably
(C) is released　　(D) has not yet been caught

(　　)50. The airline company finally broke even last year.

(A) was highly profitable　　(B) went bankrupt
(C) stopped losing money　　(D) had an accident

(　　)51. You will need to brush up on your Spanish if you want to do business with people from South American countries.

(A) improve　(B) learn painting　(C) pretend to master　(D) withdraw

(　　)52. All proceeds from the auction will go to charities.

(A) profits　(B) bargains　(C) costs　(D) losses

(　　)53. As the flight to the Bahamas was delayed for eight hours, all passengers were going bananas.

(A) buying fruits　(B) going to the market

(C) getting very angry　(D) disappointed

(　　)54. He got his visa at the eleventh hour.

(A) at the last moment　(B) at eleven o'clock

(C) before noon　(D) by midnight

(　　)55. I was supposed to meet John at the concert hall, but he stood me up.

(A) kept his promise　(B) knew it well

(C) canceled the reservation　(D) didn't show up

III. Cloze. Please choose the best answer for each blank in the following passages.
段落填空：請選出下列段落中各句空格的最佳答案。

Now (56) as a clinical condition, the symptoms of jet lag include (57) of exhaustion, disorientation, forgetfulness and fuzziness, not to mention headaches, bad moods, and a reduced sex drive. Some people's circadian rhythms are so (58) disrupted that they are on the (59) of true depression. But while it's generally accepted that there is no "cure" for jet lag, an increasing number of treatments and products are said to be able to minimize its (60) , which can last anything from a few days to several weeks.

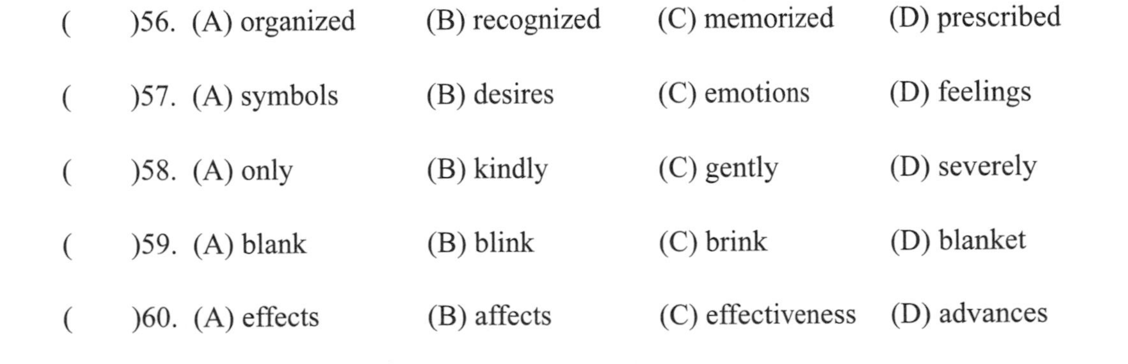

(　　)56. (A) organized　(B) recognized　(C) memorized　(D) prescribed

(　　)57. (A) symbols　(B) desires　(C) emotions　(D) feelings

(　　)58. (A) only　(B) kindly　(C) gently　(D) severely

(　　)59. (A) blank　(B) blink　(C) brink　(D) blanket

(　　)60. (A) effects　(B) affects　(C) effectiveness　(D) advances

When you (61) a foreign purchase to a bank credit card, such as MasterCard or Visa, all you lose with most cards is the 1 percent the issuer charges for the actual exchange. Other banks, (62) , add a surcharge of 2 to 3 percent on transactions in foreign currencies. Even (63) a surcharge, you generally lose less with a credit card (64) with currency or traveler's checks.

Therefore, don't use traveler's checks as your primary (65) of foreign payment. But do take along a few $20 checks or bills to exchange at retail for those last minute or unexpected needs.

( )61. (A) exchange (B) charge (C) recharge (D) claim

( )62. (A) as a result (B) as a consequence
(C) however (D) moreover

( )63. (A) when (B) with (C) as (D) about

( )64. (A) than (B) then (C) there (D) theme

( )65. (A) mean (B) means (C) meaning (D) material

All societies have dress codes, most of which (66) unwritten but understood by most members of the society. The dress code has (67) rules or signals indicating how a person's clothing should be (68) . This message may (69) indications of the person's social class, income, occupation, ethnic and religious affiliation, attitude, marital status, sexual availability, and sexual orientation. Clothes convey other social messages, including personal or cultural identity. (70) , wearing expensive clothes can communicate wealth or the image of wealth.

( )66. (A) is (B) are (C) be (D) had

( )67. (A) build (B) been built (C) built-in (D) building

( )68. (A) wear (B) wore (C) worn (D) warm

( )69. (A) accuse (B) exclude (C) include (D) confess

( )70. (A) In addition (B) In summary (C) For example (D) In contrast

IV. Reading Comprehension. 閱讀測驗

Railways were the first form of mass transportation and had an effective monopoly on land transport until the development of the motorcar in the early 20th century. Railway companies in Europe and the United States used streamlined trains since 1933 for high-speed services with an average speed of up to 130 km/h (80 mph) and a top speed of more than 160 km/h (100 mph).

The first high-speed train was the Italian ETR 200 that in July 1939 went from Milan to Florence at 165 km/h, with a top speed of 203 km/h. With this service, these trains were able to compete with the upcoming airplanes. In 1957, the Odakyu Electric Railway in Greater Tokyo launched its Romancecar 3000 SSE. This set a world record for narrow gauge trains at 145 km/h (90 mph), giving Japanese designers confidence that they could safely build even faster trains at standard gauge. Desperate for transport solutions due to overloaded trains between Tokyo and Osaka, the idea of high-speed rail was born in Japan.

There is no globally accepted standard separating high-speed rail from conventional railroads; however, a number of widely accepted variables have been acknowledged by the industry in recent years. Generally, high-speed rail is defined as having a top speed in regular use of over 200 km/h (125 mph).

(　　)71. According to the first paragraph of this passage, what is true about the development of mass transportation?

(A) Railways used to be the primary means of land transportation before the 20th century.
(B) Motorcars were designed to monopolize land transport in the early 20th century.
(C) High-speed services derived from motorcar racing.
(D) The high-speed train was first built by Japanese engineers.

(　　)72. According to the passage, which country introduced the first high-speed train?

(A) Italy.　(B) France.　(C) Japan.　(D) The USA.

(　　)73. What is the top record speed ever achieved by high-speed trains before 1960?

(A) 90 km/h　(B) 145 km/h　(C) 165 km/h　(D) 203 km/h

(　　)74. What was the driving force for the Japanese to first build the high-speed rail?

(A) To compete with airplane transportation.
(B) To share the train transport loadings between Tokyo and Osaka.
(C) To attract foreign tourists to Japan.
(D) To show off their hi-tech achievement.

(　　)75. Which of the following statements is true?

(A) Traditional railroads are no longer in use.
(B) Airlines will lose their customers to high-speed rails because of speed.
(C) High-speed rail is defined as having a speed of over 200 kilometers per hour.
(D) High-speed rail companies will replace all land transporters.

A tour manager has individual duties to perform to run a tour smoothly and successfully. For instance, the tour manager should always be the first one up every morning in order to make sure each team member is ready before the bus leaves for the next scenic spot each day.

The tour manager will also check for possible changes to the itinerary. Most days of a tour require a long bus trip to the next venue. The traveling time may be the only opportunity for the tour manager to undertake much of the administrative chores: paper work, phone calls, and planning for the next few days. This may include confirming and reconfirming hotel reservations, return flights, and arrival time at restaurants and scenic spots.

It usually falls to the tour manager to keep the team members and the service crew happy while they are hundreds, or thousands, of miles away from their homes and their families. The tour manager shall keep everyone working as a team and deal with individual problems, such as stolen passports, physical ailments and medical emergencies. Most importantly, the tour manager must take the group members home safe and sound at the end of the journey and get ready for the next trip.

(　　)76. What is this passage mainly about?

(A) Running a profitable tour.
(B) Tips on booking cheap hotel rooms.
(C) Enjoying tours.
(D) The duties of a tour manager.

(　　)77. Which of the following is generally NOT considered a tour manager's responsibility?

(A) Keep everyone happy.
(B) Drive the tour bus.
(C) Visit the resorts as scheduled.
(D) Confirm hotel reservations.

(　　)78. Which of the following words is closest in meaning to the word "venue" in the passage?

(A) Stand
(B) Spot
(C) Sport
(D) Sigh

(　　)79. What will a responsible tour manager most likely do on the bus during the tour?

(A) Make phone calls to friends.
(B) Buy discounted souvenirs for team members.
(C) Find seats with the best view for team members.
(D) Reconfirm return flights for team members.

(　　)80. What can be inferred from this passage?

(A) Most tours become mental and physical burdens for a tour manager.
(B) Most tours require tour members to pay extra fees for services.
(C) Most tour managers don't change their original itinerary.
(D) Most tour managers ask their group members to help with chores.

★標準答案

1. (A)	2. (C)	3. (A)	4. (A)	5. (D)
6. (C)	7. (B)	8. (B)	9. (B)	10. (B)
11. (C)	12. (B)	13. (A)	14. (B)	15. (B)
16. (B)	17. (D)	18. (C)	19. (A)	20. (D)
21. (C)	22. (A)	23. (A)	24. (B)	25. (C)
26. (C)	27. (C)	28. (D)	29. (B)	30. (B)
31. (A)	32. (D)	33. (D)	34. (D)	35. (B)
36. (D)	37. (C)	38. (C)	39. (C)	40. (C)
41. (B)	42. (B)	43. (A)	44. (B)	45. (C)
46. (B)	47. (B)	48. (C)	49. (D)	50. (C)
51. (A)	52. (A)	53. (C)	54. (A)	55. (D)
56. (B)	57. (D)	58. (D)	59. (C)	60. (A)
61. (B)	62. (C)	63. (B)	64. (A)	65. (B)
66. (B)	67. (C)	68. (C)	69. (C)	70. (C)
71. (A)	72. (A)	73. (D)	74. (B)	75. (C)
76. (D)	77. (B)	78. (B)	79. (D)	80. (A)

98 年外語領隊英文試題中譯與解析

I. Vocabulary and Grammar. Choose the best answer for each test item.
單字與文法：替每個測驗項目選出最適合的答案。

1. The plane leaving for Tokyo from Hong Kong will depart at seven p.m..

(A) depart（原形動詞） (B) departing（現在分詞）
(C) departure（名詞） (D) departed（過去分詞）
以上皆為起飛之意。

中譯 從香港飛往東京的班機將於晚上7點起飛。

解析 will後面加原形動詞，故選depart 起飛。

2. You will have to pay extra fees for overweight baggage.

(A) tags 標籤 (B) badges 徽章 (C) fees 費用 (D) credits 信用

中譯 你必須替超重的行李支付額外的費用。

解析 由pay可以直接推知答案為fees。fee為通稱的費用，而tuition fees則是學費。charge為收取費用之意，No charge則為不需收費。fee的例句：The museum charges adults a small fee, but children can go in for free. 博物館向成人收取少許入場費，但小孩則可以免費參觀。98導遊

3. If you want to become a successful tour manager, you have to work hard and learn from the seniors.

(A) hard 努力地 (B) hardly 幾乎不地 (C) harshly 嚴厲地 (D) easily 容易地

中譯 如果你想成為一名成功的領隊，你必須很努力地工作並向資深領隊學習。

解析 常聽到的play hard, work hard 認真玩樂、認真工作，也是同樣用法。the seniors 長者，也可作前輩、資深人士。

4. You will get a boarding pass after completing the check-in.

(A) pass 通行證 (B) post 郵件 (C) plan 計劃 (D) past 過去

中譯 在完成登機報到手續之後，你將會拿到一張登機證。

解析 boarding pass 登機證。

5. May I have two hundred U.S. dollars in small denominations?

(A) accounts 帳目 (B) balance 餘額 (C) numbers 號碼 (D) denominations 面額

中譯 我可以兌換200美元的小額鈔票嗎？

解析 denomination 面額，例句：In what denominations? 要什麼面額的？

6. I would like to withdraw $500 from my savings account.

(A) give in 屈服 (B) put out 熄滅 (C) withdraw 提領 (D) reject 拒收

中譯 我想從我的儲蓄帳戶內提500美元。

解析 withdraw 提領；deposit 存入；savings account 儲蓄存款戶頭。

7. The flight to Chicago has been cancelled due to heavy snow.

(A) concealed 隱含 (B) cancelled 取消

(C) compared 比起 (D) consoled 安慰

中譯 因為大雪，到芝加哥的班機被取消了。

解析 cancel 取消，由heavy snow可推知班機被取消了。其他類似例句：Due to the impending disaster, we have to cancel our flight to Bangkok. 因為即將到來的災害，我們必須取消到曼谷的航班。100領隊

8. Please keep your seat belt fastened during the flight for safety.

(A) fasten（原形動詞） (B) fastened（過去分詞）

(C) fastening（現在式） (D) fastener（名詞）

以上皆為束緊之意。

中譯 為了安全，飛行途中請束緊你的安全帶。

解析 keep後面接過去分詞，其實就是讓此過去分詞當形容詞用，也就是讓「某物」（此處為seat belt 安全帶）維持在「某狀態」（此處為fastened 束緊狀態）。因為東西是「被束緊」，故選過去分詞。

9. You will need to take a connecting flight from Taoyuan to Kaohsiung.

(A) contacting 聯繫 (B) connecting 連接

(C) competing 比賽 (D) computing 計算

中譯 從桃園到高雄，你必須搭接駁班機。

解析 connecting flight 轉機班機，例句：Due to the delay, we are not able to catch up with our connecting flight. 因為延遲，我們無法趕上我們的轉機班機。102領隊

10. Many tourists are fascinated by the natural spectacles of Taroko Gorge.

(A) sparkles 火花 (B) spectacles 奇觀

(C) spectators 觀眾 (D) sprinklers 灑水機

中譯 許多觀光客為太魯閣的自然奇觀所著迷。

解析 spectacles 奇觀；fascinate 迷住、強烈地吸引，fascinating用來形容某事，fastened則是指人被迷住了的意思。

11. City maps are always available at the local tourist information center.

(A) floors 樓層 (B) streets 街道 (C) maps 地圖 (D) tickets 票

中譯 城市地圖可在當地觀光旅遊中心取得。

解析 重點單字：available 可得到的；unavailable 不可得的。

12. The American government has decided to provide financial assistance to bail out the automobile industry. Car makers are relieved at the news.

(A) accommodate 適應 (B) bail out 保釋、紓困

(C) cash in on 利用 (D) detect 偵測

中譯 美國政府決定提供財務援助來紓困汽車工業。汽車業者對此新聞感到欣慰。

解析 bail out 保釋、紓困，例句：I asked for a rise of salary so I could bail out. 我要求加薪以便渡過困難。

13. Tourists are advised to avoid traveling to areas with landslides.

(A) avoid 避免 (B) assume 假設

(C) assist 協助 (D) accompany 陪伴

中譯 觀光客被通知避免旅行到有山崩的地方。

解析 avoid + Ving 避免某事；landslide 山崩。

14. All transportation vehicles should be well-maintained and kept in good running condition.

(A) retrained 再訓練 (B) maintained 維護

(C) entertained 招待 (D) suspended 中止

中譯 所有的交通工具都該有完善的維護，且保持良好的運作狀態。

解析 由kept in good running condition可推知為maintained，過去分詞表「被」維護。vehicle 運載工具。

15. Migratory birds are suspected to be major carriers of avian flu.

(A) Immigrating 移來的
(B) Migratory 遷移的
(C) Seasoning 調味品
(D) Motivating 刺激的

中譯 會遷移的鳥類被懷疑是禽流感的主要帶原者。

解析 migratory bird 候鳥（會遷移的鳥類）；avian flu 禽流感。

16. My boss is very demanding; he keeps asking us to complete assigned tasks within the limited time span.

(A) luxurious 豪華的
(B) demanding 苛求的
(C) obvious 明顯的
(D) relaxing 令人輕鬆的

中譯 我的老闆很嚴苛，他一直要求我們在有限的時間內完成指定任務。

解析 由assigned tasks within the limited time span可推知為demanding 苛求的（現在分詞當形容詞，形容人）；assign 分配、分派。

17. I missed the early morning train because I overslept.

(A) overbooked 超額訂購
(B) overcooked 煮得過久
(C) overtook 趕上
(D) overslept 睡過頭

中譯 因為我睡過頭，所以錯過早班火車。

解析 由missed train可推知為oversleep 睡過頭（overslept為過去式）。

18. In time of economic recession, many small companies will downsize their operation.

(A) appreciation 鑑賞力
(B) progression 發展
(C) recession 不景氣
(D) reduction 減少

中譯 在經濟不景氣時期，很多小公司都會縮減他們的經營。

解析 由downsize 裁減（員工）人數，可推知為recession 不景氣。economic recession經濟蕭條為慣用說法，而非economic reduction 經濟減少，無此說法。

19. You will be fined for littering in public places.

(A) fined 處以……罰金
(B) found 建立
(C) founded 被……建立
(D) funded 被……挹注資金

中譯 在公共場所亂丟垃圾會被罰錢。

解析 fine 處以……罰金；litter 亂扔廢棄物。國外路邊常見的標示為：Do not litter、No littering都是不要隨意丟棄的意思。

20. The police officer needs to direct the traffic during the rush hours.

(A) assign 分配 (B) break 打破 (C) compete 比賽 **(D) direct 指揮**

中譯 警察須在尖峰時刻指揮交通。

解析 direct 指揮，此處當動詞。rush 匆忙的、繁忙的。

21. We look forward to hearing from you soon.

(A) seeing 看到 (B) hear 聽到 **(C) hearing 聽到** (D) listen 傾聽

中譯 我們很期望很快地聽到你的消息。

解析 look forward的用法有兩種：① look forward to + N；② look forward to + Ving。

22. Reservations for hotel accommodation should be made in advance to make sure rooms are available.

(A) advance (B) advanced (C) advances (D) advancing

中譯 旅館的訂房應提早訂，才能確保有房間。

解析 in advance 事先，為必考片語。

23. People traveling to a foreign country may need to apply for a visa.

(A) for (B) of (C) on (D) to

中譯 人們到國外旅行可能需要申請簽證。

解析 visa 簽證，例句：If you're travelling to the United States, you may need a visa. 如果你到美國旅行，你可能需要簽證。100領隊

24. He likes to travel. He is very interested in learning foreign languages and cultures.

(A) interest 興趣 **(B) interested 感興趣的**
(C) interesting 有趣的 (D) interestingly 抱持興趣地

中譯 他喜歡旅遊。他對學習外國語言和文化很有趣的。

解析 interested 人對某事有興趣；interesting 某事是有趣的。

25. This is a non-smoking restaurant. Please put out your cigarette at once.

(A) put in 提交 (B) put on 穿上 **(C) put out 熄滅** (D) put up 建造

中譯 這裡是非吸菸餐廳。請立刻熄滅你的香菸。

解析 put out 熄滅；at once 立刻、馬上。

26. The hotel services are far from satisfactory. I need to file a complaint with the manager.

(A) pay 支付 (B) claim 聲稱 (C) file 申訴 (D) add 添加

中譯 旅館的服務完全稱不上滿意。我需要向經理客訴。

解析 file a complaint 投訴；satisfactory 令人滿意的、符合要求的；unsatisfactory 不令人滿意的，例句：People might refuse to tip if they find the service is unsatisfactory. 如果他們覺得服務不滿意的話，人們可能會拒絕給小費。99領隊

27. The company is promoting the new products now, so you can buy one and get the second one free.

(A) forwarding 轉寄 (B) progressing 進步
(C) promoting 推銷 (D) pretending 假裝

中譯 公司現在正在推廣新產品，所以你可享買一送一的優惠。

解析 promote 推銷（動詞）；promotion 推銷（名詞）。

28. Beware of strangers at the airport and do not leave your luggage unattended.

(A) unanswered 未答覆的 (B) uninterested 無利害關係的
(C) unimportant 不重要的 (D) unattended 沒人照顧的

中譯 小心機場的陌生人，不要讓你的行李無人看管（在視線之外）。

解析 國外常見告示牌寫Please do not leave personal belongings unattended.。

29. If you have the receipts for the goods you have purchased, you can claim a tax rebate at the airport upon departure.

(A) relief 減輕 (B) rebate 折扣 (C) involve 包含 (D) reply 回答

中譯 如果你有購物收據，離境時可於機場要求退稅。

解析 rebate 折扣；goods 商品；purchase 購買；departure 出發、起程。

30. We are sorry. All lines are currently busy. Please hold on for the next available agent.

(A) keep 保持 (B) hold 握住 (C) call 呼叫 (D) take 拿

中譯 很抱歉。所有電話都忙線中。請等候下一位服務人員。

解析 hold on（打電話時用語）別掛斷；currently 現在。

31. All passengers shall go through security check before boarding.

(A) security 安全 (B) activity 活動 (C) insurance 保險 (D) deficiency 缺乏

中譯 上機前所有旅客都應該通過安全檢查。

解析 security 安全；flight security 飛安。

32. The time difference is thirteen hours between Taipei and New York.

(A) decision 決定 (B) division 區分 (C) diligence 勤奮 (D) difference 差別

中譯 台北與紐約的時差為13個小時。

解析 time difference 時差。

33. This artist's masterpieces are on exhibition at the museum.

(A) workouts 練習 (B) presences 出席
(C) masterminds 智囊 (D) masterpieces 傑作

中譯 藝術家的傑作正於博物館展出。

解析 masterpiece 傑作；exhibition 展覽。

34. You will pay a fare of fifty dollars for your ferry ride.

(A) fan 電風扇 (B) fate 命運 (C) fair 博覽會 (D) fare 費用

中譯 你要付50元的費用來搭乘渡輪。

解析 fee和fare的差別：
① fee 服務費
- pay the lawyer's fees 付律師費
- a bill for school fees 學費帳單
② fare（大眾運輸）票價
- What is the bus fare to London? 到倫敦的公共汽車費是多少？
- travel at half / full / reduced fare 半價 / 全價 / 減價
- Most taxi drivers in Kinmen prefer to ask for a flat fare rather than use the meter.
大部分金門的計程車司機喜歡使用單一費率而非使用計程表。100導遊

35. People have to learn to cope with their problems.

(A) find fault with 批評 (B) cope with 應對
(C) come up with 趕上 (D) end up with 以……作為結束

中譯 人們必須學習處理自己的問題。

解析 cope with their problems 處理問題，solve則是解決。

36. Public indifference to voting is a problem in many democratic countries with low turnouts in elections.

(A) interpretation 解釋 (B) intervention 調停
(C) contribution 貢獻 (D) indifference 不重視

中譯 大眾對於投票的漠不關心且投票率低是許多民主國家的問題。

解析 democratic 民主的；indifference 漠不關心；difference 不同之處，例句：Her daughter's indifference to her makes her very sad. She wishes her daughter would show more concern for her. 她女兒對她的漠不關心讓她相當難過。她希望女兒能夠更關心她。98導遊

37. The news was too good to be true.

(A) to.....is (B) two.....to be (C) too.....to be (D) so.....that is

中譯 這個消息好到不像真的。

解析 too...to...是太……所以不能的意思，to後面的句子要用否定來解釋。

38. The fresh cake appears so inviting.

(A) flash.....inviting 閃光……誘人的 (B) flesh.....invited 肌肉……邀請
(C) fresh.....inviting 新鮮……誘人的 (D) flush.....invited 沖洗……邀請

中譯 這個新鮮蛋糕看起來太吸引人了。

解析 當現在分詞inviting是描述感受時，表達的是修飾的名詞給人的感受。此處的修飾對象為the fresh cake，而inviting為吸引人的（像是邀請人來吃的意思）。appear 似乎、看來好像。

39. Because of a fire, the heritage building was burned down.

(A) It is because.....burned down (B) Because.....burned down
(C) Because of.....was burned down (D) That because of.....had burned down

中譯 由於這場大火，這座古蹟被燒毀了。

解析 because of + 名詞，fire為名詞，故選because of。building是「被」燒掉，故選burned down。heritage 遺產、世襲財產。

40. Jumbo jet had made it possible for people to travel for a long distance comfortably.

(A) possible.....to travel
(B) possible it.....travel
(C) it possible.....to travel
(D) it is possible.....travel

中譯 波音747飛機使人長途旅行得以舒適成真。

解析 make it possible to V 「使V……成為可能」的意思，使得V（動作）可以執行。此處make不是使役動詞，其中的it是假主詞，代替後面的to V。原句應為make to travel for a long distance comfortably possilble。但是受詞（to travel for a long distance comfortably）太長，改成make it possible to travel for a long distance comfortably。

41. Those who have survived a quake will cherish life more.

(A) survives.....cherishes 生存……珍惜
(B) have survived.....will cherish
(C) are surviving.....are cherished
(D) are survivals of .....had cherished

中譯 那些從地震中存活的人會更珍惜生命。

解析 此題從中文意思推論即可解題，因為已經存活（have survived），所以將來更珍惜生命（will cherish）。

II. Word meaning. Choose the best answer for the underlined word or phrase in each sentence. 詞意測驗：請選出詞意與每題以底線標示之字詞最接近的答案。

42. Government officials have overlooked the impact of inflation on the economy.

(A) highly expected 高度的期待
(B) failed to notice 沒有注意到
(C) found ways of 找到方法
(D) forgave 原諒

中譯 政府官員忽略了通貨膨脹對經濟的影響。

解析 考題中常見以over開頭的單字：oversleep 睡過頭；overweight 過重。impact 衝擊；inflation 通貨膨脹。

43. I came across my high school classmate when I traveled to Los Angeles.

(A) met by chance 偶遇　(B) planned to visit 計劃去訪問

(C) moved to see 前去探訪　(D) was glad to find 高興地找到

中譯 當我到洛杉磯旅行時，我碰巧遇見我的高中同學。

解析 come across、meet by chance都是偶遇的意思。

44. John's families moved to the United States. They intended to live there for good.

(A) comfortably 舒服地　(B) permanently 永久地

(C) mostly 大多　(D) temporarily 暫時地

中譯 約翰全家搬到美國。他們打算永遠住在那邊。

解析 intend 想要、打算；for good = permanently 永久地。

45. All drinks served on the airplane are complimentary.

(A) for extra cost 額外費用

(B) of self service 自助服務

(C) free of charge 免費

(D) first come, first served 先到者優先服務

中譯 所有在飛機上所供應的飲料都是免費的。

解析 complimentary 免費，例句：A complimentary breakfast of coffee and rolls is served in the lobby between 7 and 10 am. 有咖啡和捲餅的免費早餐於早上7點到10點在大廳供應。102領隊 charge名詞為費用，動詞為收費，把帳掛在……。Breakfast is provided at no extra charge. 提供早餐，不另收費（此處charge為名詞）。I would like to charge this to my American Express card, please. 我希望可以用我的美國運通卡付費，麻煩了（此處charge為動詞）。102領隊

46. The airplane is cruising at an altitude of 30,000 feet at 700 kilometers per hour.

(A) detecting 偵查　(B) moving 移動　(C) showing 顯示　(D) speeding 加速

中譯 飛機目前以每小時700公里的速度，航行於30,000英呎的海拔上。

解析 curise 飛行，例句：Airliners now cruise the ocean at great speed. 飛機目前以高速來越洋飛行。

47. Many people have put on some pounds during the New Year vacation.

(A) dressed up 打扮　　(B) gained 獲得

(C) gambled 賭博　　(D) turned into 使變成

中譯 於新年假期期間，許多人體重增加不少磅。

解析 gain weight、put on weight都是增重之意。例句：Please don't order so much food! I have been putting on weight for the last two months. 拜託別點太多食物！這兩個月我已經開始變胖了。100領隊

48. I think you are paying too much for the bells and whistles of this new car.

(A) important equipment 重要的設備

(B) basic ingredients 基本的原料

(C) unnecessary features 不重要的特點

(D) visual difference 視覺的不同

中譯 我認為你花太多的錢在添加這部新車所不必要的附加功能。

解析 由paying too much可推知為unnecessary features 不重要的特點，因為通常不需要的才會paying too much。

49. After three years, the most wanted criminal is still at large.

(A) is finally kept in prison 最終被關在監獄

(B) is living miserably 淒慘地生活

(C) is released 被釋放

(D) has not yet been caught 還沒有被抓

中譯 3年之後，頭號通緝犯仍逍遙法外。

解析 still at large 逍遙法外。

50. The airline company finally broke even last year.

(A) was highly profitable 高利潤　　(B) went bankrupt 破產

(C) stopped losing money 停止賠錢　　(D) had an accident 出了車禍

中譯 這家航空公司去年終於損益兩平。

解析 break even 不賺不賠、收支平衡。

51. You will need to brush up on your Spanish if you want to do business with people from South American countries.

(A) improve 改進 (B) learn painting 學習繪畫
(C) pretend to master 妄想要控制 (D) withdraw 提領

中譯 如果你想和南美國家的人做生意的話，你將需要改進你的西班牙文。

解析 brush up on 改進、溫習。

52. All proceeds from the auction will go to charities.

(A) profits 利潤 (B) bargains 特價品
(C) costs 花費 (D) losses 損失

中譯 全部從拍賣所得來的利潤，將會捐給慈善機構。

解析 proceed = profit 收益、利潤；auction 拍賣。

53. As the flight to the Bahamas was delayed for eight hours, all passengers were going bananas.

(A) buying fruits 買水果 (B) going to the market 去市場
(C) getting very angry 非常生氣 (D) disappointed 失望

中譯 因為飛往巴哈馬的班機延誤8小時，所有乘客都快氣瘋了。

解析 going bananas 氣瘋了。

54. He got his visa at the eleventh hour.

(A) at the last moment 在最後一刻 (B) at eleven o'clock 11點
(C) before noon 中午前 (D) by midnight 在午夜

中譯 他在最後一刻拿到簽證。

解析 at the eleventh hour 最後一刻。

55. I was supposed to meet John at the concert hall, but he stood me up.

(A) kept his promise 守承諾
(B) knew it well
(C) canceled the reservation 取消預約
(D) didn't show up 沒有出現

中譯 我原本和約翰約在音樂廳見面，但他放我鴿子。

解析 stand sb. up 爽某人約。

III. Cloze. Please choose the best answer for each blank in the following passages.
段落填空：請選出下列段落中各句空格的最佳答案。

Now recognized as a clinical condition, the symptoms of jet lag include feelings of exhaustion, disorientation, forgetfulness and fuzziness, not to mention headaches, bad moods, and a reduced sex drive. Some people's circadian rhythms are so severely disrupted that they are on the brink of true depression. But while it's generally accepted that there is no "cure" for jet lag, an increasing number of treatments and products are said to be able to minimize its effects, which can last anything from a few days to several weeks.

中譯 現今公認時差為臨床狀況，症狀包含精疲力竭、失去方向感、健忘和模糊不清，更別說是頭痛、情緒不好還有性慾減低。有些人的生理時鐘被嚴重打亂，以至於處於憂鬱沮喪的邊緣。雖然普遍認為時差無法被「治療」，但越來越多的療法和藥品據說可以使時差的影響減到最低，這樣的療效可以持續幾天甚至幾星期。

單字 clinical condition 臨床狀況　symptom 症狀
jet lag 時差　circadian rhythm 生理時鐘
treatment 治療法　minimize 使減到最少

56. (A) organized 有組織的　(B) recognized 公認的
(C) memorized 記下的　(D) prescribed 處方的

57. (A) symbols 象徵　(B) desires 慾望
(C) emotions 情緒　(D) feelings 情懷

58. (A) only 只有　(B) kindly 親切地
(C) gently 溫和地　(D) severely 嚴重地

59. (A) blank 使無效　(B) blink 眨眼睛
(C) brink 邊緣　(D) blanket 毯子

60. (A) effects 效果　(B) affects 影響
(C) effectiveness 效力　(D) advances 前進

When you charge a foreign purchase to a bank credit card, such as MasterCard or Visa, all you lose with most cards is the 1 percent the issuer charges for the actual exchange. Other banks, however, add a surcharge of 2 to 3 percent on transactions in foreign currencies. Even with a surcharge, you generally lose less with a credit card than with currency or traveler's checks.

中譯 當你用信用卡支付國外購物，像是MasterCard卡或是Visa卡，簽帳購物的損失是多收實際消費的1%附加費用。然而，其他銀行於外幣交易時則加收2-3%的附加費用。即便有附加費用，相較於付現或是旅行支票的損失還是比較少。

Therefore, don't use traveler's checks as your primary means of foreign payment. But do take along a few $20 checks or bills to exchange at retail for those last minute or unexpected needs.

中譯 所以不要以旅行支票當成國外付款的主要工具。但還是要準備幾張20美元面額的旅行支票或鈔票，以便最後一刻或是臨時購物之需。

單字 transaction 交易
foreign currency 外幣
surcharge 額外費

61. (A) exchange 交換 (B) charge 索價
(C) recharge 再索費 (D) claim 聲稱

62. (A) as a result 結束 (B) as a consequence 後果
(C) however 然而 (D) moreover 此外

解析 看到other banks可知是以however 然而來做比較。

63. (A) when (B) with (C) as (D) about

解析 with a surcharge 有著附加費用，with為「與」的意思。

64. (A) than 比 (B) then 然而 (C) there 那裡 (D) theme 主題

解析 從lose less可知有比較的意味，故選than。

65. (A) mean 苛薄 (B) means 方法
(C) meaning 意思 (D) material 原料

解析 此處考的是means 方法、方式之意，而mean當動詞是意思，meaning則是當名詞，mean當形容詞則是苛薄的意思。

All societies have dress codes, most of which are unwritten but understood by most members of the society. The dress code has built-in rules or signals indicating how a person's clothing should be worn. This message may include indications of the person's social class, income, occupation, ethnic and religious affiliation, attitude, marital status, sexual availability, and sexual orientation. Clothes convey other social messages, including personal or cultural identity. For example, wearing expensive clothes can communicate wealth or the image of wealth.

中譯 所有社會都有穿衣規範，大部分是沒有被書寫下來的，但卻被大多數的社會成員所了解。穿衣規範有內定的規則與訊息，指出一個人的衣服該怎麼穿。這類訊息隱含了人們的社會地位、收入、職業、種族和宗教信仰、態度、婚姻狀態、發生性行為的意願以及性傾向。服裝傳達其他社會訊息，包含個人以及文化的認同。比如說，穿很昂貴的衣服可以和別人表達自己的財富，或是富有的印象。

單字 dress code 著裝標準　　indicate 指出
occupation 職業　　religious affiliation 宗教信仰
marital status 婚姻狀況　　convey 傳達

66. (A) is　(B) are　(C) be　(D) had

解析 此處的most of which為dress codes，故為複數。

67. (A) build　(B) been built　(C) built-in　(D) building 建築物

解析 built-in 內建、內定的。

68. (A) wear 穿　(B) wore　(C) worn　(D) warm 暖的

解析 wear – wore – worn 現在式、過去式、過去分詞。

69. (A) accuse 控告　(B) exclude 除外　(C) include 包含　(D) confess 坦白

70. (A) In addition 另外　(B) In summary 總而言之
(C) For example 例如　(D) In contrast 與……相比

解析 in contrast with 與……相比（與with並用）。

IV. Reading Comprehension. 閱讀測驗

Railways were the first form of mass transportation and had an effective monopoly on land transport until the development of the motorcar in the early 20th century. Railway companies in Europe and the United States used streamlined trains since 1933 for high-speed services with an average speed of up to 130 km/h (80 mph) and a top speed of more than 160 km/h (100 mph).

中譯 鐵路是最早的大眾運輸工具，也是最有效率的陸上交通工具，霸主地位直到20世紀初汽車發展後為止。歐洲和美國的鐵路公司從1933年開始使用流線型火車提供平均時速130公里（80英里）的高速服務，最高速可超過160公里（100英里）。

單字 mass transportation 大眾交通工具
monopoly 壟斷

The first high-speed train was the Italian ETR 200 that in July 1939 went from Milan to Florence at 165 km/h, with a top speed of 203 km/h. With this service, these trains were able to compete with the upcoming airplanes. In 1957, the Odakyu Electric Railway in Greater Tokyo launched its Romancecar 3000 SSE. This set a world record for narrow gauge trains at 145 km/h (90 mph), giving Japanese designers confidence that they could safely build even faster trains at standard gauge. Desperate for transport solutions due to overloaded trains between Tokyo and Osaka, the idea of high-speed rail was born in Japan.

中譯 第一台高速火車誕生於1939年7月，為義大利的ETR 200，從米蘭開往佛羅倫斯，時速為165公里，最高速可達203公里。鑒於這樣的服務，這些火車能夠和接下來的飛機競爭。1957年，東京的小田急電鐵株式會社發表了浪漫特快SSE 3000。這個創下當時窄軌火車時速145公里（90英里）的世界紀錄，這讓日本的設計師有信心可以安全打造更快的正常軌道火車。由於日本急於紓解東京到大阪超載的載量，於是誕生了高速鐵路的概念。

單字 overload 超載
high-speed rail 高速鐵路

There is no globally accepted standard separating high-speed rail from conventional railroads; however, a number of widely accepted variables have been acknowledged by the industry in recent years. Generally, high-speed rail is defined as having a top speed in regular use of over 200 km/h (125 mph).

中譯 其實國際上沒有區分傳統鐵路和高速鐵路的標準，不過這幾年業界有大多數人所接受的差異。一般來說，高速鐵路定義為最高速超過時速200公里（125英里）。

單字 acknowledge 承認

71. According to the first paragraph of this passage, what is true about the development of mass transportation?

(A) Railways used to be the primary means of land transportation before the 20th century.
20世紀之前，鐵路為陸上主要的交通工具。

(B) Motorcars were designed to monopolize land transport in the early 20th century.
在20世紀初，汽車被設計來獨佔陸上交通。

(C) High-speed services derived from motorcar racing.

高速服務被賽車所剝奪。

(D) The high-speed train was first built by Japanese engineers.

第一個高速火車由日本工程師所建。

中譯 根據本文第一段，對於大眾運輸的發展哪個正確？

解析 由本文第一段第一句Railways were the first form of mass transportation and had an effective monopoly on land transport until the development of the motorcar in the early 20th century. 即可知。

72. According to the passage, which country introduced the first high-speed train?

(A) Italy. 義大利。 (B) France. 法國。

(C) Japan. 日本。 (D) The USA. 美國。

中譯 根據本文，哪個國家最早有高速火車？

解析 由The first high-speed train was the Italian ETR 200.可知。

73. What is the top record speed ever achieved by high-speed trains before 1960?

(A) 90 km/h (B) 145 km/h (C) 165 km/h (D) 203 km/h

中譯 在1960年之前高速火車最快的速度為多少？

解析 由The first high-speed train was the Italian ETR 200 that in July 1939 went from Milan to Florence at 165 km/h, with a top speed of 203 km/h.可知。

74. What was the driving force for the Japanese to first build the high-speed rail?

(A) To compete with airplane transportation.

為了打敗航空運輸。

(B) To share the train transport loadings between Tokyo and Osaka.

要分散東京到大阪的運輸量。

(C) To attract foreign tourists to Japan.

為了吸引外國遊客到日本。

(D) To show off their hi-tech achievement.

為了炫耀他們的高科技成果。

中譯 是哪個原因讓日本人首先想要打造高速鐵路？

解析 由Desperate for transport solutions due to overloaded trains between Tokyo and Osaka, the idea of high-speed rail was born in Japan.可知。

75. Which of the following statements is true?

(A) Traditional railroads are no longer in use.
傳統鐵路不再被使用了。

(B) Airlines will lose their customers to high-speed rails because of speed.
航空業會流失旅客是因為其速度。

(C) High-speed rail is defined as having a speed of over 200 kilometers per hour.
高速鐵路的定義為時速超過200公里。

(D) High-speed rail companies will replace all land transporters.
高速鐵路公司將會全面取代陸上交通工具。

中譯 以下哪項為真？

解析 由Generally, high-speed rail is defined as having a top speed in regular use of over 200 km/h (125 mph).可知。

A tour manager has individual duties to perform to run a tour smoothly and successfully. For instance, the tour manager should always be the first one up every morning in order to make sure each team member is ready before the bus leaves for the next scenic spot each day.

中譯 領隊有很多個人的職責需要去執行，才能讓整個旅程順利且成功地結束。例如，領隊應該總是每天都第一個早起，在巴士開往下一個景點之前，確保每個團員都準備上車。

The tour manager will also check for possible changes to the itinerary. Most days of a tour require a long bus trip to the next venue. The traveling time may be the only opportunity for the tour manager to undertake much of the administrative chores: paper work, phone calls, and planning for the next few days. This may include confirming and reconfirming hotel reservations, return flights, and arrival time at restaurants and scenic spots.

中譯 領隊也要確認行程上可能會有的改變。旅行大多數的時間都需要搭長途巴士前往下一個景點。在旅途中的時間有可能是領隊唯一可以處理行政事務的機會，像是紙本工作、打電話聯絡，以及替之後幾天做計劃。這個可能包含了確認以及再確認飯店的訂房、回程班機，以及餐廳和景點的到達時間。

單字 itinerary 旅程
administrative chore 行政工作
confirm reservation 確認預約

It usually falls to the tour manager to keep the team members and the service crew happy while they are hundreds, or thousands, of miles away from their homes and their families. The tour manager shall keep everyone working as a team and deal with individual problems, such as stolen passports, physical ailments and medical emergencies. Most importantly, the tour manager must take the group members home safe and sound at the end of the journey and get ready for the next trip.

中譯 領隊通常很難讓每個團員和服務人員都開心，特別是大家都離自己的家與家庭幾百、幾千英里遠時。領隊應該要讓每個人都如團隊般運作，並處理個人的問題，像是護照被偷、身體不舒服或是醫療緊急事件。最重要的是，領隊必須確保團員在旅程結束時安然無恙，並準備好迎接下一趟旅行。

單字 physical ailment 身體上的病痛
safe and sound 安然無恙

76. What is this passage mainly about?

(A) Running a profitable tour. 經營有利潤的旅行團。

(B) Tips on booking cheap hotel rooms. 訂便宜飯店房間的訣竅。

(C) Enjoying tours. 享受旅程。

(D) The duties of a tour manager. 領隊的職責。

中譯 本文的主旨為何？

解析 由本文第一句可得知A tour manager has individual duties to perform to run a tour smoothly and successfully.

77. Which of the following is generally NOT considered a tour manager's responsibility?

(A) Keep everyone happy. 讓每個人開心。

(B) Drive the tour bus. 開觀光巴士。

(C) Visit the resorts as scheduled. 按行程參訪名勝。

(D) Confirm hotel reservations. 確認飯店訂位。

中譯 哪一項不被認為是領隊的責任？

解析 本文內沒提及(B)。

78. Which of the following words is closest in meaning to the word "venue" in the passage?

(A) Stand 站　(B) Spot 點　(C) Sport 運動　(D) Sigh 嘆息

中譯 哪個字最接近本文中「venue」的意思？

解析 scenic spot 景點。

79. What will a responsible tour manager most likely do on the bus during the tour?

(A) Make phone calls to friends.
打電話給朋友。

(B) Buy discounted souvenirs for team members.
幫團員買打折的紀念品。

(C) Find seats with the best view for team members.
幫團員找到最好欣賞風景的座位。

(D) Reconfirm return flights for team members.
幫團員們再次確認回程班機。

中譯 在旅程期間，什麼是一個負責任的領隊最有可能在巴士上做的？

解析 由第二段The traveling time may be the only opportunity for the tour manager to undertake much of the administrative chores: paper work, phone calls, and planning for the next few days. This may include confirming and reconfirming hotel reservations, return flights, and arrival time at restaurants and scenic spots.可知。

80. What can be inferred from this passage?

(A) Most tours become mental and physical burdens for a tour manager.
大部分的旅程對領隊來說都是心理和生理上的負擔。

(B) Most tours require tour members to pay extra fees for services.
大部分的旅程需要團員多付服務費。

(C) Most tour managers don't change their original itinerary.
大部分的領隊不需要改變原來的行程。

(D) Most tour managers ask their group members to help with chores.
大部分的領隊要求團員幫忙行政工作。

中譯 由本文可推論以下哪件事？

解析 由第二、三段的領隊職責可推知。

99 年外語領隊英文試題＋標準答案

★99年專門職業及技術人員普通考試導遊人員、領隊人員考試試題

類科：外語領隊人員（英語）

科 目：外國語（英語）

考試時間：1 小時 20 分

※注意：（一）本試題為單一選擇題，請選出一個正確或最適當的答案，複選作答者，該題不予計分。

（二）本科目共80題，每題1.25分，須用2Ｂ鉛筆在試卡上依題號清楚劃記，於本試題上作答者，不予計分。

（三）本試題禁止使用電子計算器。

(　　)1. Our hotel provides free ______ service to the airport every day.

(A) accommodation　(B) communication
(C) transmission　(D) shuttle

(　　)2. Rescuers from many countries went to the ______ of the earthquake to help the victims.

(A) capital　(B) refuge　(C) epicenter　(D) shelter

(　　)3. Tourists enjoy visiting night markets around the island to taste ______ local snacks.

(A) authentic　(B) blend　(C) inclusive　(D) invisible

(　　)4. Mike forgot to save the file and the computer ______ suddenly. It was a real disaster.

(A) broke up　(B) was broke　(C) was plugged in　(D) crashed

(　　)5. Expo 2010 ______ in Shanghai, China from May 1 to October 31, 2010.

(A) will hold　(B) will be holding　(C) will be held　(D) is holding

(　　)6. Although the unemployment rate reached an all-time high in mid-2009, it has fallen for four ______ months by December.

(A) consecutive　(B) connecting　(C) continual　(D) temporary

(　　)7. ______ has become a very serious problem in the modern world. It's estimated that there are more than 1 billion overweight adults globally.

(A) Depression　(B) Obesity　(C) Malnutrition　(D) Starvation

( )8. Living in a highly ______ society, some Taiwanese children are forced by their parents to learn many skills at a very young age.

(A) compatible (B) prospective (C) threatened (D) competitive

( )9. There is clear ______ that the defendant committed the murder of the rich old man.

(A) research (B) evidence (C) statistics (D) vision

( )10. If Scott had studied hard enough, he ______ the midterm exam. Now he has to burn the midnight oil to pass the final exam.

(A) would pass (B) will pass
(C) have passed (D) would have passed

( )11. John has to ______ the annual report to the manager before this Friday; otherwise, he will be in trouble.

(A) identify (B) incline (C) submit (D) commemorate

( )12. Millions of people are expected to ______ in the 2010 Taipei International Flora Expo.

(A) participate (B) adjust (C) emerge (D) exist

( )13. It is said that there are only a few lucky days ______ for getting married in 2010.

(A) elated (B) available (C) elected (D) resentful

( )14. Tom was ______ from his school for stealing and cheating on the exams.

(A) exempted (B) expelled (C) exported (D) evacuated

( )15. Many customers complained that they had difficulty assembling the M-20 mountain bicycle, because the instructions in the manual were not ______.

(A) implicit (B) explicit (C) complex (D) exquisite

( )16. There are eight ______ for the Academy Award for the best picture this year.

(A) attendants (B) nominees (C) conductors (D) producers

( )17. Our company has been on a very tight ______ since 2008.

(A) deficit (B) management (C) budget (D) debt

( )18. Please remain ______ while the plane takes off.

(A) seated (B) sitting (C) sat (D) seating

( )19. Mary is ______ divorce because her husband is having an affair with his secretary.

(A) controling to (B) filing for (C) calling for (D) accustomed to

( )20. I want to make a/an ______ with Dr. Johnson tomorrow morning. I think I've caught a cold.

(A) reservation (B) arrangement (C) meeting (D) appointment

( )21. Since the economy is improving, many people are hoping for a ______ in salary in the coming year.

(A) raise (B) rise (C) surplus (D) bonus

( )22. The birth rate in Taiwan was at a/an ______ low last year.

(A) record (B) recorded (C) recording (D) accordingly

( )23. I need some ______ for taking buses around town.

(A) checks (B) exchange (C) change (D) savings

( )24. All my friends are recommending the movie, Avatar; ______, I am too busy to see it.

(A) but (B) therefore (C) so (D) however

( )25. Remember to ______ some sunscreen before you go to the beach.

(A) drink (B) scrub (C) wear (D) move

( )26. These ancient porcelains are very ______ and might break easily, so please handle them carefully.

(A) wicked (B) infirm (C) fragile (D) stout

( )27. The Department of Health urged the public to receive H1N1 flu shot as a ______ against potential outbreaks.

(A) prohibition (B) preparation (C) presumption (D) precaution

( )28. The Ministry of the Interior has decided to ______ telephone fraud.

(A) dismiss (B) discharge (C) eliminate (D) execute

( )29. Our guided ______ around the farm lasted for two and a half hours.

(A) voyage (B) journey (C) tour (D) crossing

(　　)30. All the ______ on the city rail map are color-coded so that a traveler knows which direction she/he should take.

(A) routes　(B) roads　(C) sights　(D) systems

(　　)31. We arrived at the airport ______, so we had plenty of time for checking in and boarding.

(A) at the best of times　(B) in our own time
(C) dead on time　(D) in good time

(　　)32. To use a TravelPass, you have to insert it ______ the automatic stamping machine when you get off.

(A) through　(B) between　(C) off　(D) into

(　　)33. Guest: What ______ do you have in your hotel?
Hotel clerk: We have a fitness center, a swimming pool, two restaurants, a beauty parlor, and a boutique.

(A) facilities　(B) benefits　(C) itineraries　(D) details

(　　)34. Guest: ______
Hotel clerk: Our standard room costs NT$3,500 per night.

(A) Is room service included in your price?
(B) What is your room rate?
(C) How much do you charge for a luxury room?
(D) Do I have to pay for an extra bed?

(　　)35. Go to the office at the Tourist Information Center and they will give you a ______ about sightseeing.

(A) destination　(B) deposit　(C) baggage　(D) brochure

(　　)36. Guest: Hello, this is room 205. The faucet in our bathroom is dripping and I can't turn it off.
Hotel clerk: ______

(A) I'm terribly sorry about that. I'll get it cleaned for you right away.
(B) OK, I'll have it changed by the electrician.
(C) Is it? I'm sorry, I'll get it fixed by a plumber.
(D) I do apologize. If you tell me which one, I'll send someone to open it.

(　　)37. It's difficult to find a hotel with a/an ______ room in high season.

(A) occupied　(B) vacant　(C) lank　(D) unattended

(　　)38. If you're looking for Greek food in this area, sorry to say, there is very ______ choice.

(A) few　(B) any　(C) much　(D) little

(　　)39. This express train ______ at 9:30 am every day. You can plan a short walk before that in the itinerary.

(A) is about to leave　(B) will leave

(C) will be leaving　(D) leaves

(　　)40. Cathedrals, mosques, and temples are all ______ buildings.

(A) religious　(B) natural　(C) political　(D) rural

(　　)41. If you take a ______ holiday, all your transport, accommodation, and even meals and excursions will be taken care of.

(A) leisure　(B) business　(C) package　(D) luxury

(　　)42. Tourism has helped ______ the economy for many countries, and brought in considerable revenues.

(A) boast　(B) boost　(C) receive　(D) recall

(　　)43. The number of independent travelers ______ steadily since the new policy was announced.

(A) rose　(B) has risen　(C) arose　(D) has arisen

(　　)44. If you want to work in tourism, you need to know how to work as part of a team. But sometimes, you also need to know how to work ______.

(A) separately　(B) confidently　(C) creatively　(D) independently

(　　)45. Jane completely missed the ______ of what the guest was complaining about.

(A) line　(B) goal　(C) point　(D) plan

(　　)46. Many restaurants in Paris offer a ______ of snails for guests to taste.

(A) plate　(B) group　(C) chunk　(D) loaf

( )47. Slices of lamb are ______ or fried in butter and served with mushrooms, onions, and chips.

(A) added (B) mixed (C) grilled (D) stored

( )48. Waiter: Are you ready to order, sir?
Guest: ______

(A) Your food looks tasty.
(B) OK, I'll have that!
(C) I don't eat meat.
(D) I think so. But what is your specialty?

( )49. A kimono is a kind of clothing ______ the Japanese wear during special ceremonies.

(A) where (B) who (C) when (D) that

( )50. People ______ fireworks to celebrate New Year.

(A) get off (B) take off (C) let off (D) put off

( )51. The caller: Can I speak to Ms. Taylor in room 612, please?
The operator: Please wait a minute. (pause) I'm sorry. There's no answer. May I ______ a message?

(A) bring (B) take (C) leave (D) send

( )52. This trip starts ______ Easter Sunday and lasts for five days.

(A) at (B) on (C) in (D) for

( )53. The guest is given a ______ after he makes a complaint to the restaurant.

(A) change (B) profit (C) refund (D) bonus

( )54. I'm afraid your credit card has already ______. Would you like to pay in cash instead?

(A) cancelled (B) booked (C) expired (D) exposed

( )55. The ______ at the information desk in a hotel provides traveling information to guests.

(A) bellhop (B) concierge (C) butler (D) bartender

Studies of the brain show that there is a __56__ basis for general intelligence. The brains of intelligent people use less energy during problem __57__. The brain waves of people with higher intelligence show a quicker __58__. Some researchers conclude that differences in intelligence __59__ differences in the speed and __60__ of information processing by the brain.

( )56. (A) psychological (B) biological (C) logical (D) chemical

( )57. (A) spiraling (B) saving (C) solving (D) soaking

( )58. (A) reaction (B) request (C) remorse (D) reply

( )59. (A) consist of (B) are made up of (C) result in (D) result from

( )60. (A) loudness (B) epic (C) effectiveness (D) affection

For those who travel on a __61__, flying with a low-cost airline might be an option because you pay so much less than what you would be expected to pay with a traditional airline. Companies such as Ryanair, Southwest Airlines and Easyjet are some good examples. It's so easy to fly with these low-cost __62__. From booking the tickets, checking in to boarding the plane, everything has become hassle-free. You only need to book online even if there are only two hours left before departure. You can also just __63__ the check-in desk and buy the tickets two hours before the plane takes off. Checking in is also easy and quick, and you're only required to arrive at the airport one hour before departure. But since traveling with these low-cost airlines has been so __64__, you cannot expect to get free food, drinks or newspapers on board. There is also no classification regarding your seats and the flight attendants, who might be wearing casual clothing as their uniform, won't certainly serve you. As most of these low-cost airlines are __65__, you might need to get ready for landing even after you have only gone on board for a few minutes.

( )61. (A) schedule (B) budget (C) routine (D) project

( )62. (A) forms (B) means (C) cruises (D) carriers

( )63. (A) pop in (B) break in (C) fill in (D) come in

( )64. (A) inexpensive (B) inconvenient (C) inefficient (D) inappropriate

( )65. (A) good-haul (B) huge-haul (C) short-haul (D) long-haul

"That's £3.25 altogether," said a taxi driver. "Keep the change, please," replied a young lady when she handed over the money to the driver. "Thank you. Have a pleasant stay in York," said the driver after she received it with delight. This brief dialogue demonstrates ___66___ pleasant the giving and receiving of tipping could be. Tipping has been a common way of showing appreciation to people who have served you. It is the kind of courtesy ___67___ mostly to people who are serving in the travel and tourism industry. But sometimes things might not turn out to be so perfect. People might refuse to tip if they find the service is ___68___ . They might have no idea about what would be the appropriate amount for tipping. In some countries, tipping is included in the service when you pay for the bill in a restaurant and that amount will be 10 or 15% of your total bill. ___69___ they like it or not, some people might still be asked to tip or be overcharged ___70___ tipping if there is no stipulation about how much one should tip. In cases like these, tipping might not be an enjoyable experience at all.

( )66. (A) why (B) what (C) how (D) which

( )67. (A) targeting (B) targeted (C) directing (D) directed

( )68. (A) ungrateful (B) unsatisfactory (C) undeniable (D) unexceptional

( )69. (A) Whether (B) Where (C) What (D) While

( )70. (A) for (B) from (C) on (D) of

Even a small reduction of salt in the diet can be a big help to the heart. A new study published in the New England Journal of Medicine used a computer model to predict how just three grams less a day would affect heart disease in the United States.

The result: Thirteen percent fewer heart attacks. Eight percent fewer strokes. Four percent fewer deaths. Eleven percent fewer new cases of heart disease. And two hundred forty billion dollars in health care savings. Researchers found less salt intake could prevent one hundred thousand heart attacks and ninety-two thousand deaths every year.

According to the U.S. government, the average American man eats, on average, ten grams of salt a day; however, the American Heart Association advises no more than three grams for healthy people. It says salt in the American diet has increased fifty percent since the 1970s, while blood pressures have also risen. Less salt can mean a lower blood pressure.

New York City Mayor, Michael Bloomberg, is leading an effort called the National Salt Reduction Initiative. The idea is to put pressure on food companies and restaurants. Critics call it government interference.

( )71. What is the best title for this passage?

(A) The disadvantages of salt (B) Less salt can mean longer life
(C) How to consume less salt (D) How to cure heart disease

( )72. According to the prediction of the study, how many grams of salt less a day can reduce the risk of heart disease?

(A) three (B) ten (C) fifteen (D) eleven

( )73. Which of the following statement is NOT true?

(A) Eight percent fewer strokes was predicted by the study if people take less salt.
(B) The results of the study were predicted by a computer model.
(C) The study was conducted in New England.
(D) About two hundred forty billion dollars in health care could be saved by eating less salt.

( )74. Which of the following statements is NOT true?

(A) The average American man eats 10 grams of salt a day.
(B) Less salt could prevent ninety-two thousand deaths a year.
(C) No more than three grams of salt are good for healthy people.
(D) Americans have increased the amount of salt in their diet by fifteen percent since the 1970s.

( )75. What can be inferred from the last paragraph?

(A) Mayor Michael Bloomberg's National Salt Reduction Initiative is widely supported by Americans.
(B) The purpose of National Salt Reduction Initiative is to promote gourmet cuisines in New York City.
(C) Mayor Bloomberg is concerned about the health of American people.
(D) Mayor Bloomberg has an ambition to run for the next presidency of the United States.

Recently, a new type of tourism, or what is called 'alternative tourism', has emerged and become more and more popular among people who feel tired of the same old holidays and hope to gain real or authentic experiences from traveling. This new kind of tourism takes the form of individual custom-made or independent holidays that take people to remote and exotic destinations, and cater to their different needs and interests. These holidays are basically designed and arranged at a personal level. They often have different themes and offer a variety for people to choose from. As the market for this new form of tourism has expanded greatly, newer topics and programs will also appear as long as people begin to develop newer interests and needs in the future.

But what exactly can people get out of alternative tourism? For ecology-minded people, they can go whale-watching or take a conservation trip to help restore the damaged coastline. For people who like adventure and outdoor activities, the choices could range from mountain climbing, scuba diving, windsurfing, white-water rafting to cycling in the mountains and deserts. For people who simply like to relax and gain a peace of mind, they can spend a week at spa and health resorts to relax and de-stress, or take yoga and meditation lessons at country retreats in India. For people who are fond of culture and heritage, they can visit museums and art galleries in New York, take a weekend break at the Edinburgh International Festival, or tour around France to visit historic castles.

Other programs under alternative tourism include holidays that are taken for educational, artistic or religious purposes. These contain learning English on a four-week trip to Australia, learning survival skills in the jungles, learning how to paint or handle dogs during a few days' holiday, and go on a pilgrimage to holy places and sites. The lists to these different kinds of programs are endless and cater to different customers' needs and interests. But the messages this emergence of new holidays signals for the travel and tourism industry are that alternative tourism not only reflects the changing faces of tourism, but also brings both challenges and opportunities to the industry.

(　　)76. What is the main idea of this passage?

(A) the contents of alternative tourism
(B) the significance of mass tourism
(C) the popularity of alternative tourism
(D) the reasons for the emergence of tourism

(　　)77. In paragraph 1, what does the word 'custom-made' mean?

(A) It means customers designing their own holidays to meet their own interests.
(B) It means holidays arranged according to different cultural customs.
(C) It means travelers getting the approval from customs officers.
(D) It means holidays designed individually and can vary from person to person.

(　　)78. If you plan to go bungee-jumping, what type of tourism does it belong to?

(A) Ecotourism.　　(B) Adventure tourism.

(C) Cultural tourism.　　(D) Escape tourism.

(　　)79. Which of the following holidays can be seen as educational?

(A) A weekend break in a country house for beauty treatments.

(B) A trip to Vancouver for the 2010 Winter Olympics.

(C) A one-week holiday in Paris on how to cook delicacies.

(D) Riding camels in the Sahara for a six-day holiday.

(　　)80. According to this passage, what does the appearance of alternative tourism signify to the travel and tourism industry?

(A) Tourism is about caring for people.

(B) People working in the travel and tourism industry should love their jobs.

(C) Tourism keeps changing and it is both demanding and rewarding.

(D) It is important to learn about different cultures and customs.

★標準答案

1. (D)	2. (C)	3. (A)	4. (D)	5. (C)
6. (A)	7. (B)	8. (D)	9. (B)	10. (D)
11. (C)	12. (A)	13. (B)	14. (B)	15. (B)
16. (B)	17. (C)	18. (A)	19. (B)	20. (D)
21. (#)	22. (A)	23. (C)	24. (D)	25. (C)
26. (C)	27. (D)	28. (C)	29. (C)	30. (A)
31. (D)	32. (D)	33. (A)	34. (B)	35. (D)
36. (C)	37. (B)	38. (D)	39. (D)	40. (A)
41. (C)	42. (B)	43. (B)	44. (D)	45. (C)
46. (A)	47. (C)	48. (D)	49. (D)	50. (C)
51. (B)	52. (B)	53. (C)	54. (C)	55. (B)
56. (B)	57. (C)	58. (A)	59. (D)	60. (C)
61. (B)	62. (D)	63. (A)	64. (A)	65. (C)
66. (C)	67. (D)	68. (B)	69. (A)	70. (A)
71. (B)	72. (A)	73. (C)	74. (D)	75. (C)
76. (A)	77. (D)	78. (B)	79. (C)	80. (C)

備註：第21題答A或B或AB者均給分。

99 年外語領隊英文試題中譯與解析

1. Our hotel provides free shuttle service to the airport every day.

(A) accommodation 住宿　(B) communication 溝通
(C) transmission 傳輸　(D) shuttle 接駁工具

中譯 我們飯店每天免費提供到機場的接駁巴士服務。

解析 THSR Shuttle Bus 台灣高鐵接駁巴士，如從車站至機場兩點固定來回的，即稱 shuttle bus。

2. Rescuers from many countries went to the epicenter of the earthquake to help the victims.

(A) capital 首都　(B) refuge 避難所
(C) epicenter 震央　(D) shelter 避難所

中譯 來自許多國家的救援者到震央去幫忙受害者。

解析 由epicenter中間的center可推知為震央。為什麼不是選shelter 避難所？因為由題目of the earthquake 地震的，可將shelter 避難所刪去。

3. Tourists enjoy visiting night markets around the island to taste authentic local snacks.

(A) authentic 真正的　(B) blend 融合
(C) inclusive 包含的　(D) invisible 無形的

中譯 遊客喜歡在島上到處參訪夜市，嚐嚐真正的道地小吃。

解析 local snacks 道地小吃。由local可推知為authentic 真正的。

★authentic 真正的，例句：This restaurant features authentic Northern Italian dishes that reflect the true flavors of Italy. 這間餐廳的特色為反映義大利口味的道地北義大利菜。101導遊

★其他關於夜市的考題

Night markets in Taiwan have become popular tourist destinations. They are great places to shop for bargains and eat typical Taiwanese food. 台灣的夜市已經成為受歡迎的觀光景點。他們是討價還價和吃傳統台灣料理的好地方。101導遊

4. Mike forgot to save the file and the computer crashed suddenly. It was a real disaster.

(A) broke up 結束　(B) was broke 被打破

(C) was plugged in 插入　(D) crashed 當機

中譯 麥克忘了存檔，而電腦忽然當機。真是慘不忍睹。

解析 disaster 災害、災難。

★file除了當名詞「檔案」外，當動詞有「提出」的意思，如以下兩個考古題，都將file當動詞使用。

- Mary is filing for divorce because her husband is having an affair with his secretary. 瑪莉提出離婚訴訟是因為她的丈夫與其祕書有染。
- The hotel services are far from satisfactory. I need to file a complaint with the manager. 飯店的服務讓人無法滿意，我需要向經理客訴。98領隊

5. Expo 2010 will be held in Shanghai, China from May 1 to October 31, 2010.

(A) will hold 舉行　(B) will be holding

(C) will be held　(D) is holding

中譯 2010年的世界博覽會將於中國上海舉行，從5月1日到10月31日。

解析 活動是「被」舉辦的，故選will be held。

★舉辦活動的兩個常見單字：

① host 主辦（帶有主辦人的意思）

- Rio will host the 2016 Summer Olympic Games. 里約將主辦2016年夏季奧運。
- An open-minded city, Taipei hosted Asia's first Gay Pride parade which has now become an annual autumn event. 身為一座心胸開放的都市，台北主辦亞洲第一屆同志遊行，並且成為每年於秋天所舉辦的活動。100導遊

② hold 舉行、舉辦

- The Olympic Games are held every four years. 奧運每4年（被）舉辦一次。
- The first Taipei Lantern Festival was held in 1990. Due to the event's huge popularity, the festival has been expanded every year. 第一屆的台北燈籠節於1990年舉行。而因為這場活動受到極大的歡迎，慶祝活動一年比一年盛大。98導遊

6. Although the unemployment rate reached an all-time high in mid-2009, it has fallen for four consecutive months by December.

(A) consecutive 連續不斷的 (B) connecting 連接
(C) continual 多次重複的 (D) temporary 暫時的

中譯 雖然失業率於2009年年中一直都很高，但到12月時已經連續下降4個月。

解析 unemployment 失業；reach 抵達、伸手及到、達到，在此指達到。

7. Obesity has become a very serious problem in the modern world. It's estimated that there are more than 1 billion overweight adults globally.

(A) Depression 沮喪 (B) Obesity 肥胖
(C) Malnutrition 營養失調 (D) Starvation 飢餓

中譯 肥胖已經成為現代世界很嚴重的問題。預估全球有超過十億成人過胖。

解析 由overweight可推知為obesity 肥胖。estimate 估計、估量；globally 全球地。

8. Living in a highly competitive society, some Taiwanese children are forced by their parents to learn many skills at a very young age.

(A) compatible 能共處的 (B) prospective 預期的
(C) threatened 受到威脅的 (D) competitive 競爭性的

中譯 生活在高度競爭的社會，有些台灣小孩從小就被逼著學很多技能。

解析 由learn many skills可知社會是很competitive 競爭性的。

9. There is clear evidence that the defendant committed the murder of the rich old man.

(A) research 調查 (B) evidence 證據
(C) statistics 統計量 (D) vision 遠見

中譯 鐵證證明被告殺了這名有錢的老男人。

解析 defendant 被告；commit 犯（罪）。

10. If Scott had studied hard enough, he would have passed the midterm exam. Now he has to burn the midnight oil to pass the final exam.

(A) would pass (B) will pass 通過
(C) have passed (D) would have passed

中譯 如果史考特念書夠用功的話，他應該會通過期中考。現在他必須熬夜才能通過期末考。

解析 與過去事實相反的假設，條件子句動詞須用「had + p.p.」，主要子句則是「主詞 + 助動詞 + have + p.p.」，故選would have passed。

11. John has to submit the annual report to the manager before this Friday; otherwise, he will be in trouble.

(A) identify 識別　(B) incline 傾斜
(C) submit 提交　(D) commemorate 慶祝

中譯 約翰必須在這週五之前提交年度報告給經理，不然他就完蛋了。

解析 submit 提交；submit a plan 提出一項計劃；otherwise 否則、不然。

12. Millions of people are expected to participate in the 2010 Taipei International Flora Expo.

(A) participate 參加　(B) adjust 調整
(C) emerge 浮現　(D) exist 存在

中譯 幾百萬人期待參加2010年的台北國際花卉博覽會。

解析 participate in 參加。

13. It is said that there are only a few lucky days available for getting married in 2010.

(A) elated 興高采烈的　(B) available 可獲得的
(C) elected 當選的　(D) resentful 忿恨的

中譯 據說2010年只有幾天好日子可以結婚。

解析 available 可獲得的；stock available 貨源充足；unavailabe 不可獲得的；Goods unavailable 無貨可供。

14. Tom was expelled from his school for stealing and cheating on the exams.

(A) exempted 免除　(B) expelled 開除
(C) exported 輸出　(D) evacuated 疏散

中譯 湯姆被學校開除是因為偷竊以及考試作弊。

解析 expel 開除；expel from a country 驅逐出境。

15. Many customers complained that they had difficulty assembling the M-20 mountain bicycle, because the instructions in the manual were not explicit.

(A) implicit 含蓄的
(B) explicit 明確的
(C) complex 複雜的
(D) exquisite 精緻的

中譯 許多客戶抱怨他們對於組裝M-20登山腳踏車有問題，因為操作指令沒有寫得很清楚。

解析 explicit 明確的；implicit 不明確的；assemble 組合、裝配；instructions 指令。

16. There are eight nominees for the Academy Award for the best picture this year.

(A) attendants 隨行人員
(B) nominees 入圍者
(C) conductors 領導者
(D) producers 製片人

中譯 今年奧斯卡的最佳影片共有8名入圍者。

解析 nominate 提名；nominee 入圍者。

17. Our company has been on a very tight budget since 2008.

(A) deficit 虧損
(B) management 管理
(C) budget 預算
(D) debt 債務

中譯 自從2008年，我們公司的預算就很緊縮。

解析 budget 預算，為名詞，亦可當成動詞，為編列預算。例句：Parents should teach their children to budget their money at an early age. Otherwise, when they grow up, they will not know how to manage their money. 父母應該在孩子還小時就教導他們如何控制花費，否則當小孩長大時，將不知如何理財。98導遊 budget在此為動詞。我們俗稱的廉價航空公司即為budget airline或是low-cost airline。

18. Please remain seated while the plane takes off.

(A) seated 就坐的
(B) sitting 就坐
(C) sat 坐
(D) seating 座位數

中譯 當飛機起飛時，請保持就坐。

解析 remain + 狀態，故選seated（過去分詞當成形容詞）。

19. Mary is filing for divorce because her husband is having an affair with his secretary.

(A) controling to 操控
(B) filing for 申請
(C) calling for 需要
(D) accustomed to 習慣於

中譯 瑪莉提出離婚訴訟是因為她的丈夫與其祕書有染。

解析 file除了當名詞「檔案」外，當動詞有「提出」的意思。例句：The hotel services are far from satisfactory. I need to file a complaint with the manager. 飯店的服務讓人無法滿意。我需要向經理客訴。98領隊
divorce 離婚；have an affair with 與……有染。

20. I want to make a/an appointment with Dr. Johnson tomorrow morning. I think I've caught a cold.

(A) reservation 預約　(B) arrangement 安排
(C) meeting 會議　(D) appointment 預約

中譯 我想預約強生醫生明天早上的時間。我想我感冒了。

解析 和醫生預約是用make an appointment，預約飯店或是餐廳則是make a reservation。

21. Since the economy is improving, many people are hoping for a raise in salary in the coming year.

(A) raise 提高　(B) rise 升高　(C) surplus 過剩　(D) bonus 獎金

中譯 既然經濟已經好轉，許多人希望明年能加薪。

解析 raise此處當名詞，為加薪，例句：Since our economy has been improving recently, I hope that my boss will give me a big raise this year. 因為我們的經濟情況最近一直持續好轉，我希望我的老闆今年可以幫我大加薪。99導遊
salary 薪資、薪水。

★raise（raised, raised）是及物動詞，必須接受詞。
- Please raise your hand if you know the answer. 如果你知道答案，請舉手。
- The company will raise salaries by 5%. 公司將加薪5%。
- Many concerns were raised about South Africa hosting the World Cup in 2010, but in the end South Africa pulled it off and did an excellent job. 對於南非舉辦2010年世界盃的疑慮升高，但最後南非消除了這些疑慮且表現出色。101導遊

22. The birth rate in Taiwan was at a/an record low last year.

(A) record 紀錄　(B) recorded 記錄
(C) recording 錄影　(D) accordingly 因此

中譯 台灣的出生率和去年比起來達到低點的紀錄。

解析 看到birth rate可知道是record 紀錄的比較。

23. I need some change for taking buses around town.

(A) checks 支票　(B) exchange 匯率

(C) change 零錢　(D) savings 儲蓄

中譯 我需要一些零錢搭公車到鎮上。

解析 change 零錢；bill 紙鈔。

24. All my friends are recommending the movie, Avatar; however, I am too busy to see it.

(A) but 但是　(B) therefore 因此

(C) so 所以　(D) however 然而

中譯 我所有的朋友都推薦《阿凡達》這部電影，然而我太忙而無法去看。

解析 recommend 推薦、介紹。因為主詞沒去看，所以選however。

25. Remember to wear some sunscreen before you go to the beach.

(A) drink 喝　(B) scrub 使勁地擦洗

(C) wear 塗抹　(D) move 移動

中譯 在你去海灘之前，記得擦一些防曬乳。

解析 wear 穿，除了衣服外，香水和防曬乳都是用「wear」，例句：wear perfume 噴香水。

26. These ancient porcelains are very fragile and might break easily, so please handle them carefully.

(A) wicked 邪惡的　(B) infirm 虛弱的　(C) fragile 易碎的　(D) stout 肥胖的

中譯 這些古代的瓷器很脆弱，很容易打破，所以請小心處理。

解析 porcelain （總稱）瓷器，但由break easily即可推知為fragile 易碎的。

27. The Department of Health urged the public to receive H1N1 flu shot as a precaution against potential outbreaks.

(A) prohibition 禁令　(B) preparation 藥劑

(C) presumption 推測　(D) precaution 預防

中譯 衛生處勸導公眾接受H1N1流感疫苗作為預防，以對抗潛在的爆發。

解析 precaution 預防；caution 警告，例句：Motorists are strongly advised to take caution when they drive along windy mountainous roads to avoid plunging into a ravine. 強烈告誡摩托車騎士當行經風很大的深山時，要特別注意避免墜入深谷。100導遊 urge 催促、力勸；outbreak 暴動。

28. The Ministry of the Interior has decided to eliminate telephone fraud.

(A) dismiss 解散　　(B) discharge 釋放
(C) eliminate 消滅　　(D) execute 實行

中譯 內政部長決定消滅電話詐欺。

解析 telephone fraud 電話詐欺；fraud 欺騙（行為）、詭計、騙局。eliminate 消滅；eliminate errors 消除錯誤。

29. Our guided tour around the farm lasted for two and a half hours.

(A) voyage 航行　(B) journey 旅程　(C) tour 觀光　(D) crossing 交叉點

中譯 我們的農場導覽共持續2個半小時。

解析 guided tour 有導遊的遊覽；guided 被引導。

30. All the routes on the city rail map are color-coded so that a traveler knows which direction she/he should take.

(A) routes 路線　(B) roads 道路　(C) sights 景觀　(D) systems 系統

中譯 城市鐵路地圖的所有路線用顏色區分，這樣旅人才知道他們要搭哪個方向。

解析 routes 路線；a train / bus route 火車 / 公車路線。例句：The hiking route of the Shitoushan Trail is not steep and so is suitable for most people, including the elderly and young children. 獅頭山步道的健行路線不太陡峭，所以適合大多數的人，包含老人和小孩。100導遊

31. We arrived at the airport in good time, so we had plenty of time for checking in and boarding.

(A) at the best of times 在最好的情況下
(B) in our own time 在自己的時間裡
(C) dead on time 準時
(D) in good time 及時地

中譯 我們及時抵達機場，所以還有很多時間可以辦理登機。

解析 plenty of 大量的。和good有關的時間用法：in good time 及時地；for good 永久地，例句：John's families moved to the United States. They intended to live there for good. 約翰全家搬到美國。他們打算永遠住在那邊。98領隊

32. To use a TravelPass, you have to insert it into the automatic stamping machine when you get off.

(A) through 穿過　(B) between 在……之內
(C) off 在……之外　(D) into 進入……之內

中譯 當你下車時，要用TravelPass，你必須將票插入自動剪票機。

解析 insert into 插入；get on 上車；get off 下車。

33. Guest: What facilities do you have in your hotel?
Hotel clerk: We have a fitness center, a swimming pool, two restaurants, a beauty parlor, and a boutique.

(A) facilities 設備　(B) benefits 利益
(C) itineraries 遊記　(D) details 細節

中譯 客人：你們飯店有什麼設施？
飯店服務員：我們有健身中心、游泳池、兩間餐廳、一間美容室和女裝店。

解析 parlor 休息室、接待室；boutique 流行女裝商店、精品店，例句：Sara bought a beautiful dress in a in a fashionable boutique district in Milan. 莎拉在米蘭的流行時尚區的一間精品店買了一件漂亮的洋裝。101導遊

34. Guest: What is your room rate?
Hotel clerk: Our standard room costs NT$3,500 per night.

(A) Is room service included in your price? 客房服務有包含在價錢裡嗎？
(B) What is your room rate? 你們的房價是多少？
(C) How much do you charge for a luxury room? 對於豪華房間你們收費多少？
(D) Do I have to pay for an extra bed? 我需要替多餘的床付費嗎？

中譯 客人：你們的房價是多少？
飯店人員：我們的標準房每晚要價3,500元。

解析 由NT$3,500 per night可推知為詢問房價。standard 標準。

35. Go to the office at the Tourist Information Center and they will give you a brochure about sightseeing.

(A) destination 目的地 (B) deposit 存款

(C) baggage 行李 (D) brochure 手冊

中譯 去旅遊中心他們會給你一本觀光手冊。

解析 Tourist Information Center通常會提供brochure 手冊以及map 地圖。

36. Guest: Hello, this is room 205. The faucet in our bathroom is dripping and I can't turn it off.

Hotel clerk: Is it? I'm sorry, I'll get it fixed by a plumber.

(A) I'm terribly sorry about that. I'll get it cleaned for you right away.
我感到非常抱歉。我會立刻清理乾淨。

(B) OK, I'll have it changed by the electrician.
沒問題，我會請電工來修改。

(C) Is it? I'm sorry, I'll get it fixed by a plumber.
這樣嗎？很抱歉，我會請水電工修好。

(D) I do apologize. If you tell me which one, I'll send someone to open it.
我向您道歉。如果您告訴我哪一間，我會請人去開門。

中譯 客人：您好，這裡是205號房。我們浴室的水龍頭一直滴，我關不了。
飯店服務員：這樣嗎？很抱歉，我會請水電工修好。

解析 由faucet 水龍頭可推論為請plumber 水電工來修。

37. It's difficult to find a hotel with a/an vacant room in high season.

(A) occupied 已占滿的 (B) vacant 空著的

(C) lank 細長的 (D) unattended 沒人照顧的

中譯 很難在旺季找到有空房的飯店。

解析 vacant 形容詞，空的；vacancy 名詞，空房、空位。

38. If you're looking for Greek food in this area, sorry to say, there is very little choice.

(A) few 少許的 (B) any 任何的 (C) much 很多的 (D) little 很少的

中譯 如果你要在這區找希臘食物，很抱歉，沒什麼選擇。

解析 little 很少、幾乎沒有；a little 有一些。

39. This express train leaves at 9:30 am every day. You can plan a short walk before that in the itinerary.

(A) is about to leave (B) will leave

(C) will be leaving (D) leaves 離開

中譯 這班快車每天9點半出發。在那行程之前，你可以計劃散個步。

解析 leave for 前往某處；leaves 從哪邊離開。

重點：express 快的、直達的；itinerary 旅程、路線。

40. Cathedrals, mosques, and temples are all religious buildings.

(A) religious 宗教性的 (B) natural 自然的

(C) political 政治的 (D) rural 鄉村的

中譯 教堂、清真寺、寺廟都是宗教的建築。

解析 religion 宗教；religious 宗教性的。

41. If you take a package holiday, all your transport, accommodation, and even meals and excursions will be taken care of.

(A) leisure 空閒 (B) business 事業 (C) package 包裹 (D) luxury 奢侈

中譯 如果你選擇套裝行程，你所有的交通、住宿和餐食、旅遊都會被打點好。

解析 package holiday 套裝行程；excursion 遠足。

42. Tourism has helped boost the economy for many countries, and brought in considerable revenues.

(A) boast 自誇 (B) boost 提振 (C) receive 收到 (D) recall 想起

中譯 旅遊業在許多國家已經幫忙振興經濟，且帶來許多可觀的收入。

解析 boost the economy 振興經濟；economic recession 經濟蕭條；revenue 稅收。

43. The number of independent travelers has risen steadily since the new policy was announced.

(A) rose 上升 (B) has risen 上升 (C) arose 出現 (D) has arisen 出現

中譯 因為新政策的頒布，有越來越多的自助旅行者。

解析 steadily 穩固地、平穩地。

文法小教室

rise、raise、arise都有升起的意思，但各有不同：

① rise（rose, risen）是非及物動詞，其後不可有受詞。

- The sun always rises in the east. 太陽從東方升起。

② raise（raised, raised）是及物動詞，必須接受詞。

- Please raise your hand if you know the answer. 如果你知道答案，請舉手。

The company will raise salaries by 5%. 公司將加薪5%。

③ arise是非及物動詞，其後不可有受詞，常指事情的發生。arise from / out of...即「由…造成」。

- Accidents always arise from the carelessness. 許多事故都源於粗心。

44. If you want to work in tourism, you need to know how to work as part of a team. But sometimes, you also need to know how to work independently.

(A) separately 個別地　(B) confidently 確信地

(C) creatively 創造性地　(D) independently 獨立地

中譯 如果你想要在旅遊業工作，你需要知道如何和團體工作，但有時候你也需要知道如何獨立作業。

解析 work as a team 團體工作；work independently 獨立工作。

45. Jane completely missed the point of what the guest was complaining about.

(A) line 線　(B) goal 目標　(C) point 重點　(D) plan 計劃

中譯 珍完全搞不清楚客戶抱怨的重點。

解析 point 重點，就像時下年輕人常說的，你的（重）點在哪？

46. Many restaurants in Paris offer a plate of snails for guests to taste.

(A) plate 盤　(B) group 團體　(C) chunk 大塊　(D) loaf 條

中譯 巴黎的許多餐廳提供一整盤的蝸牛給客戶吃。

解析 plate 盤子；bowl 碗。

47. Slices of lamb are grilled or fried in butter and served with mushrooms, onions, and chips.

(A) added 附加的 (B) mixed 混合的 (C) grilled 烤的 (D) stored 儲存

中譯 一片片的烤羊肉或是用奶油炸的羊肉，佐上蘑菇、洋蔥和薯片。

解析 grill 烤，通常熱源只有單面，像是中秋烤肉。

48. Waiter: Are you ready to order, sir?
Guest: I think so. But what is your specialty?

(A) Your food looks tasty. 你的食物看起很好吃。

(B) OK, I'll have that! 好的，我要這個！

(C) I don't eat meat. 我不吃肉。

(D) I think so. But what is your specialty? 應該是。你們的招牌菜是什麼？

中譯 服務生：你準備好要點了嗎，先生？
客人：應該是。你們的招牌菜是什麼？

解析 specialty 招牌菜；set meal 套餐。

49. A kimono is a kind of clothing that the Japanese wear during special ceremonies.

(A) where (B) who (C) when (D) that

中譯 和服是一種日本人在傳統儀式穿的衣服。

解析 用that來連接子句。

50. People let off fireworks to celebrate New Year.

(A) get off 離開 (B) take off 脫去 (C) let off 引爆 (D) put off 延遲

中譯 人們點燃煙火來慶祝新年。

解析 煙火是考古題常出現的主題，像是Spectacular fireworks shows lit up the sky of cities around the world as people celebrated the start of 2012. 壯觀的煙火照亮了世界上許多城市的天空，來慶祝2012年的開始。101導遊

51. The caller: Can I speak to Ms. Taylor in room 612, please?
The operator: Please wait a minute. (pause) I'm sorry. There's no answer.
May I take a message?

(A) bring 帶 (B) take 拿 (C) leave 留下 (D) send 寄

中譯 來電者：我可以和612號房的泰勒女士說話嗎？
接線生：等一下。（停頓）我很抱歉。沒有人應答。我可以幫你留話嗎？

解析 leave a message 留話給某人；take a message 幫某人留話。

52. This trip starts on Easter Sunday and lasts for five days.

(A) at (B) on (C) in (D) for（皆為介係詞）

中譯 這趟旅程始於復活節並持續5天。

解析 由Sunday可知選on，on ＋ 星期幾。

53. The guest is given a refund after he makes a complaint to the restaurant.

(A) change 零錢 (B) profit 利潤 (C) refund 退款 (D) bonus 獎金

中譯 這名客人在他和餐廳抱怨之後拿到退款。

解析 此題的refund為名詞，亦可當動詞使用，例：If I cancel the trip, will I be refunded? 如果我取消行程，我可以退費嗎？100領隊

54. I'm afraid your credit card has already expired. Would you like to pay in cash instead?

(A) cancelled 取消 (B) booked 預定 (C) expired 屆期 (D) exposed 揭穿

中譯 恐怕你的信用卡已經過期了。你希望改以付現代替嗎？

解析 expired 屆期、過期的；expiry date 到期日。

55. The concierge at the information desk in a hotel provides traveling information to guests.

(A) bellhop 旅館侍者 (B) concierge 旅館服務台人員
(C) butler 領班 (D) bartender 酒保

中譯 旅館服務台人員提供旅遊資訊給客人。

解析 concierge 旅館服務台人員、門房。

Studies of the brain show that there is a biological basis for general intelligence. The brains of intelligent people use less energy during problem solving. The brain waves of people with higher intelligence show a quicker reaction. Some researchers conclude that differences in intelligence result from differences in the speed and effectiveness of information processing by the brain.

中譯 大腦的研究顯示就一般智力來說是有生物學上的基礎。聰明的大腦當在解決問題時使用較少的能量。智力較高的大腦腦波也顯示有比較快的反應。有些研究認為智力的差異來自於大腦在處理訊息時的速度和效能。

片語 problem-solving 解決問題

56. (A) psychological 心理學的　(B) biological 生物學的
(C) logical 合理的　(D) chemical 化學的

57. (A) spiraling 盤旋　(B) saving 挽救
(C) solving 解決　(D) soaking 浸泡

58. (A) reaction 反應　(B) request 請求
(C) remorse 悔恨　(D) reply 答覆

59. (A) consist of 由……構成　(B) are made up of 由……組成
(C) result in 導致　(D) result from 起因於

60. (A) loudness 喧鬧　(B) epic 史詩
(C) effectiveness 有效　(D) affection 影響

For those who travel on a budget, flying with a low-cost airline might be an option because you pay so much less than what you would be expected to pay with a traditional airline. Companies such as Ryanair, Southwest Airlines and Easyjet are some good examples. It's so easy to fly with these low-cost carriers. From booking the tickets, checking in to boarding the plane, everything has become hassle-free. You only need to book online even if there are only two hours left before departure. You can also just pop in the check-in desk and buy the tickets two hours before the plane takes off. Checking in is also easy and quick, and you're only required to arrive at the airport one hour before departure. But since traveling with these low-cost airlines has been so inexpensive, you cannot expect to get free food, drinks or newspapers on board. There is also no classification regarding your seats and the flight attendants, who might be wearing casual clothing as their uniform, won't certainly serve you. As most of these low-cost airlines are short-haul, you might need to get ready for landing even after you have only gone on board for a few minutes.

中譯 對於想要低價旅行的人來說，搭廉價航空也許是個選擇，因為你所要付的比起你預期要付給傳統航空公司的錢少得多。像是瑞安航空、西南航空，以及易捷航空都是很好的例子。搭乘廉價航空非常容易。從訂票、到機場登記登機，每一件事都是輕而易舉的。甚至你只需要在出發前2個小時之前在網路上訂票。你也可以直接在起飛前2個小時跑到簽到櫃台前買票。辦理登機手續也很容易以及快速，而且你可以在起飛前一個小時到機場即可。既然廉價航空是如此廉價，你不能期望在飛機上有免費的食物、飲料和報紙。而且對於你的座位也沒有艙等之分，空服員可能還穿休閒服當成制服，當然也不會服務你。多數的廉價航空航班都是短程的，甚至可能你登機後沒幾分鐘你就要準備降落了。

單字 low-cost airline 低成本航空公司　　option 選擇
hassle-free 輕而易舉　　classification 分級

61. (A) schedule 計劃　　**(B) budget 預算**
(C) routine 慣例　　(D) project 專案

62. (A) forms 格式　　(B) means 方法
(C) cruises 航遊　　**(D) carriers 航空公司**

63. **(A) pop in 突然出現**　　(B) break in 闖入
(C) fill in 填寫　　(D) come in 進來

64. **(A) inexpensive 便宜的**　　(B) inconvenient 不方便的
(C) inefficient 無效率的　　(D) inappropriate 不適當的

65. (A) good-haul 好的長途　　(B) huge-haul 巨大的長途
(C) short-haul 短程運輸的　　(D) long-haul 持久

"That's £3.25 altogether," said a taxi driver. "Keep the change, please," replied a young lady when she handed over the money to the driver. "Thank you. Have a pleasant stay in York," said the driver after she received it with delight. This brief dialogue demonstrates how pleasant the giving and receiving of tipping could be. Tipping has been a common way of showing appreciation to people who have served you. It is the kind of courtesy directed mostly to people who are serving in the travel and tourism industry. But sometimes things might not turn out to be so perfect. People might refuse to tip if they find the service is unsatisfactory. They might have no idea about what would be the appropriate amount for tipping. In some countries, tipping is included in the service when you pay for the bill in a restaurant and that amount will be 10 or 15% of your total bill. Whether they like it or not, some people might still be asked to tip or be overcharged for tipping if there is no stipulation about how much one should tip. In cases like these, tipping might not be an enjoyable experience at all.

中譯 「總共是3.25英鎊。」計程車司機說。「不用找了！」當一名年輕小姐把錢遞給司機時這樣說著。「謝謝！祝你在約克玩得愉快」司機收下後愉快地說。這段簡短的對話展現出收送小費可以是件很愉悅的事情。小費是向人們的服務表達感謝之意的常見方法。這多半是指在旅遊業中，對替你服務的人展現出禮貌。但有時候事情不會如此完美。如果他們覺得服務令人不滿意的話，人們可能會拒絕給小費。人們也有可能不知道小費該給多少才恰當。在某些國家，小費已經包含在你所需要的餐館總帳單中佔10-15%。不論他們喜歡與否，如果沒有規定要給多少小費的話，有些人可能會被要求給小費，或是多被要小費。在這樣的情況下，給予小費可能不是一個令人愉快的經驗。

單字 hand over 交出 | delight 愉快
demonstrate 說明 | tip 小費
appreciation 感謝 | courtesy 禮貌
bill 帳單 | stipulation 規定

66. (A) why (B) what (C) how (D) which

67. (A) targeting (B) targeted 把……作為目標（或對象）
(C) directing 針對 (D) directed 經指導的

68. (A) ungrateful 忘恩負義的 (B) unsatisfactory 令人不滿意的
(C) undeniable 不可否認的 (D) unexceptional 普通的

69. (A) Whether (B) Where (C) What (D) While

70. (A) for (B) from (C) on (D) of

Even a small reduction of salt in the diet can be a big help to the heart. A new study published in the New England Journal of Medicine used a computer model to predict how just three grams less a day would affect heart disease in the United States.

中譯 其實只要飲食上少一點點鹽就能對心臟有很大的幫助。新英格蘭醫學雜誌最新研究表示，用電腦模型預測每天少3克鹽就能影響美國的心臟病。

單字 reduction 減少 | diet 飲食
affect 影響

The result: Thirteen percent fewer heart attacks. Eight percent fewer strokes. Four percent fewer deaths. Eleven percent fewer new cases of heart disease. And two hundred forty billion dollars in health care savings. Researchers found less salt intake could prevent one hundred thousand heart attacks and ninety-two thousand deaths every year.

中譯 結果：降低13%心臟病發、降低8%中風、降低4%死亡率、降低11%新的心臟病例。以及省下2,400億美元的健康照護支出。研究者發現降低鹽的攝取每年可以預防10萬件心臟病發和救回9萬2千條性命。

單字 stroke 中風
intake 吸收

According to the U.S. government, the average American man eats, on average, ten grams of salt a day; however, the American Heart Association advises no more than three grams for healthy people. It says salt in the American diet has increased fifty percent since the 1970s, while blood pressures have also risen. Less salt can mean a lower blood pressure.

中譯 根據美國政府，平均每個美國人每天吃10克鹽，然而，美國心臟協會建議健康的人每天不要超過3克。他們表示自從1970年代，美國人飲食的鹽量增加了一半，血壓也升高了。少鹽可代表較低的血壓。

New York City Mayor, Michael Bloomberg, is leading an effort called the National Salt Reduction Initiative. The idea is to put pressure on food companies and restaurants. Critics call it government interference.

中譯 紐約市市長，麥可・彭博，目前領導一項計劃叫「國家降低鹽分攝取計劃」。這項主意是向食物公司和餐廳施壓。評論稱之為政府干預。

71. What is the best title for this passage?

(A) The disadvantages of salt 鹽的壞處

(B) Less salt can mean longer life 少鹽能夠長壽

(C) How to consume less salt 如何吃少一點的鹽

(D) How to cure heart disease 如何治療心臟病

中譯 何者最適合當本文標題？

解析 由The result: Thirteen percent fewer heart attacks. Eight percent fewer strokes. Four percent fewer deaths. Eleven percent fewer new cases of heart disease.可知。

72. According to the prediction of the study, how many grams of salt less a day can reduce the risk of heart disease?

(A) three 3 (B) ten 10 (C) fifteen 15 (D) eleven 11

中譯 根據研究的預測，每天減少多少鹽可以降低心臟病的發生風險？

解析 由the American Heart Association advises no more than three grams for healthy people可知。

73. Which of the following statement is NOT true?

(A) Eight percent fewer strokes was predicted by the study if people take less salt.
研究顯示如果人們少攝取鹽，可以預計少8%的中風。

(B) The results of the study were predicted by a computer model.
研究的結果是由電腦模型所預測的。

(C) The study was conducted in New England.
這份研究是在新英格蘭做的。

(D) About two hundred forty billion dollars in health care could be saved by eating less salt.
少攝取鹽可以省下2,400億元的健康照護支出。

中譯 以下何者敘述錯誤？

解析 應是發表於新英格蘭期刊：A new study published in the New England Journal of Medicine。

74. Which of the following statements is NOT true?

(A) The average American man eats 10 grams of salt a day.
美國人平均每天吃10克鹽。

(B) Less salt could prevent ninety-two thousand deaths a year.
少鹽每年可以挽回9萬2千條性命。

(C) No more than three grams of salt are good for healthy people.
對健康的人來說，少於3公克的鹽是好的。

(D) Americans have increased the amount of salt in their diet by fifteen percent since the 1970s.
美國人自1970年代以來，鹽的攝取量增加了15%。

中譯 哪一項敘述錯誤？

解析 由It says salt in the American diet has increased fifty percent since the 1970s, while blood pressures have also risen.可知，是50%不是15%。

75. What can be inferred from the last paragraph?

(A) Mayor Michael Bloomberg's National Salt Reduction Initiative is widely supported by Americans.
紐約市長麥可・彭博的「國家降低鹽分攝取計劃」被美國人所廣泛支持。

(B) The purpose of National Salt Reduction Initiative is to promote gourmet cuisines in New York City.
「國家降低鹽分攝取計劃」是用來推廣紐約市的美食。

(C) Mayor Bloomberg is concerned about the health of American people.
紐約市長彭博關心美國人的健康。

(D) Mayor Bloomberg has an ambition to run for the next presidency of the United States.
紐約市長彭博對於參選下一屆的美國總統野心勃勃。

中譯 最後一段可推論何事？

解析 由The idea is to put pressure on food companies and restaurants.可知是關心食物所帶來的健康問題。

Recently, a new type of tourism, or what is called 'alternative tourism', has emerged and become more and more popular among people who feel tired of the same old holidays and hope to gain real or authentic experiences from traveling. This new kind of tourism takes the form of individual custom-made or independent holidays that take people to remote and exotic destinations, and cater to their different needs and interests. These holidays are basically designed and arranged at a personal level. They often have different themes and offer a variety for people to choose from. As the market for this new form of tourism has expanded greatly, newer topics and programs will also appear as long as people begin to develop newer interests and needs in the future.

中譯 近來，一種新型態的旅遊形式，名為「另類旅遊」，崛起並且越來越受到歡迎，特別是對於千篇一律的假期所感到厭煩的人，他們想要獲得真實且道地的旅遊經驗。這類新型態的旅遊是針對個人客製化的，或是獨立的假期帶人們去偏遠和富有異國風情的地方，並且滿足不同的需求和興趣。這些假期基本上安排與設計都是很個人化的。他們通常有不同的主題和選擇提供挑選。而因為這樣新型態的旅遊近來擴展迅速，未來也會出現越來越多新的主題或是企劃，來因應人們新的喜好與需求。

單字 alternative 替代的（alternative tourism 另類觀光）

emerge 出現　remote 相隔很遠的

exotic 異國情調的　cater 迎合

But what exactly can people get out of alternative tourism? For ecology-minded people, they can go whale-watching or take a conservation trip to help restore the damaged coastline. For people who like adventure and outdoor activities, the choices could range from mountain climbing, scuba diving, windsurfing, white-water rafting to cycling in the mountains and deserts. For people who simply like to relax and gain a peace of mind, they can spend a week at spa and health resorts to relax and de-stress, or take yoga and meditation lessons at country retreats in India. For people who are fond of culture and heritage, they can visit museums and art galleries in New York, take a weekend break at the Edinburgh International Festival, or tour around France to visit historic castles.

中譯 但到底人們可以從另類旅遊中獲得什麼？對於在乎生態的人來說，他們可以去賞鯨，或者去修護被破壞的海岸線。對於愛好冒險以及戶外運動的人來說，則有登山、潛水、衝浪、峽谷漂流、在山中和沙漠中騎腳踏車等選擇。對於只想放鬆以及獲得心靈平靜的人，他們可以一整個星期都在SPA和健康度假中心中放鬆和減壓，或是去印度上瑜珈和冥想的課。而喜歡文化和歷史遺跡的人，則可以造訪紐約的博物館和美術館，或是週末參加愛丁堡藝術節，又或是到法國參觀歷史古堡。

重點 restore 恢復　retreat 僻靜之處

heritage 遺跡、世襲財產

Other programs under alternative tourism include holidays that are taken for educational, artistic or religious purposes. These contain learning English on a four-week trip to Australia, learning survival skills in the jungles, learning how to paint or handle dogs during a few days' holiday, and go on a pilgrimage to holy places and sites. The lists to these different kinds of programs are endless and cater to different customers' needs and interests. But the messages this emergence of new holidays signals for the travel and tourism industry are that alternative tourism not only reflects the changing faces of tourism, but also brings both challenges and opportunities to the industry.

中譯 其他另類旅遊的行程則有不同的目的，像是教育性、藝術性或是宗教性質。這些像是到澳洲學四週英文課、在叢林中學習求生技術、在短短假期內學會畫畫或是訓練狗兒，也可去聖地或是遺跡來趟宗教之旅。各式各樣的類型多到數不清，且能滿足客戶的需求和興趣。這些都透漏了新型態的假期以及另類旅遊，對於旅遊業來說不只是反映旅遊風貌的改變，同時也對旅遊業帶來新的挑戰以及契機。

單字 pilgrimage 朝聖　　emergence 出現

76. What is the main idea of this passage?

(A) the contents of alternative tourism 另類旅遊的內容

(B) the significance of mass tourism 大眾旅遊的重要性

(C) the popularity of alternative tourism 另類旅遊的受歡迎程度

(D) the reasons for the emergence of tourism 旅遊業產生的原因

中譯 本文的主旨為何？

解析 由第二段的內容可得知。

77. In paragraph 1, what does the word 'custom-made' mean?

(A) It means customers designing their own holidays to meet their own interests.
是客人自己設計他們的假期來滿足自己興趣的意思。

(B) It means holidays arranged according to different cultural customs.
是針對不同文化習俗來設計假期的意思。

(C) It means travelers getting the approval from customs officers.
是指旅客得到海關官員同意的意思。

(D) It means holidays designed individually and can vary from person to person.
是表示依照每個人的需求來個別設計假期的意思。

中譯 第一段的「custom-made」是什麼意思？

解析 由此句This new kind of tourism takes the form of individual custom-made or independent holidays that take people to remote and exotic destinations, and cater to their different needs and interests. 的individual 個人的，可猜出意思。

78. If you plan to go bungee-jumping, what type of tourism does it belong to?

(A) Ecotourism. 生態旅遊。

(B) Adventure tourism. 冒險旅遊。

(C) Cultural tourism. 文化旅遊。

(D) Escape tourism. 生存旅遊。

中譯 如果你計劃去高空彈跳，是屬於哪一類旅遊？

79. Which of the following holidays can be seen as educational?

(A) A weekend break in a country house for beauty treatments.

週末於鄉間做美容療程。

(B) A trip to Vancouver for the 2010 Winter Olympics.

參訪2010溫哥華冬季奧運。

(C) A one-week holiday in Paris on how to cook delicacies.

去巴黎一週學烹飪。

(D) Riding camels in the Sahara for a six-day holiday.

去撒哈拉沙漠6天騎駱駝。

中譯 以下哪一種假期是富有教育性的？

解析 因為「學」烹飪，故可被視為educational 有教育性的。

80. According to this passage, what does the appearance of alternative tourism signify to the travel and tourism industry?

(A) Tourism is about caring for people.

旅遊業準備關心人們。

(B) People working in the travel and tourism industry should love their jobs.

在旅遊業工作的人們應該愛他們的工作。

(C) Tourism keeps changing and it is both demanding and rewarding.

旅遊業一直不斷改變，既累人卻也很有成就感。

(D) It is important to learn about different cultures and customs.

學習不同的文化和習俗很重要。

中譯 根據本文，另類旅遊的出現對於旅遊業來說，象徵了什麼？

解析 由最後一段But the messages this emergence of new holidays signals for the travel and tourism industry are that alternative tourism not only reflects the changing faces of tourism, but also brings both challenges and opportunities to the industry.可推知。

100 年外語領隊英文試題＋標準答案

★100年專門職業及技術人員普通考試導遊人員、領隊人員考試試題

類科：外語領隊人員（英語）

科 目：外國語（英語）

考試時間：1 小時 20 分

※注意：（一）本試題為單一選擇題，請選出一個正確或最適當的答案，複選作答者，該題不予計分。

（二）本科目共80題，每題1.25分，須用2Ｂ鉛筆在試卡上依題號清楚劃記，於本試題上作答者，不予計分。

（三）本試題禁止使用電子計算器。

(　　)1. It is not my cup of tea!

(A) I must obey the instructions.　(B) I don't like it.
(C) I am not good at making tea.　(D) It is not my imagination.

(　　)2. The prosperity of ______ tourism is related to the policy of our government.

(A) domestic　(B) duplicated　(C) dumb　(D) detour

(　　)3. We should ______ all the possibilities when solving this problem.

(A) negate　(B) ponder　(C) attack　(D) project

(　　)4. He runs away with the idea, and the other faculty members do not agree.

(A) They blame him for his irresponsibility.
(B) They do not accept his hasty conclusion.
(C) They turn down his unexpected invitation.
(D) They reject his application.

(　　)5. She can speak English and French with ______.

(A) faculty　(B) future　(C) facility　(D) frailty

(　　)6. The waiters will show you where to bed down.

(A) The waiters will tell you the place that you may put your beddings.
(B) The waiters will ask for your assistance later.
(C) The waiters will tell you where you may stay tonight.
(D) The waiters will provide everything you need.

(　　)7. Mr. Jones has got the hang of being a tour guide.

(A) Mr. Jones quit his job.
(B) Mr. Jones needs our help now.
(C) Mr. Jones met some strangers on his way home.
(D) Mr. Jones has learned the skills of being a tour guide.

(　　)8. I like those stamps, but ______.

(A) I would not like to cost lots on money to buy them
(B) I would rather buy something else
(C) they would spend much money
(D) they would waste much money

(　　)9. Mr. Brown was the president, and now Mr. Bean steps into his shoes.

(A) Mr. Bean stamps on Mr. Brown's feet.
(B) Mr. Brown orders Mr. Bean to try his own shoes.
(C) Mr. Bean has replaced Mr. Brown.
(D) Mr. Bean offends Mr. Brown.

(　　)10. Our parents were high on love and patience, and therefore we followed their instructions willingly.

(A) rejoiced (B) transcended (C) valued (D) taught

(　　)11. The rustic scenery appealed to him so much that he bought a house there.

(A) rural (B) deserted (C) urban (D) beautiful

(　　)12. Due to the impending disaster, we have to ______ our flight to Bangkok.

(A) provide (B) cancel (C) resume (D) tailor

(　　)13. His face looks like ______.

(A) a toad (B) of a toad (C) with a toad (D) that of a toad

(　　)14. His conclusion seems to insinuate that we can visit Russia very soon.

(A) report (B) imply (C) deny (D) affirm

(　　)15. The tour guide ______ him into buying some expensive souvenirs.

(A) persuaded (B) dissuaded (C) suggested (D) purified

(　　)16. The mobs were mollified when he gave a speech.

(A) wiped out (B) attended (C) pacified (D) angry

( )17. We all felt ______ when the manager got drunk.

(A) embarrassed (B) embarrassing
(C) being embarrassed (D) been embarrassed

( )18. The travel agent ______ the delay.

(A) astonished at (B) astonished (C) apologized (D) apologized for

( )19. He will tell you as soon as he ______ .

(A) knows (B) has known (C) will know (D) is knowing

( )20. He devoted himself to ______ poor children.

(A) be taught (B) teaching (C) teach (D) teaching with

( )21. She is not so stupid ______ not to understand that.

(A) so (B) with (C) as (D) for

( )22. The interpreter talked as if he ______ how to fly like a bird.

(A) knew (B) would know (C) had known (D) has known

( )23. Gaga: Let's go Dutch.
Melody: ______.

(A) Are you so rich as to pay for all of us?
(B) We had better go to Germany.
(C) Do you really want to pick it up?
(D) Good idea!

( )24. Neither you, nor I, nor he ______ in Mr. Brown's class.

(A) am (B) is (C) are (D) be

( )25. The wedding anniversary is worth ______.

(A) being celebrated (B) celebrating
(C) of celebrating (D) celebrated

( )26. Wulai (烏來) is a famous hot-spring ______.

(A) resort (B) mansion (C) pivot (D) plaque

( )27. I found myself ______ an airplane.

(A) in broad (B) on board (C) abroad (D) with boarding

( )28. You must check the ______ date of your passport. You may need to apply for a new one.

(A) explanatory (B) exploratory (C) expiry (D) expository

( )29. ______ there is a holiday, we always go hiking.

(A) During (B) Whatever (C) Whenever (D) While

( )30. Bonnie signed up ______ dancing classes in the Extension Program.

(A) on (B) in (C) for (D) about

( )31. After the plane touches down, we have to remain in our seats until we ______ to the gate.

(A) pass by (B) stop over (C) take off (D) taxi in

( )32. Our ______ wants to reserve a table for dinner tomorrow.

(A) alcoholic (B) client (C) gambler (D) retailer

( )33. If you're travelling to the United States, you may need a ______.

(A) vicar (B) villa (C) vista (D) visa

( )34. Do not be afraid to eat with your hands here. When in Rome, do ______ the Romans do.

(A) for (B) as (C) of (D) since

( )35. The ______ of Liberty, a gift from France, is erected in New York Harbor.

(A) Statuette (B) Stature (C) Status (D) Statue

( )36. Before the plane leaves the ground, we must ______ a video related to flight safety.

(A) glance (B) look (C) notice (D) watch

( )37. What shall we do ______ ?

(A) after a dinner (B) after dinner (C) after we dinner (D) after the dinner

( )38. I am so happy that Nick is coming to visit us. Please tell him to make himself ______ home.

(A) inside (B) in (C) on (D) at

(　　)39. Would you like to order a/an ______ or refer to the à la carte menu?

(A) complex meal (B) singular meal (C) set meal (D) united meal

(　　)40. The newlyweds are on their ______ tour.

(A) blossom (B) bosom (C) begotten (D) bridal

(　　)41. ______ there is more than one Paris in the world, there's really only one Paris in the world. It is the capital of France.

(A) Although (B) Already (C) However (D) And

(　　)42. Please don't order so much food! ______ for the last two months.

(A) Earned much weight was (B) I have been putting on weight

(C) My weight has put on (D) My weight was gaining

(　　)43. This group of people would like to stay in ______ hotels. They need to be five star hotels.

(A) convenient (B) leisure (C) luxurious (D) public

(　　)44. Is there any problem ______ my reservation?

(A) in (B) of (C) to (D) with

(　　)45. Do not draw attention to yourself by ______ large amounts of cash or expensive jewelry.

(A) display (B) displayed (C) displays (D) displaying

(　　)46. I enjoyed the stay here. Thank you very much for the ______.

(A) hospital (B) hospitality (C) hostilities (D) hostel

(　　)47. Jessica's customers complained because they had to pay twice for their ______ .

(A) accommodation (B) acculturation

(C) accusation (D) assimilation

(　　)48. ______ , I will try to correct it.

(A) If I've done a mistake (B) If I've done wrongly

(C) If I've done something wrong (D) If I've done something mistake

(　　)49. If I cancel the trip, will I ______ ?

(A) be refunded (B) refund (C) refunded (D) refunding

(　　)50. William Faulkner was a Nobel ______.

(A) laurel　(B) launder　(C) laureate　(D) lavatory

(　　)51. Client: I would like to change 500 US dollars into NT dollars.

Bank clerk: Certainly, sir. Please complete this form and make sure ______.

(A) you jot down the capital appreciation

(B) you put the full name in capitals

(C) you visited the capitals of other countries

(D) you vote against capital punishment

(　　)52. An ______ gambler will have a hard time when deciding to stop this bad habit.

(A) introvert　(B) invidious　(C) inveterate　(D) innocuous

(　　)53. Hotel clerk: I'm sorry, could you spell that for me, please?

Guest: Yes, certainly. ______.

(A) It's three days counting from today　(B) It's S-M-Y-T-H

(C) It's Sunday next week　(D) It's 100 US dollars

(　　)54. Guest: You have answered my questions thoroughly. Thank you very much.

Hotel clerk: You are welcome. ______.

(A) It's been my address.　(B) It's been my intention.

(C) It's been my pleasure.　(D) It's been my thinking.

(　　)55. A: Have you seen my iPod? I can't find it anywhere.

B: Don't worry. ______.

(A) It will approach eventually　(B) It will come out eventually

(C) It will turn up eventually　(D) It will turn out eventually

Even though American social relations are complex, hard to form, and hard to maintain, I managed to (56) the gap, and I was able to have close friendships with some Americans. For (57) , the first semester I attended college, I became friends with one of the American students who used to attend math class with me. We used to study together, go to parties together, and he used to help me a lot with my English. (58) he transferred to another university, we always keep (59) with each other. From my experience, I have come to understand that Americans are generally verbal and long, silent periods are (60) to them. I think conversations make a friendly atmosphere among people.

(　　)56. (A) bridge　(B) expand　(C) separate　(D) reveal

(　　)57. (A) effort (B) example (C) possibility (D) truth

(　　)58. (A) After then (B) Even though (C) Not even (D) Only if

(　　)59. (A) an eye (B) head down (C) in touch (D) nose clean

(　　)60. (A) sensible (B) suitable (C) pursuable (D) uncomfortable

In Japan, guests have to (61) their shoes at the entrance of any Japanese-style accommodation. Slippers are (62) inside, except on the *tatami* matting, so bring thick socks if the weather is cold.

Seating in the room is on cushions called *zabuton* arranged around the low table. In the (63) season, there may be a blanket around the table. You slip your feet under the blanket for the (64) of a *kotatsu* electrical heating unit.

The *futon* bedding is laid out on the floor. It (65) consists of a mattress, sheets, a thick cover, and extra blankets if needed. A thin *yukata* robe is provided. In cold weather it is supplemented by a *tanzen* gown worn over it.

(　　)61. (A) exchange (B) replace (C) remove (D) wear

(　　)62. (A) wear (B) wearing (C) wore (D) worn

(　　)63. (A) spring (B) summer (C) autumn (D) winter

(　　)64. (A) electrification (B) vitamin (C) warmth (D) wave

(　　)65. (A) extremely (B) ordinarily (C) privately (D) sensitively

Destinations can be cities, towns, natural regions, or even whole countries. The economies of all tourist destinations are (66) to a significant extent on the money produced by tourism. It is possible to (67) destinations as natural or built: *Natural destinations* (68) seas, lakes, rivers, coasts, mountain ranges, desert, and so on. *Built destinations* are cities, towns, and villages. A *resort* is a destination constructed mainly or completely to serve the needs of tourism, (69) Cancun in Mexico.

Successful destinations are seen to be unique in some way by those who visit them. *Climate* is one of the (70) that determines this uniqueness. Not surprisingly, *temperate* and *tropical* climates attract the greatest number of visitors.

( )66. (A) dependent (B) disconnected (C) repellent (D) preferred

( )67. (A) amplify (B) classify (C) signify (D) verify

( )68. (A) concern (B) consist (C) include (D) involve

( )69. (A) so on (B) so so (C) such as (D) so that

( )70. (A) conclusions (B) specializations (C) superstitions (D) features

In the early 1900s, large numbers of Neanderthal skeletons were found in the Dordogne region of southern France.And scientists decided that they finally had enough information to say what a Neanderthal Man looked like. They gave the job of rebuilding a Neanderthal Man to a French scientist called Marcellin Boule.

After studying the bones for many months, Boule began writing reports that described the Neanderthal Man as looking more like an animal than a human being. A curved spine, he said, stopped the Neanderthal Man from standing upright and forced it to hold its head forward. Nor could it fully extend its legs. And, like a monkey, it could pick up and hold things with its feet.

In 1957, however, British scientists looked again at the skeleton Boule had studied. And they decided that most of Boule's ideas were wrong. The Neanderthal's feet could not hold things, and its spine was not curved. Neanderthals could stand upright, but the skeleton Boule had studied had arthritis. And when they calculated the size of the Neanderthal's brain, they decided that it was as large as the brain of early Homo sapiens.

( )71. Which century is mentioned in this passage?

(A) the 18th century (B) the 19th century
(C) the 20th century (D) the 21st century

( )72. What is this passage mainly about?

(A) The French scientist's rebuilding of the Neanderthals
(B) The study of the Neanderthal skeletons in the 1900s
(C) The corrected knowledge on the Neanderthals
(D) The similarities between the Neanderthals and the monkeys

( )73. Which of the following is closest in meaning to the word "upright" in the passage?

(A) curved down (B) toward the right
(C) leaning backward (D) straight up

( )74. Which of the following is NOT mentioned in the passage about Marcellin Boule?

(A) He was praised for rebuilding the Neanderthal Man in the early 1900s.
(B) He was a French scientist who wrote reports about the Neanderthal Man.
(C) His ideas were later overturned by other scientists.
(D) He described the Neanderthals as more like monkeys than mankind.

( )75. What can be inferred from this passage?

(A) Most of the Neanderthals had illnesses such as arthritis.
(B) The Neanderthals were probably related to human beings.
(C) Many Neanderthals could act both as monkeys and as human beings.
(D) The brain size of the Neanderthals grew larger from 1900 to 1957.

The McDonald's hamburger company is going into the airline catering business. A Swiss charter plane will be painted in the McDonald's colors, some cabin staff will wear McDonald's outfits, and the inflight food, instead of the customary cold collation, will be Big Macs and chicken McNuggets.

The service will be introduced on April 1, which initially led some people to suspect an April Fool trick, but the company and its Swiss airline collaborator, Crossair, confirmed yesterday that the project is no hoax. It will serve charter routes from Geneva and Zurich to popular European holiday resorts.

In line with the McDonald's practice of prefixing products with "Mc", the 161-seater MD83 jet will be known officially as the McPlane. Its fuselage will be painted to depict the McDonald's golden arches, and the cabin seats will be upholstered in bright red leather. McPlane's interior will seek to create the atmosphere of a McDonald's high street outlet, complete with "Have a nice day" greetings from the cockpit. However, it is uncertain if the cabin drinks trolley would be replaced by a milkshake dispenser. Chips, or "fries" as McDonald's call them, have been ruled out because of the danger of using a deep-fat frier.

( )76. What is the best title for this passage?

(A) McDonald's and the charter plane fuselage
(B) The external and internal design of McPlane
(C) McDonald's in the airline business
(D) The types of McDonald's food in the air

( )77. Which type of McDonald's food will not be seen on McPlane?

(A) Chips (B) Big Macs (C) McNuggets (D) Coke

( )78. Why did some people doubt the reality of this report?

(A) The food on board will be the regular customary collation.

(B) Swiss airline and Crossair acknowledged this trick.

(C) Only one plane will be related to McDonald's.

(D) The service will begin on April Fool's Day.

( )79. What does a "high street" mean?

(A) a principal street (B) a countryside street

(C) a very crowded street (D) a colorful street

( )80. According to the passage, who will be greeting the passengers with "Have a nice day"?

(A) the passengers (B) the flight attendants

(C) the pilot (D) the ground staff

★標準答案

1. (B)	2. (A)	3. (B)	4. (B)	5. (C)
6. (C)	7. (D)	8. (B)	9. (C)	10. (C)
11. (A)	12. (B)	13. (#)	14. (B)	15. (A)
16. (C)	17. (A)	18. (D)	19. (A)	20. (B)
21. (C)	22. (C)	23. (D)	24. (B)	25. (B)
26. (A)	27. (B)	28. (C)	29. (C)	30. (C)
31. (D)	32. (B)	33. (D)	34. (B)	35. (D)
36. (D)	37. (B)	38. (D)	39. (C)	40. (D)
41. (A)	42. (B)	43. (C)	44. (D)	45. (D)
46. (B)	47. (A)	48. (C)	49. (A)	50. (C)
51. (B)	52. (C)	53. (B)	54. (C)	55. (C)
56. (A)	57. (B)	58. (B)	59. (C)	60. (D)
61. (C)	62. (D)	63. (D)	64. (C)	65. (B)
66. (A)	67. (B)	68. (C)	69. (C)	70. (D)
71. (C)	72. (C)	73. (D)	74. (A)	75. (B)
76. (C)	77. (A)	78. (D)	79. (A)	80. (C)

備註：第13題答A或D或AD者均給分。

100 年外語領隊英文試題中譯與解析

1. It is not my cup of tea!

   (A) I must obey the instructions. 我必須遵守指示。

   (B) I don't like it. 我不喜歡它。

   (C) I am not good at making tea. 我不太會泡茶。

   (D) It is not my imagination. 這不是我的想像。

   中譯 這杯不是我的茶。

   解析 It is not my cup of tea!其實就是時下年輕人所說的「這不是我的菜」。

2. The prosperity of domestic tourism is related to the policy of our government.

   (A) domestic 國內的 (B) duplicated 複製的

   (C) dumb 啞的 (D) detour 繞道而行

   中譯 國內旅遊業的興盛與我們政府政策有關。

   解析 domestic 國內的；internaitonal 國際的；domestic flight 國內航班；international flight 國際航班；prosperity 興旺、繁榮。可由our government推論和domestic 國內的有關。

3. We should ponder all the possibilities when solving this problem.

   (A) negate 拒絕 (B) ponder 仔細考慮

   (C) attack 攻擊 (D) project 計劃

   中譯 當解決此問題時，我們應該仔細考慮任何可能性。

   解析 由solving this problem可推論是需要ponder 仔細考慮。ponder upon the problem 仔細考慮問題；solve 解決。

4. He runs away with the idea, and the other faculty members do not agree.

   (A) They blame him for his irresponsibility. 他們指責他的不負責任。

   (B) They do not accept his hasty conclusion. 他們不接受他輕率的結論。

   (C) They turn down his unexpected invitation. 他們拒絕他意外的邀請。

   (D) They reject his application. 他們拒絕他的申請。

   中譯 他倉促地說出想法，而其他教授不同意。

   解析 run away with 不受控制；faculty 全體教員。

5. She can speak English and French with facility.

(A) faculty 全體教員　(B) future 未來

(C) facility 流利　(D) frailty 弱點

中譯 她可以說很流利的英文和法文。

解析 with facility 流利，本句可替換成She can speak English and French fluently.。fluently 流利地。

6. The waiters will show you where to bed down.

(A) The waiters will tell you the place that you may put your beddings.
服務生將會告訴你哪裡可以放寢具。

(B) The waiters will ask for your assistance later.
服務生等會兒將要求你的援助。

(C) The waiters will tell you where you may stay tonight.
服務生將告訴你今晚你會下榻在哪裡。

(D) The waiters will provide everything you need.
服務生會提供你所需的每樣東西。

中譯 服務生將告訴你今晚你會下榻在哪裡。

解析 bed down 夜宿，也就是下榻之處。

7. Mr. Jones has got the hang of being a tour guide.

(A) Mr. Jones quit his job.
瓊斯先生辭職了。

(B) Mr. Jones needs our help now.
瓊斯先生現在需要我們的幫忙。

(C) Mr. Jones met some strangers on his way home.
瓊斯先生在回家途中遇到一些陌生人。

(D) Mr. Jones has learned the skills of being a tour guide.
瓊斯先生已經學習到當一位領隊的技巧。

中譯 瓊斯先生已經學習到當一位領隊的技巧。

解析 get the hang of sth. 掌握某事的訣竅。

8. I like those stamps, but I would rather buy something else.

(A) I would not like to cost lots on money to buy them 我不想要花很多錢在買郵票上

(B) I would rather buy something else 我寧願買其他東西

(C) they would spend much money 他們會花很多錢

(D) they would waste much money 他們會浪費很多錢

中譯 我喜歡那些郵票，但我寧願買其他東西。

解析 rather 寧願，例句：I would rather you come tomorrow. 我寧願你明天來。

9. Mr. Brown was the president, and now Mr. Bean steps into his shoes.

(A) Mr. Bean stamps on Mr. Brown's feet.
豆豆先生踩在布朗先生的腳上。

(B) Mr. Brown orders Mr. Bean to try his own shoes.
布朗先生提供豆豆先生試穿他自己的鞋。

(C) Mr. Bean has replaced Mr. Brown.
豆豆先生取代布朗先生。

(D) Mr. Bean offends Mr. Brown.
豆豆先生冒犯布朗先生。

中譯 過去布朗先生是一位總統，而現在豆豆先生接替他的位子。

解析 step into sb.'s shoes 接替某人 = replace somebody。

10. Our parents were high on love and patience, and therefore we followed their instructions willingly.

(A) rejoiced 高興 (B) transcended 超越

(C) valued 重視 (D) taught 教導

中譯 我們的父母相當重視愛與耐心，因此我們願意承襲他們的教導。

解析 high on 熱衷於 = value 重視；instructions 指令、教導；willingly 自動地、欣然地。

11. The rural scenery appealed to him so much that he bought a house there.

(A) rural 鄉下的 (B) deserted 荒蕪的

(C) urban 都市的 (D) beautiful 漂亮的

中譯 鄉村風光很吸引他，因此他在那裡買了一棟房子。

解析 rural 鄉下的、田園的、鄉村風味的；urban 都市的。

12. Due to the impending disaster, we have to cancel our flight to Bangkok.

(A) provide 提供 (B) cancel 取消 (C) resume 重複 (D) tailor 裁縫

中譯 因為即將到來的災害，我們必須取消到曼谷的航班。

解析 impending 即將發生的、逼近的；disaster 災害、災難。due to 因為，例句：Due to the delay, we are not able to catch up with our connecting flight. 因為延遲，我們無法趕上我們的轉機班機。102領隊

13. His face looks like a toad. / that of a toad.

(A) a toad 討厭的傢伙 (B) of a toad
(C) with a toad (D) that of a toad

中譯 他的臉看起來像蟾蜍。

解析 toad 討厭的傢伙 / 蟾蜍，that = the face的意思，故二者皆可。

14. His conclusion seems to insinuate that we can visit Russia very soon.

(A) report 報告 (B) imply 暗示 (C) deny 否認 (D) affirm 堅稱

中譯 他的結論似乎暗示我們很快就可以參訪俄羅斯。

解析 insinuate 暗示、巧妙地潛入，例：insinuate oneself into sb.'s favour 巧妙地巴結上某人；insinuate oneself into the crowd 漸漸地擠進人群。conclusion 結論。

15. The tour guide persuaded him into buying some expensive souvenirs.

(A) persuaded 說服 (B) dissuaded 勸阻
(C) suggested 建議 (D) purified 淨化

中譯 這名導遊說服他買昂貴的紀念品。

解析 persuade into Ving 說服某事；souvenir 紀念品。

16. The mobs were pacified when he gave a speech.

(A) wiped out 去除 (B) ate nded 出席
(C) pacified 使……平靜 (D) angry 生氣的

中譯 當他演講時，暴徒們的情緒被緩和下來。

解析 mob 暴民；pacify 使（某人）安靜、在（有戰爭的地方）實現和平，例：pacify the riot 平定暴動；pacify a baby 撫慰嬰兒。

17. We all felt embarrassed when the manager got drunk.

(A) embarrassed 感到尷尬的　(B) embarrassing 使人尷尬的
(C) being embarrassed　(D) been embarrassed

中譯 當經理喝醉時，我們都感到很不好意思。

解析 embarrassing 使人尷尬的，指事物；embarrassed 感到尷尬的，形容人。由felt得知是人對此事感到尷尬，故選embarrassed。

18. The travel agent apologized for the delay.

(A) astonished at　(B) astonished
(C) apologized　(D) apologized for 道歉

中譯 旅行社因為行程延誤而道歉。

解析 apologize to 人 for 某事，意思是為某事向某人道歉，故選(D)。

19. He will tell you as soon as he knows.

(A) knows 知道　(B) has known　(C) will know　(D) is knowing

中譯 他一旦知道就會告訴你。

解析 單純未來假設，故選knows。此句也可以寫為He will tell you if he knows.。

20. He devoted himself to teaching poor children.

(A) be taught　(B) teaching　(C) teach 教導　(D) teaching with

中譯 他獻身於教育貧困兒童。

解析 devote to Ving 獻身於某事。

21. She is not so stupid as not to understand that.

(A) so　(B) with　(C) as　(D) for

中譯 她沒有笨到不瞭解這件事。

解析 so as not to 以免、免得、生怕，例句：We talked quietly so as not to be overheard. 我們低聲交談，以免別人聽到。

22. The interpreter talked as if he had known how to fly like a bird.

(A) knew (B) would know (C) had known (D) has known

中譯 口譯員講得好像他知道如何像鳥一樣飛翔。

解析 interpreter 口譯員；as if 好像、似乎，S + V as if S + had Vpp 與過去事實相反。

23. Gaga: Let's go Dutch.
Melody: Good idea!

(A) Are you so rich as to pay for all of us? 你夠有錢付我們所有人的錢嗎？

(B) We had better go to Germany. 我們最好去德國。

(C) Do you really want to pick it up? 你真的要把它撿起來嗎？

(D) Good idea! 好主意！

中譯 卡卡：我們各自付帳吧！
美樂蒂：好主意！

解析 go Dutch 各自付帳。

24. Neither you, nor I, nor he is in Mr. Brown's class.

(A) am (B) is (C) are (D) be

中譯 不是你，也不是我，更不是他在布朗先生的班級上。

解析 最近的主詞為he，故選動詞is。

25. The wedding anniversary is worth celebrating.

(A) being celebrated (B) celebrating 慶祝
(C) of celebrating (D) celebrated

中譯 結婚周年很值得慶祝。

解析 「worth of + 動名詞」與「worth + 動名詞」兩者形式不同，但意思相同。worth of + 動名詞－被動式的動名詞；而worth後面接主動式的動名詞，雖然在形式上是主動的，但其意義仍然是被動的。如 The wedding anniversary is worth of being celebrating. = The wedding anniversary is worth celebrating.。

26. Wulai (烏來) is a famous hot-spring resort.

(A) resort 名勝 (B) mansion 大廈 (C) pivot 中心點 (D) plaque 名牌

中譯 烏來是著名的溫泉度假勝地。

解析 hot-spring 溫泉；resort 休閒度假之處、名勝。

27. I found myself on board an airplane.

(A) in broad
(B) on board 在飛機上
(C) abroad 在國外
(D) with boarding

中譯 我發現我自己在飛機上。

解析 必考片語：on board 在飛機上；boarding pass 登機證。

28. You must check the expiry date of your passport. You may need to apply for a new one.

(A) explanatory 解釋的
(B) exploratory 探險的
(C) expiry 到期、滿期
(D) expository 說明性

中譯 你必須檢查您的護照的到期日。你也許需要申請一本新的。

解析 expiry 到期的；expire 到期，例句：I am afraid your credit card has already expired. Would you like to pay in cash instead? 恐怕你的信用卡已經過期了。你希望改以付現代替嗎？ 99領隊

29. Whenever there is a holiday, we always go hiking.

(A) During 在……的期間
(B) Whatever 不論什麼
(C) Whenever 無論何時
(D) While 當……時

中譯 無論何時有假，我們總是去健行。

解析 whenever 無論何時。

30. Bonnie signed up for dancing classes in the Extension Program.

(A) on
(B) in
(C) for
(D) about

中譯 邦妮報名登記了推廣教育的舞蹈課。

解析 sign up for 報名登記。

31. After the plane touches down, we have to remain in our seats until we taxi in to the gate.

(A) pass by 經過
(B) stop over 短暫停留
(C) take off 起飛
(D) taxi in 飛機在跑道上滑行

中譯 飛機降落後，我們必須待在座位上，直到滑入機坪入口。

解析 touch down 著陸；taxi in 飛機在跑道上滑行。

32. Our client wants to reserve a table for dinner tomorrow.

(A) alcoholic 酗酒者　(B) client 顧客
(C) gambler 賭徒　(D) retailer 零售商

中譯 我們的客人想要為明天晚餐預先訂桌。

解析 reserve 預約、預訂；reserve a table 訂桌；make reservation 預約。

33. If you're travelling to the United States, you may need a visa.

(A) vicar 傳教牧師　(B) villa 別墅　(C) vista 街景　(D) visa 簽證

中譯 如果你到美國旅行，你可能需要簽證。

解析 visa 簽證，例句：People traveling to a foreign country may need to apply for a visa. 人們到國外旅行可能需要申請簽證。98領隊

34. Do not be afraid to eat with your hands here. When in Rome, do as the Romans do.

(A) for　(B) as　(C) of　(D) since

中譯 在這裡不要害怕用手吃飯。要入境隨俗。

解析 When in Rome, do as the Romans do. 入境隨俗。

35. The Statue of Liberty, a gift from France, is erected in New York Harbor.

(A) Statuette 塑像　(B) Stature 身材　(C) Status 狀態　(D) Statue 雕像

中譯 自由女神像，是來自法國的禮物，豎立在紐約港。

解析 The Statue of Liberty 自由女神像；erect 豎起。

36. Before the plane leaves the ground, we must watch a video related to flight safety.

(A) glance 瀏覽　(B) look 看　(C) notice 注意　(D) watch 看

中譯 在飛機起飛前，我們必須觀看和飛安有關的影片。

解析 watch 觀看。

37. What shall we do after dinner?

(A) after a dinner　(B) after dinner　(C) after we dinner　(D) after the dinner

中譯 晚飯後我們要做什麼？

解析 dinner 晚餐為不可數名詞，不需加冠詞。

38. I am so happy that Nick is coming to visit us. Please tell him to make himself at home.

(A) inside (B) in (C) on (D) at

中譯 我很開心尼克要來拜訪我們。請告訴他把這裡當自己家。

解析 make somebody at home 讓某人不要拘束，就像在自己家一樣。

39. Would you like to order a/an set meal or refer to the à la carte menu?

(A) complex meal (B) singular meal (C) set meal 套餐 (D) united meal

中譯 你想要點套餐，還是參考菜單？

解析 set meal 套餐。

40. The newlyweds are on their bridal tour.

(A) blossom 開花 (B) bosom 胸部
(C) begotten 獨生子 (D) bridal 婚禮的

中譯 新婚夫婦正在蜜月旅行。

解析 newlyweds 新婚夫婦；bridal tour = honeymoon 蜜月旅行。

41. Although there is more than one Paris in the world, there's really only one Paris in the world. It is the capital of France.

(A) Although 儘管 (B) Already 已經 (C) However 然而 (D) And 和

中譯 雖然全世界有一個以上名叫巴黎的地方，但是世界上其實只有一個巴黎。那就是法國的首都。

解析 由more than one Paris和only one Paris比較，為轉折語氣，故選although。

42. Please don't order so much food! I have been putting on weight for the last two months.

(A) Earned much weight was I (B) I have been putting on weight
(C) My weight has put on (D) My weight was gaining

中譯 拜託別點太多食物！這兩個月我已經開始變胖了。

解析 gain weight、put on weight都是增重之意，例句：Many people have put on some pounds during the New Year vacation. 於新年假期期間，許多人體重增加不少磅。98領隊

43. This group of people would like to stay in luxurious hotels. They need to be five star hotels.

(A) convenient 方便 (B) leisure 閒暇
(C) luxurious 豪華 (D) public 公共

中譯 這群人想要住在豪華飯店。這些飯店必須是五星級的。

解析 luxurious 奢華的；luxury 奢華。

44. Is there any problem with my reservation?

(A) in (B) of (C) to (D) with

中譯 我的預約有任何問題嗎？

解析 某事有問題，用with problem。

45. Do not draw attention to yourself by displaying large amounts of cash or expensive jewelry.

(A) display 炫耀 (B) displayed (C) displays (D) displaying

中譯 不要藉由展示大量的現金和貴重首飾，引起別人對自己的注意力。

解析 draw attention to 引起對……的注意；by Ving 藉由……的動作。

46. I enjoyed the stay here. Thank you very much for the hospitality.

(A) hospital 醫院 (B) hospitality 熱情好客
(C) hostilities 敵意 (D) hostel 宿舍

中譯 我喜歡住這裡。謝謝你的熱情好客。

解析 hospitality 熱情好客。

47. Jessica's customers complained because they had to pay twice for their accommodation.

(A) accommodation 住宿 (B) acculturation 文化適應
(C) accusation 指控 (D) assimilation 吸收

中譯 潔西卡的客人有抱怨，因為他們必須支付兩次住宿費用。

解析 accommodation 住宿，例句：Reservations for hotel accommodation should be made in advance to make sure rooms are available. 旅館的訂房應提早訂，才能確保有房間。98領隊

48. If I've done something wrong, I will try to correct it.

(A) If I've done a mistake
(B) If I've done wrongly
(C) If I've done something wrong
(D) If I've done something mistake

中譯 如果我做錯事，我會試著改正。

解析 make a mistake、do something wrong都為犯錯的說法，(A)應該改成made a mistake；(B)、(D)應該改成done something wrong。

49. If I cancel the trip, will I be refunded?

(A) be refunded (B) refund 退款 (C) refunded (D) refunding

中譯 如果我取消行程，我可以退費嗎？

解析 人之於refund 退費為被動，refund在此處為動詞，亦可為名詞，如：The guest is given a refund after he makes a complaint to the restaurant. 這名客人在他和餐廳抱怨之後拿到退款。99領隊

50. William Faulkner was a Nobel laureate.

(A) laurel 殊榮
(B) launder 洗滌
(C) laureate 得獎者
(D) lavator （英文無此字）

中譯 威廉·福克納是諾貝爾獎的得主。

解析 laureate當名詞為戴桂冠的人，當動詞則為使某物戴桂冠，形容詞則為配戴桂冠的。

51. Client: I would like to change 500 US dollars into NT dollars.

Bank clerk: Certainly, sir. Please complete this form and make sure you put the full name in capitals.

(A) you jot down the capital appreciation 你記錄資產增值
(B) you put the full name in capitals 用大寫寫全名
(C) you visited the capitals of other countries 你參觀其他國家首都
(D) you vote against capital punishment 投票反對死刑

中譯 客戶：我想要將500美元換成新台幣。
銀行行員：沒問題，先生。請填此表格並且確保用大寫寫全名。

解析 in capitals 用大寫。

52. An inveterate gambler will have a hard time when deciding to stop this bad habit.

(A) introvert 個性內向的
(B) invidious 令人反感的
(C) inveterate 根深蒂固的
(D) innocuous 無害的

中譯 一個根深蒂固的賭徒要把壞習慣戒掉是很困難的。

解析 inveterate 根深蒂固的；gambler 賭徒。

53. Hotel clerk: I'm sorry, could you spell that for me, please?

Guest: Yes, certainly. It's S-M-Y-T-H.

(A) It's three days counting from today 從今天開始數是3天
(B) It's S-M-Y-T-H 是S-M-Y-T-H
(C) It's Sunday next week 下星期是星期天
(D) It's 100 US dollars 這要價100美元

中譯 飯店人員：不好意思，可以幫我拼出來嗎？
客人：好的，沒問題。S-M-Y-T-H。

解析 spell 拼字。

54. Guest: You have answered my questions thoroughly. Thank you very much.

Hotel clerk: You are welcome. It's been my pleasure.

(A) It's been my address. 這是我的地址。
(B) It's been my intention. 這是我的打算。
(C) It's been my pleasure. 這是我的榮幸。
(D) It's been my thinking. 這是我的想法。

中譯 客人：你回答問題回答地很詳細。非常謝謝你。
飯店服務員：不客氣。這是我的榮幸。

解析 thoroughly 認真仔細地，由Thank you very much.可推知答案為It's been my pleasure.。

55. A: Have you seen my iPod? I can't find it anywhere.
B: Don't worry. It will turn out eventually.

(A) It will approach eventually 它終究會抵達

(B) It will come out eventually 它終究會出來

(C) It will turn up eventually 它終究會出現

(D) It will turn out eventually 最終結果是

中譯 A：你有看到我的iPod嗎？我到處都找不到。
B：別擔心。它終究會出現。

解析 turn up 出現；turn out 結果。

Even though American social relations are complex, hard to form, and hard to maintain, I managed to bridge the gap, and I was able to have close friendships with some Americans. For example, the first semester I attended college, I became friends with one of the American students who used to attend math class with me. We used to study together, go to parties together, and he used to help me a lot with my English. Even though he transferred to another university, we always keep in touch with each other. From my experience, I have come to understand that Americans are generally verbal and long, silent periods are uncomfortable to them. I think conversations make a friendly atmosphere among people.

中譯 即便美國人的社交關係是複雜、難以形成且維持的，我還是盡量打破隔閡，並有幾位親近的美國朋友。比如說，我上大學的第一學期，我就和一名一起上數學課的美國學生成為朋友。我們經常一起念書，一起去派對，他之前常幫助我的英文。即便他轉學到其他大學，我們總是保持聯絡。就我的經驗來看，我已經了解美國人通常是比較喜歡交談的，且沉默寡言對他們來說是不舒服的。我認為會話會產生與人友好的氣氛。

單字 manage 設法　transfer 轉換
atmosphere 氣氛

56. (A) bridge 橋　(B) expand 擴張
(C) separate 分開　(D) reveal 顯露

57. (A) effort 努力　(B) example 例子
(C) possibility 可能性　(D) truth 真相

58. (A) After then 在此之後　(B) Even though 儘管
(C) Not even 甚至　(D) Only if 只有當

59. (A) an eye 注意 (B) head down 保持低調

(C) in touch 保持聯絡 (D) nose clean 不參與

60. (A) sensible 敏感的 (B) suitable 適合的

(C) pursuable 可實行的 (D) uncomfortable 不舒服的

In Japan, guests have to remove their shoes at the entrance of any Japanese-style accommodation. Slippers are worn inside, except on the tatami matting, so bring thick socks if the weather is cold.

中譯 在日本，於任何一個日式風格旅館的玄關處，客人都必須脫鞋。拖鞋是在室內穿的，除了在榻榻米上，所以如果天氣冷，要帶襪子。

Seating in the room is on cushions called zabuton arranged around the low table. In the winter season, there may be a blanket around the table. You slip your feet under the blanket for the warmth of a kotatsu electrical heating unit.

中譯 房間裡圍著矮桌，坐在稱為「沙包墊」的墊子上。冬天的時候，也許會在桌子上加上毯子。你把腳伸進電爐加熱的毯子下取暖。

The futon bedding is laid out on the floor. It ordinarily consists of a mattress, sheets, a thick cover, and extra blankets if needed. A thin *yukata* robe is provided. In cold weather it is supplemented by a tanzen gown worn over it.

中譯 睡覺時被子是鋪在地板上的。通常有一個床墊、床單、厚被，如果有需要會提供額外的毯子。房內提供薄浴衣。在寒冷的天氣時再添加一件睡袍。

重點 accommodation 住處 consist of 由某事物組成或構成

supplement 增補、補充

61. (A) exchange 交換 (B) replace 取代

(C) remove 移除 (D) wear 穿

62. (A) wear 穿 (B) wearing

(C) wore (D) worn

63. (A) spring 春天 (B) summer 夏天

(C) autumn 秋天 (D) winter 冬天

64. (A) electrification 電氣化 (B) vitamin 維生素
(C) warmth 溫暖 (D) wave 浪

65. (A) extremely 非常地 (B) ordinarily 通常地
(C) privately 私下地 (D) sensitively 敏銳地

Destinations can be cities, towns, natural regions, or even whole countries. The economies of all tourist destinations are dependent to a significant extent on the money produced by tourism. It is possible to classify destinations as natural or built: *Natural destinations* include seas, lakes, rivers, coasts, mountain ranges, desert, and so on. *Built destinations* are cities, towns, and villages. A *resort* is a destination constructed mainly or completely to serve the needs of tourism, such as Cancun in Mexico.

中譯 旅遊地點，可以是城市、小鎮、自然區域甚至整個國家。所有旅遊景點的經濟有很大一部分是依賴旅遊業所帶來的收益。旅遊景點可被區分為自然以及人為的：自然旅遊景點包含海洋、湖泊、河流、海岸、山脈和沙漠等等。人為的景點則是城市、小鎮以及鄉村。度假勝地就是大部分或是完全用來因應旅遊業的需求，像是墨西哥的坎昆。

Successful destinations are seen to be unique in some way by those who visit them. Climate is one of the features that determines this uniqueness. Not surprisingly, temperate and *tropical* climates attract the greatest number of visitors.

中譯 熱門的旅遊景點對於參訪的旅客來說是具有獨特性的。氣候就是決定獨特性的因素之一。無庸置疑地，溫帶以及熱帶氣候是最受青睞的。

單字 region 地區、地帶
extent 程度、限度
and so on 等等
determine 決定
uniqueness 獨一無二、獨特性

66. (A) dependent 依靠的 (B) disconnected 不相連的
(C) repellent 相斥的 (D) preferred 偏好的

67. (A) amplify 放大 (B) classify 分類
(C) signify 象徵 (D) verify 驗證

68. (A) concern 關心 (B) consist 組成
(C) include 包含 (D) involve 牽涉

69. (A) so on 等
(B) so so 還好
(C) such as 例如
(D) so that 以便

70. (A) conclusions 結論
(B) specializations 專業
(C) superstitions 迷信
(D) features 特色

In the early 1900s, large numbers of Neanderthal skeletons were found in the Dordogne region of southern France. And scientists decided that they finally had enough information to say what a Neanderthal Man looked like. They gave the job of rebuilding a Neanderthal Man to a French scientist called Marcellin Boule.

中譯 1900年代初期，在法國南部的多爾多涅省發現了大量的尼安德人骨頭。而科學家終於決定他們有足夠的資訊描繪尼安德人的樣貌。他們將這項重建的工作交給了一名法國科學家，馬西林．布爾。

After studying the bones for many months, Boule began writing reports that described the Neanderthal Man as looking more like an animal than a human being. A curved spine, he said, stopped the Neanderthal Man from standing upright and forced it to hold its head forward. Nor could it fully extend its legs. And, like a monkey, it could pick up and hold things with its feet.

中譯 經過了數個月研究骨頭之後，布爾開始著手寫報告描述尼安德人的樣子，看起來比較像動物，而非人類。他說彎曲的脊椎讓尼安德人無法直立且迫使它的頭往前。並且也不能完全伸展雙腳。以及像是猴子一樣，可以用腳拿與抓東西。

In 1957, however, British scientists looked again at the skeleton Boule had studied. And they decided that most of Boule's ideas were wrong. The Neanderthal's feet could not hold things, and its spine was not curved. Neanderthals could stand upright, but the skeleton Boule had studied had arthritis. And when they calculated the size of the Neanderthal's brain, they decided that it was as large as the brain of early Homo sapiens.

中譯 在1957年，一名英國科學家又看了布爾研究過的骨頭。他們覺得布爾大部分的想法是錯的。尼安德人的腳不能抓東西，它的脊椎沒有彎曲。尼安德人可以直立站著，但是布爾研究的骨頭有關節炎。以及，當他們計算尼安德人的大腦尺寸後，他們認為大小和早期人類是一樣的。

單字 skeleton 骨骼、骸骨
spine 脊柱、脊椎
curve 彎曲
calculate 計算

71. Which century is mentioned in this passage?

(A) the 18th century 18世紀 (B) the 19th century 19世紀

(C) the 20th century 20世紀 (D) the 21st century 21世紀

中譯 本文主要是描述哪一世紀的事？

解析 由第一段的In the early 1900s以及最後一段的In 1957可知為20世紀。

72. What is this passage mainly about?

(A) The French scientist's rebuilding of the Neanderthals
法國科學家重建尼安德人

(B) The study of the Neanderthal skeletons in the 1900s
1900年代尼安德人的骨頭研究

(C) The corrected knowledge on the Neanderthals
有關尼安德人修正後的知識

(D) The similarities between the Neanderthals and the monkeys
尼安德人與猴子的相似性

中譯 本文的主旨為何？

解析 由最後一段可知。

73. Which of the following is closest in meaning to the word "upright" in the passage?

(A) curved down 向下彎曲 (B) toward the right 朝向右邊

(C) leaning backward 後傾 (D) straight up 站直

中譯 哪個比較接近「upright」的意思？

解析 upright 挺直、筆直。

74. Which of the following is NOT mentioned in the passage about Marcellin Boule?

(A) He was praised for rebuilding the Neanderthal Man in the early 1900s.
他於1900年代早期因重建尼安德人而被稱讚。

(B) He was a French scientist who wrote reports about the Neanderthal Man.
他是名法國科學家，寫了關於尼安德人的報告。

(C) His ideas were later overturned by other scientists.

他的概念之後被其他科學家所推翻。

(D) He described the Neanderthals as more like monkeys than mankind.

他形容尼安德人比較像猴子而非人類。

中譯 關於馬西林・布爾，以下哪項未曾被提及？

解析 除了(A)之外皆在本文中提及。

75. What can be inferred from this passage?

(A) Most of the Neanderthals had illnesses such as arthritis.

多數尼安德人有關節炎。

(B) The Neanderthals were probably related to human beings.

尼安德人和人類可能有關。

(C) Many Neanderthals could act both as monkeys and as human beings.

許多尼安德人行為像猴子和人。

(D) The brain size of the Neanderthals grew larger from 1900 to 1957.

尼安德人的腦袋從1900到1957漸漸變大。

中譯 由本文可推論以下何者？

解析 由And when they calculated the size of the Neanderthal's brain, they decided that it was as large as the brain of early Homo sapiens.可知。

The McDonald's hamburger company is going into the airline catering business. A Swiss charter plane will be painted in the McDonald's colors, some cabin staff will wear McDonald's outfits, and the inflight food, instead of the customary cold collation, will be Big Macs and chicken McNuggets.

中譯 麥當勞漢堡公司即將跨入航空餐飲事業。一架瑞士飛機將會被漆上麥當勞的顏色，有些機艙人員會穿上麥當勞的制服，而機上餐飲不再是傳統整套的冰冷點心，而會是大麥克和麥克雞塊。

The service will be introduced on April 1, which initially led some people to suspect an April Fool trick, but the company and its Swiss airline collaborator, Crossair, confirmed yesterday that the project is no hoax. It will serve charter routes from Geneva and Zurich to popular European holiday resorts.

中譯 這項服務將於4月1日開始，起初會讓人聯想到是愚人節的把戲，但麥當勞以及合作夥伴——瑞士的羅莎爾航空公司，昨天證實了這項計劃並非謠言。這將提供從日內瓦到蘇黎世等歐洲受歡迎的度假航班中服務。

In line with the McDonald's practice of prefixing products with "Mc", the 161-seater MD83 jet will be known officially as the McPlane. Its fuselage will be painted to depict the McDonald's golden arches, and the cabin seats will be upholstered in bright red leather. McPlane's interior will seek to create the atmosphere of a McDonald's high street outlet, complete with "Have a nice day" greetings from the cockpit. However, it is uncertain if the cabin drinks trolley would be replaced by a milkshake dispenser. Chips, or "fries" as McDonald's call them, have been ruled out because of the danger of using a deep-fat frier.

中譯 與麥當勞的縮寫「Mc」一樣，161人座的MD83會正式改名為麥克機。它的機身將會畫上代表麥當勞的金黃色拱門，機艙內的座位也會被套上亮紅色的皮椅套。麥克機的內裝會追求創造出麥當勞主要商店街的氛圍，駕駛座艙會以「祝你擁有愉快的一天」的問候語來完工。不過，這還不確定飲料餐車是否會被改成奶昔機。由於油炸鍋的危險性，洋芋片或是麥當勞所說的「薯條」，會排除在外。

單字 staff 職員、工作人員　　outfit 全套服裝
confirm 確定

76. What is the best title for this passage?

(A) McDonald's and the charter plane fuselage 麥當勞與包機機身

(B) The external and internal design of McPlane 麥克機內外裝的設計

(C) McDonald's in the airline business 麥當勞跨入航空業

(D) The types of McDonald's food in the air 飛機上麥當勞食物的類型

中譯 何者最適合當本文標題？

解析 由The McDonald's hamburger company is going into the airline catering business.可知。

77. Which type of McDonald's food will not be seen on McPlane?

(A) Chips 薯條　　(B) Big Macs 大麥克

(C) McNuggets 麥克雞塊　　(D) Coke 可樂

中譯 不會在麥克機上見到哪項食物？

解析 由Chips, or "fries" as McDonald's call them, have been ruled out because of the danger of using a deep-fat frier.可知。

78. Why did some people doubt the reality of this report?

(A) The food on board will be the regular customary collation.
飛機上提供的食物是一般的食物。

(B) Swiss airline and Crossair acknowledged this trick.
瑞士航空與羅莎爾航空公司承認這個騙局。

(C) Only one plane will be related to McDonald's.
只有一架飛機和麥當勞有關。

(D) The service will begin on April Fool's Day.
這項服務於愚人節開始。

中譯 為什麼有些人質疑這篇報導的真實性？

解析 由The service will be introduced on April 1此段可知。

79. What does a "high street" mean?

(A) a principal street 主要街道

(B) a countryside street 鄉村街道

(C) a very crowded street 非常擁擠的街道

(D) a colorful street 色彩繽紛的街道

中譯 「high street」是什麼意思？

解析 high street 主要街道、大街。

80. According to the passage, who will be greeting the passengers with "Have a nice day"?

(A) the passengers 乘客

(B) the flight attendants 空服人員

(C) the pilot 飛行員

(D) the ground staff 地勤人員

中譯 根據本文，誰會和乘客打招呼說「祝你擁有愉快的一天」？

解析 由以下這句可知是駕駛員座艙內的人：complete with "Have a nice day" greetings from the cockpit。

101 年外語領隊英文試題＋標準答案

★101年專門職業及技術人員普通考試導遊人員、領隊人員考試試題

類科：外語領隊人員（英語）

科目：外國語（英語）

考試時間：1 小時 20 分

※注意：（一）本試題為單一選擇題，請選出一個正確或最適當的答案，複選作答者，該題不予計分。

（二）本科目共80題，每題1.25分，須用2Ｂ鉛筆在試卡上依題號清楚劃記，於本試題上作答者，不予計分。

（三）本試題禁止使用電子計算器。

(　　)1. If the tapes do not meet your satisfaction, you can return them within thirty days for a full ______.

(A) fund　(B) refund　(C) funding　(D) fundraising

(　　)2. There was a slight departure delay at the airport due to ______ weather outside.

(A) forbidden　(B) inclement　(C) declined　(D) mistaken

(　　)3. For safety reasons, radios, CD players, and mobile phones are banned on board, and they must remain ______ until the aircraft has landed.

(A) switched on　(B) switch on　(C) switch off　(D) switched off

(　　)4. During take-off and landing, carry-on baggage must be placed in the overhead compartments or ______ the seat in front of you.

(A) parallel　(B) down　(C) underneath　(D) lower

(　　)5. While many couples opt for a church wedding and wedding party, a Japanese groom and a Taiwanese bride ______ in a traditional Confucian wedding in Taipei.

(A) tied the knot　(B) knocked off　(C) wore on　(D) stepped down

(　　)6. If the air conditioner should ______ , call this number immediately.

(A) break up　(B) break down　(C) break into　(D) break through

(　　)7. ______, the applicant was not considered for the job.

(A) Due to his lack of experience　　(B) Because his lack of experience
(C) His lack of experience　　(D) Due to his experience lack

(　　)8. The company ______ by a nationally-known research firm.

(A) the surveyed market had　　(B) had the surveyed market
(C) had the market surveyed　　(D) the market had surveyed

(　　)9. ______ the first computers, today's models are portable and multifunctional.

(A) Alike　　(B) Unlike　　(C) Dislike　　(D) Unlikely

(　　)10. The hotel ______ for the conference featured a nine-hole golf course.

(A) that he selected　　(B) that he selected it
(C) that selected　　(D) he selected it

(　　)11. Now you can purchase a seat and pick up your boarding pass at the airport on the day of departure ______ simply showing appropriate identification.

(A) together　　(B) for　　(C) by　　(D) with

(　　)12. The downtown bed-and-breakfast agency has ______.

(A) a two-night minimum reservation policy
(B) a policy two-night minimum reservation
(C) a reservation two-night policy minimum
(D) a minimum policy two-night reservation

(　　)13. Finding an accountant ______ specialty and interests match your needs is critically important.

(A) who　　(B) which　　(C) whose　　(D) whom

(　　)14. Smokers who insist on lighting up in public places are damaging not only their own health but also that of ______.

(A) another　　(B) each other　　(C) one another　　(D) others

(　　)15. The Internet is creating social isolation ______ people are spending more time on computers.

(A) unless　　(B) so that　　(C) though　　(D) as

(　　)16. ______ the offer is, the more pressure we will have to bear.

(A) The greatest　　(B) The greater　　(C) More of　　(D) Most of

( )17. Ecotourism is not only entertaining and exotic; it is also highly educational and ______.

(A) rewarded (B) rewards (C) reward (D) rewarding

( )18. Readers ______ to the magazine pay less per issue than those buying it at a newsstand.

(A) subscribe (B) subscribing (C) subscribed (D) are subscribing

( )19. Passengers ______ to other airlines should report to the information desk on the second floor.

(A) have transferred (B) transfer
(C) are transferred (D) transferring

( )20. ______ is first to arrive in the office is responsible for checking the voice mail.

(A) The person (B) Who (C) Whoever (D) Whom

( )21. Members of the design team were not surprised that Ms. Wang created the company logo ______.

(A) itself (B) herself (C) themselves (D) himself

( )22. In the interests of safety, passengers should carry ______ dangerous items nor matches while on board.

(A) either (B) or (C) neither (D) not

( )23. I am sure that if he ______ the flight to Paris, he would have arrived there by now.

(A) makes (B) made (C) is making (D) had made

( )24. "We are approaching some turbulence. For your safety, please keep your belts ______ until the 'seat belt' sign goes off."

(A) fasten (B) fastened (C) fastening (D) be fastened

( )25. Each country has its own regulations ______ fruit and vegetable imports.

(A) pertaining (B) edible (C) allowable (D) regarding

( )26. Those wishing to be considered for paid leave should put ______ requests in as soon as possible.

(A) they (B) them (C) theirs (D) their

(　　)27. The convenience store ______ owner just won the grand lottery will be closed next month.

(A) which　(B) who　(C) whose　(D) that

(　　)28. The flight will make a ______ in Paris for two hours.

(A) stopover　(B) stepover　(C) flyover　(D) crossover

(　　)29. All of the students cried out excitedly ______ knowing that the midterm examination had been canceled.

(A) for example　(B) because　(C) as long as　(D) upon

(　　)30. If you carry keys, knives, aerosol cans, etc., in your pocket when you pass through the security at the airport, you may ______ the alarm, and then the airport personnel will come to search you.

(A) let on　(B) let off　(C) set on　(D) set off

(　　)31. My father always asks everyone in the car to ______ for safety, no matter how short the ride is.

(A) tight up　(B) fast up　(C) buckle up　(D) stay up

(　　)32. Client: What are this hotel's ______?
Agent: It includes a great restaurant, a fitness center, an outdoor pool, and much more, such as in-room Internet access, 24-hour room service, and trustworthy babysitting, etc.

(A) installations　(B) utilities　(C) amenities　(D) surroundings

(　　)33. Tourist: What is the baggage allowance?
Airline clerk: ______.

(A) Please fill out this form.
(B) Sorry, cash is not suggested to be left in the baggage.
(C) It is very cheap.
(C) It is 20 kilograms per person.

(　　)34. The manager gave a copy of his to his ______ secretary and asked her to arrange some business meetings for him during his stay in Sydney.

(A) visa　(B) boarding pass
(C) itinerary　(D) journey

( )35. A tour guide is ______ informing tourists about the culture and the beautiful sites of a city or town.

(A) afraid of (B) responsible for (C) due to (D) dependent on

( )36. A bus used for public transportation runs a set route; however, a ______ bus travels at the direction of the person or organization that hires it.

(A) catering (B) chatter (C) charter (D) cutter

( )37. I was overjoyed to learn that I had accumulated enough ______ to upgrade myself from coach to business class.

(A) loyalty points (B) credit cards (C) grades (D) degrees

( )38. Palm Beach is a coastline ______ where thousands of tourists from all over the world spend their summer vacation.

(A) airport (B) resort (C) pavement (D) passage

( )39. Before you step out for a foreign trip, you should ______ about the accommodations, climate, and culture of the country you are visiting.

(A) insure (B) require (C) inquire (D) adjust

( )40. Our flight ______ to Los Angeles due to the stormy weather in Long Beach.

(A) was landed (B) had averted
(C) had been transformed (D) was diverted

( )41. After disembarking the flight, I went directly to the ______ to pick up my bags and trunks.

(A) airport lounge (B) cockpit (C) runway (D) baggage claim

( )42. Disobeying the airport security rules will ______ a civil penalty.

(A) result in (B) make for (C) take down (D) bring on

( )43. I would like to express our gratitude to you ______ behalf of my company.

(A) at (B) on (C) by (D) with

( )44. The security guards carefully patrol around the warehouse at ______ throughout the night.

(A) once (B) odds (C) intervals (D) least

( )45. ______ the father came into the bedroom did the two little brothers stopped fighting.

(A) Only when (B) Only if (C) If only (D) While

( )46. Working as a hotel ______ means that your focus is to ensure that the needs and requests of hotel guests are met, and that each guest has a memorable stay.

(A) commander (B) celebrity (C) concierge (D) candidate

( )47. Mount Fuji is considered ______; therefore, many people pay special visits to it, wishing to bring good luck to themselves and their loved ones.

(A) horrifying (B) scared (C) sacred (D) superficial

( )48. The non-smoking policy will apply to any person working for the company ______ of their status or position.

(A) regardless (B) regarding (C) in regard (D) as regards

( )49. This puzzle is so ______ that no one can figure it out.

(A) furry (B) fuzzy (C) fury (D) futile

( )50. If I had called to reserve a table at Royal House one week earlier, we ______ a gourmet reunion dinner last night.

(A) can have (B) will have had
(C) would have had (D) would have eating

( )51. ______ unemployed for almost one year, Henry has little chance of getting a job.

(A) Having been (B) Be (C) Maybe (D) Since having

( )52. The school boys stopped ______ the stray dog when their teacher went up to them.

(A) bully (B) bullied (C) to be bullying (D) bullying

( )53. The teacher had asked several students to clean up the classroom, but ______ of them did it.

(A) all (B) both (C) none (D) either

( )54. Before the applicant left, the interviewer asked him for a current ______ number so that he could be reached if he was given the job.

(A) connection (B) concert (C) interview (D) contact

( )55. If you have to extend your stay at the hotel room, you should inform the front desk at least one day ______ your original departure time.

(A) ahead to (B) forward to (C) prior to (D) in front of

( )56. I will be very busy during this weekend, so please do not call me ______ it is urgent.

(A) except (B) besides (C) while (D) unless

( )57. Prohibited items in carry-on bags will be confiscated at the checkpoints, and no ______ will be given for them.

(A) argument (B) recruitment (C) compensation (D) decision

( )58. All the employees have to use an electronic card to ______ in when they arrive for work.

(A) clock (B) access (C) enter (D) apply

( )59. I called to ask about the schedule of the buses ______ to Kaoshiung.

(A) leaving (B) heading (C) binding (D) taking

( )60. As for the delivery service of our hotel, FedEx and UPS can make ______ at the front desk Monday through Friday, excluding holidays.

(A) posts (B) pickups (C) picnics (D) practices

Many visitors to Italy avoid its famous cities, preferring instead the quiet countryside of Tuscany, located in the rural heart of the country. Like the rest of Italy, Tuscany has its share of art and architectures, __61__ travelers are drawn more by its gentle hills, by its country estates, and by its hilltop villages. This is not an area to rush through but to enjoy slowly, like a glass of fine wine produced here. Many farmhouses offer simple yet comfortable __62__. From such a base, the visitors can __63__ the nearby towns and countryside, __64__ up the sunshine, or just __65__ in the company of a good book.

( )61. (A) if (B) once (C) but (D) because

( )62. (A) accommodations (B) replacements (C) customs (D) privileges

( )63. (A) explain (B) explore (C) explode (D) expose

( )64. (A) leap (B) mount (C) soak (D) creep

(　　)65. (A) register　(B) relax　(C) reduce　(D) repeat

Vancouver Island is one of the most beautiful places in the world. It is situated off the west __66__ of Canada, about one and a half hour by ferry from Vancouver on the mainland. Victoria, the capital city, __67__ over one hundred and fifty years ago and is famous for its old colonial style buildings and beautiful harbor. It is the center of government for the province of British Columbia, so many of the people living there are __68__ as public servants. The lifestyle is very relaxed, __69__ to other cities in Canada, and this is __70__ a lot of people to move there after they retire. The island is also popular with tourists because of the magnificent mountain scenery and the world-renowned Butchart Gardens.

(　　)66. (A) quarter　(B) position　(C) coast　(D) site

(　　)67. (A) was founded　(B) founded　(C) was founding　(D) found

(　　)68. (A) regarded　(B) employed　(C) included　(D) treated

(　　)69. (A) compared　(B) to compare　(C) comparing　(D) compare

(　　)70. (A) hindering　(B) demanding　(C) attracting　(D) prohibiting

After 16 weeks of labor contract disputes, Wang Metals workers say they have had enough. At 10:30 this morning, hundreds of workers walked out of work and onto the picket line. Wang Metals has more than 800 workers, and the union says about 90 percent of them are participating in the strike. They plan to continue to picket factory office here in four-hour shifts. The union representative claims workers have taken these measures as a last resort. " We had met and decided to wait for the company to put a decent offer on the table, and when it finally did last night, it turned out to be unacceptable. So, we voted to strike."The representative said that union members will strike as long as necessary. Extra security has been ordered by the plant, and guards are blocking passage through the main entrance to the factory. Local business leaders are concerned because any kind of prolonged dispute could have a negative effect on other sectors of the community as well. "Wang Metals is the backbone of our local economy. Everything from food to entertainment, to houses...it all connects to the plant," says one business owner.

(　　)71. Which of the following is the best headline for this news report?

(A) Wang Plant Orders Extra Security

(B) 800 Workers Stage Walkout at Wang

(C) Wang Metals Loses Money During Strike

(D) Wang Workers Start Strike Today

(   )72. What triggered the strike?

(A) The company being the backbone of the local economy.

(B) An offer by the company that the union found unacceptable.

(C) 90 percent of the workers picketing the factory offices.

(D) The company ordering extra security guards.

(   )73. How long do the workers intend to strike?

(A) For four weeks. (B) A number of weeks.

(C) Indefinitely. (D) Late into the night.

(   )74. If some of the plant workers were to lose their jobs, what might be the effect on the community as a whole?

(A) Hardly any effect. Things would stay the same.

(B) There would be more houses available for other people to live in.

(C) The economy of the community would suffer.

(D) The economy of the community would prosper.

(   )75. Who blocked the passage through the main entrance to the factory?

(A) Security guards. (B) Local business leaders.

(C) Union representatives. (D) Company officials.

Vacation rentals are fully private homes whose owners rent them out on a temporary basis to tourists as an alternative to hotels. They are available in all kinds of destinations, from a rustic cabin in the mountains to a downtown apartment in a major city. They can be townhouses, single-family-style homes, farms, beach houses, or even villas.

Vacation rentals are generally appealing for many reasons. They are, to name some on the top, cost-saving, spacious, great for large groups, separated from crowds, and no tips or service charges. Besides, they have kitchens for cooking, living rooms for gathering, outdoor spaces for parties or barbeques, and they offer the appeal of living like locals in a real community. They are usually equipped with facilities such as sports and beach accessories, games, books and DVD libraries, and in warmer locations, a swimming pool. Many vacation rentals are pet-friendly, so people can take their pets along with them when traveling.

Customers who choose hotels often enjoy the advantages of brand recognition, familiar reservation processes, and on-site service, while booking a vacation rental may mean stepping out of that comfort zone in order to get privacy, peace and quietness they offer -- things that are hard to obtain in a hotel room. For tourists, choosing a vacation rental over a hotel means more than short-term lodging -- vivid experiences and lifelong memories are what they value.

(　　)76. What is this reading mainly about?

(A) Planning leisure trips.
(B) The values of different vacation destinations.
(C) Alternative accommodations for tourists.
(D) Booking accommodations for fun trips.

(　　)77. What is the major concept of a vacation rental?

(A) Private houses rent out on weekdays only.
(B) Private homes rent out to tourists.
(C) Furnished homes for rent when owners are on vacations.
(D) Furnished rooms for short-term homestays.

(　　)78. Which of the following is NOT considered the reason that makes vacation rentals appealing?

(A) Familiar booking processes.
(B) Being economic.
(C) Being equipped with many useful facilities.
(D) Being pet-friendly.

(　　)79. What is the major advantage when tourists choose hotels rather than vacation rentals?

(A) Fame and wealth.　　(B) Living like locals.
(C) Fair prices.　　(D) On-site service.

(　　)80. Which of the following statements is a proper description of vacation rentals?

(A) They are shared by many owners.
(B) Tipping is not necessary at vacation rentals.
(C) They are built for business purpose.
(D) Daily cleaning is usually included in the rental contract.

★標準答案

1. (B)	2. (B)	3. (D)	4. (C)	5. (A)
6. (B)	7. (A)	8. (C)	9. (B)	10. (A)
11. (C)	12. (A)	13. (C)	14. (D)	15. (D)
16. (B)	17. (D)	18. (B)	19. (D)	20. (C)
21. (B)	22. (C)	23. (D)	24. (B)	25. (D)
26. (D)	27. (C)	28. (A)	29. (D)	30. (D)
31. (C)	32. (C)	33. (D)	34. (C)	35. (B)
36. (C)	37. (A)	38. (B)	39. (C)	40. (D)
41. (D)	42. (A)	43. (B)	44. (C)	45. (A)
46. (C)	47. (C)	48. (A)	49. (B)	50. (C)
51. (A)	52. (D)	53. (C)	54. (D)	55. (C)
56. (D)	57. (C)	58. (A)	59. (B)	60. (B)
61. (C)	62. (A)	63. (B)	64. (C)	65. (B)
66. (C)	67. (A)	68. (B)	69. (A)	70. (C)
71. (D)	72. (B)	73. (C)	74. (C)	75. (A)
76. (C)	77. (B)	78. (A)	79. (D)	80. (B)

101 年外語領隊英文試題中譯與解析

1. If the tapes do not meet your satisfaction, you can return them within thirty days for a full refund.

(A) fund 資金 (B) refund 退款
(C) funding 提供資金 (D) fundraising 募款

中譯 如果這些膠帶不能讓你滿意，你可以在30天內退還並獲得全額退款。

解析 refund 退款為常考單字，例句：We can refund the price difference. 我們可以退還差價。meet satisfaction 達到滿意的程度。

2. There was a slight departure delay at the airport due to inclement weather outside.

(A) forbidden 禁止的 (B) inclement 狂風暴雨的
(C) declined 衰落的 (D) mistaken 弄錯的

中譯 因為外面惡劣的天氣，導致機場班機起飛有些延誤。

解析 due to由於，由delay 延誤可得知天氣為inclement 狂風暴雨的。slight 微小的；departure 出發、起飛。類似考題：Due to the impending disaster, we have to cancel our flight to Bangkok. 因為即將到來的災害，我們必須取消到曼谷的航班。100領隊

3. For safety reasons, radios, CD players, and mobile phones are banned on board, and they must remain switched off until the aircraft has landed.

(A) switched on 開機 (B) switch on 開機
(C) switch off 關機 (D) switched off 關機

中譯 由於飛安的因素，收音機、CD播放器、手機都禁止在飛機上使用，且必須保持關機的狀態直到飛機降落。

解析 on board以及in flight都是在飛機上的意思。ban 禁止，例：There is a ban on smoking. 有一個禁菸令。此處選擇switched off表關機的「狀態」，故選switched。

4. During take-off and landing, carry-on baggage must be placed in the overhead compartments or underneath the seat in front of you.

(A) parallel 平行 (B) down 下方
(C) underneath 在……下面 (D) lower 較低的

中譯 在飛機起飛和降落其間，隨身行李都必須放置於頭頂上的行李隔間內，或是在你前方的座位底下。

解析 通常carry-on baggage 隨身行李會放於前方的座位下，故選underneath。

5. While many couples opt for a church wedding and wedding party, a Japanese groom and a Taiwanese bride tied the knot in a traditional Confucian wedding in Taipei.

(A) tied the knot 結婚　(B) knocked off 敲昏

(C) wore on 時間推移　(D) stepped down 降低

中譯 當許多情侶選擇教堂婚禮以及婚宴時，一對日本新郎以及台灣新娘在台北選擇傳統的儒家婚禮互訂終身。

解析 tie the knot為結婚的慣用說法，若不熟此片語，仍可由關鍵字wedding將其他選項剔除。groom 新郎；bride 新娘。

6. If the air conditioner should break down, call this number immediately.

(A) break up 打碎、分手　(B) break down 停止運轉

(C) break into 破門而入　(D) break through 突破

中譯 如果冷氣機壞了，請立即撥打這電話號碼。

解析 break 打破，以下許多片語請牢記：break up 打碎、分手；break down 停止運轉；break into 破門而入；break through 突破。

7. Due to his lack of experience, the applicant was not considered for the job.

(A) Due to his lack of experience　(B) Because his lack of experience

(C) His lack of experience　(D) Due to his experience lack

中譯 由於他的經驗不足，這名申請者不被考慮錄取這份工作。

解析 此題以剔除法即能選出答案，先刪除His lack of experience，名詞片語不能放於句首；再刪除Because his lack of experience，because後應接句子，故不符；剩下兩個due to開頭的選項，但由於experience lack明顯錯誤（lack為形容詞，應放於名詞之前），故選Due to his lack of experience。consider 考慮。

8. The company had the market surveyed by a nationally-known research firm.

(A) the surveyed market had　(B) had the surveyed market

(C) had the market surveyed　(D) the market had surveyed

中譯 這間公司請了全國知名的研究公司來做市場調查。

解析 the company主詞之後應接名詞，故只考慮(B)、(C)，而市場「被調查」故選 market surveyed。firm 公司。

9. Unlike the first computers, today's models are portable and multifunctional.

(A) Alike 相似的 (B) Unlike 不像的 (C) Dislike 不喜歡 (D) Unlikely 不像地

中譯 不同於第一代的電腦，今日的電腦是可攜式且多功能的。

解析 此題為今日和第一代電腦之比較，故選unlike 兩方不同的。

10. The hotel that he selected for the conference featured a nine-hole golf course.

(A) that he selected (B) that he selected it

(C) that selected (D) he selected it

中譯 他為這次記者會所選的旅館是以九洞的高爾夫球場為特色。

解析 that he selected為形容詞子句，用來修飾hotel，故不需要代名詞it。feature 特色，此當動詞。

11. Now you can purchase a seat and pick up your boarding pass at the airport on the day of departure by simply showing appropriate identification.

(A) together 一起 (B) for 為了

(C) by 藉由 (D) with 和……一起

中譯 現在你只需出示適當證件就可以買票（購買座位），並於出發當天於機場領取登機證。

解析 by表示手法、原因；此處為藉由showing appropriate identification 出示適當證件，而得以pick up your boarding pass 領取登機證。purchase 購買。

12. The downtown bed-and-breakfast agency has a two-night minimum reservation policy.

(A) a two-night minimum reservation policy

(B) a policy two-night minimum reservation

(C) a reservation two-night policy minimum

(D) a minimum policy two-night reservation

中譯 市中心的民宿代理中心有至少入住兩晚的住宿政策。

解析 reservation policy 住宿政策，為一個概念，兩個單字不得分開。

13. Finding an accountant whose specialty and interests match your needs is critically important.

(A) who (B) which (C) whose (D) whom

中譯 找到一位符合你需求與利益的專長的會計師非常重要。

解析 accountant的專長，故選whose。直譯則為：找到一位會計師，他的專長和利益符合你需求是非常重要的。

14. Smokers who insist on lighting up in public places are damaging not only their own health but also that of others.

(A) another 另一個 (B) each other 彼此
(C) one another 彼此 (D) others 其他人

中譯 在公共場所堅持要抽菸的人，不僅傷到他們自己的健康，也傷害到其他人的。

解析 their own（自己），和他人，故選others。

15. The Internet is creating social isolation as people are spending more time on computers.

(A) unless 除非 (B) so that 以便 (C) though 儘管 (D) as 當……的時候

中譯 當人們花更多的時間在電腦上時，網路正造成社會隔離。

解析 as 正當，這裡的as和when、while一樣，所對應的中文都是「當……的時候」。

16. The greater the offer is, the more pressure we will have to bear.

(A) The greatest 最大的 (B) The greater 較大的
(C) More of 較多的 (D) Most of 最多的

中譯 出價越大，我們將要承受的壓力也越多。

解析 the greater, the more由the more可推知為the greater。

17. Ecotourism is not only entertaining and exotic; it is also highly educational and rewarding.

(A) rewarded 被獎賞的 (B) rewards 獎品
(C) reward 獎賞 (D) rewarding 有價值的

中譯 生態旅遊不只富有娛樂性和具有異國情調，更有高度教育性和有價值的。

解析 reward 獎賞；rewarding 有價值的。

18. Readers subscribing to the magazine pay less per issue than those buying it at a newsstand.

(A) subscribe （現在簡單式） (B) subscribing （現在分詞）

(C) subscribed （過去式） (D) are subscribing （現在進行式）

以上皆為訂閱之意

中譯 訂閱雜誌的讀者每期所付的錢比在書報攤零買的錢來得少。

解析 subscribe to 訂閱，最簡單的方式為看到句中的buying，來猜答案為subscribing（同樣都是以現在分詞來形容讀者）。

★簡化形容詞子句的步驟：

(1) 去關係代名詞

(2) 將形容詞子句中的動詞改為現在分詞Ving

(3) 如遇be動詞改為being，則將being省略

例句：Readers who subscribe to the magazine pay less per issue than those readers who buy it at a newsstand.

= Readers subscribing to the magazine pay less per issue than those buying it at a newsstand.

19. Passengers transferring to other airlines should report to the information desk on the second floor.

(A) have transferred（現在完成式） (B) transfer （現在簡單式）

(C) are transferred （被動式） (D) transferring （現在分詞）

以上皆為轉乘之意。

中譯 要轉搭其他班機的旅客請到2樓的櫃台報到。

解析 本題如前題考一樣的文法，即簡化形容詞子句的步驟：

(1) 去關係代名詞

(2) 將形容詞子句中的動詞改為現在分詞Ving

(3) 如遇be動詞改為being，則將being省略

例句：Passengers transferring to other airlines should report to the information desk on the second floor.

= Passengers who transfer to other airlines should report to the information desk on the second floor.

20. Whoever is first to arrive in the office is responsible for checking the voice mail.

(A) The person 這個人 (B) Who 誰

(C) Whoever 不論是誰 (D) Whom 誰（受詞）

中譯 不論是誰第一個進到辦公室，要負責檢查語音信箱。

解析 這裡是選「人」且「不論是誰」，故選Whoever。

21. Members of the design team were not surprised that Ms. Wang created the company logo herself.

(A) itself 它自己
(B) herself 她自己
(C) themselves 他們自己
(D) himself 他自己

中譯 設計團隊的成員並不驚訝王女士她自己設計出公司的商標。

解析 由Ms. Wang可知為herself 她自己。

22. In the interests of safety, passengers should carry neither dangerous items nor matches while on board.

(A) either （兩者中）任一的
(B) or 或
(C) neither 也不
(D) not 不

中譯 為了安全考量，乘客不能帶危險物品或是火柴登機。

解析 in the interests of 因為……的考量；neither...nor為對等連接詞，為既不……也不……的意思。若連接兩個主詞，動詞的數與後者一致。

23. I am sure that if he had made the flight to Paris, he would have arrived there by now.

(A) makes
(B) made
(C) is making
(D) had made

中譯 我確定如果他當時趕上飛往巴黎的班機，他應該現在就到那裡了。

解析 由would have arrived可知是與過去相反，故選had made，與過去事實相反的假設。在假設語氣裡，當所敘述的事情和「過去」有關時，條件子句動詞須用「had + p.p.」如本題if he had made the flight to Paris，主要子句則是「主詞 + 助動詞 + have + p.p.」如本題he would have arrived there by now。

24. "We are approaching some turbulence. For your safety, please keep your belts fastened until the 'seat belt' sign goes off."

(A) fasten （現在簡單式）
(B) fastened （過去分詞）
(C) fastening （現在分詞）
(D) be fastened （被動式）

中譯 「我們正接近某個亂流。為了你的安全，請繫緊安全帶直到座位安全帶的指示燈熄滅。」

解析 fasten為繫緊之意。keep 維持（某事某物的狀態），接受詞以及受詞補語，故選fastened過去分詞。過去分詞當補語的例句：She had her photo taken. 她照了相。過去分詞taken當受詞her photo 的補語。

25. Each country has its own regulations regarding fruit and vegetable imports.

(A) pertaining 附屬的　　(B) edible 可食的

(C) allowable 可允許的　　(D) regarding 關於

中譯 關於水果與蔬菜的進口，每個國家都有其規定。

解析 regarding 關於。關於某事的三種用法「regarding something」、「with regard to something」、「as regards something」。

26. Those wishing to be considered for paid leave should put their requests in as soon as possible.

(A) they 他們　　(B) them 他們

(C) theirs 他們（的東西）　　(D) their 他們的

中譯 想要申請有薪假的人應該盡快提出申請。

解析 由Those可知為their requests 「那些人」的請求。they是用來當主詞（主格），them是用來當they的受格。their是形容詞，後面必須接名詞；theirs已經是代名詞，後面不接名詞。

27. The convenience store whose owner just won the grand lottery will be closed next month.

(A) which　　(B) who　　(C) whose　　(D) that

中譯 便利商店的主人剛剛贏了樂透大獎，商店將於下週關門。

解析 「便利商店的」主人，故選whose。whose為所有格。whose用於人 / 人以外的事物。

of which用於人以外的事物。which / who / whose / that皆為關係代名詞，是「代名詞」，亦是「連接詞」，代替了先前出現的人事物，同時具有連接詞的功能，將數個短的句子，連接成一個長句。who代替人，which代替事或物，that可與who / which替換，但是that之前不可以有逗號或介系詞。

28. The flight will make a stopover in Paris for two hours.

(A) stopover 中途停留　　(B) stepover 跨距

(C) flyover 天橋　　(D) crossover 臨界

中譯 飛機將短暫停留巴黎2個小時。

解析 重點單字：stopover 中途停留，transit則是轉機。

29. All of the students cried out excitedly upon knowing that the midterm examination had been canceled.

(A) for example 例如　(B) because 因為
(C) as long as 只要　(D) upon 一旦

中譯 在一知道期中考被取消後，所有學生立刻高聲呼叫。

解析 upon 一旦，後面接Ving。
補充：一……就……；立即……的用法
S + V as soon as S + V （連接詞用法） = S + V upon Ving （介系詞用法）
因此本題可替換成All of the students(s) cried(v) out excitedly as soon as they(s) know(v) that the midterm examination had been canceled.

30. If you carry keys, knives, aerosol cans, etc., in your pocket when you pass through the security at the airport, you may set off the alarm, and then the airport personnel will come to search you.

(A) let on 洩漏祕密　(B) let off 寬恕
(C) set on 開啟　(D) set off 引發

中譯 如果你帶著鑰匙、小刀、噴霧罐等東西在你的口袋，當你通過機場的安檢區時，你可能會引發警報器，接著機場的人員會來搜查你。

解析 set off 引發。其他安檢例句為Please examine your luggage carefully before leaving. At the security counter, every item in the luggage has to go through inspection. 在出發前請仔細檢查你的行李。在安檢櫃台時，行李內的每一項物品都會被檢查。99導遊

31. My father always asks everyone in the car to buckle up for safety, no matter how short the ride is.

(A) tight up 繃緊一點　(B) fast up （無此片語）
(C) buckle up 繫好安全帶　(D) stay up 熬夜

中譯 不管路程多短，為了安全著想，我爸爸總是要求車上每個人都繫好安全帶。

解析 buckle up ＝ fasten seatbelt 繫好安全帶。Please keep your seat belt fastened during the flight for safety. 為了安全，飛行途中請束緊你的安全帶。

32. Client: What are this hotel's amenities?

Agent: It includes a great restaurant, a fitness center, an outdoor pool, and much more, such as in-room Internet access, 24-hour room service, and trustworthy babysitting, etc.

(A) installations 裝置　　(B) utilities 實用

(C) amenities 設施　　(D) surroundings 環境

中譯 客戶：這間飯店有什麼設施？

代理商：有一間很棒的餐廳、健身房、戶外游泳池、和其他設施，像是室內網路、24小時客房服務，和值得信賴的保母服務。

解析 由a great restaurant、a fitness center、an outdoor pool可推知是amenities 設施。

33. Tourist: What is the baggage allowance?

Airline clerk: It is 20 kilograms per person.

(A) Please fill out this form. 請填這表格。

(B) Sorry, cash is not suggested to be left in the baggage.

抱歉，不建議現金放在行李內。

(C) It is very cheap. 這很便宜。

(D) It is 20 kilograms per person. 每個人20公斤。

中譯 旅客：行李的限額是多少？

航空公司職員：每個人20公斤。

解析 ibaggage allowance 行李的限額，故選It is 20 kilograms per person.。

34. The manager gave a copy of his itinerary to his secretary and asked her to arrange some business meetings for him during his stay in Sydney.

(A) visa 簽證　　(B) boarding pass 登機證

(C) itinerary 行程　　(D) journey 旅程

中譯 經理交給他的祕書一份旅行計畫（行程），並且要求她幫他在雪梨安排一些業務會議。

解析 itinerary 行程，具有詳細計劃的含意，而非比較廣泛的journey 旅程。

35. A tour guide is responsible for informing tourists about the culture and the beautiful sites of a city or town.

(A) afraid of 害怕
(B) responsible for 對……有責任
(C) due to 由於
(D) dependent on 依靠

中譯 導遊應負責介紹該城鎮的文化和美麗景點給旅客。

解析 responsible for 對……有責任。take responsibility to do = be responsible for doing sth.。

36. A bus used for public transportation runs a set route; however, a charter bus travels at the direction of the person or organization that hires it.

(A) catering 餐飲 (B) chatter 閒聊 (C) charter 租賃 (D) cutter 切割機

中譯 用來當大眾運輸工具的巴士有固定的路線，然而，承租的巴士（遊覽車）依照租車的人或團體來行駛。

解析 charter bus 遊覽車；set route 固定的路線。

37. I was overjoyed to learn that I had accumulated enough loyalty points to upgrade myself from coach to business class.

(A) loyalty points 會員點數
(B) credit cards 信用卡
(C) grades 等級
(D) degrees 度數

中譯 我感到超級開心，因為我已經累積足夠的會員點數讓我從普通艙升級到商務艙。

解析 loyalty points 會員點數；points 點數。

38. Palm Beach is a coastline resort where thousands of tourists from all over the world spend their summer vacation.

(A) airport 機場
(B) resort 名勝
(C) pavement 人行道
(D) passage 通過

中譯 棕櫚灘是海岸度假勝地，來自世界各地的上千名遊客都到此來度過暑假。

解析 必考單字：resort 名勝。常見的retreat則是僻靜之地。

39. Before you step out for a foreign trip, you should inquire about the accommodations, climate, and culture of the country you are visiting.

(A) insure 保險 (B) require 需要 (C) inquire 詢問 (D) adjust 調整

中譯 在你踏出國外旅程之前，你應該先詢問有關那個國家的住宿、天氣和文化。

解析 step out 踏出；inquire 詢問；accommodations 住宿。

40. Our flight was diverted to Los Angeles due to the stormy weather in Long Beach.

(A) was landed 被登陸　(B) had averted 已經避免
(C) had been transformed 已經被轉換　(D) was diverted 被轉向

中譯 因為長灘的大風暴，我們的航班被迫轉向到洛杉磯。

解析 diverted 被轉向；stormy weather = inclement weather 天氣惡劣。

41. After disembarking the flight, I went directly to the baggage claim to pick up my bags and trunks.

(A) airport lounge 機場貴賓室　(B) cockpit 駕駛員座艙
(C) runway 逃亡　(D) baggage claim 行李認領處

中譯 下飛機後，我直接走向行李認領處拿我的包包和行李箱。

解析 常考單字：baggage claim 行李認領處。

42. Disobeying the airport security rules will result in a civil penalty.

(A) result in 導致　(B) make for 走向
(C) take down 寫下、病倒　(D) bring on 引起

中譯 違反機場安全規定會導致民法的刑責。

解析 result in / lead to皆為導致的意思。

43. I would like to express our gratitude to you on behalf of my company.

(A) at　(B) on　(C) by　(D) with

中譯 我代表公司對你表達我們的感激。

解析 四個選項皆為介系詞。常考片語：on behalf of 代表，其他例句：The Union has filed a protest on behalf of the terminated workers. 公會已經代表被資遣的員工發起抗議。102領隊

44. The security guards carefully patrol around the warehouse at intervals throughout the night.

(A) once 一次（at once 立刻）　(B) odds 優勢
(C) intervals 間隔　(D) least 至少

中譯 警衛晚上定時仔細地巡邏倉庫。

解析 at intervals 時不時；Interval 間隔。

45. Only when the father came into the bedroom did the two little brothers stopped fighting.

(A) Only when (B) Only if (C) If only (D) While

中譯 只有當爸爸進到臥房時，兩名小弟弟才會停止打架。

解析 only（只要……）放句首時，後方句須用倒裝句型，可還原成It is only when the father came into the bedroom the two little brothers stopped fighting.。

46. Working as a hotel concierge means that your focus is to ensure that the needs and requests of hotel guests are met, and that each guest has a memorable stay.

(A) commander 指揮官 (B) celebrity 名人
(C) concierge 門房 (D) candidate 候選人

中譯 身為飯店的門房，表示你的重點是要確保客戶的需求與要求被滿足，讓每位房客有個難忘的停留回憶。

解析 concierge 門房；concierge service 管家服務，其他例句：The concierge at the information desk in a hotel provides traveling information to guests. 旅館服務台人員提供旅遊資訊給客人。99領隊

47. Mount Fuji is considered sacred; therefore, many people pay special visits to it, wishing to bring good luck to themselves and their loved ones.

(A) horrifying 恐懼的 (B) scared 害怕的
(C) sacred 神聖的 (D) superficial 膚淺的

中譯 富士山被視為神聖的，因此許多人會特別拜訪，希望可以替自己以及所愛的人帶來好運。

解析 sacred 神聖的，亦常用來形容廟宇。

48. The non-smoking policy will apply to any person working for the company regardless of their status or position.

(A) regardless 無論 (B) regarding 關於
(C) in regard 關於 (D) as regards 至於

中譯 禁菸政策將適用於任何在公司工作的人，不管其地位或職位。

解析 regardless 無論如何；regarding 關於某事的三種用法「regarding something」、「with regard to something」、「as regards something」。

49. This puzzle is so fuzzy that no one can figure it out.

(A) furry 毛茸茸的 (B) fuzzy 模稜兩可的
(C) fury 憤怒的 (D) futile 無用的

中譯 這個謎題是如此的模稜兩可，以至於沒人能理解。

解析 figure out 理解，為常考片語。

50. If I had called to reserve a table at Royal House one week earlier, we would have had a gourmet reunion dinner last night.

(A) can have (B) will have had
(C) would have had (D) would have eating

中譯 如果我早一個星期打電話去皇家餐廳預約，我們昨晚可能就有美味的團圓飯。

解析 與過去事實相反，條件子句動詞須用「had + p.p.」，主要子句則是「主詞 + 助動詞 + have + p.p.」。

51. Having been unemployed for almost one year, Henry has little chance of getting a job.

(A) Having been (B) Be (C) Maybe (D) Since having

中譯 因為亨利已經幾乎一年沒有工作了，他找到工作的機會很小

解析 在副詞子句的主詞與主要子句的主詞相同時（此題為Henry），我們可將副詞子句中的連接詞及主詞去掉，並將動詞改為Ving（動詞為主動語態，須為「現在分詞」（Ving）；被動語態，須變為「過去分詞」（PP）），即為簡單分詞構句。原句的副詞子句為Since he has been unemployed，故可簡化成Having unemployed。little chance 幾乎毫無機會。

52. The school boys stopped bullying the stray dog when their teacher went up to them.

(A) bully (B) bullied (C) to be bullying (D) bullying

中譯 當他們的老師走向他們時，這些男學生停止欺負流浪狗。

解析 動詞bully意為欺負，stop + Ving表停止做某事，stop to V表停下手邊之事，去做某事。

53. The teacher had asked several students to clean up the classroom, but none of them did it.

(A) all 全部 (B) both 兩者 (C) none 都沒有 (D) either 或

中譯 這名老師要求幾位學生去清掃教室，但都沒有人去。

解析 none 都沒有。none既可指人也可指物，其後通常接of。none當主詞時，動詞可用單數形或複數形。

54. Before the applicant left, the interviewer asked him for a current contact number so that he could be reached if he was given the job.

(A) connection 連接　(B) concert 演唱
(C) interview 面試　(D) contact 聯絡

中譯 在應徵者離開之前，面試人員和他要他的聯絡電話，若是他有錄取便得以聯絡。

解析 contact number 聯絡電話。其他面試相關的例句：Beatrix's friend had given her a mock interview before she actually went to meet the personnel manager of the company she was applying to. 貝翠絲的朋友給她一個模擬的面試，在她真的要和所申請工作公司的人事主管面試之前。100導遊

55. If you have to extend your stay at the hotel room, you should inform the front desk at least one day prior to your original departure time.

(A) ahead to 提前　(B) forward to 期待
(C) prior to 在……之前　(D) in front of 正前方

中譯 如果你必須延長在飯店房間的時間，你至少應該在原定離開時間的前一天告知櫃台。

解析 prior to 在……之前；A is prior to B A在B之前。

56. I will be very busy during this weekend, so please do not call me unless it is urgent.

(A) except 除了　(B) besides 此外　(C) while 當　(D) unless 除非

中譯 我在這週末將會非常忙碌，所以請不要打給我，除非是很緊急的事情。

解析 unless為除非，except…只用於表達不包含在內的「除外」。

57. Prohibited items in carry-on bags will be confiscated at the checkpoints, and no compensation will be given for them.

(A) argument 爭論　(B) recruitment 招聘
(C) compensation 補償　(D) decision 決定

中譯 隨身行李中的違禁品將會於檢查站被沒收，且沒有任何的補償。

解析 compensate 補償。安檢的延伸考題會有Please examine your luggage carefully before leaving. At the security counter, every item in the luggage has to go through inspection. 在出發前請仔細檢視你的行李。在安檢櫃台時，行李內的每一項物品都會被檢查。99導遊

58. All the employees have to use an electronic card to clock in when they arrive for work.

(A) clock 打卡　(B) access 訪問　(C) enter 進入　(D) apply 申請

中譯 當抵達辦公室時，所有的員工都必須使用電子卡來打卡。

解析 clock in / clock out 打卡上班 / 打卡下班，clockless worke 彈性工時員工，clock + less也就是不用打卡的意思。

59. I called to ask about the schedule of the buses heading to Kaoshiung.

(A) leaving 離開　(B) heading 前往　(C) binding 綁住　(D) taking 拿起

中譯 我打電話過來問關於開往高雄的巴士時刻表。

解析 heading to 前往某處。head for 對準目標去；head to 向著目標方向去。

60. As for the delivery service of our hotel, FedEx and UPS can make pickups at the front desk Monday through Friday, excluding holidays.

(A) posts 郵件　(B) pickups 取件　(C) picnics 野餐　(D) practices 練習

中譯 關於我們飯店的寄件服務，聯邦快遞公司以及聯合包裹速遞公司會於週一至週五於櫃台取件，假日除外。

解析 pickups 取件服務，為hotel service飯店服務之一，常見的飯店服務例句：Airport limousine service, valet parking service, and concierge service are some of the most popular items among our guest services. 機場禮車接送服務、代客泊車、管家服務是我們最受歡迎的客戶服務項目之一。102領隊

Many visitors to Italy avoid its famous cities, preferring instead the quiet countryside of Tuscany, located in the rural heart of the country. Like the rest of Italy, Tuscany has its share of art and architectures, but travelers are drawn more by its gentle hills, by its country estates, and by its hilltop villages. This is not an area to rush through but to enjoy slowly, like a glass of fine wine produced here. Many farmhouses offer simple yet comfortable accommodations. From such a base, the visitors can explore the nearby towns and countryside, soak up the sunshine, or just relax in the company of a good book.

中譯 許多到義大利旅遊的旅客避免到有名的大城市，反而到托斯卡尼寧靜的鄉間，此處位於義大利的鄉村中心。不像義大利的其他地方，托斯卡尼雖然在藝術與建築占有一席之地，但卻是以和緩的山丘、鄉間的莊園以及山頂上的村落吸引旅人。這裡不須匆忙，反而可以慢慢享受生活，就像是一杯此處所產的美酒一般。許多農家提供簡單但舒適的住處。以此為基地，旅客還能探索附近的城鎮與鄉間，擁抱陽光，或只是放輕鬆與書為伴。

單字 rural 農村的　　the rest of 其餘的、剩下的
estates 財產、資產

61. (A) if 如果　(B) once 一旦　(C) but 但是　(D) because 因為

62. (A) accommodations 住宿　(B) replacements 替代品
(C) customs 海關　(D) privileges 特權

63. (A) explain 解釋　(B) explore 探索　(C) explode 爆炸　(D) expose 曝光

64. (A) leap 跳越　(B) mount 乘馬　(C) soak 吸收　(D) creep 爬行

65. (A) register 註冊　(B) relax 放鬆　(C) reduce 減少　(D) repeat 重複

Vancouver Island is one of the most beautiful places in the world. It is situated off the west coast of Canada, about one and a half hour by ferry from Vancouver on the mainland. Victoria, the capital city, was founded over one hundred and fifty years ago and is famous for its old colonial style buildings and beautiful harbor. It is the center of government for the province of British Columbia, so many of the people living there are employed as public servants. The lifestyle is very relaxed, compared to other cities in Canada, and this is attracting a lot of people to move there after they retire. The island is also popular with tourists because of the magnificent mountain scenery and the world-renowned Butchart Gardens.

中譯 溫哥華島是世界上最美麗的地方之一。坐落在加拿大的西岸，從溫哥華搭渡輪需一個半小時。其首都維多利亞，建立於150年前，以其舊式的殖民時期建築以及美麗的港灣而聞名。它是卑詩省的政府中心，許多居民都是公務人員。和加拿大其他城市比起來，這裡的生活方式非常令人放鬆，也吸引很多人退休後遷居於此。因為有許多壯麗的山景和世界知名的布查花園，這是很受遊客歡迎的小島。

單字 rcolonial 殖民地的
harbor 港灣
public servants 公務員（= civil servant）
magnificent 壯麗的

66. (A) quarter 季 (B) position 位置
(C) coast 海岸 (D) site 地點

67. (A) was founded（過去簡單式被動） (B) founded（過去式）
(C) was founding（過去進行式） (D) found（現在式）
以上都為found 建立的意思

68. (A) regarded 被視為 (B) employed 被受雇
(C) included 被包含 (D) treated 被對待

69. (A) compared（過去分詞） (B) to compare（不定詞）
(C) comparing（現在分詞） (D) compare（現在簡單式）
以上皆為compare 比較的意思

70. (A) hindering 阻礙 (B) demanding 要求
(C) attracting 吸引 (D) prohibiting 禁止

After 16 weeks of labor contract disputes, Wang Metals workers say they have had enough. At 10:30 this morning, hundreds of workers walked out of work and onto the picket line. Wang Metals has more than 800 workers, and the union says about 90 percent of them are participating in the strike. They plan to continue to picket factory office here in four-hour shifts. The union representative claims workers have taken these measures as a last resort. "We had met and decided to wait for the company to put a decent offer on the table, and when it finally did last night, it turned out to be unacceptable. So, we voted to strike. "The representative said that union members will strike as long as necessary. Extra security has been ordered by the plant, and guards are blocking passage through the main entrance to the factory. Local business leaders are concerned because any kind of prolonged dispute could have a negative effect on other sectors of the community as well. "Wang Metals is the backbone of our local economy. Everything from food to entertainment, to houses... it all connects to the plant," says one business owner.

中譯 16週的勞工契約糾紛之後，王氏金屬公司的員工表示他們早已受夠了。今天早上10點半，數百名工人離開工作崗位參加罷工。王氏金屬公司有超過800名工人，工會表示有90%的人參加這次罷工。他們計劃持續每隔4小時輪班，組成罷工封鎖線圍住工廠辦公室。工會代表宣稱工人已經把這些當成最後手段了。「我們和公司見面並且等待合理的價錢，但到昨晚我們發現所提出的條件是無法接受的。因此我們投票決議罷工。」代表說工會成員會罷工多久是多久。工廠方面則是新增保全，警衛擋住了通往工廠的主要通道。當地商業領袖則擔憂任何爭議的延長都會對當地社區其他面向產生負面的影響。「王氏金屬公司是我們當地的經濟支柱。從食物到娛樂、到房屋的每一個面向都和它有關」一名做生意的老闆表示。

單字
labor 勞工	dispute 爭論
picket line 示威（罷工）者的糾察線	strike 打擊、罷工，在此作罷工
last resort 最後的手段	representative 代表
prolonged 延長的	backbone 支柱

71. Which of the following is the best headline for this news report?

(A) Wang Plant Orders Extra Security 王氏工廠雇用更多的警衛

(B) 800 Workers Stage Walkout at Wang 800名工人舉行聯合罷工

(C) Wang Metals Loses Money During Strike 王氏金屬於罷工期間損失金錢

(D) Wang Workers Start Strike Today 王氏金屬工人今日開始罷工

中譯 哪一項最適合當成新聞報導的標題？

解析 由At 10:30 this morning, hundreds of workers walked out of work and onto the picket line.可知。

72. What triggered the strike?

(A) The company being the backbone of the local economy.
這間公司是當地經濟的重要支柱。

(B) An offer by the company that the union found unacceptable.
公司所提出的條件工會無法接受。

(C) 90 percent of the workers picketing the factory offices.
90%的工人將工廠辦公室用封鎖線封起。

(D) The company ordering extra security guards.
公司雇用更多的警衛。

中譯 什麼事情引起了罷工？

解析 由" We had met and decided to wait for the company to put a decent offer on the table, and when it finally did last night, it turned out to be unacceptable. So, we voted to strike."可知。

73. How long do the workers intend to strike?

(A) For four weeks. 4個星期。 (B) A number of weeks. 幾個星期。

(C) Indefinitely. 無限期。 (D) Late into the night. 到晚上。

中譯 工人們打算罷工多久？

解析 由The representative said that union members will strike as long as necessary. 可知。

74. If some of the plant workers were to lose their jobs, what might be the effect on the community as a whole?

(A) Hardly any effect. Things would stay the same. 沒什麼影響，情況都一樣。

(B) There would be more houses available for other people to live in. 會有更多的房子讓其他人入住。

(C) The economy of the community would suffer. 經濟會惡化。

(D) The economy of the community would prosper. 經濟會好轉。

中譯 如果工廠工人失去工作，對社區整體會有什麼影響？

解析 由Local business leaders are concerned because any kind of prolonged dispute could have a negative effect on other sectors of the community as well.可知。

75. Who blocked the passage through the main entrance to the factory?

(A) Security guards. 警衛。

(B) Local business leaders. 當地生意人。

(C) Union representatives. 工會代表。

(D) Company officials. 公司代表。

中譯 誰堵住了通往工廠的主要入口通道？

解析 由Extra security has been ordered by the plant, and guards are blocking passage through the main entrance to the factory.可知。

Vacation rentals are fully private homes whose owners rent them out on a temporary basis to tourists as an alternative to hotels. They are available in all kinds of destinations, from a rustic cabin in the mountains to a downtown apartment in a major city. They can be townhouses, single-family-style homes, farms, beach houses, or even villas.

中譯 假期租屋是完全的私人住宅，其屋主短暫地將屋子出租給遊客當成是飯店以外的選擇。依目的地的不同也有不同的選擇，像是山中的小木屋，或是大城市中的市中心公寓。可以是連棟的住宅，也可以是獨棟透天屋、農場、海邊住宅甚至是別墅。

Vacation rentals are generally appealing for many reasons. They are, to name some on the top, cost-saving, spacious, great for large groups, separated from crowds, and no tips or service charges. Besides, they have kitchens for cooking, living rooms for gathering, outdoor spaces for parties or barbeques, and they offer the appeal of living like locals in a real community. They are usually equipped with facilities such as sports and beach accessories, games, books and DVD libraries, and in warmer locations, a swimming pool. Many vacation rentals are pet-friendly, so people can take their pets along with them when traveling.

中譯 假期租屋在很多方面都是很吸引人的。比如說，從最吸引人的來說，就是省錢、空間大、適合一大群人、和其他人群隔開，以及沒有小費和服務費。此外，還有廚房可以煮菜，客廳可以聚會，戶外空間可用來舉辦派對和烤肉，就像真實住在當地社區的居民一樣。這些租屋通常會有運動設施、海灘設備、遊戲、書本，和許多DVD，氣候溫暖的地方甚至會有游泳池。許多假期租屋是可以帶寵物入住的，所以很多人會帶著寵物一起旅行。

Customers who choose hotels often enjoy the advantages of brand recognition, familiar reservation processes, and on-site service, while booking a vacation rental may mean stepping out of that comfort zone in order to get privacy, peace and quietness they offer -- things that are hard to obtain in a hotel room. For tourists, choosing a vacation rental over a hotel means more than short-term lodging -- vivid experiences and lifelong memories are what they value.

中譯 客戶選擇飯店常是享受品牌知名度、熟悉的訂房流程和現場服務，然而假期租屋則意味著要走出舒適圈，以獲得隱私、平和與安靜，這些都很難從飯店住宿中獲得。對於遊客來說，選擇假期租屋而非飯店，表示比短期住宿更重要的是道地的生活體驗以及一輩子的記憶，才是他們所重視的。

單字 rental 租賃　　spacious 廣闊的
separate 區分　　advantage 優勢
brand 商標、牌子　　recognition 贊譽認可

76. What is this reading mainly about?

(A) Planning leisure trips. 計劃休閒旅遊。

(B) The values of different vacation destinations. 不同假期目的地的價值。

(C) Alternative accommodations for tourists. 觀光客另外的食宿選擇。

(D) Booking accommodations for fun trips. 預定有趣旅程的住宿。

中譯 本文的主旨為何？

解析 由第一段They are available in all kinds of destinations可知。

77. What is the major concept of a vacation rental?

(A) Private houses rent out on weekdays only.
私有的房屋只在平日出租。

(B) Private homes rent out to tourists.
私有的房屋出租給觀光客。

(C) Furnished homes for rent when owners are on vacations.
已布置好的房子在屋主度假時出租。

(D) Furnished rooms for short-term homestays.
已布置好的房間給短期的寄宿家庭。

中譯 短期租屋的主要概念是什麼？

解析 由Vacation rentals are fully private homes whose owners rent them out on a temporary basis to tourists as an alternative to hotels.可知。

78. Which of the following is NOT considered the reason that makes vacation rentals appealing?

(A) Familiar booking processes. 熟悉的訂房程序。

(B) Being economic. 便宜。

(C) Being equipped with many useful facilities. 備有許多有用的設施。

(D) Being pet-friendly. 對寵物友善。

中譯 哪一項不是短期租屋吸引人的地方？

解析 由Customers who choose hotels often enjoy the advantages of brand recognition, familiar reservation processes可知familiar reservation processes為飯店的優點，而非假期租屋的優點。

79. What is the major advantage when tourists choose hotels rather than vacation rentals?

(A) Fame and wealth. 名聲和財富。

(B) Living like locals. 像當地人一樣生活。

(C) Fair prices. 平價。

(D) On-site service. 現場服務。

中譯 當遊客選擇飯店而非短期租屋時，最大的優點是什麼？

解析 由最後一段第一句可知。

80. Which of the following statements is a proper description of vacation rentals?

(A) They are shared by many owners. 他們為很多主人所有。

(B) Tipping is not necessary at vacation rentals. 短期租屋不一定要付小費。

(C) They are built for business purpose. 他們因商業用途而建。

(D) Daily cleaning is usually included in the rental contract.
每天的清掃通常包含於租賃合約內。

中譯 以下哪項對於短期租屋的敘述為正確的？

解析 由Vacation rentals are generally appealing for many reasons. They are, to name some on the top, cost-saving, spacious, great for large groups, separated from crowds, and no tips or service charges.可知。

102 年外語領隊英文試題＋標準答案

★102年專門職業及技術人員普通考試導遊人員、領隊人員考試試題

等別：普通考試

類科：外語領隊人員（英語）

科目：外國語（英語）

考試時間：1 小時 20 分

※注意：（一）本試題為單一選擇題，請選出一個正確或最適當的答案，複選作答者，該題不予計分。
（二）本科目共80題，每題1.25分，須用2Ｂ鉛筆在試卡上依題號清楚劃記，於本試題上作答者，不予計分。
（三）本試題禁止使用電子計算器。

(　　)1. The ______ of touring in this city is that it's very pricey.
(A) convenience　(B) downside　(C) confusion　(D) opportunity

(　　)2. Seeing the rise of new media technology, many people predict newspapers will soon be ______.
(A) widespread　(B) prevalent　(C) obsolete　(D) accessed

(　　)3. Am I ______ to compensation if my ferry is canceled?
(A) asked　(B) entitled　(C) qualified　(D) requested

(　　)4. It is the high season, and I'm not sure whether the hotel could provide enough ______ for the whole group.
(A) vacation　(B) locations
(C) recommendation　(D) accommodations

(　　)5. Due to the delay, we are not able to catch up with our ______ flight.
(A) connecting　(B) connected　(C) connect　(D) connectional

(　　)6. ______ of the death penalty say it is an important tool for preserving law and order in the society.
(A) Components　(B) Respondents　(C) Opponents　(D) Proponents

( )7. Even though John has returned from Bali for two weeks, he is still ______ the memories of his holidays.

(A) missing (B) forgetting (C) savoring (D) remembering

( )8. The park does not allow pets; ______, we would have brought our puppy with us.

(A) unless (B) therefore (C) likewise (D) otherwise

( )9. This traveler's check is not good because it should require two ______ by the user.

(A) insurances (B) accounts (C) signatures (D) examinations

( )10. Shelly has adhered ______ a low-fat diet for over two months and succeeded in losing 12 pounds.

(A) on (B) at (C) in (D) to

( )11. Violent video games have been ______ for school shootings, increases in bullying, and violence towards women.

(A) influenced (B) acclaimed (C) decided (D) blamed

( )12. My car wouldn't start this morning, and then I realized the battery was ______.

(A) empty (B) low (C) weak (D) dead

( )13. Recently, extreme weather and climate events in the form of heat waves, droughts and floods seem to have become the norm rather than the ______.

(A) condition (B) objection (C) exception (D) question

( )14. Many ______ users of mobile phones would get anxious and panic once the phone is missing.

(A) friendly (B) familiar (C) heavy (D) careful

( )15. After looking at the map, Tom suggested that we ______ heading east.

(A) continue (B) continued

(C) have continued (D) are continuing

( )16. In 2060, people over 65 will account ______ more than 41 percent of the population in Taiwan.

(A) for (B) no (C) in (D) at

(　　)17. Despite his effort to combat fear of height, the dip and turn of the roller coaster still ______ Jeff.

(A) excited　(B) terrified　(C) convinced　(D) stimulated

(　　)18. We have seen a marked increase in the number of visitors to the theme park, but cannot understand why the total income indicates ______.

(A) a demand　(B) a decline　(C) a distinction　(D) a disruption

(　　)19. The Union has filed a protest ______ behalf of the terminated workers.

(A) for　(B) In　(C) on　(D) at

(　　)20. Paul didn't go to the baseball game yesterday; ______, he went fishing.

(A) not to mention　(B) instead
(C) in that case　(D) moreover

(　　)21. The manager lacked coordination and communication skills; likewise, his crew was altogether ______.

(A) disciplined　(B) disjointed　(C) dismayed　(D) discriminated

(　　)22. The chemicals in these cleaning products can be ______ to our health.

(A) hazardous　(B) hapless　(C) rueful　(D) pitiful

(　　)23. It took us no time to clear ______ at the border.

(A) costume　(B) costumes　(C) custom　(D) customs

(　　)24. Good luck for your interview today. I'll keep my fingers ______ and wish you the best.

(A) bent　(B) crossed　(C) pointed　(D) knitted

(　　)25. Our new neighbors next door will have a ______ party this weekend.

(A) homecoming　(B) homebasing　(C) housewarming　(D) housemoving

(　　)26. Aliens who overstay their visas would be ______ back to their country of birth.

(A) deported　(B) discharged　(C) departed　(D) disclaimed

(　　)27. Computer chess games are getting cheaper all the time; ______, their quality is improving.

(A) indeed　(B) in short　(C) therefore　(D) meanwhile

( )28. Stay calm and clear-minded. I'm sure you'll have no problem ______ the exam.

(A) to pass (B) passing (C) pass (D) passed

( )29. Sorry, we don't have these shoes in size seven. They are out of ______. Would you like to try a different style?

(A) order (B) business (C) stock (D) sale

( )30. A: How often do you eat out?

B: ______

(A) Five times a week. (B) For thirty minutes.

(C) Every one hour. (D) In a second.

( )31. A: Sir, you just triggered the security alarm. Are you carrying any metal item?

B: ______

(A) No, I have emptied all my coins from my pockets.

(B) No, I didn't pull the trigger.

(C) Yes, it's a very sensitive detector.

(D) Yes, you can never be too careful.

Recently a cheating scandal has rocked the world: Lance Armstrong, an American professional road racing cyclist, finally admitted that he had used performance-enhancing drugs in his seven Tour de France wins. In the past, he persistently denied the (32) of doping, even under oath, and persecuted former close associates who went public (33) him. Now, he confesses his years of denial as "one big lie" for keeping up a fairy tale image: a hero who overcame cancer, a winner of the Tour repeatedly, and a father with a happy marriage and children. Armstrong's cheat has rekindled the long-term debate on (34) performance-enhancing drugs should be accepted in sports. On one side, it is argued that these drugs' harmful health effects have been overstated, and using drugs is part of the (35) of sports much like improved training techniques and new technologies. On the other side, it is argued that these drugs are harmful and potentially fatal, and that athletes who use them are cheaters who gain an unfair (36) and violate the spirit of competition.

( )32. (A) implementation (B) exploitation (C) persecution (D) allegation

( )33. (A) for (B) upon (C) over (D) against

( )34. (A) how (B) lest (C) whether (D) which

( )35. (A) evolution (B) satisfaction (C) cooperation (D) distribution

( )36. (A) viewpoint (B) advantage (C) share (D) control

( )37. Jennifer is very good with specific details, but she doesn't always get the ______.

(A) big frame (B) big image (C) big picture (D) big book

( )38. Do they have a ______ plan if it rains tomorrow and they can't go hiking?

(A) convenience (B) contingency (C) continuous (D) constituent

( )39. The past years have seen many ______ in the telecommunications industry, such as the development of phones that can receive e-mail and images.

(A) innovations (B) invitations (C) Instructions (D) installations

( )40. Joe works around the clock. He's really ______ to make money and get ahead in the company.

(A) deluded (B) driven (C) disappointed (D) depressed

( )41. Most of my friends don't eat meat. ______ we always go to vegetarian restaurants when we go out for dinner.

(A) Because (B) As a result (C) If (D) When

( )42. We decided to take our vacation during the winter this year ______ we realized that we could save a lot of money that way.

(A) till (B) then (C) so (D) because

( )43. When you stay in a hotel, what basic ______ do you think are necessary?

(A) activities (B) capabilities (C) facilities (D) abilities

( )44. Airport limousine service, valet parking service, and concierge service are some of the most poplar items among our ______.

(A) car services (B) guest services (C) sales services (D) retail services

( )45. The "Ambassador" is centrally located in Hsinchu, a few minutes by car from the station. It offers a ______view of the metro Hsinchu area.

(A) panoramic (B) pacific (C) pastoral (D) premodern

( )46. I would like to ______ my American Express card, please.

(A) choose this to (B) charge this to (C) chain this to (D) change this to

( )47. Guest: I have made a reservation for a suite overnight.

Clerk: Yes, we have your reservation right here. Would you please fill out this ______ form and show me your ID?

(A) reimbursement (B) registration (C) refund (D) registrar

( )48. He's got a new job in Paris. He has been ______ there for three months.

(A) live (B) lived (C) living (D) life

( )49. As Tim has no experience at all, I ______ he is qualified for this job.

(A) describe (B) deliberate (C) develop (D) doubt

( )50. How ______ you feel if your best friends from high school mistook you for someone thirty years older at the reunion?

(A) would (B) would have (C) will (D) will have

( )51. Taiwan Mountain Tea and Red Sprout Mountain Tea are ______ subspecies of the island. They were discovered in Taiwan in the 17th century.

(A) inscribed (B) indigenous (C) incredible (D) industrial

( )52. A group of young students has taken the ______ through social media to organize a rally against the austerity plans.

(A) invitation (B) initiative (C) instruction (D) inscription

( )53. Wild Formosa Sika deer became ______ due to extensive hunting of the animal during the Dutch colonization period.

(A) extinct (B) excite (C) exact (D) explicit

( )54. Many emerging countries are facing economic uncertainty after the ______ with former union.

(A) making up (B) breaking up (C) setting up (D) taking up

( )55. Would you please pick up the groceries from the store ______ your way home?

(A) on (B) in (C) through (D) of

( )56. Releasing the prisoners for fear of overcrowding might ______ the current rule of law.

(A) understand (B) undermine (C) underdevelop (D) underfund

( )57. Getting ______ the city in a foreign country can be tricky as many locals don't speak English or welcome foreigners.

(A) around (B) up (C) with (D) along

( )58. Your detailed ______ is as follows: leaving Taipei on the 14th of June and arriving at Tokyo on the same day at noon.

(A) item (B) identification (C) itinerary (D) inscription

(　　)59. ______ you listen to the conclusion, you should continue to take notes as completely as possible.

(A) But　(B) Whether　(C) How　(D) As

(　　)60. Many people engage in risky tasks only for personal satisfaction—they are ______ only with their self-esteem.

(A) concerned　(B) contained　(C) complained　(D) completed

(　　)61. The term *rites of passage* was introduced by the Flemish anthropologist Arnold van Gennep in 1090 to describe the ______ that make important transitions in people's lives.

(A) cemeteries　(B) certainties　(C) celebrities　(D) ceremonies

(　　)62. With the same consumption of fuel, this motorbike goes ______ that one.

(A) as twice fast as　(B) twice fast as

(C) as fast as twice of　(D) twice as fast as

(　　)63. One of the most important parts of these activities is for students to share the ______ of a group discussion with the rest of the class.

(A) lowlights　(B) brightlights　(C) highlights　(D) headlights

(　　)64. Still to come ______ BBC World News, our Paris correspondent will update us on the Euro crisis.

(A) by　(B) on　(C) through　(D) in

(　　)65. Many people have made "getting in shape" one of their new year ______.

(A) recreations　(B) revolutions　(C) revelations　(D) resolutions

(　　)66. Upon ______ to the plan, the organizers are to set out the procedures.

(A) agreeing　(B) agree　(C) agreed　(D) agreeable

(　　)67. Client: Are there any direct flights to Paris?

Clerk: No, you would have to ______ in Amsterdam.

(A) transfer　(B) transport　(C) translate　(D) transform

(　　)68. Client: Could you give us a table ______?

Waiter: Certainly. Follow me, please.

(A) with the window　(B) to the window

(C) through the window　(D) by the window

( )69. Pineapple cakes and local teas are some of the most popular ______ of Taiwan.

(A) sights (B) souvenirs (C) services (D) surprises

( )70. A ______ breakfast of coffee and rolls is served in the lobby between 7 and 10am.

(A) complete (B) complimentary (C) continuous (D) complicate

( )71. The hotels in the resort areas are fully booked in the summer. It would be very difficult to find any ______ then.

(A) vacations (B) visitors (C) views (D) vacancies

( )72. ______ on the board for more than two decades, the president knows all the details necessary to persuade the new members.

(A) Having served (B) Serving (C) Services (D) Served

( )73. On occasions of loss and grief, we should use the most appropriate words to express our ______.

(A) considerations (B) contemplations (C) condolences (D) complacency

( )74. ______ the use of personal pronouns such as he or she, it can be used to refer to an entire idea or concept that is comprehensive and complex.

(A) In order to (B) In reference to (C) In contrast to (D) In speaking to

( )75. Steve created quite ______ when he introduced that controversial idea at the advisory meeting.

(A) a stock (B) a stare (C) a stir (D) a star

( )76. This sleek and sophisticated design might be ______ to some of you who don't believe in the aesthetics of products.

(A) an eye opener (B) a can opener (C) an ear opener (D) a beer opener

Mount Rushmore is perhaps one of North America's most distinguished and famous landmarks, right after the Statue of Liberty. It features the busts of four U.S. Presidents, Washington, Jefferson, Lincoln and Roosevelt.

This place has an interesting story. First, a New York lawyer named Charles E. Rushmore visited the Black Hills in 1885. He asked a local the name of the granite mountain before them. Since the peak had no name, the man replied humorously, "Mount Rushmore." The name has never been changed since! In 1923 state historian Doane Robinson suggested carving some giant statues in South Dakota's Black Hills. However, the formations chosen, known as the Needles, were too fragile, and the sculptor, Mr. Gutzon Borglum, decided to use the granite mountain instead. Born in a family of Danish Mormons in Idaho in 1867, Borglum studied art in Paris and enjoyed moderate fame as a sculptor after remodeling the torch for the Statue of Liberty. Borglum chose the presidents "in commemoration of the foundation, preservation and continental expansion of the United States." President Calvin Coolidge dedicated the memorial in 1927.

At this very moment, near this mountain, there is another colossal monument **in progress:** the Crazy Horse Memorial, to honor this courageous Indian leader. In this way, history is preserved, as big as the heritage is, to be shared with everyone in an attractive way.

(　　)77. What is the second paragraph mainly about?

(A) A brief history of Mount Rushmore.
(B) The geographical features of Mount Rushmore.
(C) Other attractions near Mount Rushmore.
(D) A comparison between Mount Rushmore and the Statue of Liberty.

(　　)78. What does "**in progress**" imply about the Crazy Horse Memorial in the last paragraph?

(A) It is better than the other monuments.
(B) It will change to an Indian name.
(C) It is still under construction.
(D) It gives more fun to the tourists.

(　　)79. Mr. Gutzon Borglum ______.

(A) was an unknown artist before he carved the giant statues
(B) suggested carving some statues in South Dakota's Black Hills
(C) chose the subjects for his sculptures
(D) was a sculptor from France

(　　)80. The four U.S. presidents featured in Mount Rushmore do NOT include ______.

(A) Jefferson　(B) Coolidge　(C) Roosevelt　(D) Washington

★標準答案

1. (B)	2. (C)	3. (B)	4. (D)	5. (A)
6. (D)	7. (C)	8. (D)	9. (C)	10. (D)
11. (D)	12. (D)	13. (C)	14. (C)	15. (A)
16. (A)	17. (B)	18. (B)	19. (C)	20. (B)
21. (B)	22. (A)	23. (D)	24. (B)	25. (C)
26. (A)	27. (D)	28. (B)	29. (C)	30. (A)
31. (A)	32. (D)	33. (D)	34. (C)	35. (A)
36. (B)	37. (C)	38. (B)	39. (A)	40. (B)
41. (B)	42. (D)	43. (C)	44. (B)	45. (A)
46. (B)	47. (B)	48. (C)	49. (D)	50. (A)
51. (B)	52. (B)	53. (A)	54. (B)	55. (A)
56. (B)	57. (A)	58. (C)	59. (D)	60. (A)
61. (D)	62. (D)	63. (C)	64. (B)	65. (D)
66. (A)	67. (A)	68. (D)	69. (B)	70. (B)
71. (D)	72. (A)	73. (C)	74. (C)	75. (C)
76. (A)	77. (A)	78. (C)	79. (C)	80. (B)

102 年外語領隊英文試題中譯與解析

1. The downside of touring in this city is that it's very pricey.

(A) convenience 方便
(B) downside 缺點
(C) confusion 困惑
(D) opportunity 機會

中譯 這座城市觀光的缺點就是物價昂貴。

解析 pricey 貴的；tour 旅遊，可為名詞及動詞。

2. Seeing the rise of new media technology, many people predict newspapers will soon be obsolete.

(A) widespread 廣泛的
(B) prevalent 盛行的
(C) obsolete 過時的
(D) accessed 存取的

中譯 看見了新媒體科技的崛起，很多人預測報紙很快就會過時。

解析 obsolete 過時的，相似詞有：outdated、old-fashioned 舊式的。

3. Am I entitled to compensation if my ferry is canceled?

(A) asked 要求
(B) entitled 有權享有
(C) qualified 有資格
(D) requested 要求

中譯 如果我的遊輪行程被取消了，我有權力要求補償嗎？

解析 entitled to 有……資格的；compensation 補償、彌補。相關考題例句：Prohibited items in carry-on bags will be confiscated at the checkpoints, and no compensation will be given for them. 隨身行李中的違禁品將會於檢查站被沒收，且沒有任何的補償。101領隊

4. It is the high season, and I'm not sure whether the hotel could provide enough accommodations for the whole group.

(A) vacation 假期
(B) locations 位子
(C) recommendation 推薦
(D) accommodations 住宿

中譯 現在是旺季，我不確定飯店是否可以提供足夠的住宿給整個旅行團。

解析 high season是旺季，而It's high time則是時間剛好。

5. Due to the delay, we are not able to catch up with our connecting flight.

(A) connecting (B) connected
(C) connect (D) connectional

中譯 因為延遲，我們無法趕上我們的轉機班機。

解析 connect為連接之意。catch up 趕上；connecting flight 轉機班機。以現在分詞當形容詞，故選connecting。

6. Proponents of the death penalty say it is an important tool for preserving law and order in the society.

(A) Components 元件 (B) Respondents 受訪者
(C) Opponents 反對者 (D) Proponents 支持者

中譯 死刑的支持者說這是一項維護法律以及社會秩序很重要的工具。

解析 proponents 支持者。提到死刑的其他考題例句：The support for suspending death penalty has gained momentum, and it is very likely that someday the congress of the country will pass its suspension. 支持廢死已越來越有勢力，某天很有可能國會通過廢死。102導遊

7. Even though John has returned from Bali for two weeks, he is still savoring the memories of his holidays.

(A) missing 想念 (B) forgetting 忘記
(C) savoring 細細品味 (D) remembering 記得

中譯 即便約翰已經從峇里島回來2個星期了，他仍然對他的假期回憶念念不忘。

解析 savor 細細品味，savor在此即為enjoy的意思。

8. The park does not allow pets; otherwise, we would have brought our puppy with us.

(A) unless 除非 (B) therefore 因此 (C) likewise 同樣 (D) otherwise 否則

中譯 這座公園不讓寵物進入，不然我們就會帶我們的寵物了。

解析 would have brought表示與事實相反，故選otherwise。

9. This traveler's check is not good because it should require two signatures by the user.

(A) insurances 保險 (B) accounts 帳戶
(C) signatures 簽名 (D) examinations 考試

中譯 旅行支票不好用是因為它需要持有者的兩份簽名。

解析 sign 簽名，動詞；signatures 簽名，名詞。

10. Shelly has adhered to a low-fat diet for over two months and succeeded in losing 12 pounds.

(A) on (B) at (C) in (D) to

中譯 雪麗遵循低卡飲食兩個多月，並且成功瘦下12磅。

解析 adhered to 堅持；英文領隊考題經常出現關於減重的主題。
- Please don't order so much food! I have been putting on weight for the last two months. 拜託別點太多食物！這兩個月我已經開始變胖了。100領隊
- Many people have put on some pounds during the New Year vacation. 於新年假期期間，許多人體重增加不少磅。98領隊

11. Violent video games have been blamed for school shootings, increases in bullying, and violence towards women.

(A) influenced 影響 (B) acclaimed 讚譽
(C) decided 決定 (D) blamed 責怪

中譯 暴力的遊戲被歸咎於導致校園槍械、增加霸凌，以及對於女性的暴力。

解析 blame for 歸咎於；blame sb for sth 因為某事而責備某人。

12. My car wouldn't start this morning, and then I realized the battery was dead.

(A) empty 空 (B) low 低 (C) weak 弱 (D) dead 死亡

中譯 我的車子早上無法發動，然後我瞭解原來是電池沒電了。

解析 口語上dead經常用來表示電池沒電了。

13. Recently, extreme weather and climate events in the form of heat waves, droughts and floods seem to have become the norm rather than the exception.

(A) condition 狀況 (B) objection 反對
(C) exception 例外 (D) question 問題

中譯 最近，極端的天氣氣候像是熱浪、乾旱以及水災似乎都成了常態而非例外。

解析 droughts 乾旱；norm 基準；exception 例外，名詞；except for 例外。

14. Many users of mobile phones would get heavy anxious and panic once the phone is missing.

(A) friendly 友善地 (B) familiar 相似 (C) heavy 重的 (D) careful 小心

中譯 一旦手機不見時，許多手機的使用者都會重度焦慮或慌張。

解析 heavy users 重度使用者。

15. After looking at the map, Tom suggested that we continue heading east.

(A) continue (B) continued (C) have continued (D) are continuing

中譯 看過了地圖之後，湯姆建議我們應該持續往東。

解析 suggest + Ving 建議某事，或是suggest that S + V 建議某人做某事。continue 持續。

16. In 2060, people over 65 will account for more than 41 percent of the population in Taiwan.

(A) for (B) no (C) in (D) at

中譯 2060年，65歲以上的人口將會超過台灣人口總數的41%。

解析 account for 說明（原因、理由等）、導致、引起、（在數量、比例上）占、對……負責。例句：How do you account for the company's alarmingly high staff turnover? 你怎麼解釋這家公司高得令人憂心的人員流動率？

17. Despite his effort to combat fear of height, the dip and turn of the roller coaster still terrified Jeff.

(A) excited 興奮 (B) terrified 嚇壞了

(C) convinced 說服 (D) stimulated 刺激

中譯 即便他對於懼高症做了許多的努力，雲霄飛車的俯衝和轉彎還是嚇壞了傑夫。

解析 combat 戰鬥、搏鬥；terrify 使驚嚇，動詞。例句1：Flying terrifies him. 坐飛機讓他害怕得要命。例句2：He was terrified of heights. 他懼高。

18. We have seen a marked increase in the number of visitors to the theme park, but cannot understand why the total income indicates a decline.

(A) a demand 需求 (B) a decline 下降

(C) a distinction 區別 (D) a disruption 中斷

中譯 我們看到主題樂園的遊客數已有顯著的增加，但卻不懂為何總收入卻下滑。

解析 decline、decrease都是下降、減少的意思。

19. The Union has filed a protest on behalf of the terminated workers.

(A) for (B) in (C) on (D) at

中譯 公會已經代表被資遣的員工發起抗議。

解析 on behalf of 代表……。I would like to express our gratitude to you on behalf of my company. 我代表公司對你表達我們的感激。101領隊

20. Paul didn't go to the baseball game yesterday; instead, he went fishing.

(A) not to mention 不用提 (B) instead 反而
(C) in that case 在這種情況下 (D) moreover 此外

中譯 保羅昨天沒去棒球比賽，反而是釣魚去了。

解析 instead 替代、反而，為副詞，所帶出的事情是要做的、會做的，且會帶出子句；instead of 代替，所引導的事情則是不要做的、沒有做的，instead of + N or Ving。

21. The manager lacked coordination and communication skills; likewise, his crew was altogether disjointed.

(A) disciplined 紀律 (B) disjointed 脫節
(C) dismayed 驚惶 (D) discriminated 歧視

中譯 這名經理缺乏統整以及溝通技巧，同樣地，他的人員也都很散亂。

解析 disjointed 脫節鬆散的、支離破碎的；coordination 協調；crew 工作人員。

22. he chemicals in these cleaning products can be hazardous to our health.

(A) hazardous 有害的 (B) hapless 不幸的
(C) rueful 悔恨的 (D) pitiful 可憐的

中譯 清潔用品中的化學物質對我們的健康可能有害。

解析 hazardous 有害的，例句：Smoking can be hazardous to health. 吸菸對健康有害。

23. It took us no time to clear customs at the border.

(A) costume 服裝 (B) custumes 服裝 (C) custom 風俗 (D) customs 海關

中譯 於邊界通關沒有花我們什麼時間。

解析 clear customs 結關、清關或者通關，指進口貨物、出口貨物和轉運貨物在進入一國海關關境或國境時，必須向海關申報，並辦理海關規定的各項手續。custom為風俗；customary為約定俗成的；customs為海關，考題常出現此三個單字。

24. Good luck for your interview today. I'll keep my fingers crossed and wish you the best.

(A) bent 彎曲 (B) crossed 交叉 (C) pointed 尖 (D) knitted 針織的

中譯 祝你今天的面試順利。我會祈禱好運以及祝福你一切順利。

解析 fingers crossed為祈求好運的常用用法。

25. Our new neighbors next door will have a housewarming party this weekend.

(A) homecoming (B) homebasing

(C) housewarming 喬遷之喜 (D) housemoving

中譯 我們隔壁的新鄰居本週末將會有一個喬遷派對。

解析 housewarming party 喬遷派對，把房子炒熱，充滿人氣之意。

26. Aliens who overstay their visas would be deported back to their country of birth.

(A) deported 被驅逐出境 (B) discharged 出院

(C) departed 起飛 (D) disclaimed 否認

中譯 超過簽證時間的外國人會被驅逐送回他們的出生國家。

解析 deport 將……驅逐出境；departed 飛機起飛，兩者請勿搞混！

27. Computer chess games are getting cheaper all the time; meanwhile, their quality is improving.

(A) indeed 的確 (B) in short 總之 (C) therefore 因此 (D) meanwhile 同時

中譯 電腦的象棋遊戲越來越便宜了，同時他們的品質也在進步。

解析 meanwhile的基本意思是「其間、與此同時」，指在一件事情發生的過程中或者一段時間內另一件事也在發生。

28. Stay calm and clear-minded. I'm sure you'll have no problem passing the exam.

(A) to pass (B) passing (C) pass 過 (D) passed

中譯 保持冷靜和清晰的思路。我敢保證你會沒有問題地通過考試。

解析 have no problem + Ving 做某事沒有問題；have problems + Ving 做某事有問題 / 困難 = have trouble / difficulty + Ving。

29. Sorry, we don't have these shoes in size seven. They are out of stock. Would you like to try a different style?

(A) order 點　(B) business 商業　(C) stock 存貨　(D) sale 銷售

中譯 抱歉，這些鞋子我們沒有7號尺寸。他們都賣完存貨了。你要不要試試看其他款式？

解析 stock 存貨，例句：We have a fast turnover of stock. 我們的貨物周轉快。

30. A: How often do you eat out?
B: Five times a week.

(A) Five times a week. 1週5次。　(B) For thirty minutes. 持續30分鐘。
(C) Every one hour. 每小時1次。　(D) In a second. 在1秒內。

中譯 A：你多常外食？
B：1週5次。

解析 問how often（頻率），故選Five times a week.。

31. A: Sir, you just triggered the security alarm. Are you carrying any metal item?
B: No, I have emptied all my coins from my pockets.

(A) No, I have emptied all my coins from my pockets.
沒有，我已經清空口袋內的所有硬幣。
(B) No, I didn't pull the trigger. 沒有，我沒有扣動板機。
(C) Yes, it's a very sensitive detector. 對，他是非常敏銳的偵查器。
(D) Yes, you can never be too careful. 對，你再小心也不為過。

中譯 A: 先生，你剛觸動了安全警示。你有攜帶任何金屬物品嗎？
B: 沒有，我已經清空口袋內的所有硬幣。

解析 trigger 觸發、引起，相似的意思還有set off。empty形容詞是空的，指房間等時，意思是「空的」、「裡面沒裝東西的」；指座位時，意思是「沒有人佔據的」；指人心理時，意思是「空虛的」；作動詞是「把……倒空」。

Recently a cheating scandal has rocked the world: Lance Armstrong, an American professional road racing cyclist, finally admitted that he had used performance-enhancing drugs in his seven Tour de France wins. In the past, he persistently denied the allegation of doping, even under oath, and persecuted former close associates who went public against him. Now, he confesses his years of denial as "one big lie" for keeping up a fairy tale image: a hero who overcame cancer, a winner of the Tour repeatedly, and a father with a happy marriage and children. Armstrong's cheat has rekindled the long-term debate on whether performance-enhancing drugs should be accepted in sports. On one side, it is argued that these drugs' harmful health effects have been overstated, and using drugs is part of the evolution of sports much like improved training techniques and new technologies. On the other side, it is argued that these drugs are harmful and potentially fatal, and that athletes who use them are cheaters who gain an unfair advantage and violate the spirit of competition.

中譯 最近一樁欺騙的醜聞震驚世界：藍斯．阿姆斯壯，一名美國公路自行車賽職業車手，最終承認他曾在七次環法冠軍賽中使用過增強表現的藥物。過去，他不斷否認使用藥物，甚至發誓，以及迫害公開反對他的前親密戰友。現在，他坦承這幾年的否認都是「大謊言」來保持他傳奇般的形象，一名戰勝癌症、不停在比賽中奪冠的贏家、以及有著美滿婚姻和小孩的爸爸。阿姆斯壯的欺瞞點燃了長期以來的爭論，增強表現的藥物是否能運用於運動中。一則說法為這些藥物對於健康的傷害其實被高估了，使用這些藥只是運動的某部分的進化，像是改進過的訓練技巧以及新的科技。另一說則為，這些藥物都是有害且有致命危機的，而這些用藥的運動員都是欺騙者，得到不公平的優勢並且違反競爭的精神。

單字

cheat 行騙	scandal 醜聞
admit 承認	persistently 持續不斷地
deny 否認	persecute 迫害
confess 承認	fairy tale 童話故事
overcome 戰勝	rekindle （使）再振作

32. (A) implementation 實施　(B) exploitation 開發　(C) persecution 迫害　(D) allegation 指控

33. (A) for　(B) upon　(C) over　(D) against
以上皆為介系詞

34. (A) how 如何　(B) lest 免得　(C) whether 是否　(D) which 哪個

35. (A) evolution 進化　(B) satisfaction 滿意　(C) cooperation 合作　(D) distribution分配

36. (A) viewpoint 觀點 (B) advantage 優勢
(C) share 分享 (D) control 控制

37. Jennifer is very good with specific details, but she doesn't always get the big picture.
(A) big frame 大框架 (B) big image 大圖像
(C) big picture 大局 (D) big book 大書

中譯 珍妮佛對於特定細節非常在行，但她總是不瞭解整體的狀況。

解析 big picture 大局，也就是一件事的全貌。

38. Do they have a contingency plan if it rains tomorrow and they can't go hiking?
(A) convenience 方便 (B) contingency 應變
(C) continuous 連續 (D) constituent 成分

中譯 如果明天下雨他們不能健行的話，他們有緊急備案嗎？

解析 考contingency plan 緊急備案的用法。

39. The past years have seen many innovations in the telecommunications industry, such as the development of phones that can receive e-mail and images.
(A) innovations 創新 (B) invitations 邀請
(C) instructions 指令 (D) installations 安裝

中譯 過去幾年在電信通訊產業上有許多創新，像是手機可以收電子郵件和照片這樣的進步。

解析 innovations 創新、革新。這幾年常考科技相關的考題，例句1：The cellphone is very handy because it connects us with the world at large and even provides us with the necessary information on crucial moments. 手機非常的方便，因為它讓我們充分和世界溝通，甚至在重要時刻提供我們所需的資訊。102導遊
例句2：Technology, such as cellphones, often fosters equality and helps lift people out of poverty. 科技，像是手機，常常促進平等並且幫助人們脫貧。102導遊

40. Joe works around the clock. He's really driven to make money and get ahead in the company.
(A) deluded 迷惑 (B) driven 驅動
(C) disappointed 失望的 (D) depressed 沮喪的

中譯 夙日以繼夜地工作。他真的極度想賺錢和走在公司的最前面。

解析 driven （人）受到驅策的、有動力的。

41. Most of my friends don't eat meat. As a result, we always go to vegetarian restaurants when we go out for dinner.

(A) Because 因為 (B) As a result 所以
(C) If 如果 (D) When 當

中譯 我大部分的朋友不吃肉。所以當我們一起外出用晚餐時，我們總是去素食餐廳。

解析 as a result 結果、因此；as a result of... 由於……的結果。

42. We decided to take our vacation during the winter this year because we realized that we could save a lot of money that way.

(A) till 直到 (B) then 然後 (C) so 所以 (D) because 因為

中譯 我們決定今年冬天度假，因為我們發現這樣我們可以省很多錢。

解析 We decided to take our vacation during the winter this year為果，we realized that we could save a lot of money that way為因，故選because。

43. When you stay in a hotel, what basic facilities do you think are necessary?

(A) activities 活動 (B) capabilities 能力
(C) facilities 設施 (D) abilities 能力

中譯 當你住在飯店時，你認為哪些基本的設備是必須的？

解析 facilities 設施，為重點單字。考題例句如：Guest: What facilities do you have in your hotel? 客人：你們飯店有什麼設施？ Hotel clerk: We have a fitness center, a swimming pool, two restaurants, a beauty parlor, and a boutique. 飯店服務員：我們有健身中心、游泳池、兩間餐廳、一間美容室和女裝店。99領隊

44. Airport limousine service, valet parking service, and concierge service are some of the most poplar items among our guest services.

(A) car services 汽車服務 (B) guest services 客戶服務
(C) sales services 銷售服務 (D) retail services 零售服務

中譯 機場接送服務、代客泊車、管家服務是我們最受歡迎的客戶服務項目之一。

解析 guest services 客戶服務；room service 客房服務。

45. The "Ambassador" is centrally located in Hsinchu, a few minutes by car from the station. It offers a panoramic view of the metro Hsinchu area.

(A) panoramic 全景 (B) pacific 太平洋
(C) pastoral 田園 (D) premodern 前現代

中譯 國賓飯店位於新竹的正中央，距離車站開車只要幾分鐘。它提供了新竹市區的全景。

解析 panoramic 全景，例句：Most rooms enjoy panoramic views of the sea. 大多數房間都能看到海的全景。

46. I would like to charge this to my American Express card, please.

(A) choose this to 選擇 (B) charge this to 付費
(C) chain this to 鍊 (D) change this to 交換

中譯 我希望可以用我的美國運通卡付費，麻煩了。

解析 charge名詞為費用，動詞為收費、把帳掛在……，此題為動詞。charge為名詞的例句：All drinks served on the airplane are free of charge. 所有在飛機上所供應的飲料都是免費的。動詞例句：The hospitals charge the patients for every aspirin. 醫院的每一片阿斯匹靈都要病人付錢。

47. Guest: I have made a reservation for a suite overnight.
Clerk: Yes, we have your reservation right here. Would you please fill out this registration form and show me your ID?

(A) reimbursement 報銷 (B) registration 註冊
(C) refund 退款 (D) registrar 註冊員

中譯 客人：我已經訂了今晚的套房。
服務生：是的，我們這邊已經有您的訂位紀錄。麻煩您填上這個登記表格並出示您的身分證件。

解析 由fill out form可知為填寫某個表格，通常住宿時都要填寫registration form 登記表格。

48. He's got a new job in Paris. He has been living there for three months.

(A) live 生活 (B) lived (C) living (D) life 生命

中譯 他得到了一份在巴黎的新工作。他已經住在那邊3個月了。

解析 由has been可知要接living。

49. As Tim has no experience at all, I doubt he is qualified for this job.

(A) describe 形容 (B) deliberate 故意的
(C) develop 發展 (D) doubt 懷疑

中譯 因為提姆沒有任何經驗，我懷疑他是否有資格勝任這份工作。

解析 由no experience和qualified for this job對比，可知答案為doubt 懷疑。

50. How would you feel if your best friends from high school mistook you for someone thirty years older at the reunion?

(A) would (B) would have (C) will (D) will have

中譯 如果你高中最好的朋友在同學會上將你誤認為比你老30歲的人，你做何感想？

解析 「would」常被用於可能性小並且與事實相反的情況下，或者是用在「if」引導的條件句中。

51. Taiwan Mountain Tea and Red Sprout Mountain Tea are indigenous subspecies of the island. They were discovered in Taiwan in the 17th century.

(A) inscribed 落款 (B) indigenous 本地的
(C) incredible 難以置信的 (D) industrial 產業

中譯 台灣高山茶和紅芽高山茶是島上土生土長的品種。他們被發現於17世紀的台灣。

解析 indigenous 土生土長的、本地的，例句：Kangaroos are indigenous to Australia. 袋鼠是澳洲本地的動物。

52. A group of young students has taken the initiative through social media to organize a rally against the austerity plans.

(A) invitation 邀請 (B) initiative 倡議
(C) instruction 指令 (D) inscription 題詞

中譯 一群年輕學生透過社群媒體提出倡議以組織策劃來對抗撙節計劃。

解析 此處為名詞，為主動性，若為形容詞，意思則為初步的。

53. Wild Formosa Sika deer became extinct due to extensive hunting of the animal during the Dutch colonization period.

(A) extinct 滅絕 (B) excite 使興奮 (C) exact 準確 (D) explicit 明確

中譯 因為荷蘭殖民時期的濫捕，台灣野鹿已經絕種。

解析 extinct 滅絕的、破滅的，也作熄滅的。

54. Many emerging countries are facing economic uncertainty after the breaking up with former union.

(A) making up 化妝 (B) breaking up 打破

(C) setting up 設定 (D) taking up 佔用

中譯 很多新興國家在瓦解前聯盟後，都面對經濟的不確定性。

解析 關於break的片語如下：break 打破。以下許多片語請牢記：break up 打碎、分手、瓦解；break down 停止運轉；break into 破門而入；break through 突破。

55. Would you please pick up the groceries from the store on your way home?

(A) on (B) in (C) through (D) of

中譯 你可以在回家的路上順道到商店拿雜貨嗎？

解析 on the way home 在回家的路上。

56. Releasing the prisoners for fear of overcrowding might undermine the current rule of law.

(A) understand 瞭解 (B) undermine 破壞

(C) underdevelop 不發達 (D) underfund 缺乏資金

中譯 因為害怕監獄過擠而釋放犯人會破壞現有的法律。

解析 undermine 破壞；undermine law 破壞法律；preserve law 維護法律；within law 合乎法律。

57. Getting around the city in a foreign country can be tricky as many locals don't speak English or welcome foreigners.

(A) around (B) up (C) with (D) along

中譯 在國外的城市隨意走走可能會有問題，因為當地人可能不會說英文或是不歡迎外國人。

解析 get around 隨意走走，亦有說服、避開（規章）之意。

58. Your detailed itinerary is as follows： leaving Taipei on the 14th of June and arriving at Tokyo on the same day at noon.

(A) item 物件 (B) identification 識別

(C) itinerary 行程 (D) inscription 碑文

中譯 你詳細的行程如下：6月14日離開台北，當天中午抵達東京。

解析 itinerary 行程，例句：The manager gave a copy of his itinerary to his secretary and asked her to arrange some business meetings for him during his stay in Sydney. 經理交給他的祕書一份旅行計畫（行程），並且要求她幫他在雪梨安排一些業務會議。101領隊

59. As you listen to the conclusion, you should continue to take notes as completely as possible.

(A) But 但是
(B) Whether 不論
(C) How 如何
(D) As 正當……的時候

中譯 當你聽結論時，你應該要做筆記，做得越完整越好。

解析 這裡的as和when、while一樣，所對應的中文，都是「當……的時候」。
The Internet is creating social isolation as people are spending more time on computers. 當人們花更多的時間在電腦上，網路正造成社會隔離。101領隊

60. Many people engage in risky tasks only for personal satisfaction—they are concerned only with their self-esteem.

(A) concerned 關心
(B) contained 包含
(C) complained 抱怨
(D) completed 完成

中譯 許多人冒險只是為了個人慾望，他們只關心自己的自尊。

解析 concern 關心、擔心，此處為動詞，concern亦可為名詞，例句：She wishes her daughter would show more concern for her. 她希望女兒能夠更關心她。98導遊

61. The term rites of passage was introduced by the Flemish anthropologist Arnold van Gennep in 1090 to describe the ceremonies that make important transitions in people's lives.

(A) cemeteries 公墓
(B) certainties 確定性
(C) celebrities 名人
(D) ceremonies 儀式

中譯 通過儀式這名詞是由法蘭德斯的考古學家阿諾・範・基尼於1090年所提出，用來形容人生進入一個重要階段所舉行的儀式。

解析 ceremony 儀式、典禮，例句：A kimono is a kind of clothing that the Japanese wear during special ceremonies. 和服是一種日本人在特別儀式時穿的衣服。99領隊

62. With the same consumption of fuel, this motorbike goes twice as fast as that one.

(A) as twice fast as
(B) twice fast as
(C) as fast as twice of
(D) twice as fast as

中譯 有著一樣的油耗，這台摩托車跑的是那台摩托車的兩倍快。

解析 倍數 + as...as ……是……的幾倍，例句：This cat is twice tall as that one. 這隻貓是那隻貓的兩倍高。

63. One of the most important parts of these activities is for students to share the highlights of a group discussion with the rest of the class.

(A) lowlights 弱光
(B) brightlights （無此字）
(C) highlights 重點
(D) headlights 大車燈

中譯 這些活動最重要的部分之一就是讓學生和班上分享團體討論的重點。

解析 highlights 重點、最精彩的部分，為最常考的單字之一，例句：The highlight of our trip to Southern Taiwan was A Taste of Tainan where we had a lot of delicious food. 南台灣之旅的亮點就是台南小吃，我們在那吃了很多美食。101導遊

64. Still to come on BBC World News, our Paris correspondent will update us on the Euro crisis.

(A) by
(B) on
(C) through
(D) in

中譯 稍後將回到英國廣播公司世界新聞，我們的巴黎特派員將會持續報導歐洲危機。

解析 在哪個電視頻道的「在」都用on。still to come表示will come soon。

65. Many people have made "getting in shape" one of their new year resolutions.

(A) recreations 娛樂活動
(B) revolutions 革命
(C) revelations 啟示
(D) resolutions 決心

中譯 很多人的新年新願望都希望可以減肥。

解析 resolutions 決心、解答、解決。

66. Upon agreeing to the plan, the organizers are to set out the procedures.

(A) agreeing
(B) agree 同意
(C) agreed
(D) agreeable

中譯 一旦同意計劃，負責人員就開始設定步驟。

解析 upon Ving 一……即……、一……就……。
補充：一……就……、立即……的用法
S + V as soon as S + V （連接詞用法） = S + V upon Ving （介系詞用法）

67. Client： Are there any direct flights to Paris?
Clerk： No, you would have to transfer in Amsterdam.

(A) transfer 轉移 (B) transport 運輸 (C) translate 翻譯 (D) transform 轉變

中譯 客人：有到巴黎的直飛班機嗎？
服務員：沒有，你必須到阿姆斯特丹轉機。

解析 transfer flights 轉機。例句：Passengers transferring to other airlines should report to the information desk on the second floor. 要轉搭其他班機的旅客請到2樓的櫃台報到。101領隊

68. Client: Could you give us a table by the window?
Waiter: Certainly. Follow me, please.

(A) with the window
(B) to the window
(C) through the window
(D) by the window

中譯 客人：可以給我靠窗的位子嗎？
服務員：當然可以。請跟我來。

解析 by the window表示在窗戶旁，用by。

69. Pineapple cakes and local teas are some of the most popular souvenirs of Taiwan.

(A) sights 景點
(B) souvenirs 紀念品
(C) services 服務
(D) surprises 驚喜

中譯 鳳梨酥和當地的茶葉是台灣最受歡迎的紀念品。

解析 souvenirs 紀念品為常考重點單字，例句：The tour guide persuaded him into buying some expensive souvenirs. 這名導遊說服他買昂貴的紀念品。100領隊

70. A complimentary breakfast of coffee and rolls is served in the lobby between 7 and 10 am.

(A) complete 完成
(B) complimentary 免費
(C) continuous 連續
(D) complicate 複雜

中譯 免費的早餐有咖啡和捲餅於早上7點到10點在大廳供應。

解析 complimentary 免費，例句：All drinks served on the airplane are complimentary. 所有在飛機上所供應的飲料都是免費的。98領隊

71. The hotels in the resort areas are fully booked in the summer. It would be very difficult to find any vacancies then.

(A) vacations 假期 (B) visitors 旅客 (C) views 觀點 (D) vacancies 空缺

中譯 度假勝地的飯店在夏天時被訂滿了。那時很難找到空房。

解析 經常考訂房相關議題，如：Reservations for hotel accommodation should be made in advance to make sure rooms are available. 旅館的訂房應提早訂，才能確保有房間。98領隊

72. Having served on the board for more than two decades, the president knows all the details necessary to persuade the new members.

(A) Having served (B) Serving
(C) Services (D) Served

中譯 由於主席在委員會服務超過20年，主席知道說服新委員的所有必要細節。

解析 在副詞子句的主詞與主要子句的主詞相同時（此題為president），我們可將副詞子句中的連接詞及主詞去掉，並將動詞改為Ving（動詞為主動語態，須為「現在分詞」（Ving）；被動語態，須變為「過去分詞」（PP）），即為簡單分詞構句。Having served應被還原為Since he has served on the board for more than two decades（副詞子句）, the president knows all the details necessary to persuade the new members.（主要子句）。

73. On occasions of loss and grief, we should use the most appropriate words to express our condolences.

(A) considerations 考慮 (B) contemplations 思索
(C) condolences 慰問 (D) complacency 自滿

中譯 在悲傷且失去的場合，我們應該使用最適當的字眼來表達我們的慰問。

解析 condolences 哀悼 = 慰問。

74. In contrast to the use of personal pronouns such as he or she, it can be used to refer to an entire idea or concept that is comprehensive and complex.

(A) In order to 為了 (B) In reference to 關於
(C) In contrast to 相較之下 (D) In speaking to 說話

中譯 和人稱代名詞他或她相較之下，它可以被用來代表整個全面且複雜的主意或概念。

解析 因為是對比she / he以及it，故選in contrast to 相較之下。

75. Steve created quite a stir when he introduced that controversial idea at the advisory meeting.

(A) a stock 股票　(B) a stare 瞪眼　(C) a stir 騷動　(D) a star 星星

中譯 當史提芬於建議會議上提出爭議性的概念時，他引起了騷動。

解析 stir可當名詞與動詞，此處為名詞騷亂、騷動。

76. This sleek and sophisticated design might be an eye opener to some of you who don't believe in the aesthetics of products.

(A) an eye opener 大開眼界　(B) a can opener 開罐器

(C) an ear opener　(D) a beer opener 開瓶器

中譯 這個時髦精緻的設計對某些不相信產品美學的人可能會大開眼界。

解析 an eye opener 大開眼界；broaden horizons 開闊眼界。

Mount Rushmore is perhaps one of North America's most distinguished and famous landmarks, right after the Statue of Liberty. It features the busts of four U.S. Presidents, Washington, Jefferson, Lincoln and Roosevelt.

中譯 拉什莫爾山可能是緊接在自由女神像之後，北美最著名的地標。它有著美國總統華盛頓、傑佛遜、林肯以及羅斯福的半身像。

This place has an interesting story. First, a New York lawyer named Charles E. Rushmore visited the Black Hills in 1885. He asked a local the name of the granite mountain before them. Since the peak had no name, the man replied humorously, "Mount Rushmore." The name has never been changed since! In 1923 state historian Doane Robinson suggested carving some giant statues in South Dakota's Black Hills. However, the formations chosen, known as the Needles, were too fragile, and the sculptor, Mr. Gutzon Borglum, decided to use the granite mountain instead. Born in a family of Danish Mormons in Idaho in 1867, Borglum studied art in Paris and enjoyed moderate fame as a sculptor after remodeling the torch for the Statue of Liberty. Borglum chose the presidents "in commemoration of the foundation, preservation and continental expansion of the United States." President Calvin Coolidge dedicated the memorial in 1927.

中譯 這個地方有段有趣的歷史。首些，一名叫查爾斯．拉什莫爾的紐約律師於1885年拜訪黑崗。他站在山丘前問這座花崗岩山的名字為何。既然這座山丘沒有名字，他自己便笑稱他為拉什莫爾山，從此之後名稱就沒改過！1923年，南達科他州的歷史學家多安．羅賓森建議刻些巨大雕像於南達科他州的黑崗上。然而，形式上的選擇有，針狀，但太脆弱了；雕刻家卡曾．波格蘭決定使用花崗岩山來代替。卡曾波．格蘭出生於1867，愛達荷州的丹麥的摩門教家庭；波格蘭於巴黎念藝術，並且享受再重新朔造自由女神像所帶來的雕刻家名聲。波格蘭選擇總統以「紀念美國的建立、守成、擴張。」卡爾文．柯立芝總統於1927年為其舉行典禮。

At this very moment, near this mountain, there is another colossal monument in progress： the Crazy Horse Memorial, to honor this courageous Indian leader. In this way, history is preserved, as big as the heritage is, to be shared with everyone in an attractive way.

中譯 在此非常時期，山的附近，也有其他的巨大的紀念碑正在進行：瘋馬酋長紀念雕像，用來紀念充滿勇氣的印地安領袖。這樣一來，歷史被保存下來，就像這巨大的遺跡一樣，以吸引人的方式與每個人分享。

單字 distinguished 卓越的
bust 半身像
commemoration 慶典
feature 以……為特色（動詞）
granite 花崗石
continental 洲的

77. What is the second paragraph mainly about?

(A) A brief history of Mount Rushmore. 拉什莫爾山的簡史。

(B) The geographical features of Mount Rushmore. 拉什莫爾山的地理特色。

(C) Other attractions near Mount Rushmore. 拉什莫爾山附近其他景點。

(D) A comparison between Mount Rushmore and the Statue of Liberty.
拉什莫爾山和自由女神的比較。

中譯 第二段的主旨為何？

解析 由最後一句In this way, history is preserved, as big as the heritage is, to be shared with everyone in an attractive way.可知。

78. What does "in progress" imply about the Crazy Horse Memorial in the last paragraph?

(A) It is better than the other monuments. 它比其他古蹟好。

(B) It will change to an Indian name. 它會換一個印地安的名字。

(C) It is still under construction. 它尚在建造當中。

(D) It gives more fun to the tourists. 它帶給遊客更多歡樂。

中譯 最後一段關於瘋馬酋長紀念雕像中的「in progress」是什麼意思？

解析 in progress為進行中的意思。

79. Mr. Gutzon Borglum ______.

(A) was an unknown artist before he carved the giant statues
在雕刻聖像之前是個默默無名的藝術家

(B) suggested carving some statues in South Dakota's Black Hills
建議在南達科他州黑崗雕刻雕像

(C) chose the subjects for his sculptures 選擇雕塑作品的主題

(D) was a sculptor from France 法國的雕刻家

中譯 雕刻家卡曾・波格蘭 ______。

解析 由Borglum chose the presidents "in commemoration of the foundation, preservation and continental expansion of the United States."可知。

80. The four U.S. presidents featured in Mount Rushmore do NOT include Coolidge.

(A) Jefferson 傑佛遜
(B) Coolidge 科立芝
(C) Roosevelt 羅斯福
(D) Washington 華盛頓

中譯 拉什莫爾山所刻的4位總統不包含以下哪位？

解析 由It features the busts of four U.S. Presidents, Washington, Jefferson, Lincoln and Roosevelt.可知。

Part 3

歷屆外語導遊 英文試題＋中譯與解析

98 年外語導遊英文試題＋標準答案

★98年專門職業及技術人員普通考試導遊人員、領隊人員考試試題

類科：外語導隊人員（英語）

科目：外國語（英語）

考試時間：1 小時 20 分

※注意：（一）本試題為單一選擇題，請選出一個正確或最適當的答案，複選作答者，該題不予計分。

（二）本科目共80題，每題1.25分，須用2Ｂ鉛筆在試卡上依題號清楚劃記，於本試題上作答者，不予計分。

（三）本試題禁止使用電子計算器。

(　　)1. Being a tour guide is a very important job. In many cases, the tour guide is the traveler's first ______ of our country.

(A) difference　(B) impression　(C) dictation　(D) influence

(　　)2. Parents should teach their children to ______ their money at an early age. Otherwise, when they grow up, they will not know how to manage their money.

(A) inspire　(B) budget　(C) instill　(D) assert

(　　)3. The members of the older ______ do not understand why young people like to go to such noisy places as MTVs and KTVs.

(A) destruction　(B) identification　(C) glorification　(D) generation

(　　)4. Her daughter's ______ to her makes her very sad. She wishes her daughter would show more concern for her.

(A) institution　(B) preference　(C) indifference　(D) addition

(　　)5. The museum charges adults a small ______ , but children can go in for free.

(A) fee　(B) tuition　(C) loan　(D) ticket

(　　)6. The first Taipei Lantern Festival was held in 1990. Due to the event's huge ______, the festival has been expanded every year.

(A) personality　(B) popularity　(C) exports　(D) expenses

(　　)7. It is a custom for some Taiwanese to eat a bowl of long noodles on New Year's Eve. They feel that doing so will ______ their chances of living long lives.

(A) save　(B) waste　(C) delete　(D) increase

(　　)8. When we get to the airport, we first go to the check-in desk where the airline representatives ______ our luggage.

(A) pack　(B) move　(C) weigh　(D) claim

(　　)9. The National Palace Museum opens daily from 9 a.m. to 5 p.m.. However, for Saturdays, the hours are ______ to 8:30 p.m..

(A) closed　(B) moved　(C) lasted　(D) extended

(　　)10. I love getting up at ______. Watching the sunrise is the best way to start the day.

(A) dawn　(B) noon　(C) midnight　(D) night

(　　)11. The museum has a marvelous ______ of art works from all over the world.

(A) distance　(B) mixture　(C) connection　(D) degree

(　　)12. The driver has made a ______ that you throw all your garbage in the bin at the front on your way out.

(A) license　(B) fence　(C) fossil　(D) request

(　　)13. In order to ______ the architecture of the building, you really need to get off the bus and get closer to it.

(A) absorb　(B) exhaust　(C) beware　(D) appreciate

(　　)14. Giant pandas are among the ______ animals in the world. There are only some 1,860 in the world, and two are residing in Taipei Zoo now.

(A) busiest　(B) rarest　(C) smartest　(D) barest

(　　)15. We're going to be driving through farmland for the next twenty minutes or so, so just ______ and relax until we're closer to the city.

(A) sit back　(B) pull over　(C) fall through　(D) wind up

(　　)16. Taking photographs inside the museum is ______. However, you can take pictures of the grounds and the outside of the buildings.

(A) diagnosed　(B) prohibited　(C) recruited　(D) exploded

(　　)17. We don't recommend exchanging your money at the hotel because you won't get a ______ rate.

(A) humble　(B) partial　(C) dull　(D) fair

(　　)18. Baseball is the number one team sport here in Taiwan. The most accomplished player, New York Yankees' Wang Chien-ming, is ______ referred to as a national treasure.

(A) barely　(B) frequently　(C) hardly　(D) thinly

(　　)19. The first sign of autumn is that the temperature has a ______ change between morning and night, coming down from 30 degrees to around 20 degrees Celsius.

(A) small　(B) trivial　(C) significant　(D) mild

(　　)20. Caused by the ______ of our "body clock," jet lag can be a big problem for most travelers in the first few days after they have arrived at their destination.

(A) aspiration　(B) inspiration　(C) disruption　(D) motivation

(　　)21. More and more Taiwanese have come to view cycling not only as a form of recreation but as a way of being environmentally ______.

(A) friendly　(B) guilty　(C) ignorant　(D) bizarre

(　　)22. Hotels are ______ internationally from one to five stars, depending on the services they offer and the prices of rooms.

(A) decorated　(B) elevated　(C) ranked　(D) advised

(　　)23. The travel agent says that we have to pay a deposit of $2,000 in advance in order to ______ the reservation for our hotel room.

(A) cancel　(B) protect　(C) remove　(D) secure

(　　)24. Display this parking ______ on your window to show that you are a hotel guest.

(A) grant　(B) privilege　(C) garage　(D) pass

(　　)25. When I take a flight, I always ask for ______ seat, so it is easier for me to get up and walk around.

(A) a window　(B) a cabinet　(C) a middle　(D) an aisle

( )26. With 49 shops around the island, Eslite Bookstore was ______ by Time magazine in 2004 as a must-see for visitors to Taiwan.

(A) charged (B) selected (C) discredited (D) accused

( )27. Because of its inexpensive yet high-quality medical services, medical tourism is ______ in Taiwan.

(A) declining (B) blowing (C) booming (D) collapsing

( )28. Table manners differ from culture to culture. In Italy, it is considered ______ for a woman to pour her neighbor a glass of wine.

(A) inappropriate (B) inconsistent (C) incomplete (D) infinite

( )29. For a lot of foreigners, the hardest thing about learning Mandarin is its tones. If you use the wrong one, you ______ saying the wrong word.

(A) take off (B) break down (C) end up (D) set out

( )30. "Flight AB123 to Tokyo has been delayed. Please check the monitor for ______ information about your departure time."

(A) further (B) optional (C) fluent (D) inside

( )31. Ku-Kuan, east of Tai-Chung City, with its steep cliffs, has become a ______ for rock climbers here in Taiwan.

(A) victory (B) paradise (C) competition (D) factory

( )32. The $3,600 shopping voucher program was ______ to spur domestic consumption, and for most people, these vouchers are really "gifts from heaven."

(A) inspected (B) complied (C) contained (D) designed

( )33. When Americans shake hands, they do so firmly, not loosely. In the American culture, a weak handshake is a sign of weak ______.

(A) personnel (B) currency (C) character (D) parade

( )34. When Latin Americans and Middle Easterners ______ each other, they tend to stand closer together when talking than Americans do.

(A) ignore (B) greet (C) criticize (D) plow

( )35. In most western countries, it's ______ for you to bring a bottle of wine or a box of candy as a gift when you are invited for dinner at someone's home.

(A) temporary (B) invalid (C) customary (D) stubborn

( )36. It takes both experience and careful ______ in order to become aware of what people in different cultures see as a "normal" or "natural" behavior.

(A) obstruction (B) paradox (C) prevention (D) observation

( )37. During the holidays, most major hotels will be fully booked. An ______ is to try and find a guest house near your desired destination.

(A) exchange (B) alternative (C) equivalent (D) applause

( )38. A total of 3,965 athletes from 81 countries will compete in the 21st Summer Deaflympics to be ______ by Taipei City from September 5 to September15 this year.

(A) fastened (B) hosted (C) offered (D) anchored

( )39. Barcelona is beautiful but it's always ______ with tourists in the summer.

(A) packed (B) steamed (C) frequented (D) patronized

( )40. We were asked by our tour guide on the shuttle bus to ______ seated until we reached our destination.

(A) endure (B) maintain (C) remain (D) adhere

( )41. Travelers should familiarize themselves with their destinations, both to get the most enjoyment out of the visit and to ______ known dangers.

(A) neglect (B) interrupt (C) avoid (D) anticipate

( )42. Some tourists like to make plans and reservations for local tours after they have arrived. They prefer not to have every day of their vacation planned ______.

(A) behind (B) afterward (C) late (D) ahead

( )43. Taiwan has more than 400 museums. The most famous of these is the National Palace Museum, which holds the world's largest ______ of Chinese art treasures.

(A) supply (B) catalogue (C) collection (D) addition

( )44. Starting in 2005, the Taipei City Government began holding its annual international Beef Noodle Soup Festival to ______ the local favorite to visitors.

(A) encourage (B) promote (C) develop (D) abandon

( )45. A website set up by the Taipei Zoo for the two pandas crashed at times as too many Taiwanese tried to catch a ______ of the two cute animals.

(A) glimpse (B) hold (C) glammer (D) photo

( )46. The ______ of the New Seven Wonders of the World campaign were announced on July 7th, 2007, and the Great Wall of China is one of the winners.

(A) sources (B) results (C) revolts (D) shelters

( )47. *One Million Star* is a popular televised singing competition in Taiwan. Every week, the contestants are graded, and the one that performs the worst will be ______.

(A) accepted (B) eliminated (C) conserved (D) congratulated

( )48. The Louvre's Tactitle Gallery, specifically designed for the blind and visually ______, is the only museum in France where visitors can touch the sculptures.

(A) discounted (B) conducted (C) instructed (D) impaired

( )49. The World Games of 2009 will take place in Kaohsiung, Taiwan, from July 16th to July 26th, 2009. The games will ______ sports that are not contested in the Olympic Games.

(A) feature (B) exclaim (C) bloom (D) appeal

( )50. People with a low ______ for spicy food should not try the "Hot and Spicy Chicken Soup" served by this restaurant: it brings tears to my eyes.

(A) prejudice (B) insistence (C) tolerance (D) indulgence

( )51. Formed in 1991 and having toured internationally in Europe and Asia, the Formosa Aboriginal Dance Troupe is a group that ______ Taiwanese folk music.

(A) performs (B) results (C) achieves (D) occurs

( )52. The two friends wanted to spend their vacation quietly, so they chose a ______ village far from busy tourist places.

(A) noisy (B) bustling (C) remote (D) violent

( )53. A store named "Come In and Look Around" sold a ______ of things. There were shoes, toys, food, books, and even cameras.

(A) dose (B) shortage (C) fume (D) variety

( )54. Opened in May 2008, the Children's Gallery of the National Palace Museum is ______ children between the ages of 7 and 12.

(A) aimed at (B) turned to (C) derived from (D) described as

( )55. With the international car exhibition on this week, it may be ______ to find parking spaces.

(A) legal (B) smooth (C) tough (D) practical

( )56. This monument ______ the men and women who died during the war.

(A) presides (B) honors (C) monitors (D) memorizes

( )57. The hostess ______ the guests to the living room where drinks were served.

(A) clutched (B) resided (C) ushered (D) derived

( )58. The doctor thought she could never walk. But now she can not only walk but run as well. It is really a ______.

(A) priority (B) miracle (C) balance (D) gesture

( )59. The strange and frightening house is said to be ______. No one has lived in it for fifty years or more.

(A) sought (B) pounded (C) haunted (D) relieved

( )60. I haven't been to Prague yet. But I am ______ to go there one day.

(A) planning (B) forming (C) predicting (D) framing

( )61. You are ______ to have a beverage on the bus, but please do not eat any food.

(A) attained (B) denied (C) permitted (D) expired

( )62. John: If you have any questions while we're going along, please don't ______ to ask.

Bob: I have a question actually. Where's the best place to have dinner around here?

(A) remain (B) hesitate (C) delay (D) remind

( )63. As a tour guide, you will face new ______ every day. One of the hardest parts of your job may be answering questions.

(A) dooms (B) challenges (C) margins (D) floods

( )64. One difference between the theatre and cinema is that you usually book tickets ______ if you are going to the theatre.

(A) in motion (B) on leave (C) in advance (D) in shape

下列第 65～67 及 68～70 題各為一個題組，請從各相關題號下之(A)、(B)、(C)、(D)四個選項中，選出一個正確或最適當的答案。

"Good evening, ladies and gentlemen. This is the pre-boarding __65__ for flight 67B to Vancouver. We are now inviting those passengers with small children, and any passenger __66__ special assistance, to begin boarding at this time. Please have your boarding pass and identification ready. Regular boarding will begin in __67__ ten minutes. Thank you."

( )65. (A) forecast (B) announcement (C) denouncement (D) definition

( )66. (A) depending (B) digesting (C) requiring (D) including

( )67. (A) approximately (B) separately (C) indirectly (D) indefinitely

Unlike bird watching, which is often most __68__ in the very early morning or just before dusk, butterfly watching is best done between around 10:00 a.m. and 4:00 p.m.. Moreover, butterflies are more __69__ than birds because they are less sensitive to sound. For these reasons, butterfly appreciation is perhaps a more __70__ hobby than bird watching.

( )68. (A) competent (B) extinct (C) successful (D) diplomatic

( )69. (A) approachable (B) edible (C) unbearable (D) affordable

( )70. (A) portable (B) curious (C) available (D) moral

What kind of job description would fit your idea of "the best job in the world"? Tourism Queensland (TQ) lately launched a talent hunt as a part of massive tourism campaign worldwide.

They are looking for a caretaker to live on Hamilton Island of the Great Barrier Reef, whose major responsibility is to be their spokesperson on the island. The contract starts from this July to January next year, and the salary for the six months is AU$150,000, around NT$3.38 million.

"The caretaker is required to do some basic chores, such as cleaning the pool, feeding over 1,500 species of fish, and sending out the mails by plane," said Kimberly Chien,

Marketing Manager of TQ. "The major task is to explore islands in Barrier Reef and keep updating an online journal with photos to share a caretaker's life with the world." The position is open to anyone who is over 18, a good swimmer and communicator.

Applicants are required to make a one-minute video explaining why he or she is the best candidate for the job. Tourism Queensland will organize a group of referees to select 11 candidates, including one from an internet voting which will be held in March. The 11 candidates will then be invited to Hamilton Island for the final interview; only one of them will win the position to do "the best job in the world."

( )71. According to the passage, what is the purpose for the state government of Queensland, Australia, to offer people a job like this?

(A) To make money. (B) To seek foreign aid.
(C) To promote tourism. (D) To provide entertainment.

( )72. Which of the following job requirements is NOT mentioned in the passage?

(A) Over 18 years old (B) A good swimmer.
(C) A good communicator. (D) A native English speaker.

( )73. According to the passage, which of the following is on the job description for this position?

(A) To host a TV talk show.
(B) To meet with international leaders.
(C) To let people know what life is like on the island.
(D) To produce a formal documentary about the island.

( )74. According to the passage, what is the application procedure for this job?

(A) To provide an overseas passport.
(B) To make a self-introduction video.
(C) To call and make a reservation for an interview.
(D) To submit a completed application form by post.

( )75. According to the passage, which of the following is true?

(A) It is a permanent job.
(B) The job begins this coming July.
(C) Twelve candidates will be selected for the final interview.
(D) The winner will be decided by an internet voting.

Loy Krathong is a favorite festival in Thailand because it is very beautiful and romantic. This is the celebration of the full moon in November. In Thai, Loy means "float" and *Krathong* means "small, lotus-shaped boat." This is the day when people float *krathongs*, wash their sins away, and make wishes for the future.

Originally, the *krathong* was made of banana leaves. A *krathong* contains food, flowers, candles and coins. The making of a *krathong* is much more creative these days as many more materials are available. When the day of the festival comes, one lights the candles, makes one's wishes and lets it float away with the current of a river.

Some believe the festival originates from Buddhism. They say the offering of flowers and candles is a tribute of respect to the footprint of the Lord Buddha on the sandy beach of the Narmaha River in India, as well as to the great Serpent and dwellers of the underwater world, after the Lord Buddha's visit to their watery realm. It is possible that this is derived from a Hindu festival that pays tribute to the god Vishnu, who meditates at the center of the ocean.

Today, Thais clean the rivers to prepare for this day. Some people do good deeds—for example, giving money to the poor. There are contests, such as *krathong*-making contests and beauty contests. The most important part of the celebration is making *krathongs* and floating them with candles in the moonlight. Also, couples or lovers believe that if they float *krathongs* together and the boats stay together in the water, their love will last forever.

(　　)76. According to the passage, typical *Loy Krathong* activities include all of the following EXCEPT ______.

(A) giving a gift to the king　　(B) making *krathongs*

(C) holding beauty contests　　(D) giving money to poor people

(　　)77. Which of the following would be the most appropriate title for this passage?

(A) Living in Thailand.　　(B) Thailand Night Life.

(C) Loy *Krathong* Festival.　　(D) How to Make a *Krathong*.

(　　)78. Which of the following is NOT mentioned in the passage about *Loy Krathong*?

(A) The festival probably originated from India.

(B) The origin of the ceremony is to honor Buddha.

(C) It is a day for people to make wishes for the future.

(D) The krathong is offered to pay respect to one's ancestors.

( )79. According to the passage, which of the following is true about krathong-making?

(A) Originally, the *krathong* was made of bamboo leaves.

(B) Fewer materials are available for making *krathongs* now.

(C) The making of *krathongs* is much more creative now.

(D) *Krathongs* come in one size only.

( )80. Altogether, for couples or lovers, *Loy Krathong* is a festival with a ______ touch.

(A) comic (B) religious (C) romantic (D) philosophical

★標準答案

1. (B)	2. (B)	3. (D)	4. (C)	5. (A)
6. (B)	7. (D)	8. (C)	9. (D)	10. (A)
11. (B)	12. (D)	13. (D)	14. (B)	15. (A)
16. (B)	17. (D)	18. (B)	19. (C)	20. (C)
21. (A)	22. (C)	23. (D)	24. (D)	25. (D)
26. (B)	27. (C)	28. (A)	29. (C)	30. (A)
31. (B)	32. (D)	33. (C)	34. (B)	35. (C)
36. (D)	37. (B)	38. (B)	39. (A)	40. (C)
41. (C)	42. (D)	43. (C)	44. (B)	45. (A)
46. (B)	47. (B)	48. (D)	49. (A)	50. (C)
51. (A)	52. (C)	53. (D)	54. (A)	55. (C)
56. (B)	57. (C)	58. (B)	59. (C)	60. (A)
61. (C)	62. (B)	63. (B)	64. (C)	65. (B)
66. (C)	67. (A)	68. (C)	69. (A)	70. (C)
71. (C)	72. (D)	73. (C)	74. (B)	75. (B)
76. (A)	77. (C)	78. (D)	79. (C)	80. (C)

98 年外語導遊英文試題中譯與解析

1. Being a tour guide is a very important job. In many cases, the tour guide is the traveler's first impression of our country.

   (A) difference 不同、差異　(B) impression 印象
   (C) dictation 口述　(D) influence 影響

   中譯 導遊是一份很重要的工作。在許多情形下，導遊是遊客對我們國家的第一印象。

   解析 first impression 第一印象；traveler亦可替換為tourist，皆為遊客之意。

2. Parents should teach their children to budget their money at an early age. Otherwise, when they grow up, they will not know how to manage their money.

   (A) inspire 鼓舞　(B) budget 編列預算
   (C) instill 注入　(D) assert 聲稱

   中譯 父母應該在孩子還小時就教導他們如何控制花費。否則，當小孩長大時，他們將不知如何理財。

   解析 budget在此為動詞；budget亦可作為名詞。我們俗稱的「廉價航空公司」即為budget airline或是low-cost airline。

3. The members of the older generation do not understand why young people like to go to such noisy places as MTVs and KTVs.

   (A) destruction 破壞　(B) identification 識別
   (C) glorification 光榮　(D) generation 世代

   中譯 老一輩（一代）的人不懂為何年輕人喜歡去這麼吵雜的地方，像是MTV或是KTV。

   解析 The older generation 老一輩的人，亦可做the elderly，或是senior citizens。

4. Her daughter's indifference to her makes her very sad. She wishes her daughter would show more concern for her.

   (A) institution 制度、習俗　(B) preference 偏好
   (C) indifference 漠不關心　(D) addition 附加

   中譯 她女兒對她的漠不關心讓她相當難過。她希望女兒能夠更關心她。

解析 indifference 漠不關心，例句：Public indifference to voting is a problem in many democratic countries with low turnouts in elections. 大眾對於投票的漠不關心且投票率低是許多民主國家的問題。98領隊
常混淆單字為difference 不同之處；concern 關心在此為名詞，show concern for someone / something 對某人 / 某事表示關心，但concern也常作為動詞，亦為關心之意。

5. The museum charges adults a small fee, but children can go in for free.

(A) fee 費用 (B) tuition 講授 (C) loan 貸款 (D) ticket 入場

中譯 博物館向成人收取少許入場費，但小孩則可以免費入場。

解析 fee為通稱的費用，例句：You will have to pay extra fees for overweight baggage. 你必須替超重的行李支付額外的費用。98導遊 而tuition fees則是學費，charges為收取費用之意，No charge則為不需收費。

6. The first Taipei Lantern Festival was held in 1990. Due to the event's huge popularity, the festival has been expanded every year.

(A) personality 個性 (B) popularity 歡迎
(C) exports 輸出 (D) expenses 花費

中譯 第一屆的台北燈籠節於1990年舉行。而因為這場活動受到極大的歡迎，慶祝活動一年比一年盛大。

解析 hold an event 舉辦活動，而此處活動名稱當主詞，故為被動式，was held為過去被舉辦之意；has been expanded 每年一直被擴張；popular為形容詞，popularity則為名詞。

7. It is a custom for some Taiwanese to eat a bowl of long noodles on New Year's Eve. They feel that doing so will increase their chances of living long lives.

(A) save 保留 (B) waste 浪費 (C) delete 刪除 (D) increase 增加

中譯 對一些台灣人來說，除夕吃碗長壽麵是項習俗。他們覺得如此一來能夠延年益壽。

解析 此題考生可能會誤選為save 保留，但此處為增加長壽的機率，故為increase the chances。custom為風俗；customary為約定俗成的；customs為海關，此三個單字常出現於考題中。

8. When we get to the airport, we first go to the check-in desk where the airline representatives weigh our luggage.

(A) pack 包 (B) move 移動 (C) weigh 秤重 (D) claim 認領

中譯 當我們到達機場，首先我們到登機櫃台，此處的航空公司工作人員會將我們的行李秤重。

解析 check-in desk 登機櫃台；claim baggage 認領行李，在check-in desk時服務人員會給你baggage claim tag 行李存根，若行李遺失則可到行李領取中心baggage claim office / counter / center請求幫忙。

9. The National Palace Museum opens daily from 9 a.m. to 5 p.m.. However, for Saturdays, the hours are extended to 8:30 p.m..

(A) closed 關門 (B) moved 移動 (C) lasted 持續 (D) extended 延長

中譯 故宮博物院每天從早上9點開放至下午5點。但每個星期六開放時間則延長到晚上8點半。

解析 此處考生可能會誤選為lasted 持續；但extended才能表達延長之意。daily 每天；opening hours 營業 / 開放時間。

10. I love getting up at dawn. Watching the sunrise is the best way to start the day.

(A) dawn 日出 (B) noon 中午 (C) midnight 午夜 (D) night 晚上

中譯 我喜歡在日出時起床。欣賞日出是開啟一天的最佳方式。

解析 若是不認識dawn的意思，從start the day也能猜出為早晨，而非其他選項的時間。

11. The museum has a marvelous mixture of art works from all over the world.

(A) distance 距離 (B) mixture 綜合
(C) connection 連結 (D) degree 程度

中譯 這間博物館有著來自世界各地神奇的藝術作品的組合。

解析 此題可能會誤看為connection，通常館藏會以collection 收藏來表示，但此題的marvelous為神奇、奇妙之意，則可猜出是不同風格的綜合，因此正確答案為mixture。

12. The driver has made a request that you throw all your garbage in the bin at the front on your way out.

(A) license 執照 (B) fence 圍籬 (C) fossil 化石 (D) request 要求

中譯 這位駕駛要求你們下車時將垃圾丟入前方的桶子內。

解析 made a request也可作為ask，都為要求別人之意。

13. In order to appreciate the architecture of the building, you really need to get off the bus and get closer to it.

(A) absorb 吸收　(B) exhaust 精疲力盡
(C) beware 當心　**(D) appreciate 欣賞**

中譯 為了欣賞建築物的結構，你真的需要下車，並靠它近一點。

解析 In order to + V 為了做某事；appreciate 欣賞（動詞）；appreciation of art 藝術鑑賞力。

14. Giant pandas are among the rarest animals in the world. There are only some 1,860 in the world, and two are residing in Taipei Zoo now.

(A) busiest 最忙碌　**(B) rarest 最稀少**
(C) smartest 最聰明　(D) barest 最裸露

中譯 大貓熊是世界上最稀有的動物之一。世界上只有1,860隻，其中2隻現在住在台北市立動物園。

解析 從題目中的There are only some 1,860 in the world可推知，giant pandas是非常rare 稀有的，rarest是rare的最高級。

15. We're going to be driving through farmland for the next twenty minutes or so, so just sit back and relax until we're closer to the city.

(A) sit back 休息　(B) pull over 靠邊停
(C) fall through 失敗　(D) wind up 結束

中譯 接下來的20分鐘我們會駛經農田，所以在接近市區之前，請輕鬆就坐。

解析 sit back直譯為坐好，口語上則為relax 放鬆、rest 休息之意；在飛機上常可聽到廣播「sit back and fasten your seatbelt」，就是請坐好，以及繫緊安全帶之意。

16. Taking photographs inside the museum is prohibited. However, you can take pictures of the grounds and the outside of the buildings.

(A) diagnosed 診斷　**(B) prohibited 禁止**
(C) recruited 招募　(D) exploded 爆炸

中譯 於博物館內攝影是被禁止的。但你可以拍建築物的周圍以及外觀。

解析 考題常見的「禁止」相關字詞有not allow、ban、prohibit，允許則是allow、permit。

17. We don't recommend exchanging your money at the hotel because you won't get fair rate.

(A) humble 謙虛的 (B) partial 部分的 (C) dull 遲鈍的 (D) fair 公平的

中譯 我們不建議你在飯店兌換你的錢，因為你不會有公平的匯率。

解析 exchange money 換匯；exchange rate 匯率；recommend + V-ing 推薦做某事。

18. Baseball is the number one team sport here in Taiwan. The most accomplished player, New York Yankees' Wang Chien-ming, is frequently referred to as a national treasure.

(A) barely 幾乎沒有 (B) frequently 頻繁
(C) hardly 幾乎不 (D) thinly 稀薄

中譯 棒球在台灣是第一名的團體運動。最有成就的球員一紐約洋基隊的王建民，常常被稱為台灣之光。

解析 national treasure 直譯為國家寶藏，也就是我們常說的「台灣之光」。

19. The first sign of autumn is that the temperature has a significant change between morning and night, coming down from 30 degrees to around 20 degrees Celsius.

(A) small 微小的 (B) trivial 不重要的
(C) significant 顯著的 (D) mild 溫和的

中譯 秋天的第一個徵兆為早晚溫差的顯著變化，從攝氏30度降到約20度。

解析 significant 顯著、顯而易見的。

20. Caused by the disruption of our "body clock," jet lag can be a big problem for most travelers in the first few days after they have arrived at their destination.

(A) aspiration 志向 (B) inspiration 靈感
(C) disruption 中斷 (D) motivation 刺激

中譯 由於生理時鐘被打斷，對於大多數的旅旅客來說，在抵達目的地的前幾天時差會是一大問題。

解析 此題易誤選為生理時鐘遭受motivation 刺激，但jet lag 時差則是因為時鐘被打斷disruption而造成。

21. More and more Taiwanese have come to view cycling not only as a form of recreation but as a way of being environmentally friendly.

(A) friendly 友善的　(B) guilty 罪惡的
(C) ignorant 無知的　(D) bizarre 怪異的

中譯 越來越多台灣人不只將單車視為一項休閒活動，也是友善環境的一項作法。

解析 environmentally friendly 環境友善；常見的還有user friendly 使用者友善，通常用來形容軟硬體的操作介面。

22. Hotels are ranked internationally from one to five stars, depending on the services they offer and the prices of rooms.

(A) decorated 裝飾　(B) elevated 提高
(C) ranked 排名、分類　(D) advised 建議

中譯 國際上將飯店分級成一至五星級，是根據飯店所提供的服務以及房價所分類。

解析 be ranked 被排名；be graded 被評分；be categorized 被分類，以上3個都是常見的評分字詞。

23. The travel agent says that we have to pay a deposit of $2,000 in advance in order to secure the reservation for our hotel room.

(A) cancel 取消　(B) protect 保護　(C) remove 除去　(D) secure 確保

中譯 旅行社說我們必須事先支付$2,000訂金，來確保飯店訂房。

解析 常考單字：travel agent 旅行社；deposit 訂金；make reservation 訂位；secure reservation 確保訂位 / 房；re-confirmation 再確認。

24. Display this parking pass on your window to show that you are a hotel guest.

(A) grant 批准　(B) privilege 特權　(C) garage 車庫　(D) pass 准許證

中譯 展示這張停車准許證於窗戶上，來表示你是此飯店的貴賓。

解析 pass（動詞）有許多種不同的意思如「通過、傳遞、消逝、批准」。而此處為名詞，為通行證、入場證之意，例No pass, no passage. 沒有通行證不得通過。

25. When I take a flight, I always ask for an aisle seat, so it is easier for me to get up and walk around.

(A) a window 窗戶 (B) a cabinet 機艙 (C) a middle 中間 (D) an aisle 走道

中譯 當我搭飛機時，我總是要求靠走道的座位，這讓我比較容易起身走動。

解析 當於機場櫃台check-in時，通常可要求劃以下的座位：window seat 靠窗的座位、aisle seat 靠走道的座位、middle seat 中間的座位，由題意easier for me to get up and walk around可得知為走道的座位。

26. With 49 shops around the island, Eslite Bookstore was selected by Time magazine in 2004 as a must-see for visitors to Taiwan.

(A) charged 被指控 (B) selected 被挑選
(C) discredited 被破壞名聲 (D) accused 被控告

中譯 在這座島上有49間營業據點，誠品書店於2004年被時代雜誌選為台灣的必遊景點。

解析 be selected 被選為；selection 選舉。

27. Because of its inexpensive yet high-quality medical services, medical tourism is booming in Taiwan.

(A) declining 衰退 (B) blowing 吹氣
(C) booming 蓬勃發展 (D) collapsing 倒塌

中譯 因為價格不貴又高品質的醫療服務，台灣的醫療觀光正蓬勃發展中。

解析 booming為景氣好的；而另一常見的blooming 開花，常用於興榮、興盛之意，如a blooming business 興隆的事業。

28. Table manners differ from culture to culture. In Italy, it is considered inappropriate for a woman to pour her neighbor a glass of wine.

(A) inappropriate 不適宜的 (B) inconsistent 不一致的
(C) incomplete 不完整的 (D) infinite 無限的

中譯 每個文化的餐桌禮儀都不同。在義大利，女士幫鄰座倒酒就被視為不恰當的行為。

解析 table manners 餐桌禮儀；appropriate / inappropriate 合宜 / 不合宜；polite / impolite 禮貌 / 不禮貌。Watch your table manners 注意你的餐桌禮儀。

29. For a lot of foreigners, the hardest thing about learning Mandarin is its tones. If you use the wrong one, you end up saying the wrong word.

(A) take off 脫下　(B) break down 故障
(C) end up 結束、結果　(D) set out 開始

中譯 對大多數的外國人來說，學習中文最難的就是音調。如果你發錯音調，結果說出來的字也是錯的。

解析 end up 最後變成……，為結束之意。

30. "Flight AB123 to Tokyo has been delayed. Please check the monitor for further information about your departure time."

(A) further 進一步的　(B) optional 選擇性的
(C) fluent 流暢的　(D) inside 內部

中譯 「飛往東京的AB123班機已延誤了。請查看螢幕上關於您的起飛時間的進一步訊息。」

解析 check有各類的用法，考生務必牢記，此處的check為查看、確認，check亦可作為帳單，check-in則為登機手續。

31. Ku-Kuan, east of Tai-Chung City, with its steep cliffs, has become a paradise for rock climbers here in Taiwan.

(A) victory 勝利　(B) paradise 天堂
(C) competition 競爭　(D) factory 工廠

中譯 谷關，位於台中市的東部，有著陡峭的懸崖，已經成為台灣攀岩者的天堂。

解析 paradise 天堂，亦常用heaven替代。兩者雖在口語上經常相互使用，但paradise這個字其實是人間仙境的意思；而heaven則是另一個世界的天堂。常考單字：steep 陡峭的。

32. The $3,600 shopping voucher program was designed to spur domestic consumption, and for most people, these vouchers are really "gifts from heaven."

(A) inspected 檢查　(B) complied 遵從
(C) contained 從容　(D) designed 設計

中譯 每人$3,600的消費券是設計來刺激國內消費的方案，對於大多數的人來說，這些消費券真的是「天上掉下來的禮物」。

解析 spur domestic consumption 刺激消費，亦可作為spur domestic spending。

33. When Americans shake hands, they do so firmly, not loosely. In the American culture, a weak handshake is a sign of weak character.

(A) personnel 人員　(B) currency 貨幣

(C) character 性格　(D) parade 遊行

中譯 當美國人握手時，會握得較為強而有力。在美國人的文化中，蜻蜓點水的握手方式則為軟弱特質的象徵。

解析 此題可能會將personnel 人員誤看成personality 人格；character指的是內在的特質，如價值觀，而personality則指外在的性格，像是內向、外向、活潑等。為一般大眾所接受的是，孩子於早期所得的經驗大部分決定其內在character 價值觀，隨後所得的經驗才決定其外在personality 人格。

34. When Latin Americans and Middle Easterners greet each other, they tend to stand closer together when talking than Americans do.

(A) ignore 忽略　(B) greet 問候　(C) criticize 批評　(D) plow 犁地

中譯 當拉丁美洲人和中東人彼此打招呼時，他們傾向站得比美國人交談時更近。

解析 greet 問候（動詞）；greetings 問候語（名詞）；greeting cards 賀卡。

35. In most western countries, it's customary for you to bring a bottle of wine or a box of candy as a gift when you are invited for dinner at someone's home.

(A) temporary 臨時的　(B) invalid 有病的；無效的

(C) customary 約定俗成的　(D) stubborn 固執的

中譯 在大多數的西方國家中，當你被邀請去其他人家作客時，帶一瓶紅酒或是一盒糖果當作伴手禮是種基本禮儀。

解析 custom為風俗；customary為約定俗成的；customs為海關。此3個單字常出現於考題中。而符合約定俗成的意思，也就是符合基本禮儀。

36. It takes both experience and careful observation in order to become aware of what people in different cultures see as a "normal" or "natural" behavior.

(A) obstruction 阻礙　(B) paradox 似是而非

(C) prevention 防止　(D) observation 觀察

中譯 需要經驗以及細心的觀察，才能夠了解在不同的文化當中哪些行為是「正常」或是「自然」的。

解析 It takes sth. in order to V 「為了某件事，而需要……」為常見句型。

37. During the holidays, most major hotels will be fully booked. An alternative is to try and find a guest house near your desired destination.

(A) exchange 交換　(B) alternative 選擇
(C) equivalent 相當於　(D) applause 鼓掌

中譯 假期期間，大部分的主要飯店都被訂滿了。要有其他的選擇，只得試著找看看接近你目的地附近的民宿。

解析 alternative常見的同義詞有choice、substitute、replacement。

38. A total of 3,965 athletes from 81 countries will compete in the 21st Summer Deaflympics to be hosted by Taipei City from September 5 to September15 this year.

(A) fastened 束緊　(B) hosted 主辦　(C) offered 提供　(D) anchored 停泊

中譯 來自81個國家，總共3,965位運動員將一同競技於第21屆夏季聽障奧林匹克運動會，此次將由台北市政府於今年9月5日至15日主辦。

解析 hold 舉辦活動；host 主辦。Olympics 奧運；Deaflympics 聽障奧運；Paralympic 殘障奧運。

39. Barcelona is beautiful but it's always packed with tourists in the summer.

(A) packed 塞滿　(B) steamed 蒸氣
(C) frequented 時常　(D) patronized 贊助

中譯 巴塞隆納很漂亮但夏天總是塞滿遊客。

解析 此處的packed with tourists也可以用full of tourists來替換。

40. We were asked by our tour guide on the shuttle bus to remain seated until we reached our destination.

(A) endure 忍受　(B) maintain 維護、保持
(C) remain 維持　(D) adhere 黏著

中譯 導遊要求我們在接駁車上維持就坐，直到我們抵達目的地。

解析 此題考生易誤選為maintain 維護，maintain通常是維護、保持某物；故選擇remain 維持。shuttle bus為接駁車、交通車之意，各類的飯店或是景點則會提供shuttle bus service 接駁車的服務。

41. Travelers should familiarize themselves with their destinations, both to get the most enjoyment out of the visit and to avoid known dangers.

(A) neglect 忽略　(B) interrupt 打斷　**(C) avoid 避免**　(D) anticipate 預測

中譯 旅客應熟悉所前往的目的地，可以享受觀光外也能避免已知的危險。

解析 familiarize with 熟悉，常見的用法也有get familiar with。

42. Some tourists like to make plans and reservations for local tours after they have arrived. They prefer not to have every day of their vacation planned ahead.

(A) behind 之後　(B) afterward 之後　(C) late 晚　**(D) ahead 之前**

中譯 有些觀光客喜歡在抵達目的地時，才安排當地的旅遊計畫以及預約相關事宜。他們不喜歡事先安排好假期的每天計畫。

解析 依照題意，觀光客喜歡到當地才安排計畫，因此不喜歡事先安排，故選ahead 之前。而ahead亦可以in advance 事先，來替換。

43. Taiwan has more than 400 museums. The most famous of these is the National Palace Museum, which holds the world's largest collection of Chinese art treasures.

(A) supply 供應　(B) catalogue 目錄
(C) collection 收藏、收集　(D) addition 附加

中譯 台灣有超過400間以上的博物館。其中最有名的為故宮博物院，擁有世界上最多的中華文物收藏品。

解析 hold除了手握，亦可為舉辦，此處則為擁有。

44. Starting in 2005, the Taipei City Government began holding its annual international Beef Noodle Soup Festival to promote the local favorite to visitors.

(A) encourage 鼓勵　**(B) promote 推廣**
(C) develop 發展　(D) abandon 放棄

中譯 台北市政府從2005年開始舉辦年度國際牛肉麵節，藉此推廣本地最愛的美食給觀光客。

解析 此題考生可能會誤選為encourage 鼓勵，或是develop 發展，但promote才有行銷推廣之意。hold 舉辦活動，為常考單字。而此處為開始舉辦，故為began holding。

45. A website set up by the Taipei Zoo for the two pandas crashed at times as too many Taiwanese tried to catch a glimpse of the two cute animals.

(A) glimpse 一瞥　(B) hold 握住　(C) glamour 魅力　(D) photo 照片

中譯 台北市立動物園替兩隻貓熊所架設的網站經常當機，因為太多的台灣人想要一睹兩隻可愛動物的風采。

解析 catch a glimpse of 某物，為捕捉某物的風采。此題考生可能會誤選為photo 照片，但photo為名詞，故應予刪除。

46. The results of the New Seven Wonders of the World campaign were announced on July 7th, 2007, and the Great Wall of China is one of the winners.

(A) sources 來源　(B) results 結果　(C) revolts 反叛　(D) shelters 遮蔽物

中譯 新世界七大奇景的結果於2007年7月7日公布，中國的萬里長城為優勝者之一。

解析 Wonders of the world為世界奇景，announce為宣布。此題為宣布結果，故選result。考生可能誤選為source 來源，但以最後一句的winners即可推論是結果出爐。

47. One Million Star is a popular televised singing competition in Taiwan. Every week, the contestants are graded, and the one that performs the worst will be eliminated.

(A) accepted 接受　(B) eliminated 排除
(C) conserved 保存　(D) congratulated 恭喜

中譯 《超級星光大道》是台灣很受歡迎的電視歌唱比賽節目。每週，參賽者都會被評分，表現最差的就會被淘汰。

解析 比賽相關字詞有contest 比賽；contestants 參賽者；judges 評審；be grades 被評分；be eliminated 被淘汰。

48. The Louvre's Tactitle Gallery, specifically designed for the blind and visually impaired, is the only museum in France where visitors can touch the sculptures.

(A) discounted 打折　(B) conducted 帶領
(C) instructed 指示　(D) impaired 受損

中譯 羅浮宮的觸感畫廊，專門替盲人以及視障所設計，這是法國唯一一個可以讓遊客觸摸雕像的博物館。

解析 visually impaired 視障；physically impaired 殘障。

49. The World Games of 2009 will take place in Kaohsiung, Taiwan, from July 16th to July 26th, 2009. The games will feature sports that are not contested in the Olympic Games.

(A) feature 特色　(B) exclaim 呼喊　(C) bloom 開花　(D) appeal 呼籲

中譯 2009年的世界運動大會將於7月16至26日在台灣的高雄舉辦。此運動大會是以奧運未舉辦的比賽項目為特色。

解析 feature 特色（名詞）、以……為特色（動詞），此處為動詞。某事件take place = be held 發生、被舉辦，若是主辦單位為主詞，則可換成Kaohsiung will host the World Games of 2009。

50. People with a low tolerance for spicy food should not try the "Hot and Spicy Chicken Soup" served by this restaurant： it brings tears to my eyes.

(A) prejudice 偏見　(B) insistence 堅持
(C) tolerance 容忍　(D) indulgence 放縱

中譯 對於辛辣食物容忍度低的人不應該試此餐廳供應的麻辣雞湯，它讓我眼淚直流。

解析 tolerance 容忍度為名詞，tolerable則為可容忍的（形容詞）。

51. Formed in 1991 and having toured internationally in Europe and Asia, the Formosa Aboriginal Dance Troupe is a group that performs Taiwanese folk music.

(A) performs 表演　(B) results 結果　(C) achieves 實現　(D) occurs 發生

中譯 成立於1991年，也曾於歐洲以及亞洲國際巡迴表演過，福爾摩沙原住民舞蹈團是演奏台灣民俗音樂的團體。

解析 form當動詞時為成立，當名詞時為表格，常見fill out the form 填妥表格，此處的perform亦可替換為play。

52. The two friends wanted to spend their vacation quietly, so they chose a remote village far from busy tourist places.

(A) noisy 吵雜　(B) bustling 繁忙　(C) remote 遙遠　(D) violent 激烈

中譯 兩位朋友想要安靜地度假，所以他們選擇了遠離繁忙觀光區的偏僻鄉村。

解析 remote為遙遠、遠端之意，因此遙控器為remote control。

53. A store named "Come In and Look Around" sold a variety of things. There were shoes, toys, food, books, and even cameras.

(A) dose 劑量　(B) shortage 短缺　(C) fume 氣味　(D) variety 變化

中譯 一間名為「進來看看」的商店賣各式各樣的東西。有鞋子、玩具、食物、書本，甚至相機。

解析 由題意可知商店賣各式各樣的物品，因此選variety 變化，vary亦可當成動詞，意為變化。

54. Opened in May 2008, the Children's Gallery of the National Palace Museum is aimed at children between the ages of 7 and 12.

(A) aimed at 為目標　(B) turned to 轉至
(C) derived from 源自　(D) described as 形容為

中譯 2008年5月開幕，故宮博物院的兒童畫廊是以7-12歲的兒童為對象。

解析 此處的aimed at也可替換成designed for children between the ages of 7 and 12替7-12歲的兒童所設計。

55. With the international car exhibition on this week, it may be tough to find parking spaces.

(A) legal 合法　(B) smooth 平順　(C) tough 困難　(D) practical 實際

中譯 因為本週有國際車展，可能會很難找到停車位。

解析 正因為有展覽，所以停車會很tough 困難，而非smooth 順利。

56. This monument honors the men and women who died during the war.

(A) presides 主持　(B) honors 榮耀
(C) monitors 監控　(D) memorizes 熟記

中譯 此紀念碑是為了榮耀在戰爭期間陣亡的男男女女。

解析 honor此處為動詞，不論為名詞、動詞，都是榮耀之意。monument為紀念碑，memorial hall為紀念堂，如Chiang Kai-shek Memorial Hall 中正紀念堂。

57. The hostess ushered the guests to the living room where drinks were served.

(A) clutched 抓住　(B) resided 居住　(C) ushered 引導　(D) derived 源自

中譯 女主人引導來賓到飲料已備妥的客廳。

解析 hostess為女主人，host為男主人；此處的usher 引導，也可替換成lead，亦為引導之意。

58. The doctor thought she could never walk. But now she can not only walk but run as well. It is really a miracle.

(A) priority 優先 (B) miracle 奇蹟 (C) balance 平衡 (D) gesture 姿態

中譯 醫生原本以為她不可能再走路了。但是她現在不但可以走，還能跑。這真的是奇蹟。

解析 not only, but (also)為「不但……，且……」的常見句型。

59. The strange and frightening house is said to be haunted. No one has lived in it for fifty years or more.

(A) sought 找尋 (B) pounded 搗毀 (C) haunted 鬧鬼 (D) relieved 放心

中譯 奇怪且恐怖的房子據說鬧鬼。已有50多年沒有人居住過了。

解析 haunt 鬼魂出沒；haunted 鬧鬼的。

60. I haven't been to Prague yet. But I am planning to go there one day.

(A) planning 計劃 (B) forming 組成 (C) predicting 預測 (D) framing 結構

中譯 我至今尚未去過布拉格。但我打算有一天要去。

解析 請特別小心不要混淆plan 計劃和predict 預測。

61. You are permitted to have a beverage on the bus, but please do not eat any food.

(A) attained 獲得 (B) denied 否認 (C) permitted 允許 (D) expired 滿期

中譯 你獲准於公車上喝飲料，但請不要吃任何東西。

解析 permitted亦可換成allowed。

62. John: If you have any questions while we're going along, please don't hesitate to ask.

Bob: I have a question actually. Where's the best place to have dinner around here?

(A) remain 剩下 (B) hesitate 猶豫 (C) delay 延遲 (D) remind 提醒

中譯 約翰：當我們進行時如果你有任何問題，請不要猶豫問我。
鮑伯：其實我有問題。這附近哪邊吃晚餐最棒？

解析 此處可能會誤選為delay 延遲，但此處為不要猶豫，故選hesitate。

63. As a tour guide, you will face new challenges every day. One of the hardest parts of your job may be answering questions.

(A) dooms 厄運　**(B) challenges 挑戰**
(C) margins 邊緣　(D) floods 水災

中譯 身為導遊，你每天會面臨到新的挑戰。工作上最困難的部分之一也許就是回答問題。

解析 此處的challenge為名詞，而challenge亦可為動詞，也為挑戰之意。

64. One difference between the theatre and cinema is that you usually book tickets in advance if you are going to the theatre.

(A) in motion 移動　(B) on leave 請假
(C) in advance 事先　(D) in shape 狀況良好

中譯 劇院和電影院其中之一的差別為：如果你要去劇院，通常需要事先訂票。

解析 theater＝theatre（英式用法）；cinema也為movie theater，都為電影院的意思。

"Good evening, ladies and gentlemen. This is the pre-boarding announcement for flight 67B to Vancouver. We are now inviting those passengers with small children, and any passenger requiring special assistance, to begin boarding at this time. Please have your boarding pass and identification ready. Regular boarding will begin in approximately ten minutes. Thank you."

中譯 「大家晚安，各位先生女士們。這是飛往溫哥華的67B班機的登機前廣播。我們現在先請帶小孩、或是需要特別協助的旅客，準備開始登機。請準備好您的登機證以及身分證件。一般旅客約將於10分鐘內開始登機。謝謝。」

65. (A) forecast 預報　**(B) announcement 宣布**
(C) denouncement 譴責　(D) definition 定義

解析 在機場候機的旅客，通常需要注意Pay attention to pre-boarding announcement。若某班機已開始登機，則會廣播flight 67B is boarding，意為已在登機中，請旅客盡速前往某號登機門（Gate No. X）。

66. (A) depending 根據　(B) digesting 消化
(C) requiring 需要　(D) including 包含

解析 航空公司所提供的special assistance，通常的服務對象為Passengers with visual impairment / hearing impairment / wheelchairs 視障 / 聽障 / 行動不便的旅客。此題中的require亦可替換為need。

67. (A) approximately 大約　(B) separately 分開
(C) indirectly 間接　(D) indefinitely 無限期

Unlike bird watching, which is often most successful in the very early morning or just before dusk, butterfly watching is best done between around 10:00 a.m. and 4:00 p.m.. Moreover, butterflies are more approachable than birds because they are less sensitive to sound. For these reasons, butterfly appreciation is perhaps a more available hobby than bird watching.

中譯 不同於賞鳥的時間通常最好為一大清早或是黃昏前，最好的賞蝶時間則是從早上10點到下午4點。此外，蝶類比鳥類更容易接近，因為他們對於聲音較不敏感。基於這些理由，賞蝶也許比賞鳥為更容易養成的習慣。

單字 before dusk 黃昏前
appreciation 欣賞

68. (A) competent 能幹的　(B) extinct 絕種的
(C) successful 成功的　(D) diplomatic 外交的

解析 賞鳥的最佳時間，也就是最容易看到鳥群的時間，故選successful。

69. (A) approachable 接近的　(B) edible 可食的
(C) unbearable 不可忍受的　(D) affordable 可負擔的

解析 由題意可知less sensitive to sound 對於聲音較不敏感，因此比較好接近。

70. (A) portable 可攜帶的　(B) curious 好奇的
(C) available 可行的　(D) moral 道德的

解析 正因蝶類對聲音比較不敏感，故更容易賞蝶，更為available 可行。

What kind of job description would fit your idea of "the best job in the world"? Tourism Queensland (TQ) lately launched a talent hunt as a part of massive tourism campaign worldwide.

中譯 什麼樣的工作是你心目中「世界上最棒的工作」？昆士蘭旅遊局最近發起了一項大型的全世界旅遊徵才活動。

They are looking for a caretaker to live on Hamilton Island of the Great Barrier Reef, whose major responsibility is to be their spokesperson on the island. The contract starts from this July to January next year, and the salary for the six months is AU$150,000, around NT$3.38million.

中譯 他們尋找一位臨時島主，要住在大堡礁的漢彌敦島上，主要責任為擔任該島的代言人。合約始於今年7月到明年1月，這半年的薪水為15萬澳幣，相當於新台幣338萬元。

單字 spokesperson 代言人
contract 合約

"The caretaker is required to do some basic chores, such as cleaning the pool, feeding over 1,500 species of fish, and sending out the mails by plane," said Kimberly Chien, Marketing Manager of TQ. "The major task is to explore islands in Barrier Reef and keep updating an online journal with photos to share a caretaker's life with the world." The position is open to anyone who is over 18, a good swimmer and communicator.

中譯 「島主必須做一些例行工作，好比清理游泳池、餵1,500種以上的魚、利用飛機寄信等等」，昆士蘭旅遊局的行銷經理金柏莉．簡表示，「主要的工作是要探索大堡礁的島嶼，並用照片更新線上日誌，和全世界分享島主的日常生活」。只要年齡18歲以上、擅長游泳、善於溝通的人都可應徵這個工作。

單字 chores 家庭雜務
task 工作

Applicants are required to make a one-minute video explaining why he or she is the best candidate for the job. Tourism Queensland will organize a group of referees to select 11 candidates, including one from an internet voting which will be held in March. The 11 candidates will then be invited to Hamilton Island for the final interview; only one of them will win the position to do "the best job in the world."

中譯 應徵者必須拍攝一分鐘的影片，解釋為什麼自己是最合適的人選。昆士蘭旅遊局會成立裁判團，先選出11名參賽者，包含3月份從網路上票選的一位。11位參賽者將被邀請到漢彌敦島上參加複賽，只有其中的一位會贏得「這世界上最棒的工作」。

單字 candidate 候選人

71. According to the passage, what is the purpose for the state government of Queensland, Australia, to offer people a job like this?

(A) To make money. 為了賺錢。

(B) To seek foreign aid. 為了尋求國外協助。

(C) To promote tourism. 為了推廣旅遊。

(D) To provide entertainment. 為了提供娛樂。

中譯 根據本文，澳洲昆士蘭政府為何要提供像這樣的工作機會？

解析 "The major task is to explore islands in Barrier Reef and keep updating an online journal with photos to share a caretaker's life with the world." 由此段得知主要是為了推廣旅遊。

72. Which of the following job requirements is NOT mentioned in the passage?

(A) Over 18 years old. 超過18歲。

(B) A good swimmer. 游泳好手。

(C) A good communicator. 好的溝通者。

(D) A native English speaker. 英語母語人士。

中譯 以下哪個工作的必要條件未於本文中提及?？

解析 The position is open to anyone who is over 18, a good swimmer and communicator. 此段文章中不含A native English speaker。

73. According to the passage, which of the following is on the job description for this position?

(A) To host a TV talk show. 主持電視節目。

(B) To meet with international leaders. 與各國領袖見面。

(C) To let people know what life is like on the island. 讓大家知道島上的生活情形。

(D) To produce a formal documentary about the island. 拍攝島上的紀錄片。

中譯 根據本文，以下哪一項工作描述符合此職位？

解析 由此段"The major task is to explore islands in Barrier Reef and keep updating an online journal with photos to share a caretaker's life with the world."，可得知答案。

74. According to the passage, what is the application procedure for this job?

(A) To provide an overseas passport. 提供外國護照。

(B) To make a self-introduction video. 製作自我介紹的影片。

(C) To call and make a reservation for an interview. 打電話預約面試。

(D) To submit a completed application form by post. 郵寄出完整的申請表格。

中譯 根據本文，哪一項是此工作的申請流程？

解析 由此段Applicants are required to make a one-minute video explaining why he or she is the best candidate for the job.，可得知答案。

75. According to the passage, which of the following is true?

(A) It is a permanent job. 這是一份永久的工作。

(B) The job begins this coming July. 工作即將從7月開始。

(C) Twelve candidates will be selected for the final interview.
共有12位候選人可能晉級到決賽。

(D) The winner will be decided by an internet voting. 由網路投票來選出優勝者。

中譯 根據本文，以下哪項屬實？

解析 由此段The contract starts from this July to January next year，可得知答案。

Loy Krathong is a favorite festival in Thailand because it is very beautiful and romantic. This is the celebration of the full moon in November. In Thai, Loy means "float" and Krathong means "small, lotus-shaped boat." This is the day when people float krathongs, wash their sins away, and make wishes for the future.

中譯 Loy Krathong是泰國最受歡迎的節慶，因為這節慶既美麗又浪漫。這是11月月圓時的慶祝節日。Loy是泰文「漂浮」的意思，Krathong則是「蓮花形狀的小船」。這是個人們放蓮花小船的日子，藉此洗淨過錯，也向未來許願。

單字 sins （違反禮節、習俗的）過錯

Originally, the krathong was made of banana leaves. A krathong contains food, flowers, candles and coins. The making of a krathong is much more creative these days as many more materials are available. When the day of the festival comes, one lights the candles, makes one's wishes and lets it float away with the current of a river.

中譯 起先，krathong是由香蕉葉所製成。krathong放上食物、鮮花、蠟燭以及銅板。目前製作krathong的材料越來越創新，因為越來越多材料更易取得。當Loy Krathong到來時，人們會點起蠟燭，許願，以及讓小船隨波漂流。

Some believe the festival originates from Buddhism. They say the offering of flowers and candles is a tribute of respect to the footprint of the Lord Buddha on the sandy beach of the Narmaha River in India, as well as to the great Serpent and dwellers of the underwater world, after the Lord Buddha's visit to their watery realm. It is possible that this is derived from a Hindu festival that pays tribute to the god Vishnu, who meditates at the center of the ocean.

中譯 有人相信這樣的節慶源自佛教。他們表示，提供獻花以及蠟燭對於佛祖走過的印度那瑪哈河岸邊的海灘足跡是種尊敬，同是也對水中世界的巨蛇以及居民的尊敬，特別是

因為佛祖走過這些水域。這也可能源自印度將貢品獻給在海洋中打坐的神明Vishnu的節慶。

單字 tribute 貢品
derived 起源
dwellers 居住者
meditate 沈思

Today, Thais clean the rivers to prepare for this day. Some people do good deeds—for example, giving money to the poor. There are contests, such as krathong-making contests and beauty contests. The most important part of the celebration is making krathongs and floating them with candles in the moonlight. Also, couples or lovers believe that if they float krathongs together and the boats stay together in the water, their love will last forever.

中譯 時至今日，泰國人清理河流來準備這節慶。有人做善事，像是救濟窮人。也有做krathong以及選美比賽。節慶最重要的部分還是製作krathongs，以及於月光中點蠟燭，讓船隨河漂流。同時，夫妻以及情侶相信如果他們一起將krathongs隨河漂流，船還是在一起漂流的話，他們的愛情就會永恆。

單字 floating 漂浮

76. According to the passage, typical Loy Krathong activities include all of the following EXCEPT ______.

(A) giving a gift to the king 給國王禮物

(B) making krathongs 製作krathongs

(C) holding beauty contests 舉辦選美比賽

(D) giving money to poor people 救濟窮人

中譯 根據本文，傳統的Loy Krathong活動不包含下列哪一項？

解析 由此段Some people do good deeds—for example, giving money to the poor. There are contests, such as krathong-making contests and beauty contests.，可得知答案。

77. Which of the following would be the most appropriate title for this passage?

(A) Living in Thailand. 住在泰國。

(B) Thailand Night Life. 泰國的夜生活。

(C) Loy Krathong Festival. Loy Krathong 節慶。

(D) How to Make a Krathong. 如何製作Krathong。

中譯 以下哪一項最適合當成本文標題？

78. Which of the following is NOT mentioned in the passage about Loy Krathong?

(A) The festival probably originated from India. 節慶可能來自於印度。

(B) The origin of the ceremony is to honor Buddha. 起源來自於對於佛祖的尊敬。

(C) It is a day for people to make wishes for the future. 是人們對於未來許願的一天。

(D) The krathong is offered to pay respect to one's ancestors. krathong是用來表示對祖先的尊敬。

中譯 以下哪一項關於Loy Krathong的事未於本文中提及？

解析 由此段Some believe the festival originates from Buddhism. They say the offering of flowers and candles is a tribute of respect to the footprint of the Lord Buddha on the sandy beach of the Narmaha River in India, as well as to the great Serpent and dwellers of the underwater world, after the Lord Buddha's visit to their watery realm. It is possible that this is derived from a Hindu festival that pays tribute to the god Vishnu, who meditates at the center of the ocean.，可得知答案。

79. According to the passage, which of the following is true about krathong-making?

(A) Originally, the krathong was made of bamboo leaves. 原本krathong是由竹葉製成。

(B) Fewer materials are available for making krathongs now. 現在製作krathong的材料更少了。

(C) The making of krathongs is much more creative now. 製作krathong的方法現在更有創意了。

(D) Krathongs come in one size only. Krathongs只有一種尺寸。

中譯 根據本文，以下哪一項對於製作krathong的敘述為真？

解析 由此段Originally, the krathong was made of banana leaves. A krathong contains food, flowers, candles and coins. The making of a krathong is much more creative these days as many more materials are available. When the day of the festival comes, one lights the candles, makes one's wishes and lets it float away with the current of a river.，可得知答案。

80. Altogether, for couples or lovers, Loy Krathong is a festival with a ______ touch.

(A) comic 漫畫　　(B) religious 宗教

(C) romantic 浪漫　　(D) philosophical 哲學

中譯 總的來說，對於夫妻以及情侶，Loy Krathong是個充滿怎樣氛圍的節日？

解析 由此段Also, couples or lovers believe that if they float krathongs together and the boats stay together in the water, their love will last forever.，可得知答案。

99 年外語導遊英文試題＋標準答案

★99年專門職業及技術人員普通考試導遊人員、領隊人員考試試題

類科：外語導遊人員（英語）

科 目：外國語（英語）

考試時間：1 小時 20 分

※注意：（一）本試題為單一選擇題，請選出一個正確或最適當的答案，複選作答者，該題不予計分。

（二）本科目共80題，每題1.25分，須用2Ｂ鉛筆在試卡上依題號清楚劃記，於本試題上作答者，不予計分。

（三）本試題禁止使用電子計算器。

(　　)1. Individuals within a group often ______ their own values in favor of those held by the group.

(A) prefer　(B) emphasize　(C) cherish　(D) compromise

(　　)2. Living near the airport, I am very much ______ by the noise of airplanes. I can not sleep well and often feel uneasy.

(A) marked　(B) bothered　(C) expected　(D) confused

(　　)3. Claire loves to buy ______ foods: vegetables and herbs from China, spices from India, olives from Greece, and cheeses from France.

(A) sea　(B) stingy　(C) tranquil　(D) exotic

(　　)4. Falling asleep in class and being drowsy at work were just two examples of his ______.

(A) energy　(B) fatigue　(C) conspiracy　(D) belief

(　　)5. Elizabeth Anker is a very ______ artist for she is not only an excellent pianist but also a great singer, painter, and poet.

(A) ethical　(B) feeble　(C) versatile　(D) classical

(　　)6. As a result of the accident, Shirley was ______ for three weeks before gradually recovered.

(A) unconscious　(B) prehistoric　(C) gorgeous　(D) fortunate

( )7. The cake was ______, and tasted bad.

(A) stale (B) nutritious (C) familiar (D) indispensable

( )8. To ______ money, buy just what you need and refrain from buying unnecessary stuff.

(A) invent (B) discard (C) save (D) exhaust

( )9. With a ______ smile, Robert showed how happy he was when he won the swimming contest yesterday.

(A) fertile (B) historic (C) pollutant (D) complacent

( )10. Susan Manning's trip to Buffalo was a/an ______ one. She took her time.

(A) hasty (B) urgent (C) rapid (D) leisurely

( )11. Professor Nelson, who is rather strange, displays some ______ behavior from time to time.

(A) ordinary (B) eccentric (C) comprehensive (D) logical

( )12. Some families have children in chronic health conditions. At times, the pressure may be ______ to every individual in the family and the challenges can affect the quality of family life.

(A) encouraging (B) convincing (C) outgoing (D) overwhelming

( )13. Christopher Reeve was ______ from the neck down and confined to a wheelchair, after the tragic accident.

(A) paralyzed (B) articulated (C) classified (D) enlightened

( )14. Many young Spaniards continued to come to the island, hoping to find gold quickly and become rich ______.

(A) backward (B) hardly (C) overnight (D) nowhere

( )15. Since our economy has been improving recently, I hope that my boss will give me a big ______ this year.

(A) conquest (B) consumption (C) rise (D) raise

( )16. John Keene's opinion has no ______ on her daughter's decision to become a professional artist. She always gets her own way.

(A) annoyance (B) revenge (C) record (D) effect

( )17. The book is about a very ______ boy who always breaks things.

(A) clumsy (B) appropriate (C) evident (D) fragrant

( )18. If something is ______, it is dull and depressing.

(A) measurable (B) dreary (C) graphic (D) hysterical

( )19. Katherine was reminded to return the book by next Monday, which she ______ from the school library three months ago.

(A) captured (B) prevented (C) borrowed (D) arrested

( )20. Sarah, who often attends symphony concerts, has a great ______ for music.

(A) anxiety (B) disregard (C) appreciation (D) headline

( )21. For some people, the fear of visiting a ______ outweighs the pain of a toothache.

(A) barbarian (B) diplomat (C) dentist (D) magician

( )22. Dr. Morales has confirmed a major ______ in the world of rock art: an ancient rock painting at a burial site from the Inca site of Machu Picchu in Peru.

(A) epidemic (B) discovery (C) flaw (D) galaxy

( )23. Some soils are extremely rich in ______ and nutrients such as iron and copper.

(A) minerals (B) mermaids (C) miniatures (D) manuscripts

( )24. Scientists have found a ______ for the rare contagious disease, and some patients now have the hope of recovery.

(A) replacement (B) penalty (C) cure (D) passion

( )25. Elaine Hadley has many ______, such as horse-back riding, dancing, and playing with animals.

(A) devices (B) sensations (C) temperaments (D) hobbies

( )26. People who have a great sense of ______ are often very popular, because they are usually intelligent, open-minded, and witty.

(A) frustration (B) humor (C) betrayal (D) inferiority

( )27. A ______ person is usually welcomed by everyone, because he never irritates people.

(A) selfish (B) naughty (C) pessimistic (D) humble

(　　)28. Petroleum production can contribute to air and water pollution; besides, drilling for ______ may disturb the fragile ecosystems.

(A) oil　　(B) light　　(C) air　　(D) truth

(　　)29. Kenneth is ______ to confide in others, because he fears that the information he reveals will be used maliciously against him.

(A) happy　　(B) thankful　　(C) reluctant　　(D) voluntary

(　　)30. ______ people are sensitive to others' wants and feelings.

(A) Blunt　　(B) Considerate　　(C) Arrogant　　(D) Dominant

(　　)31. Ms. Mead has become a media celebrity and an iconic figure who ______ a range of different ideas, values, and beliefs to a broad spectrum of the American public.

(A) alienated　　(B) buried　　(C) calculated　　(D) represented

(　　)32. For centuries, artists, historians, and tourists have been ______ by Mona Lisa's enigmatic smile.

(A) ignored　　(B) characterized　　(C) fascinated　　(D) embraced

(　　)33. ______ are small, often brightly colored, thin rubber bags that rise and float when they are filled with light gas.

(A) Balloons　　(B) Flags　　(C) Peacocks　　(D) Rainbows

(　　)34. As children grow and mature, they will leave behind ______ pursuits, and no longer be so selfish and undisciplined as they used to be.

(A) masculine　　(B) childish　　(C) philosophical　　(D) honorable

(　　)35. Dogs usually want to ______ and play with cats, whereas cats are usually afraid and defensive.

(A) chase　　(B) abandon　　(C) denounce　　(D) shun

(　　)36. Wind and sunshine are very important ______ for Penghu, attracting a large number of tourists each year.

(A) assets　　(B) quantities　　(C) propositions　　(D) materials

(　　)37. Fireworks and firecrackers are often used in Chinese communities to ______ greeting good fortunes and scaring away evils.

(A) sign　　(B) symbolize　　(C) identify　　(D) underline

( )38. Watch out for your own safety! Don't be a target of ______ while you are traveling.

(A) audience (B) thieves (C) heroes (D) clients

( )39. Scarlet fever is a/an ______ disease, which is transferable from one person to another.

(A) different (B) contagious (C) important (D) special

( )40. A ______ is a necessary document for the passenger to get on the airplane.

(A) boarding pass (B) passport
(C) identification card (D) visa

( )41. Besides participating in local cultural activities, people who desire to explore the ecology of Kenting can ______ plenty of wildlife and plants.

(A) observe (B) pick up (C) object (D) plan

( )42. Flight attendants help passengers find their seats and ______ their carry-on luggage safely in the overhead compartments.

(A) stow (B) strew (C) straighten (D) stifle

( )43. We finished the trip and the cost was well below ______. We had planned to spend three thousand dollars, but we ended up spending only half of that.

(A) reference (B) reminder (C) budget (D) permission

( )44. If there is any suspicion of contagious diseases or agricultural pests, the customs agents will impose a ______.

(A) declaration (B) duty (C) quarantine (D) predicament

( )45. When people travel to popular destinations during peak seasons, it is necessary to reserve ______ before the trip.

(A) generation (B) accommodations
(C) identification (D) confirmation

( )46. If you want to find the cheapest airplane ticket, ______ can usually be found through the Internet.

(A) bargains (B) destinations (C) reservations (D) itinerary

( )47. Tom's team won the game at the last minute, and the coach was very proud of the ______ of his players.

(A) performance (B) modulation (C) perception (D) application

( )48. Don't press the alarm bell unless in absolute ______.

(A) emergence (B) emergency (C) service (D) status

( )49. Nowadays, most information has become ______ through the use of computers.

(A) ordinal (B) fixed (C) available (D) perfect

( )50. If you have any problems or questions about our new products, you are welcome to use our ______-free service line.

(A) tax (B) toll (C) money (D) fee

( )51. The amusement park is a famous tourist ______ in Japan. Tourists of all ages love to go there.

(A) attraction (B) fascination (C) information (D) attention

( )52. Since the president of the company is absent, the general manager will ______ over the meeting.

(A) preview (B) preside (C) pledge (D) persuade

( )53. Even though you have ______ your flight with the airline, you must still be present at the check-in desk on time.

(A) informed (B) confirmed (C) required (D) given

( )54. "Don't count your chickens before they are hatched" is a ______ that reminds people not to be too optimistic before their plans succeed.

(A) story (B) proverb (C) history (D) pursuit

( )55. To increase sales of products, many companies spend huge sums of money on ______ campaigns.

(A) promotion (B) automatic (C) stable (D) solitary

( )56. Please examine your luggage carefully before leaving. At the security counter, every item in the luggage has to go through thorough ______.

(A) relation (B) invention (C) inspection (D) observation

( )57. When you are ready to get off an airplane, you will be told not to forget your personal ______.

(A) utilities (B) belongings (C) commodities (D) works

( )58. A: How can I get to the National Museum from here?
B: ______
(A) You mustn't go with your friends. (B) It is too far from here.
(C) You can take that bus. (D) I can not go with you.

( )59. Quick and friendly service at the front desk is important to the ______ of tourists.
(A) satisfaction (B) procession (C) procedure (D) prohibition

( )60. For tours in peak seasons, travel agents sometimes have to make reservations a year or more ______.
(A) above all (B) beyond all (C) in advance (D) afterwards

( )61. The flight is scheduled to ______ at eleven o'clock tomorrow. You will have to get to the airport two hours before the takeoff.
(A) land (B) depart (C) cancel (D) examine

( )62. Please see to it that all necessary ______ have been completed. Never risk your life simply for convenience's sake.
(A) possibilities (B) reservations (C) procedures (D) alternatives

( )63. You don't have to worry about where to stay tonight. My friend in downtown area will find you a night's ______.
(A) station (B) lodging (C) housekeeper (D) seat

( )64. International ______ allows countries to buy what they need from other countries.
(A) trade (B) field (C) port (D) trip

( )65. Visitors to New York often talk about the feeling of ______ there. It is a city full of energy and hope.
(A) culture (B) chat (C) excitement (D) reason

( )66. In many Western cultures, it is rude to ask about a person's age, weight, or salary. However, these topics may not be as ______ in East Asia.
(A) economical (B) polluted (C) governed (D) sensitive

( )67. I enjoy looking at ______ in museums. However, I am too poor to collect any myself.
(A) websites (B) art pieces (C) crime (D) magazines

( )68. Cathy is an outgoing and successful salesperson, but her ______ is in web design.

(A) neighborhood (B) background (C) section (D) system

( )69. Exploring the culture and history of Africa sounds like a great ______. It will be a lot of fun!

(A) research (B) abroad (C) adventure (D) space

( )70. Be sure to dress warmly when ______ in the mountains. It gets cold in the afternoon.

(A) hiking (B) shopping (C) diving (D) visiting

Clinical depression is a serious medical illness that negatively affects how you feel, the way you think and how you act. Individuals with clinical depression are unable to function as they used to. Often they have lost interest in activities that were once enjoyable to them, and feel sad and hopeless for extended periods of time. Clinical depression is not the same as feeling sad or depressed for a few days and then feeling better. It can affect your body, mood, thoughts, and behavior. It can change your eating habits, your ability to work and study, and your interaction with people.

Clinical depression is not a sign of personal weakness, or a condition that can be willed away. In fact, it often interferes with a person's ability or will to get help. It is a serious illness that lasts for weeks, months and sometimes years. It may even influence someone to contemplate or attempt suicide.

People of all ages, genders, ethnicities, cultures, and religions can suffer from clinical depression. Each year it affects over 17 million American men and women (source: American Psychiatric Association). Clinical depression is frequently unrecognized and untreated. But, with the right treatment, most people who do seek help get better within several months. Many people begin to feel better in just a few weeks.

( )71. According to the passage, which of the following statements is true?

(A) Clinical depression is not an illness but a symptom.
(B) Clinical depression may affect how people feel, think, and behave.
(C) Individuals with clinical depression function as they used to.
(D) Individuals with clinical depression are often inclined to seek external help.

(　　)72. According to the passage, how long will clinical depression affect people afflicted with the illness?

(A) It may affect them for weeks, months and sometimes years.
(B) It may affect them for a few days only.
(C) It may affect them for just several minutes.
(D) It may affect them for no longer than a couple of seconds.

(　　)73. What does the word "suicide" at the end of the second paragraph mean?

(A) the act of killing another person　(B) the act of breaking into a building
(C) the act of terminating a pregnancy　(D) the act of taking one's own life

(　　)74. Which of the following can be inferred from the passage?

(A) Clinical depression is incurable.
(B) Children are immune to clinical depression.
(C) Clinical depression is often overlooked.
(D) Old people are more likely to suffer from clinical depression than children.

(　　)75. Which of the following would be the best title for this passage?

(A) Medical Illnesses　(B) Psychological Health
(C) Medical Pathology　(D) Clinical Depression

While on vacation, not everyone likes staying at nice hotels, visiting museums, and shopping at department stores. Some would rather jump out of an airplane, speed down a river, or stay in a traditional village. They are part of a growing number of people who enjoy adventure tourism. It is a type of travel for people looking to get more out of their vacations.

With the Internet, it is easier than ever to set up an adventure tour. People can plan trips themselves, or they can find a suitable tour company online. Some popular countries to visit are Costa Rica, India, New Zealand, and Botswana. Their natural settings make them perfect for outdoor activities like hiking and diving. **Rich** in wildlife, they are also great for bird watching and safaris. Learning about the local history and culture is also popular with adventure travelers. In Peru, people love visiting the ruins of Machu Picchu. And, travelers in Tanzania enjoy meeting local tribes. In some countries, it is even possible to live and work in a village during a vacation. While building houses and helping research teams, travelers can enjoy local food and learn about the culture.

Besides being a lot of fun, these exiting trips mean big money for local economies. Tourism is already the world's largest industry, worth some $ 3 trillion. Of that, adventure tourism makes up about 20% of the market. That number is growing, as more people plan exciting vacations in their own countries and abroad.

( )76. What can we infer about adventure tourists from the passage?

(A) They like safe and comfortable vacations.

(B) They have little interest in culture.

(C) They enjoy trips that are exciting.

(D) They rarely play on sports teams.

( )77. Where would you go to visit Machu Picchu?

(A) Tanzania (B) Europe (C) Peru (D) The Himalayas

( )78. What is **NOT** a reason why people enjoy traveling to New Zealand?

(A) Tours there are cheaper than in other places.

(B) It is a great place for nature lovers.

(C) One could easily set up a bird watching trip.

(D) There are many outdoor activities.

( )79. What does the word **rich** in paragraph 2 mean?

(A) wealthy (B) plentiful (C) funny (D) heavy

( )80. What does the passage suggest about the tourism industry?

(A) It may soon be worth $3 trillion.

(B) Adventure tourism brings in the most money.

(C) Most of the industry is facing hard times.

(D) It is important to local economies.

★標準答案

1. (D)	2. (B)	3. (D)	4. (B)	5. (C)
6. (A)	7. (A)	8. (C)	9. (D)	10. (D)
11. (B)	12. (D)	13. (A)	14. (C)	15. (D)
16. (D)	17. (A)	18. (B)	19. (C)	20. (C)
21. (C)	22. (B)	23. (A)	24. (C)	25. (D)
26. (B)	27. (D)	28. (A)	29. (C)	30. (B)
31. (D)	32. (C)	33. (A)	34. (B)	35. (A)
36. (A)	37. (B)	38. (B)	39. (B)	40. (A)
41. (A)	42. (A)	43. (C)	44. (C)	45. (B)
46. (A)	47. (A)	48. (B)	49. (C)	50. (B)
51. (A)	52. (B)	53. (B)	54. (B)	55. (A)
56. (C)	57. (B)	58. (C)	59. (A)	60. (C)
61. (B)	62. (C)	63. (B)	64. (A)	65. (C)
66. (D)	67. (B)	68. (B)	69. (C)	70. (A)
71. (B)	72. (A)	73. (D)	74. (C)	75. (D)
76. (C)	77. (C)	78. (A)	79. (B)	80. (D)

99 年外語導遊英文試題中譯與解析

1. Individuals within a group often compromise their own values in favor of those held by the group.

(A) prefer 偏好　(B) emphasize 強調
(C) cherish 珍惜　(D) compromise 妥協

中譯 團體中的個人常常會因為所屬團體的利益而妥協他們自己的價值觀。

解析 此句可拆解成來看，Individuals within a group / often compromise their own values / in favor of those held by the group 團體中的個人 / 常常妥協他們的價值觀 / 為了所屬團體的利益。in favor of 贊成。因此可知答案為compromise 妥協。value 利益、價值，在此作利益。

2. Living near the airport, I am very much bothered by the noise of airplanes. I can not sleep well and often feel uneasy.

(A) marked 標記　(B) bothered 打擾
(C) expected 預期　(D) confused 困惑

中譯 住在機場附近，我深受噪音困擾。我不能睡好，而且常常感到不安。

解析 由I can not sleep well and often feel uneasy可知，深受bothered 打擾。Don't bother me! 別打擾我！uneasy 心神不安的、拘束的、不自在的。

3. Claire loves to buy exotic foods: vegetables and herbs from China, spices from India, olives from Greece, and cheeses from France.

(A) sea 海洋　(B) stingy 小氣的
(C) tranquil 鎮靜的　(D) exotic 異國風情的

中譯 克萊兒喜歡買異國風情的食物：來自中國的蔬菜和草藥、印度來的香料、希臘來的橄欖，以及法國來的起司。

解析 exotic 異國風情的；foreign則為國外的、陌生的；foreigner 外國人。由題目中提及的各個國家可知，答案為exotic 異國風情的。

4. Falling asleep in class and being drowsy at work were just two examples of his fatigue.

(A) energy 精力　(B) fatigue 疲勞　(C) conspiracy 陰謀　(D) belief 信任

中譯 於課堂上睡著以及工作時昏昏欲睡是他疲勞的症狀之一。

解析 由falling asleep以及being drowsy可知是fatigue 疲勞的症狀。
drowsy 昏昏欲睡的。

5. Elizabeth Anker is a very versatile artist for she is not only an excellent pianist but also a great singer, painter, and poet.

(A) ethical 道德的 (B) feeble 虛弱的
(C) versatile 多才多藝的 (D) classical 古典的

中譯 依莉莎白・安可是一位非常多才多藝的藝術家，因為她不但是位出色的鋼琴家，也是名優秀的歌手、畫家和詩人。

解析 pianist、singer、painter、and poet可知是非常versatile 多才多藝的。

6. As a result of the accident, Shirley was unconscious for three weeks before gradually recovered.

(A) unconscious 無意識的（不省人事的）
(B) prehistoric 史前的
(C) gorgeous 美麗的
(D) fortunate 幸運的

中譯 因為這次意外，結果雪麗逐漸恢復之前昏迷了三個星期。

解析 相關單字有unconscious 無意識的；conscious 有意識的；subconscious 潛意識的。

7. The cake was stale, and tasted bad.

(A) stale 不新鮮的（腐壞的） (B) nutritious 營養的
(C) familiar 相似的 (D) indispensable 必要的

中譯 這個蛋糕不新鮮了，且嚐起來不好吃。

解析 stale 不新鮮的；fresh 新鮮的。由tasted bad可得知蛋糕已stale 不新鮮的（腐壞的）。

8. To save money, buy just what you need and refrain from buying unnecessary stuff.

(A) invent 發明 (B) discard 拋棄 (C) save 節省 (D) exhaust 耗盡

中譯 為了省錢，只買你需要的東西，且克制不買不需要的東西。

解析 refrain from 避免，有忍住、抑制之意。unnecessary 不需要的；necessary 需要的。stuff 物品、東西。

9. With a complacent smile, Robert showed how happy he was when he won the swimming contest yesterday.

(A) fertile 富饒的　(B) historic 歷史的
(C) pollutant 汙染的　**(D) complacent 滿足的**

中譯 有著滿足的笑容，羅伯顯示出當他昨天贏了游泳比賽時有多開心。

解析 從題意可知是和開心有關的smile，故選complacent 滿足的，但若不懂第二句，光靠smile也能將其他選項刪除。

10. Susan Manning's trip to Buffalo was a/an leisurely one. She took her time.

(A) hasty 匆忙的　(B) urgent 緊急的　(C) rapid 快速的　**(D) leisurely 悠閒的**

中譯 蘇珊・曼寧去水牛城的旅程是悠閒的。她從容不迫度過她的時間。

解析 take your time就是口語上所說的「慢慢來」，因此可知這趟trip 旅程是很leisurely 悠閒的。

11. Professor Nelson, who is rather strange, displays some eccentric behavior from time to time.

(A) ordinary 普通的　**(B) eccentric 反常的**
(C) comprehensive 包容的　(D) logical 邏輯的

中譯 尼爾森教授，是一個相當奇怪的人，有時會表現出一些怪異的行為。

解析 此處的displays可換成shows，為表現之意。解題可由strange 奇怪的，來推測是eccentric behavior 怪異的行為。from time to time 有時。

12. Some families have children in chronic health conditions. At times, the pressure may be overwhelming to every individual in the family and the challenges can affect the quality of family life.

(A) encouraging 鼓勵　(B) convincing 說服
(C) outgoing 比……更快速前進　**(D) overwhelming 壓倒性的**

中譯 有些家庭的孩子有慢性疾病的情形。有時候，壓力對於每一個家庭份子來說，有如排山倒海而來這樣的挑戰也會影響家庭生活的品質。

解析 chronic 慢性（病）的。找出動詞則較易理解 The pressure may be overwhelming to every individual in the family / and the challenges can affect the quality of family life. 壓力可能是很壓倒性的（巨大的）對於家庭的每一個份子來說 / 這些挑戰會影響家庭生活的品質。

13. Christopher Reeve was paralyzed from the neck down and confined to a wheelchair, after the tragic accident.

(A) paralyzed 癱瘓的 (B) articulated 口齒清晰的
(C) classified 分類的 (D) enlightened 啟發的

中譯 因為一場悲劇性的意外，克里斯多福．李維從頸部以下都麻痺了，並且得坐在輪椅上。

解析 confined to 侷限於，由confined to a wheelchair 得坐在輪椅上推知，人已paralyzed 癱瘓的。若是看不懂confined，也能從tragic accident來猜答案。tragic 悲劇的。

14. Many young Spaniards continued to come to the island, hoping to find gold quickly and become rich overnight.

(A) backward 向後 (B) hardly 幾乎不
(C) overnight 一夜之間 (D) nowhere 毫無結果

中譯 很多年輕的西班牙人持續來到這座島上，希望可以很快地發現金礦且一夜致富。

解析 become rich overnight就是我們俗稱的「一夜致富」。Spain 西班牙（國家）；Spanish 西班牙文；Spaniard 西班牙人。

15. Since our economy has been improving recently, I hope that my boss will give me a big raise this year.

(A) conquest 克服 (B) consumption 消耗
(C) rise 上升 (D) raise 加薪

中譯 因為我們的經濟情況最近一直持續好轉，我希望我的老闆今年可以幫我大加薪。

解析 raise 加薪，例句： Since the economy is improving, many people are hoping for a raise in salary in the coming year. 既然經濟已經好轉，許多人希望明年能加薪。
99領隊
salary 薪水；由economy has been improving 經濟情況持續好轉推知，是想要求a big raise 加薪。recently 最近。

16. John Keene's opinion has no effect on her daughter's decision to become a professional artist. She always gets her own way.

(A) annoyance 使人討厭的事物　(B) revenge 復仇

(C) record 紀錄　(D) effect 影響

中譯 約翰・金尼的意見沒有辦法影響她女兒決定要成為一名專業的藝術家。她總是照著自己的步驟。

解析 effect 影響（名詞）；affect 影響（動詞），用法參見第12題題目。get one's one way 總是照著某人的步驟。get in one's way 阻擋某人的路，請注意區別。

17. The book is about a very clumsy boy who always breaks things.

(A) clumsy 笨手笨腳的　(B) appropriate 適當的

(C) evident 明顯的　(D) fragrant 芳香的

中譯 這本書是關於一名笨手笨腳的男生，他總是打破東西。

解析 由breaks things 打破東西可知，這男孩很clumsy 笨手笨腳的。句子可拆成以下來看，The book is about / a very clumsy boy / who always breaks things. 這本書是關於 / 一名笨手笨腳的男生 / 他總是打破東西。

18. If something is dreary it is dull and depressing.

(A) measurable 可測量的　(B) dreary 沉悶的

(C) graphic 生動的　(D) hysterical 歇斯底里的

中譯 如果某件事情非常的沉悶，表示是很單調且令人沮喪。

解析 由dull and depressing 單調且令人沮喪可得知，答案為dreary 沉悶的。dull 乏味的；depressing 令人沮喪的。

19. Katherine was reminded to return the book by next Monday, which she borrowed from the school library three months ago.

(A) captured 捕捉　(B) prevented 預防

(C) borrowed 借來　(D) arrested 逮捕

中譯 凱薩琳被提醒下週一還書，她三個月前從學校圖書館借的。

解析 remind 提醒；borrow from 從某處借來；return to 還。

20. Sarah, who often attends symphony concerts, has a great appreciation for music.

(A) anxiety 焦慮　　(B) disregard 忽視

(C) appreciation 鑑賞　　(D) headline 頭條

中譯 那位常常參加交響音樂會的莎拉，對於音樂有極高的鑑賞力。

解析 由often attends symphony concerts 常常參加交響音樂會可得知，對音樂有appreciation 鑑賞力。

21. For some people, the fear of visiting a dentist outweighs the pain of a toothache.

(A) barbarian 野蠻人　　(B) diplomat 外交官

(C) dentist 牙醫　　(D) magician 魔術師

中譯 對於某些人來說，看牙醫的恐懼遠大於牙痛的痛苦。

解析 從題目的toothache 牙痛，即可選出dentist 牙醫。

22. Dr. Morales has confirmed a major discovery in the world of rock art: an ancient rock painting at a burial site from the Inca site of Machu Picchu in Peru.

(A) epidemic 流行病　　**(B) discovery 發現**

(C) flaw 缺點　　(D) galaxy 銀河

中譯 莫瑞爾斯博士已經證實世界岩石藝術領域的一大發現：在祕魯的馬丘比丘地區的一處印加墓地，發現了古老的岩石繪畫。

解析 由an ancient rock painting可推知這是一項discovery 發現。confirm 證實。

23. Some soils are extremely rich in minerals and nutrients such as iron and copper.

(A) minerals 礦物質　　(B) mermaids 美人魚

(C) miniatures 縮樣　　(D) manuscripts 手稿

中譯 有些土壤富含礦物質以及營養素，像是鐵和銅。

解析 解題時若是不了解soils的意思，由iron 鐵可得知答案可能為minerals 礦物。

24. Scientists have found a cure for the rare contagious disease, and some patients now have the hope of recovery.

(A) replacement 替代法　　(B) penalty 處罰

(C) cure 治療　　(D) passion 激情

中譯 科學家已經發現治癒罕見傳染性疾病的療法，現在一些病人對於治癒懷抱希望。

解析 由the hope of recovery 對於治癒懷抱希望，可猜出答案為cure 治療。

25. Elaine Hadley has many hobbies, such as horse-back riding, dancing, and playing with animals.

(A) devices 裝置 (B) sensations 感覺

(C) temperaments 氣質 (D) hobbies 嗜好

中譯 依蓮．海德力有許多嗜好，像是騎馬、跳舞以及與動物們一起玩。

解析 hobby 嗜好（單數），hobbies（複數）；由horse-back riding, dancing, and playing with animals.得知為各類的hobbies。

26. People who have a great sense of humor are often very popular, because they are usually intelligent, open-minded, and witty.

(A) frustration 挫折 (B) humor 幽默

(C) betrayal 背叛 (D) inferiority 劣質

中譯 非常有幽默感的人通常很受歡迎，因為他們通常是聰明、開放心胸以及機智的。

解析 有這樣特質的人are often very popular 通常很受歡迎，可得知是sense of humor 幽默感。open-minded 心胸寬的、無先入為主之見的。

27. A humble person is usually welcomed by everyone, because he never irritates people.

(A) selfish 自私的 (B) naughty 調皮的

(C) pessimistic 悲觀的 (D) humble 謙虛的

中譯 謙虛的人通常受到每個人的歡迎，因為這樣的人從不激怒其他人。

解析 humble 謙虛的；down-to-earth 樸實的；irritate 使惱怒、使煩躁。

28. Petroleum production can contribute to air and water pollution; besides, drilling for oil may disturb the fragile ecosystems.

(A) oil 石油 (B) light 光線 (C) air 空氣 (D) truth 真相

中譯 石油產物會造成空氣以及水汙染，其次探鑽石油也會危害到脆弱的生態系統。

解析 petrol、oil皆為石油的意思。此題單字較難，但仍可從簡單的air and water pollution 當中猜出可能對應的單字為oil，因為石油才會產生汙染。fragile 脆弱的。

29. Kenneth is reluctant to confide in others, because he fears that the information he reveals will be used maliciously against him.

(A) happy 開心　(B) thankful 感恩的

(C) reluctant 不願意　(D) voluntary 自願的

中譯 肯尼斯不願意向他人敞開心胸，因為他怕他所吐露的心聲會被用來惡意對付他自己。

解析 confide in willing 願意 / unwilling 不願意。整句可拆成because he fears that / the information he reveals / will be used maliciously against him. 因為他怕 / 他所吐露的心聲 / 會被用來惡意對付他自己。maliciously 惡意地。

30. Considerate people are sensitive to others' wants and feelings.

(A) Blunt 遲鈍的　(B) Considerate 體貼的

(C) Arrogant 傲慢的　(D) Dominant 支配的

中譯 體貼的人通常容易察覺他人的需求以及感覺。

解析 considerate 體貼的，thoughtful也為體貼的，體貼的人對人際關係通常比較sensitive 敏感的，故選considerate 體貼的。

31. Ms. Mead has become a media celebrity and an iconic figure who represented a range of different ideas, values, and beliefs to a broad spectrum of the American public.

(A) alienated 疏遠　(B) buried 埋葬

(C) calculated 估計　(D) represented 呈現

中譯 米德小姐已經成為媒體名人以及指標人物，因為她呈現不同的想法、價值觀以及信仰於美國大眾前。

解析 此句較長，拆成以下三部分較易理解。Ms. Mead has become a media celebrity and an iconic figure / who represented a range of different ideas, values, and beliefs / to a broad spectrum of the American public. 米德小姐已經成為媒體名人以及指標人物 / 她呈現不同的想法、價值觀以及信仰 / 於美國大眾前。本句重點為iconic figure 偶像人物。

32. For centuries, artists, historians, and tourists have been fascinated by Mona Lisa's enigmatic smile.

(A) ignored 忽視　(B) characterized 特徵

(C) fascinated 迷倒　(D) embraced 擁抱

中譯 數個世紀以來，藝術家、歷史學家，以及觀光客都對蒙娜麗莎謎樣般的微笑深深著迷。

解析 fascinate 使神魂顛倒；fascinated 被迷倒的；fascinating 令人目眩神迷的。enigmatic 謎樣的；enigma 謎。

33. Balloons are small, often brightly colored, thin rubber bags that rise and float when they are filled with light gas.

(A) Balloons 氣球 (B) Flags 旗子 (C) Peacocks 孔雀 (D) Rainbows 彩虹

中譯 氣球是小型的，常常有著明亮的顏色、薄薄的橡皮袋子，當充滿輕型瓦斯時還能往上飄浮。

解析 由brightly colored、filled with light gas可猜出是balloons 氣球。

34. As children grow and mature, they will leave behind childish pursuits, and no longer be so selfish and undisciplined as they used to be.

(A) masculine 男子氣概的 (B) childish 幼稚的
(C) philosophical 哲學家的 (D) honorable 尊敬的

中譯 當小孩長大變成熟，他們將會把幼稚的行為拋下，且不再和以前一樣自私且沒有紀律。

解析 mature 變成熟；leave behind 留下；pursuit 追求；undisciplined 沒有紀律的；discipline 教條（名詞）；disciplined 有紀律的（形容詞）；no longer 不再。

35. Dogs usually want to chase and play with cats, whereas cats are usually afraid and defensive.

(A) chase 追逐 (B) abandon 拋棄 (C) denounce 譴責 (D) shun 避開

中譯 狗通常想要追貓和貓玩，反之貓咪通常會害怕且有防衛心。

解析 由dogs usually want to play with cats可猜出是chase 追逐；whereas 反之。

36. Wind and sunshine are very important assets for Penghu, attracting a large number of tourists each year.

(A) assets 資產 (B) quantities 數量
(C) propositions 提議 (D) materials 材料

中譯 風和陽光是澎湖很重要的資產，每年吸引了大批觀光客到來。

解析 由wind and sunshine attracting a large number of tourists each year可得知，是Penghu很重要的assets 資產。a large number of 很多。

37. Fireworks and firecrackers are often used in Chinese communities to symbolize greeting good fortunes and scaring away evils.

(A) sign 記號 (B) symbolize 象徵
(C) identify 確認 (D) underline 強調

中譯 煙火和鞭炮常用於華人社會中，以象徵迎接好運以及將晦氣嚇跑。

解析 symbol 符號；symbolize 象徵；greet 打招呼；scare away 將某事嚇跑。

38. Watch out for your own safety! Don't be a target of thieves while you are traveling.

(A) audience 觀眾 (B) thieves 小偷 (C) heroes 英雄 (D) clients 客戶

中譯 注意你自身的安全！當你旅遊時別成為小偷的目標！

解析 watch out 小心，常見的用法還有pay attention 注意。thief 小偷（單數），thieves（複數）。

39. Scarlet fever is a/an contagious disease, which is transferable from one person to another.

(A) different 不同的 (B) contagious 接觸傳染的
(C) important 重要的 (D) special 特別的

中譯 猩紅熱是一種接觸性的傳染病，是經由人與人接觸傳染。

解析 由transferable from one person to another 人與人接觸傳染，可得知是contagious 接觸傳染的疾病。

40. A boarding pass is a necessary document for the passenger to get on the airplane.

(A) boarding pass 登機證 (B) passport 護照
(C) identification card 身分證 (D) visa 簽證

中譯 登機證是乘客登機的必要文件。

解析 get on / get off airplane 上 / 下飛機；take off / land 起飛 / 降落。

41. Besides participating in local cultural activities, people who desire to explore the ecology of Kenting can observe plenty of wildlife and plants.

(A) observe 觀察 (B) pick up 撿起 (C) object 反對 (D) plan 計劃

中譯 除了參與當地的文化活動外，想在墾丁探訪生態環境的人也可以觀察豐富的野生動物與植物。

解析 由desire to explore the ecology of Kenting 想探訪墾丁的生態環境，可得知observe plenty of wildlife and plants 觀察豐富的野生動物與植物。

42. Flight attendants help passengers find their seats and stow their carry-on luggage safely in the overhead compartments.

(A) stow 儲藏、放置　　(B) strew 散落

(C) straighten 直立　　(D) stifle 窒息

中譯 空服員幫忙乘客找到座位，並且幫助他們將隨身行李安全地放於頭頂上的置物箱內。

解析 飛機上常見的人員：flight attendant 空服員；cabin crew 機組人員；captain 機長。

43. We finished the trip and the cost was well below budget. We had planned to spend three thousand dollars, but we ended up spending only half of that.

(A) reference 參考文獻　　(B) reminder 提醒

(C) budget 預算　　(D) permission 允許

中譯 我們結束了旅程，花費遠在預算之下。我們本來打算花3,000元，結果只花了一半。

解析 below budget 預算之下；over budget 超出預算。由題意的cost、spend可知是和「金錢」有關，故選budget 預算。

44. If there is any suspicion of contagious diseases or agricultural pests, the customs agents will impose a quarantine.

(A) declaration 聲明　　(B) duty 責任

(C) quarantine 隔離　　(D) predicament 困境

中譯 如果對於接觸傳染性疾病或是農業害蟲有任何疑慮，海關人員將會強制隔離。

解析 custom為風俗；customary為約定俗成的；customs為海關，此三個單字常出現於考題中，此處為customs 海關。contagious diseases 接觸傳染性疾病為常考名詞，務必熟記。impose 把……強加於。

45. When people travel to popular destinations during peak seasons, it is necessary to reserve accommodations before the trip.

(A) generation 世代　　(B) accommodations 住宿

(C) identification 身分　　(D) confirmation 確認

中譯 於旺季到熱門觀光景點旅遊時，一定要在旅途前先預約住宿。

解析 reserve accommodations 預約住宿；peak seasons 旺季。

46. If you want to find the cheapest airplane ticket, bargains can usually be found through the Internet.

(A) bargains 特價商品、便宜貨
(B) destinations 目的地
(C) reservations 預定
(D) itinerary 旅程

中譯 如果你想要找最便宜的機票，通常可以在網路上找到特價商品。

解析 A bargain is a bargain. 說話要算話。bargain-hunting 四處覓購便宜貨。

47. Tom's team won the game at the last minute, and the coach was very proud of the performance of his players.

(A) performance 表現
(B) modulation 調節
(C) perception 感覺
(D) application 應用

中譯 湯姆的團隊在最後一分鐘贏得比賽，教練對於選手們的表現感到非常的驕傲。

解析 coach 教練（名詞），也是巴士、普通車廂、馬車之意，當成動詞則為指導。

48. Don't press the alarm bell unless in absolute emergency.

(A) emergence 出現
(B) emergency 緊急狀況
(C) service 服務
(D) status 狀態

中譯 不要按緊急鈴，除非是非常緊急的情形。

解析 in emergency 緊急狀況；emergency room （醫院的）急診室。

49. Nowadays, most information has become available through the use of computers.

(A) ordinal 順序
(B) fixed 固定
(C) available 可獲得的
(D) perfect 完美的

中譯 現今大部分的資訊都變得容易取得，由於電腦的普及使用。

解析 由information through the use of computers可推論資訊是available 很容易到手的。

50. If you have any problems or questions about our new products, you are welcome to use our toll-free service line.

(A) tax 稅
(B) toll 通行費
(C) money 錢
(D) fee 費用

中譯 如果你對於我們的新產品有任何的問題或是疑問，歡迎撥打我們的免付費服務專線。

解析 toll-free service line 免付費服務專線，也有free call、free phone的用法。

51. The amusement park is a famous tourist attraction in Japan. Tourists of all ages love to go there.

(A) attraction 吸引　(B) fascination 魅力
(C) information 資訊　(D) attention 注意

中譯 這座遊樂園是日本很有名的觀光景點。各年齡層的觀光客都喜歡去那邊。

解析 觀光景點的幾種說法：tourist attraction、sight-seeing spot、scenic spot。amusement park 遊樂園。觀光景點相關單字：aquarium 水族館；museum 博物館。

52. Since the president of the company is absent, the general manager will preside over the meeting.

(A) preview 預覽　(B) preside 主持　(C) pledge 發誓　(D) persuade 說服

中譯 既然公司總裁缺席，總經理將會主持這場會議。

解析 preside over 主持；absent 缺席；present 出席。

53. Even though you have confirmed your flight with the airline, you must still be present at the check-in desk on time.

(A) informed 告知　(B) confirmed 確認　(C) required 要求　(D) given 給予

中譯 即便你已經和航空公司確認班機，你還是必須準時於報到櫃台報到。

解析 confirm 確認；reconfirm 再次確認。confirm flight 確認班機；confirm reservation 確認預約。

54. "Don't count your chickens before they are hatched" is a proverb that reminds people not to be too optimistic before their plans succeed.

(A) story 故事　(B) proverb 諺語　(C) history 歷史　(D) pursuit 追求

中譯 「不要太早打如意算盤」是一句提醒人們在計畫成功前不要太樂觀的諺語。

解析 Don't count your chickens before they are hatched直接翻譯為「在雞蛋孵出前不要去算會有幾隻雞」，也就是不要太早打如意算盤之意。hatch 孵。

55. To increase sales of products, many companies spend huge sums of money on promotion campaigns.

(A) promotion 促銷 (B) automatic 自動
(C) stable 穩定 (D) solitary 單獨

中譯 為了增加商品的銷售，很多公司會花大筆的金錢在促銷活動上。

解析 由to increase sales of products得知，會和promotion 促銷有關。

56. Please examine your luggage carefully before leaving. At the security counter, every item in the luggage has to go through inspection.

(A) relation 關係 (B) invention 發明
(C) inspection 檢查 (D) observation 觀察

中譯 出發前請仔細檢查你的行李。安檢櫃台會檢查行李內的每一項物品。

解析 examine以及inspect都為檢查之意，但inspect更有「權力」，因此這裡的security counter使用 inspect。

57. When you are ready to get off an airplane, you will be told not to forget your personal belongings.

(A) utilities 日常所需之物 (B) belongings 個人用品
(C) commodities 商品 (D) works 工作

中譯 當你準備下飛機時，你將會被告知別忘了帶走你的隨身物品。

解析 get off an airplane / a bus / a train 下飛機 / 巴士 / 火車；get on an airplane / a bus / a train 上飛機 / 巴士 / 火車。

58. A: How can I get to the National Museum from here?

B: You can take that bus.

(A) You mustn't go with your friends. 你絕不可和朋友一起去。
(B) It is too far from here. 離這邊太遠了。
(C) You can take that bus. 你可以搭那台公車。
(D) I can not go with you. 我不能和你一起去。

中譯 A：我該如何從這裡到國家博物館？
B：你可以搭那台公車。

解析 此題問的是「到達方式」（How... get to），故應回答使用的「交通工具」。

59. Quick and friendly service at the front desk is important to the satisfaction of tourists.

(A) satisfaction 滿意　(B) procession 行列
(C) procedure 程序　(D) prohibition 禁止

中譯 櫃台的快速以及友善服務對於觀光客的滿意度來說很重要。

解析 由quick and friendly service 快速以及友善服務可猜測，故應選satisfaction 滿意度。

60. For tours in peak seasons, travel agents sometimes have to make reservations a year or more in advance.

(A) above all 首先　(B) beyond all 超乎範圍
(C) in advance 事先　(D) afterwards 之後

中譯 對於旺季的出遊，旅行社有時必須早在一年之前、甚至更早就先預定好行程。

解析 由peak seasons得知，出發前一定得make reservations in advance 事先預約。

61. The flight is scheduled to depart at eleven o'clock tomorrow. You will have to get to the airport two hours before the takeoff.

(A) land 著陸、抵達　(B) depart 起飛
(C) cancel 取消　(D) examine 檢驗

中譯 班機預定於明天11點起飛。你必須在出發前2個小時抵達機場。

解析 depart、take off 起飛；land 著陸、抵達。

62. Please see to it that all necessary procedures have been completed. Never risk your life simply for convenience's sake.

(A) possibilities 可能性　(B) reservations 預定
(C) procedures 步驟　(D) alternatives 選擇

中譯 請留意所有所需步驟都做到完善。別只因貪圖方便而讓你的人生冒險。

解析 由Never risk your life simply for convenience's sake可推知，每一步驟都須完成，故選procedures 步驟。sake 目的。

63. You don't have to worry about where to stay tonight. My friend in downtown area will find you a night's lodging.

(A) station 車站　(B) lodging 住宿　(C) housekeeper 管家　(D) seat 座位

中譯 你不需要擔心今晚在哪過夜。我在市區的朋友會幫你找到住宿一晚的地方。

解析 由where to stay tonight可推知答案為lodging 住宿。

64. International trade allows countries to buy what they need from other countries.

(A) trade 貿易　(B) field 領域　(C) port 港口　(D) trip 旅程

中譯 國際貿易讓各個國家可以向其他國家購買所需的東西。

解析 trade可當名詞以及動詞，都為貿易、做生意之意。由buy what they need from other countries可得知為International trade 國際貿易。

65. Visitors to New York often talk about the feeling of excitement there. It is a city full of energy and hope.

(A) culture 文化　(B) chat 聊天

(C) excitement 興奮　(D) reason 理由

中譯 紐約的遊客總是討論來此的興奮感。這是個充滿活力以及希望的城市。

解析 由full of energy and hope可推知答案為excitement 興奮。

66. In many Western cultures, it is rude to ask about a person's age, weight, or salary. However, these topics may not be as sensitive in East Asia.

(A) economical 經濟的　(B) polluted 汙染的

(C) governed 管理的　(D) sensitive 敏感的

中譯 在許多西方國家，問他人的年齡、體重或是薪水是很無禮的。然而這些話題在東亞可能就不是如此敏感。

解析 sensitive 敏感的，可以是對人觀察很細微的敏感，或是需要很慎重處理的重要議題的敏感之意。

67. I enjoy looking at art pieces in museums. However, I am too poor to collect any myself.

(A) websites 網站　(B) art pieces 藝術作品

(C) crime 罪　(D) magazines 雜誌

中譯 我很享受在博物館欣賞藝術作品。然而，我太窮所以無法收藏任何作品。

解析 too poor to... 為太窮而無法做某事。

68. Cathy is an outgoing and successful salesperson, but her background is in web design.

(A) neighborhood 鄰近地區 (B) background 背景
(C) section 區段 (D) system 系統

中譯 凱西是很活潑且成功的銷售員，但她的背景是網頁設計。

解析 由salesperson和web design的反差，可知要強調background 背景的差異。

69. Exploring the culture and history of Africa sounds like a great adventure. It will be a lot of fun!

(A) research 研究 (B) abroad 國外
(C) adventure 冒險 (D) space 空間

中譯 探索非洲的文化和歷史聽起來像是個很偉大的冒險。這將會很有意思！

解析 從exploring the culture and history of Africa猜測，可能會誤選research 研究，但由It will be a lot of fun!可推測為a great adventure 偉大的冒險。

70. Be sure to dress warmly when hiking in the mountains. It gets cold in the afternoon.

(A) hiking 健行 (B) shopping 購物 (C) diving 潛水 (D) visiting 拜訪

中譯 當在山中健行時記得穿得保暖。下午會變冷。

解析 解題重點為由in the mountains可得知是hiking。

Clinical depression is a serious medical illness that negatively affects how you feel, the way you think and how you act. Individuals with clinical depression are unable to function as they used to. Often they have lost interest in activities that were once enjoyable to them, and feel sad and hopeless for extended periods of time. Clinical depression is not the same as feeling sad or depressed for a few days and then feeling better. It can affect your body, mood, thoughts, and behavior. It can change your eating habits, your ability to work and study, and your interaction with people.

中譯 臨床上的憂鬱症是種嚴重的疾病，會對你的感覺、思考方式，以及你的行為產生負面的影響。憂鬱症患者無法和之前一樣生活。他們常常對於之前感興趣的事物失去興趣，且長時間感到憂傷和絕望。憂鬱症和單純的覺得憂鬱或沮喪數天而後好轉是不一樣的。它會影響你的生理、心理、思考以及行為。也會改變你的飲食習慣、你的工作和學習能力，以及人際互動。

Clinical depression is not a sign of personal weakness, or a condition that can be willed away. In fact, it often interferes with a person's ability or will to get help. It is a serious illness that lasts for weeks, months and sometimes years. It may even influence someone to contemplate or attempt suicide.

中譯 憂鬱症並不是個人軟弱的象徵，或是可以任意而為的狀態。事實上，憂鬱症通常會影響一個人的求救的能力以及意願。這是個很嚴重的疾病，會持續好幾週、好幾個月，甚至好幾年。這甚至會影響人思考或是試圖自殺。

People of all ages, genders, ethnicities, cultures, and religions can suffer from clinical depression. Each year it affects over 17 million American men and women (source: American Psychiatric Association) . Clinical depression is frequently unrecognized and untreated. But, with the right treatment, most people who do seek help get better within several months. Many people begin to feel better in just a few weeks.

中譯 任何年齡、性別、種族、文化，甚至不同宗教的人都可能會罹患憂鬱症。美國每年有超過1,700百萬的男女罹患憂鬱症（來源：美國心理治療協會）。憂鬱症經常被忽略以及忽視。然而大部分接受適當治療的人在幾個月內都會明顯好轉。很多人甚至幾個星期內就會有起色。

71. According to the passage, which of the following statements is true?

(A) Clinical depression is not an illness but a symptom.
憂鬱症不是疾病而是症狀。

(B) Clinical depression may affect how people feel, think, and behave.
憂鬱症會影響人感覺、思考和行為。

(C) Individuals with clinical depression function as they used to.
憂鬱症患者可以和以前一樣正常生活。

(D) Individuals with clinical depression are often inclined to seek external help.
憂鬱症患者通常會傾向尋求外在幫助。

中譯 根據本文，以下哪項敘述為真？

解析 由Clinical depression is a serious medical illness that negatively affects how you feel, the way you think and how you act.可知。

72. According to the passage, how long will clinical depression affect people afflicted with the illness?

(A) It may affect them for weeks, months and sometimes years.
憂鬱症可能會影響數個星期、幾個月，甚至好幾年。

(B) It may affect them for a few days only.
只會影響幾天而已。

(C) It may affect them for just several minutes.
只會影響幾分鐘而已。

(D) It may affect them for no longer than a couple of seconds.
影響不超過幾秒。

中譯 根據本文，憂鬱症會影響人多久？

解析 由It is a serious illness that lasts for weeks, months and sometimes years.可知。

73. What does the word "suicide" at the end of the second paragraph mean?

(A) the act of killing another person 殺其他人的行為

(B) the act of breaking into a building 闖入建築的行為

(C) the act of a pregnancy 墮胎的行為

(D) the act of taking one's own life 自殺的行為

中譯 於第二段文尾的「suicide」是什麼意思？

解析 由It may even influence someone to contemplate or attempt suicide.可知。

74. Which of the following can be inferred from the passage?

(A) Clinical depression is incurable. 憂鬱症無法治癒。

(B) Children are immune to clinical depression. 小孩對憂鬱症免疫。

(C) Clinical depression is often overlooked. 憂鬱症常常被忽略。

(D) Old people are more likely to suffer from clinical depression than children.
老人比兒童很可能更容易得憂鬱症。

中譯 由本文可推知以下何者？

解析 由Clinical depression is frequently unrecognized and untreated.可知。

75. Which of the following would be the best title for this passage?

(A) Medical Illnesses 心理疾病

(B) Psychological Health 心理健康

(C) Medical Pathology 醫學病理

(D) Clinical Depression 憂鬱症

中譯 以下哪項描述最適合當本文的標題？

解析 由本文第一段第一句可知。

While on vacation, not everyone likes staying at nice hotels, visiting museums, and shopping at department stores. Some would rather jump out of an airplane, speed down a river, or stay in a traditional village. They are part of a growing number of people who enjoy adventure tourism. It is a type of travel for people looking to get more out of their vacations.

中譯 度假時，不是每個人都喜歡待在舒適的旅館、參觀博物館以及逛百貨公司。有些人寧願從飛機上跳傘、泛舟、或是待在傳統的部落中。他們是一群人數正在成長的生態探險旅遊愛好者。這是一種讓人可在假期中得到更多的旅遊模式。

With the Internet, it is easier than ever to set up an adventure tour. People can plan trips themselves, or they can find a suitable tour company online. Some popular countries to visit are Costa Rica, India, New Zealand, and Botswana. Their natural settings make them perfect for outdoor activities like hiking and diving. Rich in wildlife, they are also great for bird watching and safaris. Learning about the local history and culture is also popular with adventure travelers. In Peru, people love visiting the ruins of Machu Picchu. And, travelers in Tanzania enjoy meeting local tribes. In some countries, it is even possible to live and work in a village during a vacation. While building houses and helping research teams, travelers can enjoy local food and learn about the culture.

中譯 有了網路，比以前更容易安排一趟冒險旅程。人們可以自己安排旅程，或是他們可以在網路上找一間適合的旅行社。有些國家很受歡迎，像是哥斯大黎加、印度、紐西蘭，以及波札那。他們的自然環境非常適合戶外活動，像是健行和潛水。豐富的野生動物，也讓他們非常適合賞鳥和狩獵。學習當地的歷史以及文化也很受探險旅遊者的喜愛。在祕魯，人們喜歡去參觀馬丘比丘遺跡。在坦尚尼亞的旅行者喜歡拜訪當地部落。有些國家，甚至可以在村莊內生活或是打工度假。當建造房子和幫助研究團隊的時候，旅行者可以品嚐當地食物和學習當地文化。

Besides being a lot of fun, these exiting trips mean big money for local economies. Tourism is already the world's largest industry, worth some $ 3 trillion. Of that, adventure tourism makes up about 20% of the market. That number is growing, as more people plan exciting vacations in their own countries and abroad.

中譯 除了會有很多樂趣外，這些刺激的旅程對當地經濟也有不小助益。觀光業已經是世界上最大的產業，價值約三兆美元。其中探險旅遊占了市場的百分之二十。數字仍在成長中，越來越多人計劃在自己的國家或是國外來趟刺激的假期。

76. What can we infer about adventure tourists from the passage?

(A) They like safe and comfortable vacations. 他們喜歡舒適安全的假期。

(B) They have little interest in culture. 他們對文化不感興趣。

(C) They enjoy trips that are exciting. 他們喜歡刺激的行程。

(D) They rarely play on sports teams. 他們很少玩團體運動。

中譯 我們可以從本文推論出關於探險旅遊者的哪項資訊？

解析 由Some would rather jump out of an airplane, speed down a river, or stay in a traditional village.可知。

77. Where would you go to visit Machu Picchu?

(A) Tanzania 坦尚尼亞

(B) Europe 歐洲

(C) Peru 祕魯

(D) The Himalayas 喜馬拉雅山

中譯 你會去哪裡參觀馬丘比丘？

解析 由In Peru, people love visiting the ruins of Machu Picchu.可知。

78. What is NOT a reason why people enjoy traveling to New Zealand?

(A) Tours there are cheaper than in other places. 那裡的行程比其他地方便宜。

(B) It is a great place for nature lovers. 對愛好大自然的人來說是很棒的地方。

(C) One could easily set up a bird watching trip. 很容易安排賞鳥的行程。

(D) There are many outdoor activities. 有很多戶外活動。

中譯 以下哪項理由不是人們喜歡去紐西蘭旅遊的原因？

解析 由Their natural settings make them perfect for outdoor activities like hiking and diving. Rich in wildlife, they are also great for bird watching and safaris. Learning about the local history and culture is also popular with adventure travelers.可知。

79. What does the word rich in paragraph 2 mean?

(A) wealthy 有錢的

(B) plentiful 豐富的

(C) funny 好笑的

(D) heavy 沉重的

中譯 第二段的rich是什麼意思？

解析 由Rich in wildlife, they are also great for bird watching and safaris可知。

80. What does the passage suggest about the tourism industry?

(A) It may soon be worth $3 trillion. 很快會價值三兆美元。

(B) Adventure tourism brings in the most money. 探險旅遊業帶來最多收益。

(C) Most of the industry is facing hard times. 大部分的產業面臨危機。

(D) It is important to local economies. 對當地的經濟很重要。

中譯 本文對於旅遊業有怎樣的建議？

解析 由These exiting trips mean big money for local economies.可知。

100 年外語導遊英文試題＋標準答案

★100年專門職業及技術人員普通考試導遊人員、領隊人員考試試題

等 別：普通考試

類 科：外語導遊人員（英語）

科 目：外國語（英語）

考試時間：1 小時 20 分

※注意：（一）本試題為單一選擇題，請選出一個正確或最適當的答案，複選作答者，該題不予計分。
（二）本科目共80題，每題1.25分，須用2Ｂ鉛筆在試卡上依題號清楚劃記，於本試題上作答者，不予計分。
（三）本試題禁止使用電子計算器。

(　　)1. Hong Kong is one of the world's most thrilling Chinese New Year travel destinations. The ______ is the spectacular fireworks display on the second day of the New Year.
(A) highlight　(B) limelight　(C) insight　(D) twilight

(　　)2. Didn't you hear the ______? Come on, we need to go now or we'll miss our flight.
(A) final calling　(B) final call　(C) call final　(D) call finally

(　　)3. A ______ room or seat is being kept for someone rather than given or sold to someone else.
(A) refrained　(B) restricted　(C) reserved　(D) reversed

(　　)4. Please check your ticket and ______ that you are sitting in the correct seat.
(A) make sure　(B) be aware of　(C) find out　(D) pay attention

(　　)5. I love going away, but there's no place like ______.
(A) house　(B) home　(C) my　(D) bed outdoors

(　　)6. By 2050, Africa's population, both northern and sub-Saharan, is expected to ______ from 900 million to almost two billion.
(A) surge　(B) decrease　(C) derive　(D) descend

( )7. When you arrive at the airport, the first thing you do is go to ______.

(A) the departure lounge (B) the check-in desk
(C) the arrival desk (D) the customs

( )8. Former Japanese F2 racer Takayuki Ueda has opened the Taki Racing School on the outskirts of Bangkok. The school ______ students aged over 16 years, even if they do not have a driver's license.

(A) acquires (B) accepts (C) limits (D) arranges

( )9. As a collector, Mr. Strachwitz has built ______ is believed to be the largest private collection of Mexican-American and Mexican music.

(A) that (B) what (C) who (D) which

( )10. Because son preference has been a significant phenomenon in Asia for centuries, the Chinese actually have a term for such ______: "bare branches" – branches of the family tree that will never bear fruit.

(A) bachelors (B) barbarians (C) boycott (D) bazaar

( )11. His one ambition in life was to go on ______ to Kenya to photograph lions and tigers.

(A) safari (B) voyage (C) ferry (D) yacht

( )12. One of Hualien's long-standing traditions is stone carving, which is not surprising considering the city's main ______ is marble.

(A) mission (B) jewelry (C) leisure (D) export

( )13. Many couples live together even though they are not married. The ______ of their behavior are highly suspect, but technically they are within the law.

(A) elites (B) ethics (C) epics (D) excuses

( )14. The hiking route of the Shitoushan Trail is not ______ and so is suitable for most people, including the elderly and young children.

(A) slick (B) smooth (C) steep (D) steady

( )15. The earthquake's ______ was such that hundreds of houses were destroyed and thousands of people were killed.

(A) gratitude (B) attitude (C) latitude (D) magnitude

(　　)16. A good place to end a tour of Rome is the Trevi Fountain. Legend has it that if you toss a single coin into the Trevi, you are ______ a return to Rome.

(A) preserved　(B) obtained　(C) dedicated　(D) guaranteed

(　　)17. It is ______ time to talk about travel as the holiday season is now beginning in most countries north of the equator.

(A) last　(B) again　(C) high　(D) with

(　　)18. As a general rule, checked baggage such as golf clubs in golf bags, serfboards, baby strollers, and child car seats are not placed on a baggage ______.

(A) carnival　(B) carrier　(C) claim　(D) carousel

(　　)19. If the rain doesn't stop soon, we should consider ______ Joe's farewell party.

(A) postponing　(B) protecting　(C) proposing　(D) promoting

(　　)20. ______ you need to get in touch with me, you can reach me at 224338654 at my travel agency.

(A) Those times　(B) In case　(C) At times　(D) Sometimes

(　　)21. Motorists are strongly advised to ______ when they drive along windy mountainous roads to avoid plunging into a ravine.

(A) wear helmets　(B) take caution　(C) fasten seatbelts　(D) keep afloat

(　　)22. After singing the national ______, the President gave a speech about Taiwan's history and its people.

(A) song　(B) prayer　(C) anthem　(D) lullaby

(　　)23. The ______ consists of the usual march-past by the military and some interesting displays by the marching girls, martial arts clubs and dragon dancers.

(A) performance　(B) parade　(C) paradise　(D) paradigm

(　　)24. The students were completely ______ about their graduation trip because the school wanted it to be a surprise.

(A) under the ground　(B) in the dark
(C) off the hook　(D) against the grain

(　　)25. When ______ a conversation, it is always best to ask very broad questions such as "Where are you from?" or "How long have you been here?"

(A) innovating　(B) igniting　(C) initiating　(D) inventing

( )26. Demographers study population growth or decline and things like ______, which means the movement of populations into cities.

(A) classification (B) normalization
(C) industrialization (D) urbanization

( )27. As introductory English now begins in elementary, rather than secondary school, and classes have begun to focus more on the spoken language, travelers to Taiwan can ______ without having to attempt any Mandarin or Taiwanese.

(A) take in (B) stop off (C) get by (D) pass along

( )28. Cindy and her husband are so busy that it is difficult for them to ______ dates for a vacation.

(A) nail down (B) take up (C) bargain for (D) deal with

( )29. Most taxi drivers in Kinmen prefer to ask for a ______ fare rather than use the meter.

(A) flat (B) high (C) set (D) deal

( )30. In southern Taiwan, people's ties to rural folk culture are strongest. Local gods are more fervently worshipped. Tainan, for instance, has a temple heritage second to ______.

(A) one (B) none (C) any (D) some

( )31. An open-minded city, Taipei ______ Asia's first Gay Pride parade which has now become an annual autumn event.

(A) expanded (B) governed (C) hosted (D) portrayed

( )32. I seem to have a fever. May I have a ______ to take my temperature?

(A) thermometer (B) manometer (C) calculator (D) scale

From the end of World War II until the early 1990s, most countries in Central Europe were communist, 33 their governments controlled all aspects of their economies. However, with the end of the Cold War, and the 34 of the Berlin Wall, the situation has changed dramatically. Since that time these countries have been transitioning to market-based economies and businesses are ready to compete with developed capitalist countries for profits. 35 they can be successful has been a hot issue till today.

( )33. (A) meaning (B) demanding (C) allowing (D) witnessing

(   )34. (A) resolution   (B) revolution   (C) abolition   (D) demolition

(   )35. (A) Whenever   (B) Whether   (C) Nevertheless   (D) Consequently

(   )36 Jack was the least popular student in our class because he always enjoyed teasing and making jokes ______ others.
(A) at the expense of   (B) with the consent of
(C) in agreement with   (D) on behalf of

(   )37. Most clothes are manufactured in distant countries under ______ conditions in pollution-emitting factories before being loaded into shipping containers.
(A) hazardous   (B) hilarious   (C) ridiculous   (D) adventurous

(   )38. Middle-aged smokers are far more likely than nonsmokers to ______ dementia later in life, and heavy smokers are at more than double the risk, according to a new study.
(A) deflect   (B) demote   (C) deliberate   (D) develop

(   )39. The depth of the current economic trauma is one that the ordinary Irish man or woman has found hard to accept, ______ fully comprehend.
(A) better not   (B) rather than   (C) if only   (D) let alone

(   )40. Baked goods are not a staple of a traditional Chinese diet, but they have been quickly ______ among China's urban middle classes over the last 10 years.
(A) dashing on   (B) moving on   (C) catching on   (D) getting on

(   )41. Headlines have a ______ function when they are designed to attract the attention of the reader and interest him/her in reading the story.
(A) adhesive   (B) persuasive   (C) pervasive   (D) defensive

(   )42. Earth is unique in the universe for its ______ of water, amounting to 70 percent of its surface.
(A) benevolence   (B) abundance   (C) redundance   (D) attendance

(   )43. While courts in the U.S. generally favor the mother in the event of a divorce, Taiwan family and divorce laws will grant custody to the father, ______ some other agreement is reached.
(A) unless   (B) regardless   (C) until   (D) considering

(   )44. Despite facing an imminent labor shortage as its population ages, Japan has done ______ to open itself up to immigration.

(A) small (B) little (C) none (D) less

(   )45. The Presidential Office in Taiwan is a classic mix of European renaissance and baroque style architecture, ______ ornate with simple features.

(A) substituting (B) blazing (C) combining (D) penetrating

(   )46. Unlike other springs locations, Taian Hot Springs is relatively serene, with no more than six large-scale resorts in the area, so the place is not as ______ as Wulai and Beitou.

(A) congested (B) displaced (C) isolated (D) populated

(   )47. They ______ all around the Mediterranean for eight weeks last summer and stopped off at a number of uninhabited islands.

(A) campaigned (B) cruised (C) commuted (D) circulated

(   )48. Many foreigners who had visited Taiwan remembered the ______ of people packed into night markets and aromas floating through the air.

(A) throngs (B) sequences (C) varieties (D) whereabouts

(   )49. Jason is thinking of purchasing a new ______ because the springs in the old one have gone.

(A) thermometer (B) mattress (C) microwave (D) refrigerator

(   )50. Beatrix's friend had given her a ______ interview before she actually went to meet the personnel manager of the company she was applying to.

(A) luck (B) fake (C) mock (D) rack

(   )51. There are around 7,000 convenience stores in Taiwan, the highest concentration in the world. The ______ 7-Eleven chain offers a great range of services, from faxing and copying to bill payments for customers.

(A) customary (B) disposable (C) explicit (D) ubiquitous

(   )52. Many people consider Yangmingshan National Park a pleasant ______ from the bustle of the city.

(A) retreat (B) removal (C) departure (D) adventure

(   )53. Most ______ private schools are highly competitive – that is, they have stiffer admissions requirements.

(A) fastidious (B) obscure (C) ponderous (D) prestigious

(   )54. *Cursive II* is a recent work of Taiwan's master choreographer Lin Hwai-min. He created *Cursive*, with its title ______ from Chinese calligraphy.

(A) authorized (B) derived (C) evacuated (D) generalized

(   )55. The public education in Taiwan has been ______ from primary school through junior high school since 1968.

(A) compulsory (B) disciplinary (C) regulatory (D) ordinary

(   )56. Diabetes is a ______ disease which is difficult to cure. Management concentrates on keeping blood sugar levels as close to normal as possible without presenting undue patient danger.

(A) gigantic (B) chronic (C) lunatic (D) pandemic

(   )57. People who earn little or no income can receive public assistance, often called ______.

(A) hospitality (B) budget (C) pension (D) welfare

(   )58. The Industrial Revolution, which began in the nineteenth century, caused widespread ______ as machines replaced workers.

(A) postponement (B) curtailment (C) unemployment (D) abandonment

(   )59. ______ areas are more densely populated than rural areas. That is, they have more people per square mile.

(A) Advanced (B) Bureaucratic (C) Metropolitan (D) Spacious

(   )60. Most countries take a ______ every ten years or so in order to count the people and to know where they are living.

(A) census (B) censure (C) censor (D) censorship

(   )61. Martial law was ______ from Matsu in 1992, a number of years later than "mainland" Taiwan. Matsu residents are now allowed to travel freely to and from Taiwan.

(A) secluded (B) departed (C) expelled (D) lifted

( )62. Some people refuse to eat ______ because it is made with parts of protected animals.

(A) wonton soup (B) shark fin soup (C) saute beef (D) oyster omelet

( )63. The temple was really colorful. It had blue and red tiles all over it and there were ______ of different gods on the walls and on the roof.

(A) states (B) status (C) statues (D) stature

( )64. You can get cash from another country at the ______ at the airport.

(A) information desk (B) currency exchange
(C) customs office (D) check-in counter

( )65. There was a lot of ______ last night. At one stage there was a sudden flash of light and a tree was knocked over and caught fire.

(A) rain (B) thunder (C) storm (D) wind

( )66. Research suggests that being bilingual may boost brain power as bilingual children are found to be better at multitasking and ______ tasks, doing the most important things first.

(A) prioritizing (B) minimizing (C) eliminating (D) delimiting

( )67. ______ numerous typhoon disasters in recent years, the government has drafted a coastline law in an effort to better care for land restoration and conservation.

(A) In spite of (B) In light of (C) In terms of (D) In tune with

( )68. The Taiwan High Prosecutors Office vowed to harshly ______ anyone caught hoarding food staples as part of the government's efforts to stabilize food prices amid a string of price hikes following the Lunar New Year.

(A) take hold of (B) get a grip on (C) put an end to (D) crack down on

( )69. May I remind you not to ______ your success on an important test by watching a movie instead of studying hard.

(A) idealize (B) naturalize (C) jeopardize (D) characterize

( )70. Taiwan's premier said 2010 was a boom year for tourism in Taiwan and he ______ the success to the improvements in cross-strait relations.

(A) administered (B) advertized (C) acclaimed (D) attributed

An NGO in Malaysia has opened the country's first "baby hatch" for rescuing unwanted newborns, as authorities battle increasing cases of abandoned babies. Modeled on similar services in Germany, Pakistan and Japan, the NGO says the facility will allow mothers to leave their babies anonymously. The hatch has a small door which opens to an incubator bed on which a mother can place her baby. Once the door is closed an alarm bell will alert the NGO's staff to the baby's presence, after the mother has left. This way the baby can be kept safe, and the mother's identity never has to be known. Women, Family and Community Development Minister Shahrizat Abdul Jalil told a local newspaper that the service, to be offered by the NGO OrphanCARE, would give desperate mothers an alternative to abandoning or killing their babies.

Official statistics show 407 babies were abandoned between 2005 and 2009 in Malaysia, a Muslim-majority country where abstinence from sex is expected until marriage, and abortions are not readily available.

OrphanCARE said it had 200 prospective parents on a waiting list to adopt babies and gave an assurance that there will be no legal repercussions for those who leave their babies at the hatch. "Mothers who have babies **out of wedlock** are often in a fragile state. They don't know where to turn to or what to do with their babies," OrphanCARE president Adnan Mohamad Tahir was quoted as saying. In the country where sex is the taboo topic, it's likely that unwanted pregnancy will continue to happen. Ms. Mohamad Tahir hoped that the new baby hatch will give some children at least a better start in life.

(   )71. According to the passage, which of the following statements about the abandoned babies is true?

(A) People from Germany, Pakistan and Japan are interested in adopting them.
(B) Many of them are the results of premarital sex.
(C) Most of them are premature when first arriving at the OrphanCARE.
(D) These babies will never know their real names for the rest of their lives.

(   )72. Which does the passage suggest about Malaysia?

(A) The medical techniques of abortion develop slowly there.
(B) Malaysian women who abandon their babies will be expelled from the Muslim community.
(C) There is an increasing trend of premarital sex in that country.
(D) In Malaysia, women who have sex before marriage will receive law suits.

(　　)73. What does the phrase "out of wedlock" in the middle of paragraph 3 mean?

(A) the state of being unmarried
(B) the baby delivered outside hospital
(C) the act that is forbidden by religion
(D) the marriage that is not blessed

(　　)74. Which of the following is **NOT** true about the baby hatch?

(A) A similar device has been operated in other parts of the world.
(B) The service is meant to protect both the mother and the baby.
(C) The service is not funded by the Malaysian government.
(D) The staff will know of the baby's presence when they hear the mother press the bell.

(　　)75. Which of the following would be the best title for the passage?

(A) Increasing Newborn Babies in Malaysia
(B) Malaysia's First Baby Hatch for Abandoned Babies
(C) The Muslim Population in Malaysia Decreases
(D) Malaysian Government Rescues Unwanted Newborns

Aboriginal groups are seeking to preserve their folkways and languages as well as to return to, or remain on, their traditional lands. Eco-tourism, sewing and selling tribal carvings, jewelry and music has become a viable area of economic opportunity. However, tourism-based commercial development, such as the creation of Taiwan Aboriginal Culture Park, is not a panacea. Although these create new jobs, aborigines are seldom given management positions. Moreover, some national parks have been built on aboriginal lands against the wishes of the local tribes, prompting one Taroko activist to label the Taroko National Park as a form of "environmental colonialism." At times, the creation of national parks has resulted in forced resettlement of the aborigines.

Due to the close proximity of aboriginal land to the mountains, many tribes have hoped to cash in on hot spring ventures and hotels, where they offer singing and dancing to add to the ambience. The Wulai Atayal in particular have been active in this area. Considerable government funding has been allocated to museums and culture centers focusing on Taiwan's aboriginal heritage. Critics often call the ventures exploitative and "superficial portrayals" of aboriginal culture, which distract attention from the real problems of substandard education. Proponents of ethno-tourism suggest that such projects can positively impact the public image and economic prospects of the indigenous community.

The indigenous tribes of Taiwan are closely linked with ecological awareness and conservation issues on the island, as many of the environmental issues are spearheaded by aborigines. Political activism and sizable public protests regarding the logging of the Chilan Formosan Cypress, as well as efforts by an Atayal member of the Legislative Yuan, "focused debate on natural resources management and specifically on the involvement of aboriginal people therein." Another high-profile case is the nuclear waste storage facility on Orchid Island, a small tropical island 60 km (30 nautical miles) off the southeast coast of Taiwan. The inhabitants are the 4,000 members of the Tao (or Yami) tribe. In the 1970s the island was designated as a possible site to store low and medium grade nuclear waste. The island was selected on the grounds that it would be cheaper to build the necessary infrastructure for storage and it was thought that the population would not cause trouble. Large-scale construction began in 1978 on a site 100 m (330 ft) from the Immorod fishing fields. The Tao tribe alleges that government sources at the time described the site as a "factory" or a "fish cannery," intended to bring "jobs [to the] home of the Tao/Yami, one of the least economically integrated areas in Taiwan." When the facility was completed in 1982, however, it was in fact a storage facility for "97,000 barrels of low-radiation nuclear waste from Taiwan's three nuclear power plants." The Tao have since stood at the forefront of the anti-nuclear movement and launched several exorcisms and protests to remove the waste they claim has resulted in deaths and sickness. The lease on the land has expired, and an alternative site has yet to be selected.

(　　)76. The first two paragraphs focus on ______.

(A) the prosperity of the aboriginal tribes

(B) the heritage of Taiwan Aboriginal Culture Park

(C) the tension between tourism and environmental protection for aborigines

(D) the struggle of Taiwan aborigines for education

(　　)77. The tone of the article is ______.

(A) passionate　　(B) ironic　　(C) objective　　(D) indifferent

(　　)78. According to the article, which of the following statement is true?

(A) Few tribes attempt to invest in hot springs because of governmental policy.

(B) Eco-tourism cannot truly help the economic growth of Taiwanese aborigines.

(C) Tourism and nuclear waste are closely related on Orchid Island.

(D) The Tao people boost their economy through their influence in the Legislative Yuan.

(　　)79. The Taroko National Park is labeled as a form of "environmental colonialism" because ______.

(A) the aborigines do not get enough power and money

(B) the central government suppresses the aborigines

(C) the nuclear waste brings pollution

(D) the park was built despite the protests of local people

(　　)80. The nuclear waste on Orchid Island ______.

(A) came mainly from three nuclear plants in Taiwan

(B) created new jobs for local people

(C) will be moved to foreign countries because of anti-nuclear movement

(D) has been stored since 1978

★標準答案

1. (A)	2. (B)	3. (C)	4. (A)	5. (B)
6. (A)	7. (B)	8. (B)	9. (B)	10. (A)
11. (A)	12. (D)	13. (B)	14. (C)	15. (D)
16. (D)	17. (C)	18. (D)	19. (A)	20. (B)
21. (B)	22. (C)	23. (B)	24. (B)	25. (C)
26. (D)	27. (C)	28. (A)	29. (A)	30. (B)
31. (C)	32. (A)	33. (A)	34. (D)	35. (B)
36. (A)	37. (A)	38. (D)	39. (D)	40. (C)
41. (B)	42. (B)	43. (A)	44. (B)	45. (C)
46. (A)	47. (B)	48. (A)	49. (B)	50. (C)
51. (D)	52. (A)	53. (D)	54. (B)	55. (A)
56. (B)	57. (D)	58. (C)	59. (C)	60. (A)
61. (D)	62. (B)	63. (C)	64. (B)	65. (B)
66. (A)	67. (B)	68. (D)	69. (C)	70. (D)
71. (B)	72. (C)	73. (A)	74. (D)	75. (B)
76. (C)	77. (C)	78. (B)	79. (D)	80. (A)

100 年外語導遊英文試題中譯與解析

1. Hong Kong is one of the world's most thrilling Chinese New Year travel destinations. The highlight is the spectacular fireworks display on the second day of the New Year.

(A) highlight 亮點 (B) limelight 引人注目的中心
(C) insight 洞察力 (D) twilight 黎明

中譯 香港是世界上最令人興奮的中國新年旅遊景點之一。最精彩的部分是大年初二壯觀的煙火表演。

解析 thrilling 令人興奮的；spectacular 壯觀的、壯麗的。

2. Didn't you hear the final call? Come on, we need to go now or we'll miss our flight.

(A) final calling (B) final call (C) call final (D) call finally

中譯 你沒有聽到登機前的最後廣播嗎？快點！我們要現在過去不然就會錯過班機了。

解析 本題考final call 登機前的最後廣播的用法。

3. A reserved room or seat is being kept for someone rather than given or sold to someone else.

(A) refrained 制止的 (B) restricted 受限制的
(C) reserved 保留的 (D) reversed 顛倒的

中譯 保留的房間或是座位是替某些人保留，不能提供或出售給他人。

解析 reserved （被）保留的；reservations 預定。

4. Please check your ticket and make sure that you are sitting in the correct seat.

(A) make sure 確定 (B) be aware of 意識到
(C) find out 發現 (D) pay attention 專心

中譯 請檢查你的票並確認你坐在正確的座位上。

解析 make sure 確定。

5. I love going away, but there's no place like home.

(A) house 房子 (B) home 家 (C) my bed 我的床 (D) outdoors 戶外

中譯 我喜歡趴趴走，但沒有一個地方比得上家。

解析 為什麼選home而不選house，這是因為house為「外殼」，但home也可意指心靈上的歸屬。

6. By 2050, Africa's population, both northern and sub-Saharan, is expected to surge from 900 million to almost two billion.

(A) surge 激增　(B) decrease 減少　(C) derive 起源　(D) descend 下降

中譯 到了2050年，非洲的人口，包含北非和撒哈拉沙漠，預計會從9億激增至20億。

解析 由9億到20億，可知為surge 激增。population 人口。

7. When you arrive at the airport, the first thing you do is go to the check-in desk.

(A) the departure lounge 候機室

(B) the check-in desk 辦理登機手續的櫃台

(C) the arrival desk 入境櫃台

(D) the customs 海關

中譯 當你到達機場時，你要做的第一件事就是去辦理登機手續的櫃台。

解析 the check-in desk 辦理登機手續的櫃台。

8. Former Japanese F2 racer Takayuki Ueda has opened the Taki Racing School on the outskirts of Bangkok. The school students accepts aged over 16 years, even if they do not have a driver's license.

(A) acquires 獲得　(B) accepts 同意　(C) limits 限制　(D) arranges 安排

中譯 前日本F2賽車手上田隆幸在曼谷郊區經營了一間塔基賽車學校。這間學校接受16歲以上的學生，即便沒有駕照也可以。

解析 由even if they do not have a driver's license可知答案為accept 同意（入學）、接受之意。outskirts 郊外、郊區；driver's license 駕駛執照。

9. As a collector, Mr. Strachwitz has built what is believed to be the largest private collection of Mexican-American and Mexican music.

(A) that（關係代名詞）　(B) what（關係代名詞）

(C) who（關係代名詞）　(D) which（關係代名詞）

中譯 作為一名收藏家，史瓦辛斯先生被公認已建立了最大的私人墨西哥裔美國以及墨西哥音樂收藏。

解析 關係代名詞：what、where、when、why = 先行詞 + which

故句子可為：

As a collector, Mr. Strachwitz has built the collection that is believed to be the largest private collection of Mexican-American and Mexican music.

或是：

As a collector, Mr. Strachwitz has built the collection which is believed to be the largest private collection of Mexican-American and Mexican music.

10. Because son preference has been a significant phenomenon in Asia for centuries, the Chinese actually have a term for such bachelors: "bare branches" – branches of the family tree that will never bear fruit.

(A) bachelors 單身漢 (B) barbarians 野蠻人
(C) boycott 聯合抵制 (D) bazaar 市集

中譯 幾個世紀以來，由於重男輕女在亞洲都是很重要的現象，中國甚至稱單身漢為光棍——光棍不能為家庭開花結果。

解析 此題考bachelors 單身漢。significant 有意義的、重要的；phenomenon 現象。

11. His one ambition in life was to go on safari to Kenya to photograph lions and tigers.

(A) safari 狩獵遠征 (B) voyage 航程 (C) ferry 渡船 (D) yacht 遊艇

中譯 他畢生的雄心之一就是到非洲肯亞狩獵遠征，拍攝獅子和老虎。

解析 由lions and tigers可知為safari。ambition 雄心、抱負。

12. One of Hualien's long-standing traditions is stone carving, which is not surprising considering the city's main export is marble.

(A) mission 任務 (B) jewelry 珠寶 (C) leisure 悠閑 (D) export 出口

中譯 花蓮屹立不搖的傳統之一就是石雕，因此此城市的主要出口為大理石也就不足為奇了。

解析 此題考export為出口，進口則為import。

13. Many couples live together even though they are not married. The ethics of their behavior are highly suspect, but technically they are within the law.

(A) elites 精英 (B) ethics 道德 (C) epics 史詩 (D) excuses 藉口

中譯 許多情侶在還沒結婚前同居。他們的道德行為被高度質疑，但技術上來說他們是合法的。

解析 suspect 懷疑；within the law 合法。由but technically they are within the law來說，可得知是道德上有爭議。

14. The hiking route of the Shitoushan Trail is not steep and so is suitable for most people, including the elderly and young children.

(A) slick 光滑的　　(B) smooth 平坦的

(C) steep 陡峭的　　(D) steady 穩定的

中譯 獅頭山步道的健行路線不太陡峭，所以適合大多數的人，包含老人和小孩。

解析 由so is suitable for most people, including the elderly and young children可知是不steep 陡峭的。

15. The earthquake's magnitude was such that hundreds of houses were destroyed and thousands of people were killed.

(A) gratitude 感恩　　(B) attitude 態度

(C) latitude 緯度　　(D) magnitude 大小、震級

中譯 地震的震度能使數百間房屋被摧毀、上千人死亡。

解析 earthquake 地震，例句：Rescuers from many countries went to the epicenter of the earthquake to help the victims. 來自許多國家的救援者到震央去幫忙受害者。由earthquake可得知答案為magnitude 大小。

16. A good place to end a tour of Rome is the Trevi Fountain. Legend has it that if you toss a single coin into the Trevi, you are guaranteed a return to Rome.

(A) preserved 保存　　(B) obtained 獲得

(C) dedicated 專注　　(D) guaranteed 保證的

中譯 特雷維噴泉是結束羅馬之旅的好地方。傳說只要投一枚硬幣到噴泉內，就保證會再訪羅馬。

解析 toss 拋、頭；guarante 保證，常見用法還有refund guarantees 保證退款。

17. It is high time to talk about travel as the holiday season is now beginning in most countries north of the equator.

(A) last 最後的　　(B) again 再次　　(C) high 高的　　(D) with 以

中譯 隨著北半球國家的假期到來，是差不多該討論旅行的時候了。

解析 本題考It is high time 正是應該……的時候、是……的時候了。常見的high season則是旺季的意思。equator 赤道。

18. As a general rule, checked baggage such as golf clubs in golf bags, serfboards, baby strollers, and child car seats are not placed on a baggage carousel.

(A) carnival 嘉年華會 (B) carrier 搬運者
(C) claim 認領 **(D) carousel 轉盤**

中譯 一般來說，託運行李像是高爾夫球俱樂部的高爾夫球袋、衝浪板、嬰兒推車以及兒童汽車安全座椅不會被放在行李轉盤上。

解析 baggage carousel 行李轉盤。

19. If the rain doesn't stop soon, we should consider postponing Joe's farewell party.

(A) postponing 延期 (B) protecting 保護
(C) proposing 計劃 (D) promoting 推銷

中譯 如果雨再下不停，我們應該考慮延期喬的歡送派對。

解析 postpone 延期；delay 延遲。postpone一般指有安排的延遲，常說明延到什麼時候。例句：The meeting has been postponed to next Monday. 會議延到下星期一舉行。另外，delay則常表示由於外界的原因而拖延，如：The storm delayed the flight. 班機因風暴延遲。

20. In case you need to get in touch with me, you can reach me at 224338654 at my travel agency.

(A) Those times 這些時間 **(B) In case 萬一**
(C) At times 有時 (D) Sometimes 有時

中譯 萬一你需要和我聯繫，你可以打224338654到我的旅行社和我聯絡。

解析 get in touch with 與……取得聯繫。

21. Motorists are strongly advised to take caution when they drive along windy mountainous roads to avoid plunging into a ravine.

(A) wear helmets 戴安全帽 **(B) take caution 注意**
(C) fasten seatbelts 繫緊安全帶 (D) keep afloat 應付自如

中譯 強烈告誡摩托車騎士當行經風很大的深山時，要特別注意避免墜入深谷。

解析 plunge into 跳入、投入；ravine 溝壑、深谷。

22. After singing the national anthem, the President gave a speech about Taiwan's history and its people.

(A) song 歌曲 (B) prayer 祈禱 (C) anthem 聖歌 (D) lullaby 搖籃曲

中譯 唱完國歌之後，總統發表了一篇和台灣歷史與人民有關的演講。

解析 此題考國歌的用法：national anthem。國旗則是national flag。

23. The parade consists of the usual march- past by the military and some interesting displays by the marching girls, martial arts clubs and dragon dancers.

(A) performance 表演
(B) parade 遊行
(C) paradise 天堂
(D) paradigm 範例

中譯 此遊行的組成如同往常一樣的隊伍，有行軍隊伍，和女子儀隊、武術團體、舞龍舞獅等有趣的表演。

解析 由march 行進、行軍，或是「marching girls, martial arts clubs and dragon dancers」可推知為遊行。consists of 由某事物組成或構成。

24. The students were completely in the dark about their graduation trip because the school wanted it to be a surprise.

(A) under the ground 地底下
(B) in the dark 一無所知
(C) off the hook 擺脫危境
(D) against the grain 格格不入

中譯 學生對於畢業旅行一無所知，因為學校希望把此事當成一個驚喜。

解析 用直譯來看in the dark為在黑暗中，也就是什麼都看不到、不清楚的意思。另外，have no clue也可代表一無所知的意思。

25. When initiating a conversation, it is always best to ask very broad questions such as "Where are you from?" or "How long have you been here?"

(A) innovating 創新 (B) igniting 點燃 (C) initiating 開始 (D) inventing 發明

中譯 當開啟話題時，最好總是先問比較廣泛的問題，像是「你從哪裡來？」以及「你已經在這待多久了？」

解析 initiate 開啟，由"Where are you from?" or "How long have you been here?"可知為開啟話題。

26. Demographers study population growth or decline and things like urbanization, which means the movement of populations into cities.

(A) classification 分類　(B) normalization 正常化
(C) industrialization 工業化　**(D) urbanization 都市化**

中譯 人口統計學家研究人口的成長或是削減，以及像是都市化，就表示人口往城市移動。

解析 由populations into cities即可猜出答案urbanization 都市化，字根urban為都市。demographers 人口統計學家；decline 下降、減少。

27. As introductory English now begins in elementary, rather than secondary school, and classes have begun to focus more on the spoken language, travelers to Taiwan can get by without having to attempt any Mandarin or Taiwanese.

(A) take in 接受　(B) stop off 中途停留
(C) get by 勉強過得去　(D) pass along 路過

中譯 現在英語入門始於小學而非國中，且課程也已變得著重在口語，到台灣的旅客可以勉強用英文溝通，而不用講中文或是台語。

解析 由without having to attempt any Mandarin or Taiwanese可知為get by 勉強過得去；attempt 企圖、嘗試。

28. Cindy and her husband are so busy that it is difficult for them to nail down dates for a vacation.

(A) nail down 確定　(B) take up 拿起
(C) bargain for 指望　(D) deal with處理

中譯 辛蒂與她的丈夫是如此的忙碌，以至於難以敲定去度假的日期。

解析 nail down dates 敲定日期。

29. Most taxi drivers in Kinmen prefer to ask for a flat fare rather than use the meter.

(A) flat 平坦的　(B) high 高的　(C) set 設定的　(D) deal 買賣

中譯 大部分金門的計程車司機比較喜歡固定車資計價，而非跳表。

解析 固定車資的用法為flat fare，因為車資固定，故使用flat 平坦的。

30. In southern Taiwan, people's ties to rural folk culture are strongest. Local gods are more fervently worshipped. Tainan, for instance, has a temple heritage second to none.

(A) one 一個　(B) none 沒有　(C) any 任何　(D) some 一些

中譯 南台灣人民與民俗文化的連結是最強的。當地的神明備受崇拜。例如台南，寺廟的文化首屈一指（不亞於任何地方）。

解析 rural 農村的、田園的；second to none 不亞於任何人、首屈一指。

31. An open-minded city, Taipei hosted Asia's first Gay Pride parade which has now become an annual autumn event.

(A) expanded 使擴張　(B) governed 管理
(C) hosted 主辦　(D) portrayed 描寫

中譯 身為一座心胸開放的都市，台北主辦亞洲第一屆同志遊行，並且成為每年於秋天所舉辦的活動。

解析 舉辦活動有兩個常見單字：
① host 主辦（帶有主辦人的意思）
- Rio will host the 2016 Summer Olympic Games. 里約將主辦2016年夏季奧運。
② hold 舉行、舉辦
- The Olympic Games are held every four years. 奧運每4年（被）舉辦一次。
- The first Taipei Lantern Festival was held in 1990. Due to the event's huge popularity, the festival has been expanded every year. 第一屆的台北燈籠節於1990年舉行。而因為這場活動受到極大的歡迎，慶祝活動一年比一年盛大。98導遊

32. I seem to have a fever. May I have a thermometer to take my temperature?

(A) thermometer 溫度計　(B) manometer 壓力計
(C) calculator 計算機　(D) scale 比例尺

中譯 我好像感冒了。可以給我溫度計量溫度嗎？

解析 由fever和temperature都可猜出答案為thermometer 溫度計。

From the end of World War II until the early 1990s, most countries in Central Europe were communist, meaning their governments controlled all aspects of their economies. However, with the end of the Cold War, and the demolition of the Berlin Wall, the situation has changed dramatically. Since that time these countries have been transitioning to market-based economies and businesses are ready to compete with developed capitalist countries for profits. Whether they can be successful has been a hot issue till today.

中譯 從第二次世界大戰末期到1990年代早期，大部分中歐國家還是共產國家，也就是他們的政府控制經濟的各個層面。然而到了冷戰末期，以及柏林圍牆的倒塌，情勢有了戲劇性的轉變。自從那時開始，這些國家轉變成以市場為主的經濟，為了利潤商業也準備好和已開發的資本主義國家競爭。不論這些國家是否成功，這些議題到今天仍舊被廣泛討論。

單字 communist 共產主義者
dramatically 戲劇性地、引人注目地

33. (A) meaning 意即 (B) demanding 要求
(C) allowing 允許 (D) witnessing 見證

34. (A) resolution 決心 (B) revolution 革命
(C) abolition 廢除 (D) demolition 拆除

35. (A) Whenever 不論何時 (B) Whether 不論
(C) Nevertheless 儘管 (D) Consequently 所以

36. Jack was the least popular student in our class because he always enjoyed teasing and making jokes at the expense others.

(A) at the expense of 以……為代價 (B) with the consent of 經……的同意
(C) in agreement with 與……一致 (D) on behalf of 代表

中譯 傑克是我們班上最不受歡迎的學生，因為他總是樂於捉弄以及開他人玩笑為代價。

解析 at the expense of... 以……為代價。

37. Most clothes are manufactured in distant countries under hazardous conditions in pollution-emitting factories before being loaded into shipping containers.

(A) hazardous 危險的 (B) hilarious 歡鬧的
(C) ridiculous 可笑的 (D) adventurous 喜歡冒險的

中譯 大部分的衣服尚未裝到貨櫃船前，是在遙遠的國家的工廠排放汙染物的危險情況下所製造的。

解析 由pollution-emitting factories可知為hazardous 危險的。manufacture （大量）製造、加工。

38. Middle-aged smokers are far more likely than nonsmokers to develop dementia later in life, and heavy smokers are at more than double the risk, according to a new study.

(A) deflect 偏斜 (B) demote 使降級
(C) deliberate 仔細考慮 (D) develop 發展

中譯 根據一項新的研究，中年吸菸的人比不吸菸的人在往後的日子裡更容易引發失智症，而有菸癮的人有超過2倍以上的風險。

解析 develop a new symptom 出現新症狀。Fresh air and exercise develop healthy bodies. 新鮮空氣和運動能使身體健康。

39. The depth of the current economic trauma is one that the ordinary Irish man or woman has found hard to accept, let alone fully comprehend.

(A) better not 最好不要 (B) rather than 而不是
(C) if only 只要、但願 (D) let alone 更不用說

中譯 目前經濟創傷的深度，達到一般愛爾蘭人難以接受的程度，更別說要充分瞭解了。

解析 let alone的用法為：A, let alone B. A已經如此，更遑論B了。current 當前的、現行的；comprehend 理解、了解。

40. Baked goods are not a staple of a traditional Chinese diet, but they have been quickly catching on among China's urban middle classes over the last 10 years.

(A) dashing on 猛衝 (B) moving on 繼續前進
(C) catching on 流行 (D) getting on 進展

中譯 烘培食品並非傳統中國菜的主食，但過去10年，這些已經在中國城市的中產階級之間迅速流行。

解析 staple 主要產品、主食；catch on有2種意思：① understand 理解 ② become popular 流行起來。

41. Headlines have a persuasive function when they are designed to attract the attention of the reader and interest him/her in reading the story.

(A) adhesive 有粘性的、難忘的 (B) persuasive 善說服的
(C) pervasive 普遍的 (D) defensive 防衛的

中譯 標題有說服人的功能，它們被用來設計以吸引讀者的目光，以及讓他們有興趣讀下去。

解析 persuade 說服；persuasive 善說服的；attract 吸引。

42. Earth is unique in the universe for its abundance of water, amounting to 70 percent of its surface.

(A) benevolence 善行 (B) abundance 充裕
(C) redundance 過多 (D) attendance 出席

中譯 地球在宇宙中很獨特因為有充沛的水，大約表面70%都是水。

解析 由70 percent of its surface可知為abundance 充裕，例句：The tree yields an abundance of fruit. 這樹結果甚多。unique 唯一的、獨一無二的。

43. While courts in the U.S. generally favor the mother in the event of a divorce, Taiwan family and divorce laws will grant custody to the father, unless some other agreement is reached.

(A) unless 除非 (B) regardless 不管怎樣
(C) until 直到 (D) considering 顧及

中譯 美國法院通常於夫妻離婚時會偏向母親，但台灣的親屬法則是偏向給父親監護權，除非事先有達成協議。

解析 由美國和台灣的不同情況，可推知為unless。

44. Despite facing an imminent labor shortage as its population ages, Japan has done little to open itself up to immigration.

(A) small 小的 (B) little 很少 (C) none 沒有 (D) less 較少

中譯 即便隨著人口高齡化，勞工短缺的問題近在眼前，日本在開放移民方面還是做得很少。

解析 little表示少到幾乎沒有。imminent 逼近的、即將發生的。

45. The Presidential Office in Taiwan is a classic mix of European renaissance and baroque style architecture, combining ornate with simple features.

(A) substituting 取代 (B) blazing 強烈的
(C) combining 結合 (D) penetrating 穿透

中譯 台灣總統府是典型的歐洲文藝復興與巴洛克建築的組合，結合華麗與簡約的特徵。

解析 combine with 結合。

46. Unlike other springs locations, Taian Hot Springs is relatively serene, with no more than six large-scale resorts in the area, so the place is not as congested as Wulai and Beitou.

(A) congested 擁擠的　　(B) displaced 取代的
(C) isolated 孤立的　　(D) populated 粒子數增加的

中譯 不像其他地區，泰安溫泉相對安靜，這區域的大型度假村不超過6個，所以不像烏來和北投一樣擁擠。

解析 serene 寧靜的。由serene可知不擁擠。

47. They cruised all around the Mediterranean for eight weeks last summer and stopped off at a number of uninhabited islands.

(A) campaigned 參加活動　　(B) cruised 巡遊
(C) commuted 通勤　　(D) circulated 流通

中譯 他們去年夏天航遊地中海8週，並在一些無人島上短暫停留。

解析 由Mediterranean可知答案為cruised。cruise ship 載客長途航行的遊輪；uninhabited 無人居住的、杳無人跡的。

48. Many foreigners who had visited Taiwan remembered the throngs of people packed into night markets and aromas floating through the air.

(A) throngs 人群　　(B) sequences 順序
(C) varieties 多樣性　　(D) whereabouts 下落

中譯 許多拜訪台灣的外國人都記得人群湧進夜市，以及香氣飄在空中。

解析 由people packed into night markets可知答案為throngs 人群。

49. Jason is thinking of purchasing a new mattress because the springs in the old one have gone.

(A) thermometer 溫度計　　(B) mattress 床墊
(C) microwave 微波　　(D) refrigerator 冰箱

中譯 因為舊床墊的彈簧已經壞了，傑森在思考購買新的。

解析 此題考springs為彈簧，而非春天或溫泉。purchase 購買。

50. Beatrix's friend had given her a mock interview before she actually went to meet the personnel manager of the company she was applying to.

(A) luck 幸運 (B) fake 假的 (C) mock 模仿 (D) rack 架子

中譯 貝翠絲的朋友給她一個模擬的面試，在她實際與申請工作公司的人事主管面試之前。

解析 mock 模仿。mock-up則是作品尚未完成之前的示意圖。

51. There are around 7,000 convenience stores in Taiwan, the highest concentration in the world. The ubiquitous 7-Eleven chain offers a great range of services, from faxing and copying to bill payments for customers.

(A) customary 約定俗成的 (B) disposable 可以丟棄的
(C) explicit 清楚的 (D) ubiquitous 到處存在的

中譯 台灣大約有7,000間便利商店，是全世界密度最高的。到處都有的7-11連鎖店提供顧客各類型的服務，從傳真、影印到付款。

解析 由the highest concentration in the world可知為ubiquitous 到處存在的。concentration 集中；payment 付款。

52. Many people consider Yangmingshan National Park a pleasant retreat from the bustle of the city.

(A) retreat 僻靜之處 (B) removal 遷居
(C) departure 出發 (D) adventure 冒險

中譯 許多人認為陽明山國家公園是個遠離城市喧囂的僻靜之處。

解析 由from the bustle of the city可知為retreat。bustle 鬧哄哄地忙亂。

53. Most prestigious private schools are highly competitive – that is, they have stiffer admissions requirements.

(A) fastidious 挑剔的 (B) obscure 模糊的
(C) ponderous 沉悶的 (D) prestigious 聲望很高的

中譯 大部分有名氣的私立學校都很競爭，也就是他們有比較嚴格的入學條件。

解析 competitive 競爭的；requirements 需求。

54. Cursive II is a recent work of Taiwan's master choreographer Lin Hwai-min. He created Cursive, with its title derived from Chinese calligraphy.

(A) authorized 授權　　(B) derived 衍生出

(C) evacuated 撤離　　(D) generalized 概括

中譯 《行草貳》是台灣編舞家林懷民最近的作品。他創造行草的名稱衍生自中國書法。

解析 calligraphy 書法；derived from 衍生出。

55. The public education in Taiwan has been compulsory from primary school through junior high school since 1968.

(A) compulsory 義務的　　(B) disciplinary 訓誡的

(C) regulatory 統制的　　(D) ordinary 普通的

中譯 台灣的大眾教育自從1968年以來，從小學到國中都是義務教育。

解析 compulsory 義務的。

56. Diabetes is a chronic disease which is difficult to cure. Management concentrates on keeping blood sugar levels as close to normal as possible without presenting undue patient danger.

(A) gigantic 巨大的　　(B) chronic 慢性的

(C) lunatic 精神錯亂的　　(D) pandemic 全國流行的

中譯 糖尿病是一種慢性疾病且難以治癒。日常管理上須注意血糖高低須接近正常值，不要讓病人有過度危險的狀況發生。

解析 由difficult to cure即可推知為chronic 慢性的，cure 治癒。

57. People who earn little or no income can receive public assistance, often called welfare.

(A) hospitality 好客　　(B) budget 預算

(C) pension 退休金　　(D) welfare 福利

中譯 賺很少或沒賺錢的人可以有大眾救助，常常稱為福利。

解析 失業補助金即為welfare 福利的一種，income 收入、所得。

58. The Industrial Revolution, which began in the nineteenth century, caused widespread unemployment as machines replaced workers.

(A) postponement 延期 (B) curtailment 縮減

(C) unemployment 失業 (D) abandonment 放棄

中譯 工業革命，始於19世紀，由於機器取代勞工，導致普遍的失業。

解析 此題考unemployment 失業，延伸單字：employee 員工；employer 雇主。replace 取代。

59. Metropolitan areas are more densely populated than rural areas. That is, they have more people per square mile.

(A) Advanced 高級的 (B) Bureaucratic 官僚的

(C) Metropolitan 大都市的 (D) Spacious 廣大的

中譯 大都市區的人口密度比鄉村來得高。也就是每平方英里有比較多的人。

解析 metropolitan 大都市的，也常考urban 都會的，鄉村的則是rural。

60. Most countries take a census every ten years or so in order to count the people and to know where they are living.

(A) census 人口普查 (B) censure 責難

(C) censor 審查 (D) censorship 審查制度

中譯 大部分的國家每10年做一次人口普查，以計算人口以及了解其居住地。

解析 常考和人口相關的單字為census 人口普查，也常出現metropolitan / urban areas 都會區和rural areas 鄉村（郊區）的比較。

61. Martial law was lifted from Matsu in 1992, a number of years later than "mainland" Taiwan. Matsu residents are now allowed to travel freely to and from Taiwan.

(A) secluded 隱蔽的 (B) departed 以往的

(C) expelled 驅逐 (D) lifted 取消

中譯 馬祖在1992年解除戒嚴，比起台灣本島慢了幾年。現在馬祖居民可以自由往返台灣。

解析 此處考的lift，除了舉起，還有取消之意。lift someone out of poverty 脫貧，也曾出現於考題中。

62. Some people refuse to eat shark fin soup because it is made with parts of protected animals.

(A) wonton soup 餛飩湯　(B) shark fin soup 魚翅湯
(C) saute beef 嫩煎牛肉　(D) oyster omelet 蚵仔煎

中譯 有些人拒絕食用魚翅湯，因為它是以受保護的動物的某一部分所製成。

解析 由protected animals可知是shark fin soup。

63. The temple was really colorful. It had blue and red tiles all over it and there were statues of different gods on the walls and on the roof.

(A) states 說明　(B) status 身分　(C) statues 雕像　(D) stature 身高

中譯 寺廟非常的色彩繽紛。鋪滿藍色和紅色的磁磚，且在牆上以及屋頂上有許多不同的神明雕像。

解析 statues 雕像，如the Statue of Liberty 自由女神像。

64. You can get cash from another country at the currency exchange at the airport.

(A) information desk 服務台　(B) currency exchange 匯兌
(C) customs office 關稅局　(D) check-in counter 登機手續櫃台

中譯 你可以在機場的換匯櫃台拿到其他國家的現金。

解析 常考重點為currency exchange 匯兌、換匯。

65. There was a lot of thunder last night. At one stage there was a sudden flash of light and a tree was knocked over and caught fire.

(A) rain 雨　(B) thunder 雷　(C) storm 暴風雨　(D) wind 風

中譯 昨晚打很多雷。甚至一度有閃電將樹木擊倒並起火。

解析 由sudden flash以及caught fire可知為thunder 雷。

66. Research suggests that being bilingual may boost brain power as bilingual children are found to be better at multitasking and prioritizing tasks, doing the most important things first.

(A) prioritizing 按優先順序處理　(B) minimizing 使減到最少
(C) eliminating 排除　(D) delimiting 限定

中譯 研究顯示會說雙語的人可以增進腦力，因為發現雙語小孩對於多工以及排優先順序處理的工作上有比較好的表現，也就是先做重要的事。

解析 bilingual 雙語的；boost 提高、增加；multitasking 多重任務處理。

67. In light of numerous typhoon disasters in recent years, the government has drafted a coastline law in an effort to better care for land restoration and conservation.

(A) In spite of 不管……
(B) In light of 考慮到
(C) In terms of 就……方面來說
(D) In tune with 協調

中譯 考慮到這幾年有許多颱風災害，政府已經草擬海岸法盡力來提供土地更好的復元與保護。

解析 numerous 很多的；disaster 災難；coastline 海岸線。

68. The Taiwan High Prosecutors Office vowed to harshly crack down on anyone caught hoarding food staples as part of the government's efforts to stabilize food prices amid a string of price hikes following the Lunar New Year.

(A) take hold of 把握
(B) get a grip on 掌握
(C) put an end to 結束
(D) crack down on （對某人 / 某事物）嚴加處置或限制

中譯 隨著農曆新年的到來，台灣高等法院檢察署嚴厲地打擊任何囤積大宗食物的行為，並依此作為政府努力穩定物價上漲的一連串措施。

解析 由anyone caught hoarding food staples便可知需要crack down on，harshly 嚴厲地。

69. May I remind you not to jeopardize your success on an important test by watching a movie instead of studying hard.

(A) idealize 理想化
(B) naturalize 使歸化
(C) jeopardize 危害
(D) characterize 表現……的特色

中譯 讓我提醒你不要因為看電影而沒有用功念書，危害了你的重要考試的成功與否。

解析 jeopardize 危害；instead of 而不是某物、某事，後方須搭配「名詞」或「動名詞」（Ving），可和rather than互換。

70. Taiwan's premier said 2010 was a boom year for tourism in Taiwan and he attributed the success to the improvements in cross-strait relations.

(A) administered 管理　(B) advertised 廣告

(C) acclaimed 喝彩　**(D) attributed 歸因**

中譯 台灣的行政院長說2010年是台灣旅遊業大幅成長的一年，他將此成功歸因於兩岸關係的改善。

解析 attribute sth. to 認為某事物是……的屬性、把某事物歸功於；cross-strait relations 兩岸關係。

An NGO in Malaysia has opened the country's first "baby hatch" for rescuing unwanted newborns, as authorities battle increasing cases of abandoned babies. Modeled on similar services in Germany, Pakistan and Japan, the NGO says the facility will allow mothers to leave their babies anonymously. The hatch has a small door which opens to an incubator bed on which a mother can place her baby. Once the door is closed an alarm bell will alert the NGO's staff to the baby's presence, after the mother has left. This way the baby can be kept safe, and the mother's identity never has to be known. Women, Family and Community Development Minister Shahrizat Abdul Jalil told a local newspaper that the service, to be offered by the NGO OrphanCARE, would give desperate mothers an alternative to abandoning or killing their babies.

中譯 馬來西亞的非政府組織已設立了全國第一個「棄嬰保護艙」來拯救被遺棄的嬰孩，是政府當局對抗逐漸升高的棄嬰數的手段。以德國、巴基斯坦和日本的相似服務為範本，非政府組織說，此設施可以讓一些媽媽以匿名的方式留下他們的小孩。這個「棄嬰保護艙」有個小門，打開後有個恆溫箱，媽媽可將嬰兒留在那裡。一旦門關閉，媽媽離開後，警鈴就會向非政府組織的人員示警已經有嬰兒在恆溫箱內。這樣可以顧慮到嬰兒的安全，媽媽的身分也不會被知道。婦女、家庭與社區發展主席Shahrizat Abdul Jalil和當地報紙說非政府組織提供的孤兒關懷服務，得以讓絕望的母親有除了遺棄或殺害嬰兒的其他選擇。

Official statistics show 407 babies were abandoned between 2005 and 2009 in Malaysia, a Muslim-majority country where abstinence from sex is expected until marriage, and abortions are not readily available.

中譯 官方統計顯示，2005-2009年間馬來西亞有407個嬰兒被遺棄，一個以伊斯蘭教為主的國家，婚前性行為是不被允取的，也無法選擇墮胎。

OrphanCARE said it had 200 prospective parents on a waiting list to adopt babies and gave an assurance that there will be no legal repercussions for those who leave their babies at the hatch. "Mothers who have babies out of wedlock are often in a fragile state. They don't know where to turn to or what to do with their babies," OrphanCARE president Adnan Mohamad Tahir was quoted as saying. In the country where sex is the taboo topic, it's likely that unwanted pregnancy will continue to happen. Ms. Mohamad Tahir hoped that the new baby hatch will give some children at least a better start in life.

中譯 非政府組織的孤兒關懷服務表示有200父母在等待名單中領養小孩，也保證不會對那些將嬰兒留在保護艙的父母追究法律後果。孤兒關懷主席Adnan Mohamad Tahir表示：「在無婚姻關係生下小孩的母親通常很脆弱。她們不知道如何尋求協助，或是拿嬰兒怎麼辦。」在這個性為禁忌話題的國家，意外懷孕的情況可能會繼續發生。Mohamad Tahir希望新的棄嬰保護艙至少能提供一些兒童人生有更好的開始。

71. According to the passage, which of the following statements about the abandoned babies is true?

(A) People from Germany, Pakistan and Japan are interested in adopting them.
來自於德國、巴基斯坦和日本的人想要領養他們。

(B) Many of them are the results of premarital sex.
多數來自於婚前性行為的結果。

(C) Most of them are premature when first arriving at the OrphanCARE.
大多數到孤兒關懷服務時都是早產兒。

(D) These babies will never know their real names for the rest of their lives.
這些嬰兒永遠都不會知道他們的真實姓名。

中譯 根據本文，對於棄嬰下列哪一項陳述屬實？

解析 由Official statistics show 407 babies were abandoned between 2005 and 2009 in Malaysia, a Muslim-majority country where abstinence from sex is expected until marriage, and abortions are not readily available.可知。

72. Which does the passage suggest about Malaysia?

(A) The medical techniques of abortion develop slowly there.
那裡的墮胎醫療技術發展緩慢。

(B) Malaysian women who abandon their babies will be expelled from the Muslim community.
拋棄嬰兒的馬來西亞女人會被逐出伊斯蘭社群。

(C) There is an increasing trend of premarital sex in that country.
那個國家會有越來越多的婚前性行為發生。

(D) In Malaysia, women who have sex before marriage will receive law suits.
馬來西亞女人若有婚前性行為會由法律制裁。

中譯 由本文可得知馬來西亞什麼事？

解析 由Official statistics show 407 babies were abandoned between 2005 and 2009 in Malaysia, a Muslim-majority country where abstinence from sex is expected until marriage, and abortions are not readily available.可知。

73. What does the phrase "out of wedlock" in the middle of paragraph 3 mean?

(A) the state of being unmarried 未婚狀態

(B) the baby delivered outside hospital 嬰兒送到醫院外

(C) the act that is forbidden by religion 被宗教禁止的行為

(D) the marriage that is not blessed 不被祝福的婚姻

中譯 本文第三段中間的「out of wedlock」是什麼意思？

解析 由out of wedlock可知為不受婚姻的束縛，故為未婚狀態。

74. Which of the following is NOT true about the baby hatch?

(A) A similar device has been operated in other parts of the world.
相似的裝置在其他國家也有。

(B) The service is meant to protect both the mother and the baby.
這項服務用來保護媽媽和小孩。

(C) The service is not funded by the Malaysian government.
這個服務不是由馬來西亞所發起的。

(D) The staff will know of the baby's presence when they hear the mother press the bell.
當工作人員聽到媽媽按鈴，就會知道嬰兒的存在。

中譯 對於棄嬰保護艙的敘述下列哪項錯誤？

解析 由Once the door is closed an alarm bell will alert the NGO's staff to the baby's presence, after the mother has left.可知。

75. Which of the following would be the best title for the passage?

(A) Increasing Newborn Babies in Malaysia

馬來西亞增加新生嬰兒

(B) Malaysia's First Baby Hatch for Abandoned Babies

馬來西亞第一個棄嬰保護艙

(C) The Muslim Population in Malaysia Decreases

馬來西亞的伊斯蘭教徒減少

(D) Malaysian Government Rescues Unwanted Newborns

馬來西亞政府拯救不要的新生兒

中譯 哪一項最適合當本文的標題？

解析 由An NGO in Malaysia has opened the country's first "baby hatch" for rescuing unwanted newborns可知。

Aboriginal groups are seeking to preserve their folkways and languages as well as to return to, or remain on, their traditional lands. Eco-tourism, sewing and selling tribal carvings, jewelry and music has become a viable area of economic opportunity. However, tourism-based commercial development, such as the creation of Taiwan Aboriginal Culture Park, is not a panacea. Although these create new jobs, aborigines are seldom given management positions. Moreover, some national parks have been built on aboriginal lands against the wishes of the local tribes, prompting one Taroko activist to label the Taroko National Park as a form of "environmental colonialism." At times, the creation of national parks has resulted in forced resettlement of the aborigines.

中譯 原住民團體正在尋求保存他們的民俗和語言，還有回到或是維持在他們傳統的土地上。生態旅遊：編織以及販賣部落雕刻、飾品和音樂，以及成為可行的經濟機會。然而，以旅遊業為主的商業發展，像是台灣原住民文化園區的誕生，並非萬靈丹。雖然創造了新的工作機會，原住民卻甚少位居管理要職。甚至有些國家公園根本就蓋在當地原住民並不希望所蓋的土地上，如一名太魯閣的激進分子所提及的，太魯閣國家公園根本是一種「環境上的殖民」。有時候，國家公園的建立會導致原住民被強迫重新安置。

Due to the close proximity of aboriginal land to the mountains, many tribes have hoped to cash in on hot spring ventures and hotels, where they offer singing and dancing to add to the ambience. The Wulai Atayal in particular have been active in this area. Considerable government funding has been allocated to museums and culture centers focusing on Taiwan's aboriginal heritage. Critics often call the ventures exploitative and "superficial portrayals" of aboriginal culture, which distract attention from the real problems of substandard education. Proponents of ethno-tourism suggest that such projects can positively impact the public image and economic prospects of the indigenous community.

中譯 由於原住民的土地與高山相似，許多部落希望可從溫泉企業或飯店中牟利，他們可以唱歌跳舞以增加風情。特別是烏來泰雅這區已經很活躍。政府所資助的大量金額已經被分到以台灣原住民文化遺產為主的博物館和文化中心。批評者表示這些企業剝削以及「膚淺的表述」原住民文化，反而讓真正的不合標準的教育問題失焦。民族旅遊擁護者建議像這類的專案對於當地的社區大眾形象和經濟前景有正面的影響。

The indigenous tribes of Taiwan are closely linked with ecological awareness and conservation issues on the island, as many of the environmental issues are spearheaded by aborigines. Political activism and sizable public protests regarding the logging of the Chilan Formosan Cypress, as well as efforts by an Atayal member of the Legislative Yuan, "focused debate on natural resources management and specifically on the involvement of aboriginal people therein." Another high-profile case is the nuclear waste storage facility on Orchid Island, a small tropical island 60 km (30 nautical miles) off the southeast coast of Taiwan. The inhabitants are the 4,000 members of the Tao (or Yami) tribe. In the 1970s the island was designated as a possible site to store low and medium grade nuclear waste. The island was selected on the grounds that it would be cheaper to build the necessary infrastructure for storage and it was thought that the population would not cause trouble. Large-scale construction began in 1978 on a site 100 m (330 ft) from the Immorod fishing fields. The Tao tribe alleges that government sources at the time described the site as a "factory" or a "fish cannery," intended to bring "jobs [to the] home of the Tao/Yami, one of the least economically integrated areas in Taiwan." When the facility was completed in 1982, however, it was in fact a storage facility for "97,000 barrels of low-radiation nuclear waste from Taiwan's three nuclear power plants." The Tao have since stood at the forefront of the anti-nuclear movement and launched several exorcisms and protests to remove the waste they claim has resulted in deaths and sickness. The lease on the land has expired, and an alternative site has yet to be selected.

中譯 台灣原住民與島上的生態意識以及保護問題密不可分，許多環境問題都以原住民為矛頭。政治激進派以及許多民眾，包含泰雅族的立法委員，抗議有關棲蘭山台灣檜木的砍伐問題。「相關辯論聚焦於自然資源的管理，特別是原住民的參與。」另一個引人注目的案例為蘭嶼核廢料儲存措施，為位於台灣本島東海岸60公里（30海浬）的熱帶小島。此處有4,000名達悟族（或雅美族）的居民。1970年代，蘭嶼被選為儲藏中低階核廢料的可能地點。選上蘭嶼是因為建立必要基礎設施以及儲存比較便宜，另外人口比較不會造成麻煩。1978年開始大規模建設，距離捕魚的Immorod海域僅100公尺（330英呎）。達悟族宣稱當時政府稱所描述的地區為「工廠」或是「魚罐頭工廠」，主要是替「達悟族（或雅美族）帶來工作機會，而蘭嶼尚未與台灣本島經濟結合」。然而事實上，1982年完工時，這成為一個儲藏97,000桶來自台灣本島三個核電廠的低階放射性廢料的設施。達悟族自此開始就站在反核運動的最前端，發起數次的反核運動、以及驅逐蘭嶼惡靈抗議活動，要求移除這些已造成許多死亡與疾病的核廢料。目前土地租約已經到期，替代的土地還沒有選出來。

76. The first two paragraphs focus on ______.

(A) the prosperity of the aboriginal tribes
原住民的繁榮

(B) the heritage of Taiwan Aboriginal Culture Park
台灣原住民文化園區的遺產

(C) the tension between tourism and environmental protection for aborigines
原住民旅遊產業和環境保護的緊張關係

(D) the struggle of Taiwan aborigines for education
台灣原住民教育的掙扎

中譯 本文的前兩段聚焦於 ______？

解析 由However, tourism-based commercial development, such as the creation of Taiwan Aboriginal Culture Park, is not a panacea.可知。

77. The tone of the article is ______.

(A) passionate 熱情的　(B) ironic 冷嘲的
(C) objective 客觀的　(D) indifferent 無情的

中譯 本篇文章的語氣為 ______？

解析 由前兩段各種觀點來看，可說本文為objective。

78. According to the article, which of the following statement is true?

(A) Few tribes attempt to invest in hot springs because of governmental policy.
因為政府政策的關係，少數部落試圖投資溫泉。

(B) Eco-tourism cannot truly help the economic growth of Taiwanese aborigines.
生態旅遊不能真正幫助台灣原住民的經濟增長。

(C) Tourism and nuclear waste are closely related on Orchid Island.
旅遊和核廢料與蘭嶼是密切相關的。

(D) The Tao people boost their economy through their influence in the Legislative Yuan.
達悟族藉由他們在立法院的影響力來提升經濟。

中譯 根據本文，下列哪一項敘述正確？

解析 由本文However, tourism-based commercial development, such as the creation of Taiwan Aboriginal Culture Park, is not a panacea. Although these create new jobs, aborigines are seldom given management positions.可知。

79. The Taroko National Park is labeled as a form of "environmental colonialism" because ______.

(A) the aborigines do not get enough power and money
原住民沒有得到足夠的權力和金錢

(B) the central government suppresses the aborigines
中央政府打壓原住民

(C) the nuclear waste brings pollution
核廢料帶來汙染

(D) the park was built despite the protests of local people
即便當地居民反對仍建造公園

中譯 太魯閣國家公園被視為「環境上的殖民」，因為 ______？

解析 由本文Moreover, some national parks have been built on aboriginal lands against the wishes of the local tribes, prompting one Taroko activist to label the Taroko National Park as a form of "environmental colonialism." At times, the creation of national parks has resulted in forced resettlement of the aborigines.可知。

80. The nuclear waste on Orchid Island ______.

(A) came mainly from three nuclear plants in Taiwan

主要來自台灣的3座核電廠

(B) created new jobs for local people

替當地人製造工作機會

(C) will be moved to foreign countries because of anti-nuclear movement

因為反核運動所以會被移到其他國家

(D) has been stored since 1978

自1978年開始儲存

中譯 蘭嶼的核廢料 ______？

解析 由"97,000 barrels of low-radiation nuclear waste from Taiwan's three nuclear power plants."可知。

101 年外語導遊英文試題＋標準答案

★101年專門職業及技術人員普通考試導遊人員、領隊人員考試試題

等 別：普通考試

類 科：外語導遊人員（英語）

科 目：外國語（英語）

考試時間：1 小時 20 分

※注意：（一）本試題為單一選擇題，請選出一個正確或最適當的答案，複選作答者，該題不予計分。

（二）本科目共80題，每題1.25分，須用2 B鉛筆在試卡上依題號清楚劃記，於本試題上作答者，不予計分。

（三）本試題禁止使用電子計算器。

(　　)1. At the annual food festival, you can ______ a wide variety of delicacies.

(A) sample　(B) deliver　(C) cater　(D) reduce

(　　)2. On my flight to Tokyo, I asked a flight ______ to bring me an extra pillow.

(A) clerk　(B) employer　(C) chauffeur　(D) attendant

(　　)3. Cloud Gate, an internationally ______ dance group from Taiwan, demonstrated that the quality of modern dance inAsia could be comparable to that of modern dance in Europe and North America.

(A) refunded　(B) reflected　(C) retained　(D) renowned

(　　)4. The complex is ______ of the main building, a tennis court, and a wonderful garden.

(A) organized　(B) collected　(C) occupied　(D) comprised

(　　)5. The zoo features more than 1,000 animals in their natural ______.

(A) habitats　(B) playgrounds　(C) landmarks　(D) facilities

(　　)6. A good tour guide has to be ______ to the people in his group.

(A) considered　(B) conditioned　(C) confided　(D) committed

(　　)7. I just spent a relaxing afternoon taking a ______ along the river-walk.

(A) trot　(B) dip　(C) stroll　(D) look

( )8. In the entrance hall of the natural history museum, you can find a full-sized ______ of a dinosaur.

(A) replica (B) revival (C) remodel (D) revision

( )9. The ______ of our trip to Southern Taiwan was A Taste of Tainan where we had a lot of delicious food.

(A) gourmet (B) highlight (C) monument (D) recognition

( )10. Sara bought a beautiful dress in a ______ in a fashionable district in Milan.

(A) boutique (B) brochure (C) bouquet (D) balcony

( )11. Bopiliao, ______ in Wanhua District, Taipei, and serving as the setting for the film, Monga, is a popular tourist spot.

(A) selected (B) featured (C) located (D) directed

( )12. Before we left the hotel, our tour guide gave us a thirty-minute ______ on the local culture.

(A) exhibition (B) presentation (C) construction (D) invitation

( )13. Chichi is a town in Central Taiwan that is ______ by rail.

(A) accessible (B) approached (C) available (D) advanced

( )14. The man at the passport ______ did not seem to like the photo in my passport, but in the end he let me through.

(A) station (B) custom (C) security (D) control

( )15. Success does not happen by chance. It's achieved through hard work and ______.

(A) expiration (B) reception (C) preparation (D) irritation

( )16. If you want, I can ______ it easier for you.

(A) weigh (B) act (C) be (D) make

( )17. All resources are ______ in the sense that there are not enough to fill everyone's wants to the point of satisfaction.

(A) scarce (B) absent (C) plentiful (D) fertile

( )18. Thanks to India's economic ______ and the booming growth of its airline industry, more Indians are flying today than ever before.

(A) prosperity (B) souvenir (C) decline (D) evidence

(   )19. The tour guide is a ______ man; he is very polite and always speaks in a kind manner.

(A) careless   (B) persistent   (C) courteous   (D) environmental

(   )20. This restaurant features ______ Northern Italian dishes that reflect the true flavors of Italy.

(A) disposable   (B) confident   (C) authentic   (D) dimensional

(   )21. On my first trip to Taipei, my ______ about the city is close to zero.

(A) consensus   (B) knowledge   (C) restoration   (D) honor

(   )22. ______ excellence in running a hotel restaurant is considered by many hotel managers the most difficult challenge of all.

(A) Achieving   (B) Resembling   (C) Dictating   (D) Exhausting

(   )23. Take your time. I don't need an answer ______.

(A) consistently   (B) regularly   (C) immediately   (D) frequently

(   )24. Don't over pack when you travel because you can always ______ new goods along the way.

(A) watch   (B) acquire   (C) promote   (D) throw

(   )25. Whales are ______, like we are, and must swim to the surface to breathe air.

(A) teenagers   (B) performers   (C) giants   (D) mammals

(   )26. The landscape of this natural park is best seen on bike or foot, and there are ______ trails in the area. All paths offer breath-taking sceneries.

(A) sole   (B) simultaneous   (C) numerous   (D) indifferent

(   )27. If you need a ride to the airport, please don't ______ to call me. I'll be available all this afternoon.

(A) pursue   (B) hesitate   (C) stop   (D) think

(   )28. With crystal clear water, emerald green mountains and various outdoor activities to offer, it's not ______ that Sun Moon Lake is one of the most visited spots in Taiwan.

(A) identified   (B) apparent   (C) grateful   (D) surprising

( )29. Taiwan is well known for its mountain ______ spots and urban landmarks such as the National Palace Museum and the Taipei 101 skyscraper.

(A) scenic (B) neutral (C) vacant (D) feasible

( )30. Trash can be ______ for creatures that live in the water. Every year, plastic trash kills millions of sea birds, marine mammals and sea turtles.

(A) invaluable (B) dangerous (C) spoiling (D) tedious

( )31. Many concerns were ______ about South Africa hosting the World Cup in 2010, but in the end South Africa pulled it off and did an excellent job.

(A) surpassed (B) licensed (C) implemented (D) raised

( )32. The notion that fashionable shopping takes place only in cities is ______, thanks to the Internet.

(A) outdated (B) approximated (C) rehearsed (D) motivated

( )33. Night markets in Taiwan have become ______ tourist destinations. They are great places to shop for bargains and eat typical Taiwanese food.

(A) tropical (B) popular (C) edible (D) responsible

( )34. It has been my honor and pleasure to work with him for more than 10 years. His insight and analysis are always ______.

(A) distant (B) superficial (C) impressive (D) premature

( )35. The tragedy could have been avoided but for the ______ of the driver.

(A) carefulness (B) prediction (C) negligence (D) alertness

( )36. According to the meeting ______, three more topics are to be discussed this afternoon.

(A) agenda (B) invoice (C) recipe (D) catalog

( )37. Taroko National Park ______ high mountains and steep canyons. Many of its peaks tower above 3,000 meters in elevation.

(A) lacks (B) features (C) excludes (D) disregards

( )38. The local tour guide has a ______ personality. Everybody likes him.

(A) windy (B) stormy (C) sunny (D) cloudy

( )39. Tomorrow I will be able to let you know ______ how many people will join the trip.

(A) tremendously (B) highly (C) rationally (D) precisely

( )40. ______ fireworks shows lit up the sky of cities around the world as people celebrated the start of 2012.

(A) Invisible (B) Spectacular (C) Dull (D) Endangered

( )41. A: "Excuse me. Can I take this seat?"
B: "Sorry, it is ______."

(A) empty (B) closed (C) occupied (D) complete

( )42. Many teenagers ______ late to play online games.

(A) grow up (B) break up (C) take place (D) stay up

( )43. To ______ health and fitness, we need proper diet and exercise.

(A) maintain (B) apply (C) retire (D) contain

( )44. From the evidence, it seems quite ______ that someone broke into my office last night.

(A) humble (B) inspiring (C) obvious (D) promising

( )45. I hate to go through the ______ process of application again. I need an assistant to do it for me.

(A) interesting (B) energetic (C) fascinating (D) tedious

( )46. I was very scared when our flight was passing through ______ from the nearby storm.

(A) turbulence (B) breeze (C) currency (D) brilliance

( )47. Most critics ______ the failure of the movie to its lack of humanity.

(A) caused (B) imputed (C) rewarded (D) dedicated

( )48. It is ______ impossible to train cats to do what you want them to do, but this one called Sasha can not only shake hands with people but also use the toilet.

(A) unlikely (B) casually (C) virtually (D) secondly

( )49. My most memorable trip is climbing Mount Fuji. Getting to the ______ and seeing the sunrise from the top of theclouds was amazing.

(A) depth (B) remark (C) twig (D) peak

(　　)50. Jennifer is ______ in several languages other than her mother tongue English.

(A) fluent　(B) quiet　(C) universal　(D) tall

(　　)51. The heavy rain in the valley often affects my ______, so I sometimes have to pull my car over to the side of the roadand wait until the rain stops.

(A) landscape　(B) sight　(C) image　(D) taste

(　　)52. Costa Brava is a popular tourist destination in northeastern Spain, thanks to its ______ climate, beautiful beaches, and charming towns.

(A) dreadful　(B) contemporary　(C) moderate　(D) bitter

(　　)53. I really like your scarf. Can I ______ my hat for that?

(A) expand　(B) exist　(C) exchange　(D) expel

(　　)54. At the Welcome Center, you will find plenty of ______, including maps, brochures, and wireless internet access.

(A) resources　(B) reformation　(C) documents　(D) assistance

(　　)55. With its palaces, sculptured parks, concert halls, and museums, Vienna is a city ______ in cultures.

(A) chronic　(B) elite　(C) provincial　(D) steeped

(　　)56. The oldest of all the main Hawaiian islands, Kauai is ______ for its secluded beaches, scenic waterfalls, and jungle hikes.

(A) due　(B) known　(C) neutral　(D) ripe

(　　)57. ______ in 1730, Lancaster's Central Market is the oldest continuously operating farmers market in the United States.

(A) Demolished　(B) Established　(C) Imported　(D) Located

(　　)58. High in the mountains of Chiapas, San Cristóbal del la Casas is one of the most ______ sprots in Mexico: colorful,historic, and remarkably complex.

(A) antarctic　(B) cosmetic　(C) photogenic　(D) synthetic

(　　)59. A single visit to Rome is not enough. The city's layered complexity ______ time.

(A) assists　(B) demands　(C) evolves　(D) lingers

(　　)60. Right now, there are more tigers in ______ than there are left in the wild. We need to take action to save the big cats.

(A) captivity　(B) debt　(C) haste　(D) quality

(　　)61. After a shipwreck, cruise companies try to ______ back hesitant passengers with discounts.

(A) bounce　(B) coil　(C) lure　(D) ransom

(　　)62. A canal ______ along a leafy bike pass, through green parks, and pass the city's four remaining windmills.

(A) injects　(B) meanders　(C) pollutes　(D) rumbles

(　　)63. Tourists have a wide range of budget and tastes, and a wide variety of resorts and hotels have developed to ______ for them.

(A) cater　(B) desire　(C) mourn　(D) pray

(　　)64. The developments of technology and transport infrastructure have made many types of tourism more ______.

(A) affordable　(B) considerable　(C) exclusive　(D) illusive

(　　)65. For many, vacations and travel are increasingly being viewed as a ______ rather than a luxury and this is reflected in tourist numbers.

(A) community　(B) dynasty　(C) necessity　(D) sincerity

(　　)66. The view of ______ waterfalls in the rainforest is spectacular.

(A) ascending　(B) cascading　(C) flourishing　(D) overflowing

(　　)67. If you plan and time it right, some home ______ can let you stay somewhere for free.

(A) abiding　(B) boosting　(C) meditating　(D) swapping

(　　)68. Preservation Hall is one of the many jazz ______ in New Orleans, but some of the best music can still be found on street corners, in backyards and at funerals.

(A) ceremonies　(B) distractions　(C) habitats　(D) venues

(　　)69. As a general rule, it's best to avoid wearing white clothing and accessories when traveling. Go with darker colors that ______ dirt well.

(A) delete　(B) hide　(C) parade　(D) imply

(　　)70. People love to socialize, and Facebook makes it easier. The shy become more ______ online.

(A) modest　(B) outgoing　(C) pious　(D) timid

Let's picture a huge public gathering – like the hajj to Mecca. Think of the World Cup, the Olympics, or a rock concert. When thousands or even millions of people get together, what will be the biggest health concern? Traditionally, doctors and public health officials were most concerned about the spread of infectious diseases. Robert Steffen, a professor of travel medicine at the University of Zurich, says that infectious diseases are still a concern, but injuries are a bigger threat at so-called mass gatherings.

According to Professor Steffen, children and older people have the highest risk of injury or other health problems at mass gathering events. Children are at more risk of getting crushed in stampedes, while older people are at higher risk of heat stroke and dying from extreme heat.

Stampedes at mass gatherings have caused an estimated seven thousand deaths over the past thirty years. The design of an area for mass gathering can play a part. There may be narrow passages or other choke points that too many people try to use at once. The mood of a crowd can also play a part. Organizers of large gatherings need to avoid creating conditions that might lead to stampedes and heat stroke.

So what advice does Professor Steffen have for people attending a large gathering? First, get needed vaccinations before traveling. Then, stay away from any large mass of people as much as possible. Also, be careful with alcohol and drugs, which can increase the risk of injuries.

(　　)71. Which of the following would be the most appropriate title for this passage?

(A) How to avoid mass gatherings
(B) Mass gathering: New escape skills
(C) Infectious diseases: New cures found
(D) Health risks in a crowd: Not what you may think

(　　)72. Which of the following is closest in meaning to **stampede** in the passage?

(A) A plane crash
(B) A steamy factory
(C) A sudden rush of a crowd
(D) Heat stroke due to mass gathering events

(　　)73. According to Professor Steffen, which of the following is more threatening to the health of people attending a huge public gathering?

(A) Injuries　　(B) Infectious diseases
(C) The mood of event organizers　　(D) Insufficient budget for an event

( )74. Which of the following is clear from the passage?

(A) Infectious disease is no longer a concern of the public.
(B) Event organizers should be more careful to avoid stampedes.
(C) A proper place for mass gathering should have one narrow passage.
(D) Children and older people are prohibited to attend mass gatherings.

( )75. Which of the following statements is LEAST supported in the passage?

(A) Extreme heat can cause death at mass gatherings.
(B) Infectious diseases will not spread at mass gatherings.
(C) Alcohol can increase the risk of injuries at mass gatherings.
(D) Older people are likely to suffer from heat stroke at a large gathering.

The historic center of Hoi An looks just how Vietnam is supposed to look: narrow lanes, wooden shop houses, a charming covered bridge. Hoi An's well preserved architecture – from the 16th century onward, the harbor town attracted traders from China, India, Japan and as far as Holland and Portugal – led United Nations Educational, Scientific and Cultural Organization (UNESCO) to deem it a World Heritage site, praising it as an outstanding demonstration of cultural blending over time in an international commercial port.

When Hoi An was first recognized as a World Heritage site in 1999, the city welcomed 160,300 tourists. In 2011, 1.5 million tourists arrived. Today, tour buses crowd the edge of Hoi An's old town. Tourists flood the historic center. Hundreds of nearly identical storefronts – providing food and selling the same tailored clothes, shoes and lanterns – colonize the heritage structures. To squeeze tourism revenue, a hospital has been forced to move out. Its building, built in the 19th century, now houses a tailoring business.

While local government officials and business owners view changes in the old town positively, tourists are beginning to notice the loss of authenticity in Hoi An. A 2008 UNESCO report sounded the alarm that "unless tourism management can be improved, the economic success generated by tourism will not be sustainable in the long term."

( )76. What is the main idea of the passage?

(A) Sustainable tourism revenue in the long run should not be a concern of the government.
(B) Hoi An should sell its old town to a modern tailoring business to increase economic revenue.
(C) UNESCO should urge Hoi An to build more narrow lanes, wooden houses, and covered bridges.
(D) Tourism management of historic sites should put a focus on protecting their authenticity and integrity.

(　　)77. What country is Hoi An located in?

(A) China　(B) Vietnam　(C) Japan　(D) Thailand

(　　)78. According to the passage, the old town of Hoi An is now ______.

(A) an empty place　(B) a famous theme park

(C) a popular tourist spot　(D) a center of modern arts

(　　)79. According to the passage, UNESCO believes World Heritage sites should be ______.

(A) abandoned　(B) modernized　(C) preserved　(D) exploited

(　　)80. According to the passage, which of the following is true?

(A) Hoi An has never been influenced by foreign cultures and has never traded with other countries.

(B) Hoi An has become a UNESCO World Heritage site since the 16th century.

(C) Tourists are attracted to Hoi An to admire its modern architecture and related arts.

(D) The number of tourists to Hoi An has increased substantially after it was recognized as a World Heritage site.

★標準答案

1. (A)	2. (D)	3. (D)	4. (D)	5. (A)
6. (D)	7. (C)	8. (A)	9. (B)	10. (A)
11. (C)	12. (B)	13. (A)	14. (D)	15. (C)
16. (D)	17. (A)	18. (A)	19. (C)	20. (C)
21. (B)	22. (A)	23. (C)	24. (B)	25. (D)
26. (C)	27. (B)	28. (D)	29. (A)	30. (B)
31. (D)	32. (A)	33. (B)	34. (C)	35. (C)
36. (A)	37. (B)	38. (C)	39. (D)	40. (B)
41. (C)	42. (D)	43. (A)	44. (C)	45. (D)
46. (A)	47. (B)	48. (C)	49. (D)	50. (A)
51. (B)	52. (C)	53. (C)	54. (A)	55. (D)
56. (B)	57. (B)	58. (C)	59. (B)	60. (A)
61. (C)	62. (B)	63. (A)	64. (A)	65. (C)
66. (B)	67. (D)	68. (D)	69. (B)	70. (B)
71. (D)	72. (C)	73. (A)	74. (B)	75. (B)
76. (D)	77. (B)	78. (C)	79. (C)	80. (D)

101 年外語導遊英文試題中譯與解析

1. At the annual food festival, you can a sample wide variety of delicacies.

   (A) sample 品嚐 (B) deliver 運送 (C) cater 承辦宴席 (D) reduce 減少

   中譯 在一年一度的美食節，你可以品嚐各類佳餚。

   解析 由food festival與delicacies得知，為sample 品嚐。此處的sample也可以用taste 品嚐來替換。delicacy 美味、佳餚。

2. On my flight to Tokyo, I asked a flight attendant to bring me an extra pillow.

   (A) clerk 店員 (B) employer 雇主
   (C) chauffeur 汽車司機 (D) attendant 空服員

   中譯 在前往東京的班機，我要求空服員給我額外的枕頭。

   解析 飛機上常見的人員為flight attendant 空服員；cabin crew 機組人員；captain 機長。另外，stewardess為空姐，steward則為空少。此處由flight to Tokyo可猜出答案為attendant 空服員。

3. Cloud Gate, an internationally renowned dance group from Taiwan, demonstrated that the quality of modern dance in Asia could be comparable to that of modern dance in Europe and North America.

   (A) refunded 退還 (B) reflected 反映 (C) retained 保留 (D) renowned 有名

   中譯 雲門，來自台灣的國際知名舞蹈團體，證明亞洲現代舞水準可和歐洲以及北美的現代舞媲美。

   解析 renowned也可以用famous替換，此處由comparable to that of modern dance in Europe and North America可知為internationally renowned 國際上知名的。demonstrate 論證、證明。

4. The complex is comprised of the main building, a tennis court, and a wonderful garden.

   (A) organized 組織 (B) collected 收集
   (C) occupied 佔領 (D) comprised 構成

   中譯 這棟綜合大樓是由主要大樓、網球場，以及一座美麗的花園所組成的。

   解析 由complex 複合物可知是由各個部分所comprised 組成的。此句也可以用The complex comprises the main building, a tennis court, and a wonderful garden.替換。

5. The zoo features more than 1,000 animals in their natural habitats.

(A) habitats 棲息地
(B) playgrounds 遊樂場
(C) landmarks 地標
(D) facilities 設備

中譯 這座動物園的特色是有超過1,000種動物居住在他們天然的棲息地內。

解析 由animals 動物可得知，是居住於natural habitats 天然的棲息地內。habitat 棲息地；habitant 居民。

6. A good tour guide has to be committed to the people in his group.

(A) considered 考慮
(B) conditioned 適應
(C) confided 透露
(D) committed 承諾

中譯 一名好的導遊必須致力於照顧他的團員。

解析 tour guide的責任即為對團員負責任，故選committed。

7. I just spent a relaxing afternoon taking a stroll along the river-walk.

(A) trot 小跑
(B) dip 浸泡
(C) stroll 散步
(D) look 看

中譯 我剛剛沿著河邊散步，度過了一個悠閒的下午。

解析 由spent a relaxing afternoon可知為stroll 散步。

8. In the entrance hall of the natural history museum, you can find a full-sized replica of a dinosaur.

(A) replica 複製品
(B) revival 復活
(C) remodel 重新塑造
(D) revision 修正

中譯 在自然歷史博物館的入口大廳，你可以發現一隻大小和原物相同的複製恐龍。

解析 由full-sized可推知為replica 複製品，而非remodel 重新塑造品。hall 會堂、大廳。

9. The highlight of our trip to Southern Taiwan was A Taste of Tainan where we had a lot of delicious food.

(A) gourmet 美食家
(B) highlight 亮點、最精彩的部分
(C) monument 紀念碑
(D) recognition 承認

中譯 南台灣之旅的亮點就是台南小吃，我們在那裡吃了很多美食。

解析 由we had a lot of delicious food可推知，是此趟旅程的highlight 亮點。

10. Sara bought a beautiful dress in a boutique in a fashionable district in Milan.

(A) boutique 精品店 (B) brochure 小冊子
(C) bouquet 花束 (D) balcony 陽台

中譯 莎拉在米蘭的流行時尚區的一間精品店買了一件漂亮的洋裝。

解析 由Sara bought a beautiful dress即可推知為boutique 精品店、流行女裝店。district 區、地區。

11. Bopiliao, located in Wanhua District, Taipei, and serving as the setting for the film, Monga, is a popular tourist spot.

(A) selected 選擇 (B) featured 以……為特色
(C) located 位於 (D) directed 指揮

中譯 剝皮寮位於台北萬華區，曾是電影《艋舺》拍片的場景，是個受歡迎的觀光景點。

解析 由in Wanhua District即可推知為located 位於。tourist spots、tourist attractions為觀光景點。

12. Before we left the hotel, our tour guide gave us a thirty-minute presentation on the local culture.

(A) exhibition 展覽 (B) presentation 介紹
(C) construction 建造 (D) invitation 邀請

中譯 在我們離開旅館之前，我們的導遊做了30分鐘當地文化的簡報介紹。

解析 presentation直譯上來看是呈現，但口語中多半為簡報、介紹，在台灣報名許多旅遊行程時，旅行社多半也會提供事前的說明，亦為presentation。

13. Chichi is a town in Central Taiwan that is accessible by rail.

(A) accessible 可到達的 (B) approached 接近的
(C) available 可用的 (D) advanced先進的

中譯 集集是中台灣鐵路可達的城鎮。

解析 形容某處的交通時，經常用accessible by car / rail來形容是否能開車、搭火車到達。

14. The man at the passport control did not seem to like the photo in my passport, but in the end he let me through.

(A) station 車站 (B) custom 風俗 (C) security 安全 (D) control 管理

中譯 在護照審查管理處的人似乎不喜歡我的護照照片，但最後還是讓我通過了。

解析 此處可能誤選為custom 風俗，但海關為customs（有加s），故passport control才為正解。

15. Success does not happen by chance. It's achieved through hard work and preparation.

(A) expiration 終止　(B) reception 接待

(C) preparation 準備　(D) irritation 激怒

中譯 成功不是偶然的。它必須經由努力工作和準備而達成。

解析 由Success does not happen by chance.可知preparation 準備的重要性。by chance 意外地、偶然。

16. If you want, I can make it easier for you.

(A) weigh 秤重　(B) act 扮演　(C) be 是　(D) make 變得

中譯 如果你想，我可以幫你把它變得容易些。

解析 此處的make it easier的make為使役動詞，使某物（it）為easier 更容易的狀態。如考題People love to socialize, and Facebook makes it easier. 人們喜歡社交，而臉書讓此更容易。

17. All resources are scarce in the sense that there are not enough to fill everyone"s wants to the point of satisfaction.

(A) scarce 缺乏的　(B) absent 缺席的　(C) plentiful 豐富的　(D) fertile 肥沃的

中譯 以「無法讓每個人都滿意」的觀點來說，資源都是不足的。

解析 由not enough to fill everyone"s wants to the point of satisfaction可知資源是scarce 缺乏的。

18. Thanks to India"s economic prosperity and the booming growth of its airline industry, more Indians are flying today than ever before.

(A) prosperity 繁榮　(B) souvenir 紀念品

(C) decline 衰退　(D) evidence 證據

中譯 歸功於印度的經濟繁榮，以及該國航空業的成長，如今有更多印度人搭飛機。

解析 由the booming growth 蓬勃的成長，可推知prosperity 繁榮。I wish you all prosperity.則是「我祝你萬事如意」的意思。booming 景氣好的；growth 成長。

19. The tour guide is a courteous man; he is very polite and always speaks in a kind manner.

(A) careless 粗心的 (B) persistent 堅持不懈的

(C) courteous 禮貌的 (D) environmental 環境的

中譯 導遊是一個有教養的男生，他非常有禮貌，談吐也得宜。

解析 courteous、well-mannered、polite都有「禮貌的」的意思，而沒禮貌則為discourteous、ill-mannered、impolite。manner 態度、禮貌。

20. This restaurant features authentic Northern Italian dishes that reflect the true flavors of Italy.

(A) disposable 可丟棄的 (B) confident 有信心的

(C) authentic 道地的 (D) dimensional 尺寸的

中譯 這間餐廳的特色為反映義大利口味的道地北義大利菜。

解析 由reflect the true flavors of Italy可知，是非常authentic 道地的。reflect 反射、反映，此作反映。feature 以……為特色，為必考單字。

21. On my first trip to Taipei, my knowledge about the city is close to zero.

(A) consensus 一致 (B) knowledge 瞭解

(C) restoration 修復 (D) honor 榮譽

中譯 第一次去台北旅行時，我對該城市幾乎一無所知。

解析 考生對於knowledge都知道是「知識」，但此處可解釋為「瞭解」。knowledgable 博學的。

22. Achieving excellence in running a hotel restaurant is considered by many hotel managers the most difficult challenge of all.

(A) Achieving 達到 (B) Resembling 像

(C) Dictating 聽寫 (D) Exhausting 精疲力盡

中譯 經營飯店餐廳如何追求卓越，是許多飯店經理人視為最困難的挑戰。

解析 achieve 達到，是重點單字。例如考題Success does not happen by chance. It's achieved through hard work and preparation. 成功不是偶然的。它必須經由努力工作和準備而達成。achieving excellence即為臻於完美之意。

23. Take your time. I Don't need an answer immediately.

(A) consistently 一致地 (B) regularly 規律地

(C) immediately 立即地 (D) frequently 頻繁地

中譯 你慢慢來。我不需要你立即地給答案。

解析 由take your time可知不需immediately 立即地給答案。Take one's time.表示悠閒的意思。

24. Don't over pack when you travel because you can always acquire new goods along the way.

(A) watch 觀看 **(B) acquire 得到** (C) promote 晉升 (D) throw 投

中譯 旅行時不用帶太多東西，因為你總是可以在旅途中取得新物品。

解析 acquire 得到、獲取之意。例：We must work hard to acquire a good knowledge of English. 我們必須用功學習才能精通英語。goods 商品、貨物。

25. Whales are mammals, like we are, and must swim to the surface to breathe air.

(A) teenagers 青少年 (B) performers 表演者

(C) giants 巨人 **(D) mammals 哺乳動物**

中譯 鯨魚是哺乳動物，就像我們，需要游到水面上呼吸。

解析 由must swim to the surface to breathe air可知為mammals 哺乳動物。surface 表面、外觀。

26. The landscape of this natural park is best seen on bike or foot, and there are numerous trails in the area. All paths offer breath-taking sceneries.

(A) sole 單獨的 (B) simultaneous 同時發生的

(C) numerous 許多的 (D) indifferent 冷淡的

中譯 騎單車或是步行最能看出這個自然公園的景色，園內也有許多步道。所有路徑都能看到令人屏息的風景。

解析 numerous 許多的，其實就是常見的many。breath-taking 令人屏息的，考題中也常見用amazing 令人驚豔的、spectacular 壯觀的這兩個形容詞來描述風景。landscape 風景、景色；path 小徑、小路。

27. If you need a ride to the airport, please Don't hesitate to call me. I'll be available all this afternoon.

(A) pursue 追求 (B) hesitate 猶豫 (C) stop 停止 (D) think 思考

中譯 如果你需要搭車去機場，請不要猶豫打電話給我。我整個下午都有空。

解析 hesitate 猶豫，例句：In case you need something, please don't hesitate to ask me. 如果你需要什麼東西，請不客氣地對我說。

28. With crystal clear water, emerald green mountains and various outdoor activities to offer, it's not surprising that Sun Moon Lake is one of the most visited spots in Taiwan.

(A) identified 被識別的 (B) apparent 明顯的

(C) grateful 感恩的 (D) surprising 驚訝的

中譯 有著清澈的水、翠綠的山脈，以及多種戶外活動可選，日月潭是台灣遊客最多的景點之一並不讓人驚訝。

解析 spot 場所、地點。

29. Taiwan is well known for its mountain scenic spots and urban landmarks such as the National Palace Museum and the Taipei 101 skyscraper.

(A) scenic 風景的 (B) neutral 中立的

(C) vacant 空的 (D) feasible 行得通的

中譯 台灣以其高山風景景點以及城市的地標聞名，像是故宮博物院和台北101摩天大樓。

解析 scenic spots 風景景點，tourist spots、tourist attractions 觀光景點，此兩處景點經常出現於考題中。scenary則為風景（名詞）。well known、famous都是有名的意思，亦為常考單字。urban 城市的；rustic 鄉下的。

30. Trash can be dangerous for creatures that live in the water. Every year, plastic trash kills millions of sea birds, marine mammals and sea turtles.

(A) invaluable 無價的 (B) dangerous 危險的

(C) spoiling 破壞的 (D) tedious 乏味煩人的

中譯 垃圾對海中生物有可能是很危險的。每年塑膠垃圾殺死數百萬的海鳥、海洋哺乳類以及海龜。

解析 由kill 殺死可推知，trash can be dangerous 垃圾有可能是很危險的。

31. Many concerns were raised about South Africa hosting the World Cup in 2010, but in the end South Africa pulled it off and did an excellent job.

(A) surpassed 超越　(B) licensed 得到許可的

(C) implemented 應用的　**(D) raised 升高**

中譯 對於南非舉辦2010年世界盃的疑慮升高，但最後南非消除了這些疑慮且表現出色。

解析 concerns were raised 疑慮升高，常考的raise的用法還有get a raise 加薪。pull sth. off 成功完成。

32. The notion that fashionable shopping takes place only in cities is outdated, thanks to the Internet.

(A) outdated 過時的　(B) approximated 近似的

(C) rehearsed 排練　(D) motivated 有動機的

中譯 歸功於網路，去大城市購物才時髦這樣的觀念已經過時了。

解析 take place 發生；outdated 過時，相反詞則為modern 現代的。請注意notion為觀念、看法的意思，而不是nation 國家的意思！

33. Night markets in Taiwan have become popular tourist destinations. They are great places to shop for bargains and eat typical Taiwanese food.

(A) tropical 熱帶的　**(B) popular 受歡迎的**

(C) edible 可食用的　(D) responsible 負責任的

中譯 台灣的夜市已經成為受歡迎的觀光景點。他們是討價還價和吃傳統台灣料理的好地方。

解析 觀光景點的各類用法請務必牢記：tourist destinations、tourist spots、tourist attractions。destination 目的地。popular 受歡迎的，則是一考再考的重點單字。

34. It has been my honor and pleasure to work with him for more than 10 years. His insight and analysis are always impressive.

(A) distant 遙遠的　(B) superficial 表面的

(C) impressive 令人印象深刻的　(D) premature 早熟的

中譯 能與他共事超過10年以上是我的榮幸。他的洞見和分析總是令人印象深刻。

解析 由it has been my honor and pleasure to work with him可知其洞見和分析總是impressive 令人印象深刻的。insight 洞察力、眼光、見識。

35. The tragedy could have been avoided but for the negligence of the driver.

(A) carefulness 謹慎
(B) prediction 預測
(C) negligence 疏忽
(D) alertness 警覺

中譯 要不是司機的疏忽，這場悲劇本來可以避免的。

解析 由the tragedy could have been avoided可知悲劇還是發生了，could have been avoided為本來可以被避免，故為司機的negligence 疏忽。tragedy 悲劇、災難。

36. According to the meeting agenda, three more topics are to be discussed this afternoon.

(A) agenda 議程
(B) invoice 發票
(C) recipe 食譜
(D) catalog 目錄

中譯 根據會議議程，這個下午還有3個議題要討論。

解析 agenda為議程、應辦事項，而由meeting可將其他選項刪除。

37. Taroko National Park features high mountains and steep canyons. Many of its peaks tower above 3,000 meters in elevation.

(A) lacks 缺少
(B) features 以……為特色
(C) excludes 不包含
(D) disregards 不理會

中譯 太魯閣國家公園以高山和陡峭的峽谷為特色。許多高峰海拔超過3,000公尺。

解析 feature為重點單字，當動詞時，feature為「以……為特色」，如考題The zoo features more than 1,000 animals in their natural habitats.；當名詞時，feature為「特色」，如Her eyes are her best feature. 她的雙眼是她最大的特色。elevation 高度、海拔、提高，此作海拔。

38. The local tour guide has a sunny personality. Everybody likes him.

(A) windy 大風的
(B) stormy 暴風雨的
(C) sunny 陽光的
(D) cloudy 陰天的

中譯 這位當地的導遊有著陽光開朗的性格。每個人都喜歡他。

解析 sunny 陽光性格的；outgoing 外向；shy 害羞，都為形容個性的常考單字；humble、modest為「謙虛」的常考單字。此處的答案選項都是描述天氣的形容詞：windy 大風的；stormy 暴風雨的；sunny 陽光的；cloudy 陰天的。

39. Tomorrow I will be able to let you know precisely how many people will join the trip.

(A) tremendously 巨大地 (B) highly 非常地

(C) rationally 理性地 (D) precisely 精準地

中譯 明天我會精確地告訴你有多少人會參加這個行程。

解析 由let you know how many people will join the trip可得知是precisely 精準地。

40. Spectacular fireworks shows lit up the sky of cities around the world as people celebrated the start of 2012.

(A) Invisible 看不見的 (B) Spectacular 壯觀的

(C) Dull 遲鈍的 (D) Endangered 瀕臨絕種的

中譯 當人們慶祝2012年的開始，壯觀的煙火照亮了世界上許多城市的天空。

解析 spectacular 壯觀的，考題中也常見breath-taking 令人屏息的、amazing 令人驚豔的這兩個形容詞來描述風景。

41. A: "Excuse me. Can I take this seat?"
B: "Sorry, it is occupied."

(A) empty 空的 (B) closed 關閉的

(C) occupied 佔用 (D) complete 完整的

中譯 A：「抱歉。我可以坐這個位子嗎？」
B：「抱歉，這座位有人坐。」

解析 位子有人坐有兩種常見說法：The seat is occupied / taken.，而詢問位子是否有人坐則可以說：Is this seat taken?

42. Many teenagers stay up late to play online games.

(A) grow up 成長 (B) break up 分手

(C) take place 發生、舉行 (D) stay up 熬夜

中譯 許多年輕人熬夜玩線上遊戲。

解析 stay up 熬夜；obsessed with online game 沉迷於線上遊戲；obsessed with 著迷於某件事情。

43. To maintain health and fitness, we need proper diet and exercise.

(A) maintain 維持 (B) apply 申請 (C) retire 退休 (D) contain 包含

中譯 為了維持健康和體態，我們需要適量的節食和運動。

解析 此處的maintain 維持也可替換成keep 保持。

44. From the evidence, it seems quite obvious that someone broke into my office last night.

(A) humble 謙虛的 (B) inspiring 受啟發的

(C) obvious 明顯的 (D) promising 有希望的

中譯 從證物來看，很明顯昨晚有人闖入我的辦公室。

解析 由evidence推論someone broke into my office，可知evidence非常的obvious 明顯。

45. I hate to go through the tedious process of application again. I need an assistant to do it for me.

(A) interesting 有趣的 (B) energetic 活力的

(C) fascinating 迷人的 (D) tedious 乏味的

中譯 我痛恨再經歷一遍乏味的申請過程。我需要一位助理幫我做這些。

解析 從I hate to go through the process of application again.可推知是tedious 乏味的。

46. I was very scared when our flight was passing through turbulence from the nearby storm.

(A) turbulence 空中亂流 (B) breeze 微風

(C) currency 貨幣 (D) brilliance 光輝

中譯 當飛機通過來自附近暴風的亂流時，我真是嚇壞了。

解析 機上遇到亂流時，經常會廣播以下注意事項："We are now crossing a zone of turbulence. Please return your seats and keep your seat belts fastened. Thank you."「我們正經過亂流區。請回到座位上並保持安全帶繫緊。謝謝。」

47. Most critics imputed the failure of the movie to its lack of humanity.

(A) caused 導致 (B) imputed 歸因

(C) rewarded 獎賞 (D) dedicated 致力於

中譯 大部分的評論家將這部電影的敗筆歸因於人文的缺乏。

解析 由the failure to its lack of humanity可推知答案為imput 歸因，也就是將某事發生的原因歸到某物。lack of... 缺乏……；humanity 人性、人道。

48. It is virtually impossible to train cats to do what you want them to do, but this one called Sasha can not only shake hands with people but also use the toilet.

(A) unlikely 不太可能　(B) casually 無意地
(C) virtually 實際上　(D) secondly 第二

中譯 實際上不可能去訓練貓咪去做你想要他們做的事情，但這隻叫莎夏的貓不但能和人握手，還會在馬桶上廁所。

解析 其實由impossible to train cats就可猜出這件事為virtually impossible 實際上不可能。

49. My most memorable trip is climbing Mount Fuji. Getting to the peak and seeing the sunrise from the top of the clouds was amazing.

(A) depth 深度　(B) remark 評論　(C) twig 細枝　(D) peak 山頂

中譯 爬富士山是最令我念念不忘的旅行。登頂在雲層上看日落真是太棒了。

解析 由Mount Fuji以及seeing the sunrise，即可知為peak 山頂。

50. Jennifer is fluent in several languages other than her mother tongue English.

(A) fluent 流利的　(B) quiet 安靜的　(C) universal 宇宙的　(D) tall 高大的

中譯 珍妮佛除了自己的母語英文外，還精通數國語言。

解析 mother tongue = native language都為母語之意。fluent in several languages也可換成speak several languages with facility。

51. The heavy rain in the valley often affects my sight, so I sometimes have to pull my car over to the side of the road and wait until the rain stops.

(A) landscape 風景　(B) sight 視線
(C) image 形象　(D) taste 味覺

中譯 山谷內的大雨經常影響我的視線，所以有時候我必須停在路邊等雨停。

解析 由heavy rain以及pull my car over 把車靠邊停可知是sight 視線受影響。pull over 把……開到路邊。

52. Costa Brava is a popular tourist destination in northeastern Spain, thanks to its moderate climate, beautiful beaches, and charming towns.

(A) dreadful 可怕的　(B) contemporary 現代的
(C) moderate 溫和的　(D) bitter 苦的

中譯 西班牙東北部的布拉瓦海岸是很受歡迎的觀光景點，多虧了它溫和的氣候、美麗的海灘和迷人的小鎮。

解析 由popular tourist destination可知其氣候是moderate 溫和的。

53. I really like your scarf. Can I exchange my hat for that?

(A) expand 展開 (B) exist 存在

(C) exchange 交換 (D) expel 驅逐

中譯 我真的很喜歡你的圍巾。可以用我的帽子交換嗎？

解析 exchange 交換，另一個常見的交換為swap。兩者意思都為交換，但exchange比較正式，而swap較為口語。

54. At the Welcome Center, you will find plenty of resources, including maps, brochures, and wireless internet access.

(A) resources 資源 (B) reformation 改革

(C) documents 文件 (D) assistance 協助

中譯 在迎賓中心，你可以發現很多資源，包含地圖、小冊子，以及無線網路。

解析 map 地圖、brochure 小冊子、wireless internet access 無線網路是tourist information center 遊客中心常見的resources 資源。access 接近、進入、使用；internet access （連線）上網。

55. With its palaces, sculptured parks, concert halls, and museums, Vienna is a steeped city in cultures.

(A) chronic 長期的 (B) elite 精英

(C) provincial 省份的 (D) steeped 充滿的

中譯 有皇宮、用雕刻裝飾的公園、音樂廳和博物館，維也納是一座充滿文化的城市。

解析 be steeped in 充滿著、沉浸於，如The castle is steeped in history. 這座城堡充滿了歷史。

56. The oldest of all the main Hawaiian islands, Kauai is known for its secluded beaches, scenic waterfalls, and jungle hikes.

(A) due 由於 (B) known 知名的 (C) neutral 中立的 (D) ripe 成熟的

中譯 身為夏威夷群島最古老的島嶼，考艾島以隱密性的海灘、美景瀑布與叢林健走聞名。

解析 known for = famous for = well know for都為某事物「知名」之意。secluded 隱蔽的、僻靜的。

57. Established in 1730, Lancaster"s Central Market is the oldest continuously operating farmers market in the United States.

(A) Demolished 毀壞
(B) Established 建立
(C) Imported 進口
(D) Located 位於

中譯 設立於1730年，蘭卡斯特中央市場是美國一直持續營運、最老的農夫市場。

解析 established （被）建立，例：a newly established institution 一處新設立的機構。operate 運作、運轉、開刀，此作運作、運轉。

58. High in the mountains of Chiapas, San Cristóbal del la Casas is one of the most photogenic spots in Mexico: colorful, historic, and remarkably complex.

(A) antarctic 南極的
(B) cosmetic 化妝品
(C) photogenic 上相的
(D) synthetic 綜合性的

中譯 聖克裏斯多佛古堡位於契亞帕斯山上，是墨西哥最適於拍照的旅遊景點之一：顏色豐富，有歷史意義，並且非常地複雜。

解析 photogenic 上相的，可以是物或是人上相，例句：I'm not very photogenic. 我非常不上相。remarkably 引人注目地、明顯地、非常地，此作非常地。

59. A single visit to Rome is not enough. The city"s layered complexity demands time.

(A) assists 幫助
(B) demands 需要、要求
(C) evolves 進化
(D) lingers 逗留、徘徊

中譯 只去一次羅馬是不夠的。這座城市具有各種面向的複雜度需要時間瞭解。

解析 demands 需要、要求，例句：They demand prompt payment. 他們要求立即付款。

60. Right now, there are more tigers in captivity than there are left in the wild. We need to take action to save the big cats.

(A) captivity 囚禁 (B) debt 債務 (C) haste 急忙 (D) quality 品質

中譯 現在被囚禁的老虎比野生的多。我們必須採取行動來拯救這些大貓。

解析 和in the wild 野生相反的即為in captivity 囚禁。

61. After a shipwreck, cruise companies try to lure back hesitant passengers with discounts.

(A) bounce 跳躍 (B) coil 盤繞 (C) lure 引誘 (D) ransom 贖金

中譯 船難之後，郵輪公司試圖用折扣將猶豫的乘客吸引回來。

解析 lure 引誘；hesitant 遲疑的、躊躇的。

62. A canal meanders along a leafy bike pass, through green parks, and pass the city's four remaining windmills.

(A) injects 注射 (B) meanders 蜿蜒而流
(C) pollutes 污染 (D) rumbles 使隆隆響

中譯 一條運河沿著葉子覆蓋著的單車道蜿蜒而行，穿過綠色公園和城市剩下4座的風車。

解析 meander 蜿蜒而流，例句：The river meanders through the corn field. 這條河蜿蜒流過玉米田。

63. Tourists have a wide range of budget and tastes, and a wide variety of resorts and hotels have developed to cater for them.

(A) cater 滿足、投合 (B) desire 期望
(C) mourn 哀悼 (D) pray 祈求

中譯 觀光客有不同的預算以及品味，因此也有各式各樣的度假村和飯店來符合他們的需求。

解析 cater除了迎合的意思外，亦有承辦伙食之意。cater for the need of the customers 迎合顧客的需求。

64. The developments of technology and transport infrastructure have made many types of tourism more affordable.

(A) affordable 提供得起的 (B) considerable 值得考慮的
(C) exclusive 排外的 (D) illusive 錯覺的

中譯 科技以及交通建設的發達，讓許多型態的旅遊更讓人能夠負擔得起。

解析 afford 提供、花費、負擔得起；affordable 提供得起的，如affordable housing 買得起的房子；affordable risk 承擔得起的風險；development 生長、進化、發展，此作發達。

65. For many, vacations and travel are increasingly being viewed as a rather necessity than a luxury and this is reflected in tourist numbers.

(A) community 社區 (B) dynasty 朝代

(C) necessity 必需品 (D) sincerity 誠心誠意

中譯 對許多人來說，度假和旅行漸漸被視為一種必需品而非奢侈品，由旅遊人數就可看得出來。

解析 view as 把……當作是（= regard ... as）

66. The view of cascading waterfalls in the rainforest is spectacular.

(A) ascending 上升 (B) cascading 階梯般成瀑布落下

(C) flourishing 繁榮的 (D) overflowing 溢出的

中譯 雨林中階梯狀的瀑布景色是很壯觀的。

解析 cascade為動詞，表疊層成瀑布落下；spectacular 壯觀的。考題中也常見breath-taking 令人屏息的、amazing 令人驚豔的這兩個形容詞來描述風景。

67. If you plan and time it right, some swapping home can let you stay somewhere for free.

(A) abiding 持久的 (B) boosting 推動的

(C) meditating 沉思 (D) swapping 交換

中譯 如果你計劃且時機合適，有些交換住家可讓你免費入住。

解析 swap 交換，另一個常見的交換為exchange，如考題：I really like your scarf. Can I exchange my hat for that? 我真的很喜歡你的圍巾。我可以用我的帽子交換嗎？兩者意思都為交換，但exchange比較正式，而swap較為口語。

68. Preservation Hall is one of the many jazz venues in New Orleans, but some of the best music can still be found on street corners, in backyards and at funerals.

(A) ceremonies 典禮 (B) distractions 分心

(C) habitats 棲息地 (D) venues 演出場地

中譯 典藏廳是紐奧良許多爵士的演奏場地之一，但一些最好的音樂還是可以在街角、後院和葬禮時聽到。

解析 由be found on street corners, in backyards and at funerals可推知為各式各樣的venues 演出場地。funeral 葬禮。

69. As a general rule, it's best to avoid wearing white clothing and accessories when traveling. Go with darker colors that hide dirt well.

(A) delete 刪除 (B) hide 隱藏 (C) parade 遊行 (D) imply 暗示

中譯 一般而言，外出旅行時最好避免穿白色的衣服和飾品配件。深色服裝比較能夠隱藏汙漬。

解析 hide通常為隱瞞之意，如We've got nothing to hide. 我們沒什麼好隱瞞的。accessory 附件、配件。

70. People love to socialize, and Facebook makes it easier. The shy become more outgoing online.

(A) modest 謙虛的 (B) outgoing 外向的
(C) pious 虔誠的 (D) timid 易受驚嚇的

中譯 人們喜歡社交，而臉書讓此更為容易。害羞的人在網路上變得更外向。

解析 humble、modest都為「謙虛」的常考單字。outgoing 外向的、shy 害羞的、sunny 陽光性格的，都為形容個性的常考單字。

Let"s picture a huge public gathering – like the hajj to Mecca. Think of the World Cup, the Olympics, or a rock concert. When thousands or even millions of people get together, what will be the biggest health concern? Traditionally, doctors and public health officials were most concerned about the spread of infectious diseases. Robert Steffen, a professor of travel medicine at the University of Zurich, says that infectious diseases are still a concern, but injuries are a bigger threat at so-called mass gatherings.

中譯 讓我們想像一個大型的聚會，像去麥加朝聖的回教徒。想想世界盃、奧林匹克運動會，或是搖滾樂演唱會。當數千甚至數百萬人聚集在一起時，最大的健康問題是什麼？傳統上，醫生和公共衛生的官員最擔心的是傳染性疾病的傳播。羅伯・史提芬，蘇黎世大學的旅遊醫學教授說，傳染性疾病仍然是個問題，但其實在大規模的聚會當中受傷是更嚴重的威脅。

單字 infectious 傳染的　　mass 眾多、大量、大宗
so-called 所謂的

According to Professor Steffen, children and older people have the highest risk of injury or other health problems at mass gathering events. Children are at more risk of getting crushed in stampedes, while older people are at higher risk of heat stroke and dying from extreme heat.

中譯 根據史提芬教授所說，孩童以及老人在大型的聚會中有比較大的傷害或是其他健康問題的風險。孩童在擁擠的人群中，會有比較多受擠壓的風險；而老人面臨比較大的風險則是中暑以及死於高溫熱浪。

單字 heat stroke 中暑

Stampedes at mass gatherings have caused an estimated seven thousand deaths over the past thirty years. The design of an area for mass gathering can play a part. There may be narrow passages or other choke points that too many people try to use at once. The mood of a crowd can also play a part. Organizers of large gatherings need to avoid creating conditions that might lead to stampedes and heat stroke.

中譯 過去30年，大型人群聚會的亂竄估計已造成7,000人死亡。大型聚會的地點設計也是個問題。通道可能太擠，或是其他的障礙導致太多人試著一起湧入。群眾的情緒也會有影響。大型聚會的規劃者需要避免製造可能會引起導致亂竄擁擠以及中暑的情形。

單字 condition 情況、環境、條件、症狀，此作情況

So what advice does Professor Steffen have for people attending a large gathering? First, get needed vaccinations before traveling. Then, stay away from any large mass of people as much as possible. Also, be careful with alcohol and drugs, which can increase the risk of injuries.

中譯 那麼史提芬教授給那些參加大型聚會的人哪些建議呢？首先，旅行前先打必要的疫苗。然後盡可能遠離大型聚會的群眾。同時對於可能增加受傷風險的酒精和藥要小心。

單字 alcohol 酒精、含酒精飲料、酒
injury 傷害、損害

71. Which of the following would be the most appropriate title for this passage?

(A) How to avoid mass gatherings 如何避免大型聚會

(B) Mass gathering: New escape skills 大型聚會：新的逃生技巧

(C) Infectious diseases: New cures found 傳染性疾病：發現新處方

(D) Health risks in a crowd: Not what you may think
擁擠人群中的健康風險：和你想的可能不一樣

中譯 以下哪個敘述最適合當成本文的標題？

解析 由Robert Steffen, a professor of travel medicine at the University of Zurich, says that infectious diseases are still a concern, but injuries are a bigger threat at so-called mass gatherings.可推知。

72. Which of the following is closest in meaning to stampede in the passage?

(A) A plane crash 墜機

(B) A steamy factory 蒸氣工廠

(C) A sudden rush of a crowd 人群忽然擁入

(D) Heat stroke due to mass gathering events 因大型群眾而造成的中暑

中譯 以下哪個敘述最接近本文的stampede之意？

解析 由Stampedes at mass gatherings have caused an estimated seven thousand deaths over the past thirty years.此段可以推知。

73. According to Professor Steffen, which of the following is more threatening to the health of people attending a huge public gathering?

(A) Injuries 受傷

(B) Infectious diseases 傳染性疾病

(C) The mood of event organizers 活動主辦者的情緒

(D) Insufficient budget for an event 活動的預算不足

中譯 根據史提芬教授所說，以下哪項對於參加大型群眾聚會的人的健康較有威脅？

解析 由infectious diseases are still a concern, but injuries are a bigger threat at so-called mass gatherings可知為傷害。

74. Which of the following is clear from the passage?

(A) Infectious disease is no longer a concern of the public.
傳染病已不再是大眾關心的議題。

(B) Event organizers should be more careful to avoid stampedes.
活動主辦者應該多多注意避免人群擁擠的情形。

(C) A proper place for mass gathering should have one narrow passage.
適合大型聚會的地方應該要有狹窄的通道。

(D) Children and older people are prohibited to attend mass gatherings.
小孩和長者禁止參加大型聚會。

中譯 根據本文，可推知以下哪項？

解析 由Organizers of large gatherings need to avoid creating conditions that might lead to stampedes and heat stroke.可知。

75. Which of the following statements is LEAST supported in the passage?

(A) Extreme heat can cause death at mass gatherings.

大型聚會中的高溫會致死。

(B) Infectious diseases will not spread at mass gatherings.

大型聚會並不會散播傳染性疾病。

(C) Alcohol can increase the risk of injuries at mass gatherings.

大型聚會中酒精會增加受傷的風險。

(D) Older people are likely to suffer from heat stroke at a large gathering.

大型聚會中長者較易因熱而中暑。

中譯 以下何者為本文最不贊成的觀點？

解析 由infectious diseases are still a concern, but injuries are a bigger threat at so-called mass gatherings.可知。

The historic center of Hoi An looks just how Vietnam is supposed to look: narrow lanes, wooden shop houses, a charming covered bridge. Hoi An"s well preserved architecture – from the 16th century onward, the harbor town attracted traders from China, India, Japan and as far as Holland and Portugal – led United Nations Educational, Scientific and Cultural Organization (UNESCO) to deem it a World Heritage site, praising it as an outstanding demonstration of cultural blending over time in an international commercial port.

中譯 會安市的歷史中心看起來就和越南應有的外表一樣：狹窄的巷弄、木製的商家，以及一座迷人的廊橋。會安市的建築被完整的保留下來——從16世紀開始，這座港城就吸引了來自中國、印度、日本，甚至遠至荷蘭和葡萄牙的貿易商——因此讓聯合國教科文組織將它列為世界文化遺產，以表揚它歷年來作為文化融合的國際化商業港口的傑出典範。

單字 outstanding 顯著的、傑出的、重要的

blending 混合

commercial 商業的、商務的

When Hoi An was first recognized as a World Heritage site in 1999, the city welcomed 160,300 tourists. In 2011, 1.5 million tourists arrived. Today, tour buses crowd the edge of Hoi An"s old town. Tourists flood the historic center. Hundreds of nearly identical storefronts – providing food and selling the same tailored clothes, shoes and lanterns – colonize the heritage structures. To squeeze tourism revenue, a hospital has been forced to move out. Its building, built in the 19th century, now houses a tailoring business.

中譯 當會安市於1999年第一次被認可為世界文化遺產時，就帶來了160,300名觀光客。到了2011年，則有150萬名旅客造訪。時至今日，觀光巴士塞滿了會安市舊城區的各角落。觀光客湧進歷史中心。幾百間幾乎一樣的店面——提供食物以及販賣同樣訂做的衣服、鞋子和燈籠——佔據了這些遺跡。為了增加觀光業的收入，一間醫院被迫遷出。這棟建築建於19世紀，現在則成為成衣商店。

單字 revenue 收入、收益

While local government officials and business owners view changes in the old town positively, tourists are beginning to notice the loss of authenticity in Hoi An. A 2008 UNESCO report sounded the alarm that "unless tourism management can be improved, the economic success generated by tourism will not be sustainable in the long term."

中譯 雖然當地政府官員以及老闆對於舊城區的改變，看法相當正面，但觀光客也開始注意會安市的失真了。2008年聯合國教科文組織的一份報告提出警告：除非觀光管理有進步，不然長期來說觀光業所產生的經濟效益不會長久。

單字 authenticity 可信賴性、確實（性）
alarm 警報、鬧鐘、此作警報

76. What is the main idea of the passage?

(A) Sustainable tourism revenue in the long run should not be a concern of the government.
長期來看觀光業穩定的收入不應該為政府所擔心。

(B) Hoi An should sell its old town to a modern tailoring business to increase economic revenue.
會安市應該將其舊城區賣給現代成衣企業以增加經濟收入。

(C) UNESCO should urge Hoi An to build more narrow lanes, wooden houses, and covered bridges.
聯合國教科文組織應該力勸會安市多建造些狹窄的巷弄、木造的房子以及廊橋。

(D) Tourism management of historic sites should put a focus on protecting their authenticity and integrity.
歷史遺跡的觀光管理應該致力於保護其真實性以及完整性。

中譯 何者為本文的中心概念？

解析 由最後一段聯合國的警告，以及tourists are beginning to notice the loss of authenticity in Hoi An可推知。

77. What country is Hoi An located in?

(A) China 中國 (B) Vietnam 越南
(C) Japan 日本 (D) Thailand 泰國

中譯 會安市位於哪個國家？

解析 由第一段The historic center of Hoi An looks just how Vietnam is supposed to look可推知。

78. According to the passage, the old town of Hoi An is now ______.

(A) an empty place 空蕩蕩的地方
(B) a famous theme park 有名的遊樂園
(C) a popular tourist spot 受歡迎的觀光景點
(D) a center of modern arts 現代藝術中心

中譯 根據本文，會安市舊城區現在為？

解析 由第二段In 2011, 1.5 million tourists arrived.可知。

79. According to the passage, UNESCO believes World Heritage sites should be ______.

(A) abandoned 遺棄 (B) modernized 現代化
(C) preserved 保留 (D) exploited 剝削

中譯 根據本文，聯合國教科文組織相信世界文化遺產應該被？

解析 由最後一段unless tourism management can be improved可推知。

80. According to the passage, which of the following is true?

(A) Hoi An has never been influenced by foreign cultures and has never traded with other countries.
會安市從未被外國文化影響，也從來沒與其他國家有貿易上的往來。

(B) Hoi An has become a UNESCO World Heritage site since the 16th century.
會安市自從16世紀起就成為聯合國教科文組織的世界文化遺產。

(C) Tourists are attracted to Hoi An to admire its modern architecture and related arts.

觀光客被吸引來會安市是因為欣賞其現代建築以及相關藝術。

(D) The number of tourists to Hoi An has increased substantially after it was recognized as a World Heritage site.

自從被認可為世界文化遺產後，來到會安市的觀光客顯著增加。

中譯 根據本文，下列何項敘述為真？

解析 由When Hoi An was first recognized as a World Heritage site in 1999, the city welcomed 160,300 tourists. In 2011, 1.5 million tourists arrived.可知。

102 年外語導遊英文試題＋標準答案

★102年專門職業及技術人員普通考試導遊人員、領隊人員考試試題

等 別：普通考試

類 科：外語導遊人員（英語）

科 目：外國語（英語）

考試時間：1 小時 20 分

※注意：（一）本試題為單一選擇題，請選出一個正確或最適當的答案，複選作答者，該題不予計分。
（二）本科目共80題，每題1.25分，須用2Ｂ鉛筆在試卡上依題號清楚劃記，於本試題上作答者，不予計分。
（三）本試題禁止使用電子計算器。

( )1. Macau, a small city west of Hong Kong, has turned itself into a casino headquarters in the East. Its economy now depends very much on tourists and visitors whose number is more than double that of the local ______.

(A) man (B) shop (C) worker (D) population

( )2. Three meals a day means that ______ one will have breakfast, lunch and dinner each day.

(A) contrarily (B) nevertheless (C) normally (D) regardless

( )3. A ______ is simply another name for a small specialty shop.

(A) boutique (B) body shop (C) bonus (D) beauty

( )4. When the table filled with some ______ refreshments was removed, the host announced that dinner would be served.

(A) strong (B) heavy (C) light (D) bright

( )5. It is important to note that the brochure represents only a small ______ of a much larger bulk of rules and regulations that we have to observe.

(A) article (B) selection (C) election (D) writing

( )6. Looking back over his 50 years of living in the village, Peter does not ______ hat he did not move to a large city earlier.

(A) regret (B) remember (C) claim (D) announce

(　　)7. The easiest way to look for the shop that you want to visit in a shopping center is to go to the ______ or information desk when you fail to find out the answer from passers-by.

(A) direct (B) directory (C) dictionary (D) director

(　　)8. Taiwan is short of ______ resources but full of educational opportunities.

(A) physical (B) chemical (C) geometric (D) natural

(　　)9. Taiwan has plentiful annual ______ but unfortunately its rivers are too short and too close to the sea.

(A) cloud (B) water (C) rainfall (D) temples

(　　)10. Strictly speaking, Venice is now more of a ______ city than a maritime business city.

(A) waterfront (B) Italian (C) tourism (D) modern

(　　)11. I like Rome very much because it has many historic ______ and it is friendly to visitors.

(A) stories (B) glory (C) sites (D) giants

(　　)12. Kyoto is my ______ city because I prefer traditional Japanese culture to electronic culture.

(A) favorite (B) hobby (C) disliked (D) wonderful

(　　)13. Either the ______ or the cashier's desk of the hotel can help us figure out the exact amount of money and other details we need to join a local tour.

(A) receiving (B) reception (C) resignation (D) recognition

(　　)14. When traveling in a foreign country, we need to carry with us several important documents at all times. One of them is our passport together with the ______ permit if that has been so required.

(A) entering (B) entry (C) exit (D) ego

(　　)15. The 79 year-old Kaohsiung woman has repeatedly ______ NT$120,000 every year for some 10 years to the Home for the Aged in her hometown in Pingtung.

(A) donated (B) spent (C) borrowed (D) aided

(　　)16. I have collected so many art objects in my house that there is no more ______ for new ones.

(A) pace (B) speed (C) time (D) space

(　　)17. Though most airlines ask their passengers to check in at the airport counter two hours before the flight, some international flights ______ their passengers to be at the airport three hours before departure.

(A) revise　(B) require　(C) record　(D) reveal

(　　)18. Most cities that can date back to ancient ______ tend to either create their own myth or fabricate an unspeakable tradition that combines facts and fiction.

(A) knee　(B) history　(C) pass　(D) tool

(　　)19. Before taking a bus, it is advisable to check out its route on a computer or read carefully the route ______ at the bus stop.

(A) way　(B) chart　(C) label　(D) hostel

(　　)20. No Chinese musical instrument is like the pi-pa that has been in use for almost two thousand years either in solo performance or in ______. Critics describe the string instrument to have a unique timbre that can somewhat be matched by western lute.

(A) choir　(B) orchestra　(C) athletics　(D) chamber music

(　　)21. The question of what kind of ______ law this city upholds cannot be answered by your fallacious argument.

(A) civilized　(B) civil　(C) citizen　(D) civic

(　　)22. The Philippines is a country with more than 7000 islands and it has dozens of native languages. What is even more amazing is the ______ between the north and the south, particularly their people's religious belief and political conviction.

(A) contrast　(B) competition　(C) construction　(D) condition

(　　)23. I love to go wandering; often I take my bicycle to ______ around the country-side on weekends.

(A) tour　(B) speed　(C) stroll　(D) drive

(　　)24. The cellphone is very ______ because it connects us with the world at large and even provides us with the necessary information on crucial moments.

(A) expensive　(B) rare　(C) fashionable　(D) handy

(　　)25. When answering questions of the immigration officer, it is advisable to be straight forward and not ______.

(A) historic　(B) hesitating　(C) hospitable　(D) heroic

( )26. When a train arrives, the first thing you need to do is to check if its ______ matches with where you want to go before you step in.

(A) design (B) destination (C) destiny (D) dedication

( )27. Customs officers usually have a ______ face and they have the right to ask us to open our baggage for searching.

(A) good-looking (B) funny-looking (C) stern-looking (D) silly-looking

( )28. Some cities do not have passenger loading zones. It is advisable to follow the instruction of the tourist guide to get off or get on the tour bus to ______ safety and comfort.

(A) prevent (B) guarantee (C) keep away (D) attend to

( )29. In some airports, there is the final call announcement, but in others, they only have ______ signals on the sign board. Passengers are responsible for their own arriving at the boarding gate in time.

(A) image (B) blinking (C) faulty (D) traffic

( )30. Paris' Cultural Calendar may be bursting with fairs, salons and auctions, but nothing can quite ______ the Biennale des Antiquaires.

(A) compete with (B) comment on (C) complain about (D) compose of

( )31. Someone ______ her house last night and stole almost all her valuable things.

(A) broke through (B) broke up (C) broke in (D) broke down

( )32. ______ all the recent criticism of free trade and free markets, it's important to remember that in the last 25 years more people worldwide moved from poverty to the middle class than at any other time in history.

(A) In spite of (B) For the sake of (C) By all acounts (D) Were it not for

( )33. Mingling with tourists from different backgrounds helps tour guides ______ and learn new things in answering curious visitors' various questions.

(A) blow their own horn (B) broke up

(C) broke in (D) broke down

( )34. Pingxi District in New Taipei City of Taiwan holds an annual Lantern Festival in which releasing sky lanterns has become a tradition. ______ that sky lanterns were the invention of an ancient Chinese politician and military leader "Kong Ming."

(A) As a consequence (B) Legend has it
(C) It isn't worth the trouble (D) It is high time

( )35. I have ______ on my research project and couldn't make any progress forward, so I need to rethink my design and get some help.
(A) come to a standstill (B) come out ahead
(C) come to light (D) come through

( )36. We need to ______ how we can walk out of this maze and get home safe.
(A) figure out (B) count on (C) back up (D) give up

( )37. Money changing can be complicated. When in doubt, always ask someone who is ______.
(A) ignorant (B) shaky (C) prejudiced (D) knowledgeable

( )38. If we remember our social ______, particularly in a big crowd, we shall win people's admiration though we may not feel it.
(A) ages (B) manners (C) news (D) recruits

( )39. Dress codes are basically some ______ about what people wear in an organization or on a particular occasion.
(A) pros and cons (B) ups and downs
(C) dos and don'ts (D) ways and means

( )40. A: I'm going on a five-day trip to Thailand next week.
B: That's great! Wish ______ a wonderful trip.
(A) you (B) you have (C) you having (D) you to have

( )41. This time next year I ______ in France.
(A) am traveling (B) have been traveling
(C) will be traveling (D) have traveled

( )42. The airlines ______ to us about the long flight delay, but they just kept us waiting and did not say anything.
(A) could explain (B) had explained
(C) should be explaining (D) could have explained

( )43. When something wrong happens, ______ let me know immediately.
(A) do not manage to (B) do not hesitate to
(C) do not think to (D) do not hide to

(　　)44. A prominent survey has ranked Taipei as the second greenest metropolis among 22 major Asian cities, ______only Singapore.

(A) surpassing　(B) trailing　(C) traversing　(D) conflicting

(　　)45. Taiwan is the home of hot springs. Located along Wenshui River, the Taian Hot Springs were developed during the Japanese ______.

(A) oration　(B) operation　(C) orientation　(D) occupation

(　　)46. This is the final ______ call for China Airline Flight 009 to Hong Kong at Gate C2.

(A) landing　(B) taking off　(C) riding　(D) boarding

(　　)47. Taiwan government said yesterday it will not give up restrictions it imposes on imported beef, after a warning by U.S. lawmakers that the issue could ______ free trade talks.

(A) facilitate　(B) advance　(C) delight　(D) cripple

(　　)48. According to a new study, the continuing ______ of immigrants to American shores is encouraging business activity and producing more jobs with the supply of abundant labors.

(A) threat　(B) arrival　(C) removal　(D) selection

(　　)49. The financial ______ that started in the U.S. and swept the globe was further proof that—for better and for worse—we can't escape one another.

(A) data　(B) tadpole　(C) advent　(D) crisis

(　　)50. In order to make traveling easier, especially for those who rely on public transportation, the Tourism Bureau worked with local governments to ______ the Taiwan Tourist Shuttle Service in 2010.

(A) terminate　(B) initiate　(C) annotate　(D) depreciate

(　　)51. Technology, such as cellphones, often ______ equality and helps lift people out of poverty.

(A) fosters　(B) discourages　(C) likens　(D) diminishes

(　　)52. In the story about belling the cat, the mice know that life would be much safer if the cat were stuck with a bell around its neck. The problem is, who will ______ his life to bell the cat?

(A) achieve　(B) resolve　(C) gamble　(D) persist

( )53. Master Sheng Yen ______ his entire life to spreading the Dharma, using simple and practical language to help bring people from all walks of life closer to Buddhism.

(A) saved (B) donated (C) devoted (D) savored

( )54. Simply put, no society can truly ______ if it smothers the dreams and productivity of half its population, women.

(A) deteriorate (B) flourish (C) ravage (D) smuggle

( )55. Increasing tourism infrastructure to meet domestic and international demands has raised concerns about the ______ on Taiwan's natural environment.

(A) impact (B) input (C) itinerary (D) identity

( )56. Sweets aren't an intrinsic part of a meal, but their presence on the dining table is often a great ______ of happiness.

(A) link (B) source (C) pardon (D) ordeal

( )57. Wushantou Reservoir began its ______ in 1920 and was completed in 1930. It became the Wushantou Scenery Park in 1969.

(A) construction (B) congestion (C) contamination (D) confrontation

( )58. I'll pay a visit to the Wolfsonian, an ______ museum in Miami. I love its collection of decorative artifacts and propaganda materials from 1885 to 1945.

(A) edible (B) outrageous (C) awful (D) extraordinary

( )59. The support for suspending death penalty has gained ______, and it is very likely that someday the congress of the country will pass its suspension.

(A) monument (B) motivation (C) module (D) momentum

( )60. Thailand is a pleasure for the senses. Tourists come from around the world to visit the nation's gold-adorned temples and sample its delicious ______.

(A) sky diving (B) cuisine (C) bungee jumping (D) horseracing

( )61. The world is full of beautiful places, many with ______ stories to tell.

(A) vast (B) urgent (C) occasional (D) enchanting

( )62. If you've ever seen a jazz band ______ or tried your hand at playing a saxophone, there is a good chance that the instrument you've seen in action or handled yourself came straight from the township of Houli, Taiwan.

(A) perform (B) vanish (C) perish (D) vomit

(　　)63. Music was one of the first industries that have been disrupted by the Internet because ______ files are so easy to share, but it is found that when paying for songs is made easier than stealing them, people will pay.

(A) audio　(B) visual　(C) physical　(D) psychological

(　　)64. In a world that is ever more complex, turbulent and dangerous, Secretary Clinton has made a great ______ to strengthening the United States' relationships with allies, partners and friends.

(A) confirmation　(B) ambition　(C) contribution　(D) satisfaction

(　　)65. A bill to legalize gay marriage in Washington State has won final legislative ______ and taken effect starting 2012.

(A) approval　(B) rejection　(C) veto　(D) admission

(　　)66. One of the most painful things you may experience in life is that a friend you trust most ______ you.

(A) protects　(B) bores　(C) betrays　(D) persuades

(　　)67. Out of ignorance and selfishness, many people ______ against others based on their races, sexual orientation, age, or other reasons.

(A) falter　(B) discriminate　(C) respect　(D) beam

(　　)68. Dogs are said to be our most ______ friends because they enrich our life with their loyal company and never complain.

(A) faithful　(B) stink　(C) passive　(D) vulnerable

(　　)69. Be ______ to the people who make us happy because they are the charming gardeners who make our souls blossom.

(A) grateful　(B) resentful　(C) shameful　(D) mournful

(　　)70. Only love is powerful enough to overcome ______, an often underestimated emotion that deprives us of our happiness.

(A) passion　(B) admiration　(C) worship　(D) hatred

(　　)71. Men often give excuses to ______ their wrongdoings.

(A) justify　(B) reject　(C) knit　(D) irritate

(　　)72. Recovering from the depression of losing one's beloved, you need all the help you can get, so I very much ______ a meditation program.

(A) recruit　(B) shrug　(C) recommend　(D) shudder

( )73. When visiting Alishan, one of the most popular tourist destinations in Taiwan, it's worth spending a few days to learn about the indigenous people living in mountain villages and ______ the marvelous scenery.

(A) prick on (B) take in (C) put off (D) pick up

( )74. At 3,952 meters, Yushan is not only Taiwan's tallest ______; it is also the tallest mountain in Northeast Asia.

(A) peak (B) dip (C) vale (D) creek

( )75. Having secured political and economic stability and overcome severe flooding, Thailand's ability to bounce back is ______ to investors.

(A) annoying (B) enduring (C) appealing (D) scaffolding

( )76. ______ that much of the world is still mired in an economic slowdown, but some of the brightest examples of significant and lasting opportunity are right under our nose.

(A) All around the world (B) There is no denying

(C) In the meantime, (D) It is a turning point

Businesses often want to find out the level of service that is being providedby the employees in a particular store or place of business. In order to do this, they hire people who are known as mystery shoppers. These are people who shop at a store and secretly gather information about the store and the employees. They often also give their opinions about the overall experience they have while shopping.

Any type of business that deals with the public may be visited by a mystery shopper. These businesses include but are not limited to hotels, restaurants, retail stores, gas stations, and banks. Practically any business whose management needs to learn what the end consumer sees and experiences can benefit from mystery shopping.

Mystery shopping has become a big industry in the U.S., with estimated value of this industry at over $600 million in 2004. However, most people who work as mystery shoppers are unable to make a living doing it. Rather, they simply do it for fun and get free meals, merchandise, and sometimes money. The industry has also been hit in recent years by criminals who try to get people to pay in order to become **certified** as mystery shoppers.

( )77. According to the passage, what does a mystery shopper do?

(A) Observe how customers behave.

(B) Gather specific information about services.

(C) Visit some stores and talk with managers.
(D) Exchange information in a mysterious way.

(　　)78. According to the passage, which of the following is true?
(A) Mystery shoppers wear special costumes at work.
(B) Gas stations are among the potential places mystery shoppers will visit.
(C) There are over 600 million mystery shoppers in the U.S.
(D) Mystery shoppers are in danger because they may be beaten by criminals.

(　　)79. Which of the following is implied in the passage?
(A) Mystery shopping began in 2004.
(B) One has to look great in order to be a mystery shopper.
(C) One earns a lot of money by working as a mystery shopper.
(D) In reality, mystery shopping is just another market research tool.

(　　)80. Which of the following is closest in meaning to "**certified**" in the last line of this passage?
(A) qualified　　(B) talented　　(C) instructed　　(D) identified

★標準答案

1. (D)	2. (C)	3. (A)	4. (C)	5. (B)
6. (A)	7. (B)	8. (D)	9. (C)	10. (C)
11. (C)	12. (A)	13. (B)	14. (B)	15. (A)
16. (D)	17. (B)	18. (B)	19. (B)	20. (#)
21. (B)	22. (A)	23. (A)	24. (D)	25. (B)
26. (B)	27. (C)	28. (B)	29. (B)	30. (A)
31. (C)	32. (A)	33. (D)	34. (B)	35. (A)
36. (A)	37. (D)	38. (B)	39. (C)	40. (A)
41. (C)	42. (D)	43. (B)	44. (B)	45. (D)
46. (D)	47. (D)	48. (B)	49. (D)	50. (B)
51. (A)	52. (C)	53. (C)	54. (B)	55. (A)
56. (B)	57. (A)	58. (D)	59. (D)	60. (B)
61. (D)	62. (A)	63. (A)	64. (C)	65. (A)
66. (C)	67. (B)	68. (A)	69. (A)	70. (D)
71. (A)	72. (C)	73. (B)	74. (A)	75. (C)
76. (B)	77. (B)	78. (B)	79. (D)	80. (A)

備註：第20題答B或D或BD者均給分。

102 年外語導遊英文試題中譯與解析

1. Macau, a small city west of Hong Kong, has turned itself into a casino headquarters in the East. Its economy now depends very much on tourists and visitors whose number is more than double that of the local population.

   (A) mans 男人　(B) shop 商店　(C) worker 工人　(D) population 人口

   中譯 澳門，位於香港西邊的小城市，現在已成為東方的賭場總部。其經濟仰賴比當地人口多上兩倍的觀光客。

   解析 headquarters 總部、總公司。由tourists and visitors可推論是比較人數，故選population。

2. Three meals a day means that normally one will have breakfast, lunch and dinner each day.

   (A) contrarily 相反地　(B) nevertheless 儘管如此
   (C) normally 通常　(D) regardless 無論如何

   中譯 一天三餐表示，通常每天只會有早餐、午餐和晚餐。

   解析 normally 通常。

3. A boutique is simply another name for a small specialty shop.

   (A) boutique 精品店　(B) body shop 車身修理廠
   (C) bonus 獎金　(D) beauty parlor 美容院

   中譯 精品店也表示是賣特殊紀念品的小商店。

   解析 boutique 精品店，也是專賣流行衣服的小商店。

4. When the table filled with some light refreshments was removed, the host announced that dinner would be served.

   (A) strong 強烈的　(B) heavy 巨大的
   (C) light 輕的　(D) bright 明亮的

   中譯 當整桌的輕食都被移走時，主人宣布晚餐準備開始了。

   解析 light food 易消化的食物、輕食；refreshment 茶點。

5. It is important to note that the brochure represents only a small selection of a much larger bulk of rules and regulations that we have to observe.

(A) article 文章 (B) selection 選擇 (C) election 選舉 (D) writing 寫作

中譯 很重要必須去注意的是小冊子上只有列出我們必須遵守的龐大規則與規範的其中一小部分。

解析 brochure 小冊子；observe 遵守、奉行。

6. Looking back over his 50 years of living in the village, Peter does not regret that he did not move to a large city earlier.

(A) regret 後悔 (B) remember 記得 (C) claim 主張 (D) announce 宣布

中譯 回首過去50年的鄉村生活，彼得對於不早點搬到城市這件事並不後悔。

解析 regret的用法：

① regret to do sth.表示「對要做的事感到遺憾」，這時常用to say、to tell you、to inform you等，相當於I'm sorry to say / tell / inform you that...。

② regret doing / having done sth.表示對已經做過的事感到後悔。

③ regret + that-clause 對某件事情遺憾 / 後悔……。

7. The easiest way to look for the shop that you want to visit in a shopping center is to go to the directory or information desk when you fail to find out the answer from passers-by.

(A) direct 直接的 (B) directory 導覽 (C) dictionary 字典 (D) director 指揮者

中譯 要在購物中心找到想要逛的店家，當你問路人得不到答案時，最簡單的方式就是走到導覽區或是櫃台。

解析 passer-by 路人、經過的人。

8. Taiwan is short of natural resources but full of educational opportunities.

(A) physical 物理的 (B) chemical 化學的

(C) geometric 幾何的 (D) natural 自然的

中譯 台灣缺少天然資源但是充滿教育機會。

解析 natural 天然、自然的；educational 教育性的。

9. Taiwan has plentiful annual rainfall but unfortunately its rivers are too short and too close to the sea.

(A) cloud 雲 (B) water 水 (C) rainfall 降雨 (D) temples 寺廟

中譯 台灣有很豐沛的降雨，但很不幸的河流太短且太靠近海。

解析 plentiful 豐富的、充足的；rainfall 降雨；waterfall 瀑布。

10. Strictly speaking, Venice is now more of a tourism city than a maritime business city.

(A) waterfront 濱水地區 (B) Italian 義大利的
(C) tourism 觀光業 (D) modern 現代的

中譯 嚴格來說，威尼斯比較像觀光城市而不是海洋的商業城市。

解析 strictly speaking 嚴格地說；tourism 觀光業。

11. I like Rome very much because it has many historic sites and it is friendly to visitors.

(A) stories 故事 (B) glory 光榮 (C) sites 遺址 (D) giants 巨人

中譯 我非常喜歡羅馬，因為它有很多歷史遺跡，對遊客也很友善。

解析 historic sites 歷史遺址；site 地點、場所、網站、遺址。

12. Kyoto is my favorite city because I prefer traditional Japanese culture to electronic culture.

(A) favorite 喜愛的 (B) hobby 嗜好
(C) disliked 討厭的 (D) wonderful 奇妙的

中譯 京都是我最喜歡的城市，因為我喜歡傳統的日本文化更勝電子文化。

解析 由prefer可以知道是favorite。

13. Either the reception or the cashier's desk of the hotel can help us figure out the exact amount of money and other details we need to join a local tour.

(A) receiving 接受 (B) reception 接待處
(C) resignation 辭職 (D) recognition 讚譽

中譯 不是飯店的接待處就是收銀台，可以幫我們釐清正確的金額，以及其他我們想參加當地旅遊的細節。

解析 reception 接待處；figure out 理解、明白。

14. When traveling in a foreign country, we need to carry with us several important documents at all times. One of them is our passport together with the entry permit if that has been so required.

(A) entering 進入 (B) entry 進入 (C) exit 出口 (D) ego 自我

中譯 當在外國旅遊，我們需要隨身攜帶幾份重要的文件。其中一項就是我們的護照和入境許可證，如果有被要求的話。

解析 entry 進入（名詞）；enter 進入（動詞）；permit 允許、許可。

15. The 79 year-old Kaohsiung woman has repeatedly donated NT$120,000 every year for some 10 years to the Home for the Aged in her hometown in Pingtung.

(A) donated 捐贈 (B) spent 花費 (C) borrowed 借來 (D) aided 幫助

中譯 這名79歲的高雄婦人連續10年每年捐12萬元給她屏東家鄉的老人院。

解析 donate 捐贈（動詞）；donation（名詞）。

16. I have collected so many art objects in my house that there is no more space for new ones.

(A) pace 步調 (B) speed 速度 (C) time 時間 (D) space 空間

中譯 我在家已經收集很多藝術品了，沒有其他空間放新的了。

解析 space 空間。由many art objects in my house可知沒有space 空間了。

17. Though most airlines ask their passengers to check in at the airport counter two hours before the flight, some international flights require their passengers to be at the airport three hours before departure.

(A) revise 修正 (B) require 需要 (C) record 記錄 (D) reveal 顯示

中譯 雖然多數的航空公司要求乘客於班機起飛前2個小時到機場的櫃台登記，有些國際線班機還是需要乘客在起飛3小時前到達機場。

解析 require sb. to do sth. 要求某人做某事。

18. Most cities that can date back to ancient history tend to either create their own myth or fabricate an unspeakable tradition that combines facts and fiction.

(A) knee 膝蓋 (B) history 歷史 (C) pass 關口 (D) tool 工具

中譯 多數可以回朔到古代歷史的城市，不是傾向創造自己的神話，就是捏造結合事實以及虛幻，且無法言喻的傳統。

解析 unspeakable 無法形容的；combine 結合；fiction 虛構、捏造

19. Before taking a bus, it is advisable to check out its route on a computer or read carefully the route chart at the bus stop.

(A) way 道路 (B) chart 圖表 (C) label 標記 (D) hostel 青年旅舍

中譯 在搭公車之前，建議先在電腦上查明路線，或是在公車站時仔細閱讀路線圖。

解析 route 路線、路程；chart 圖表。

20. No Chinese musical instrument is like the pi-pa that has been in use for almost two thousand years either in solo performance or in orchestra . Critics describe the string instrument to have a unique timbre that can somewhat be matched by western lute.

(A) choir 合唱團 (B) orchestra 管絃樂隊
(C) athletics 運動 (D) chamber music 室內樂

中譯 沒有一項中國樂器像琵琶一樣被流傳超過兩千年，不是獨奏就是管絃樂隊中。評論家形容這樣弦樂器有特殊的音色，可以和西方的琵琶相配。

解析 看到musical instrument以及pi-pa，即可推知為orchestra 管絃樂隊，或是chamber music 室內樂。

21. The question of what kind of civil law this city upholds cannot be answered by your fallacious argument.

(A) civilized 文明的 (B) civil 民事的
(C) citizen 公民 (D) civic 市民的

中譯 這城市擁護哪種民法的問題，不能被你的謬論所回答。

解析 civil law 民法；uphold 贊成；fallacious 謬誤的。

22. The Philippines is a country with more than 7000 islands and it has dozens of native languages. What is even more amazing is the contrast between the north and the south, particularly their people's religious belief and political conviction.

(A) contrast 對比　　(B) competition 競爭
(C) construction 建造　　(D) condition 條件

中譯 菲律賓是一個有著超過7,000座島嶼，且有幾十種方言的國家。更令人驚訝的是南北方的對比，特別是人們的宗教信仰和政治理念都不一樣。

解析 由amazing以及between the north and the south可以推論為南北方有相當大的不同，故選contrast 對比。

23. I love to go wandering; often I take my bicycle to tour around the countryside on weekends.

(A) tour 旅行　　(B) speed 速度　　(C) stroll 漫步　　(D) drive 開車

中譯 我喜歡閒逛，我週末常常騎腳踏車到鄉間旅行。

解析 wander 漫遊、閒逛；take / have / go for a stroll 散步、漫步。

24. The cellphone is very handy because it connects us with the world at large and even provides us with the necessary information on crucial moments.

(A) expensive 昂貴的　　(B) rare 罕有的
(C) fashionable 流行的　　(D) handy 方便的、便利的

中譯 手機非常的方便，因為它讓我們充分和世界溝通，甚至在重要時刻提供我們所需的資訊。

解析 handy 方便、便利的；at large 充分地，另做「未被捕的」。

25. When answering questions of the immigration officer, it is advisable to be straight forward and not hesitating.

(A) historic 有歷史性的　　(B) hesitating 猶豫的
(C) hospitable 好客的　　(D) heroic 英勇的

中譯 當回答移民官的問題時，建議實話實說，並且不要猶豫。

解析 the immigration officer 移民局；hesitating 猶豫的。

26. When a train arrives, the first thing you need to do is to check if its destination matches with where you want to go before you step in.

(A) design 設計　　(B) destination 目的地
(C) destiny 命運　　(D) dedication 貢獻

中譯 當火車到站，在你踏進車廂前時，你需要做的第一件事就是確認目的地是否相符。

解析 必考單字為destination 目的地。

27. Customs officers usually have a stern-looking face and they have the right to ask us to open our baggage for searching.

(A) good-looking 好看的
(B) funny-looking 看起來搞笑的
(C) stern-looking 看起來嚴厲的
(D) silly-looking 看起來傻傻的

中譯 海關官員通常看起來很嚴肅，而且他們有權利為了搜查的目的而要求我們打開行李。

解析 stern 嚴厲的、嚴格的。

28. Some cities do not have passenger loading zones. It is advisable to follow the instruction of the tourist guide to get off or get on the tour bus to guarantee safety and comfort.

(A) prevent 防止
(B) guarantee 保證
(C) keep away 避開
(D) attend to 專心於

中譯 有些城市沒有乘客上下車的指定地方，因此建議遵照遊客指南來上下車來確保安全以及舒適。

解析 zone 地帶、地區；instruction 命令、指示；guarantee 保證。

29. In some airports, there is the final call announcement, but in others, they only have blinking signals on the sign board. Passengers are responsible for their own arriving at the boarding gate in time.

(A) image 圖像
(B) blinking 一閃一閃的
(C) faulty 有錯誤的
(D) traffic 交通

中譯 某些機場有最後登機的宣告，但有些沒有，只有告示牌上一閃一閃的訊號。乘客必須自行負責及時到達登機門。

解析 blink 閃爍、眨眼；blinking 一閃一閃的。

30. Paris' Cultural Calendar may be bursting with fairs, salons and auctions, but nothing can quite compete with the Biennale des Antiquaires.

(A) compete with 比得上
(B) comment on 評論
(C) complain about 抱怨
(D) compose of 由……組成

中譯 巴黎的文化盛事可能有展覽、講座和拍賣會，但沒有一個可以和巴黎古董雙年展相比。

解析 bursting with 充滿；auction 拍賣；compete with 競爭。

31. Someone broke in her house last night and stole almost all her valuable things.

(A) broke through 突圍 (B) broke up 打破

(C) broke in 闖入 (D) broke down 分解

中譯 昨晚有人闖入了她的家中，幾乎偷走所有有價值的東西。

解析 break in 打斷、強行進入、插話。

32. In spite of all the recent criticism of free trade and free markets, it's important to remember that in the last 25 years more people worldwide moved from poverty to the middle class than at any other time in history.

(A) In spite of 儘管 (B) For the sake of 為了……起見

(C) By all accounts 據大家所說 (D) Were it not for 若不是有……的話

中譯 儘管對於自由貿易與自由市場近來有所批評，很重要必須牢記的是世界各地在過去25年來，從貧窮移到中產階級的人是史上最多。

解析 in spite of 儘管；recent 近來的；criticism 評論。

33. Mingling with tourists from different backgrounds helps tour guides broaden their horizons and learn new things in answering curious visitors' various questions.

(A) blow their own horn 自吹自擂

(B) take their breath away 使他們大吃一驚

(C) fall from grace 失寵

(D) broaden their horizons 開拓視野

中譯 與不同背景的觀光客打交道讓導遊開拓視野，也學習回答好奇旅客不同的新問題。

解析 mingle 使混合、使相混；broaden their horizons 開拓視野。直譯為擴大海平面。

34. Pingxi District in New Taipei City of Taiwan holds an annual Lantern Festival in which releasing sky lanterns has become a tradition. Legend has it that sky lanterns were the invention of an ancient Chinese politician and military leader "Kong Ming."

(A) As a consequence 結果
(B) Legend has it 傳說這麼說
(C) It isn't worth the trouble 沒這個必要
(D) It is high time 該是……的時候了

中譯 台灣新北市的平溪區舉辦一年一度的燈籠節，放天燈已經是傳統。據說天燈是古代中國政治家，也是軍事領導者孔明的發明。

解析 lantern 燈籠；It is believed that... = Legend has it that...。Legend has it that + [內容] = 傳說就是[內容]。類似句型：rumor has it that 謠言這麼說。

35. I have come to a standstill on my research project and couldn't make any progress forward, so I need to rethink my design and get some help.

(A) come to a standstill 陷入停頓、停滯狀態
(B) come out ahead 出人頭地
(C) come to light 真相大白
(D) come through 到來

中譯 我的研究計畫停頓中，沒有任何進度，所以我需要重新思考我的設計並且尋找幫助。

解析 come to a standstill 停下來不前進，比喻事情不順利；rethink 重新考慮。

36. We need to figure out how we can walk out of this maze and get home safe.

(A) figure out 瞭解
(B) count on 依靠
(C) back up 支持
(D) give up 放棄

中譯 我們需要瞭解如何走出這迷宮且安全到家。

解析 figure out 估計、瞭解；maze 迷宮。

37. Money changing can be complicated. When in doubt, always ask someone who is knowledgeable.

(A) ignorant 無知的
(B) shaky 不穩固的
(C) prejudiced 有成見的
(D) knowledgeable 博學的

中譯 換匯可以是非常複雜的。當有疑慮時，請尋問了解的人。

解析 in doubt 不肯定的、不確定的；knowledgeable 博學的。

38. If we remember our social manners, particularly in a big crowd, we shall win people's admiration though we may not feel it.

(A) ages 年紀 (B) manners 禮貌
(C) news 新聞 (D) recruits 新成員

中譯 如果我們記得我們的社交禮儀，特別是在群眾中，我們應該會贏得人們的尊敬，即便我們沒有感覺到。

解析 social manners 社交禮儀；table manners 餐桌禮儀。

39. Dress codes are basically some dos and don'ts about what people wear in an organization or on a particular occasion.

(A) pros and cons 優缺點 (B) ups and downs 高低起伏
(C) dos and don'ts 注意事項 (D) ways and means 方法

中譯 關於人們在哪個機構或是特殊場合應該穿什麼樣的衣服，穿衣法則基本上有些行為準則。

解析 dos and don'ts 可做與不可做的（注意事項）。dress code 穿衣法則；occasion 場合。

40. A: I'm going on a five-day trip to Thailand next week.
B: That's great! Wish you a wonderful trip.

(A) you (B) you have (C) you having (D) you to have

中譯 A：我下星期會去泰國5天。
B：太好了！祝你有個完美的旅程。

解析 Wish you + 名詞：祝福某人某事。
補充說明：wish通常表達的是不太可能成真的事物，所以都用假設語氣；與現在事實相反wish that S + 過去式，表示的是對現在或未來的希望；與過去事實相反wish that S + had Vpp，表示的是對過去的希望。

41. This time next year I will be traveling in France.

(A) am traveling (B) have been traveling
(C) will be traveling (D) have traveled

中譯 明年此時我會在法國旅遊。

解析 未來進行式為will be Ving。

42. The airlines could have explained to us about the long flight delay, but they just kept us waiting and did not say anything.

(A) could explain (B) had explained

(C) should be explaining (D) could have explained

中譯 航空公司大可以和我們解釋班機嚴重延誤的原因，但他們只是讓我們等，什麼也不說。

解析 由they just kept us waiting表示與could have explained過去事實相反。「would、could、might」 + have + 過去分詞 → 與「過去事實」相反的假設。

43. When something wrong happens, do not hesitate to let me know immediately.

(A) do not manage to 不要設法 (B) do not hesitate to 不要猶豫

(C) do not think to 不要想 (D) do not hide to 不要躲藏

中譯 當有任何不對勁，請不要猶豫立刻和我說。

解析 由immediately可知為do not hesitate to 不要猶豫。

44. A prominent survey has ranked Taipei as the second greenest metropolis among 22 major Asian cities, only trailing Singapore.

(A) surpassing 超越 (B) trailing 落後

(C) traversing 穿越 (D) conflicting 衝突

中譯 一份卓越的調查將台北列為亞洲22個大城市中，第二綠化的大都市，僅次於新加坡。

解析 rank 把……分等、把……評級；trailing 尾隨、落後。

45. Taiwan is the home of hot springs. Located along Wenshui River, the Taian Hot Springs were developed during the Japanese occupation.

(A) oration 演說 (B) operation 手術

(C) orientation 定方位 (D) occupation 佔領時期

中譯 台灣有許多溫泉。汶水溪旁的泰安溫泉是於日本佔據時期所開發的。

解析 occupy 佔領；occupation 佔領時期。

46. This is the final boarding call for China Airline Flight 009 to Hong Kong at Gate C2.

(A) landing 著陸 (B) taking off 脱掉 (C) riding 騎乘 (D) boarding 登機

中譯 這是中華航空飛往香港的009班機於C2登機門的最後登機廣播。

解析 final boarding call、last call for boarding 最後登機廣播。

47. Taiwan government said yesterday it will not give up restrictions it imposes on imported beef, after a warning by U.S. lawmakers that the issue could cripple free trade talks.

(A) facilitate 促進 (B) advance 提出 (C) delight 喜愛 (D) cripple 破壞

中譯 台灣政府昨天表示不會放棄對於進口牛肉課稅的限制，在經過美國立法單位警告這項議題會破壞自由貿易。

解析 impose 徵（稅）；cripple 嚴重毀壞（或損害）。

48. According to a new study, the continuing arrival of immigrants to American shores is encouraging business activity and producing more jobs with the supply of abundant labors.

(A) threat 威脅 (B) arrival 到來 (C) removal 移除 (D) selection 選擇

中譯 根據新的研究，美國海岸持續到來的移民者會讓商業發展更佳，也會有更多的工作機會。

解析 arrival 到來，為名詞；arrive為動詞。

49. The financial crisis that started in the U.S. and swept the globe was further proof that — for better and for worse — we can't escape one another.

(A) data 數據 (B) tadpole 蝌蚪 (C) advent 來臨 (D) crisis 危機

中譯 金融危機始於美國，且橫掃全球，更佳證明了不論好或壞，我們誰都逃不過。

解析 financial crisis 金融危機。

50. In order to make traveling easier, especially for those who rely on public transportation, the Tourism Bureau worked with local governments to initiate the Taiwan Tourist Shuttle Service in 2010.

(A) terminate 終止 (B) initiate 開始 (C) annotate 註解 (D) depreciate 貶值

中譯 為了讓旅遊更容易，特別是針對那些仰賴大眾運輸的人，觀光旅遊局與當地政府於2010年開始執行台灣旅遊巴士。

解析 rely on 依靠、信賴 = depend on = count on；Shuttle Service 快捷公車（接駁服務）。

51. Technology, such as cellphones, often fosters equality and helps lift people out of poverty.

(A) fosters 促進　(B) discourages 鼓勵

(C) likens 比喻　(D) diminishes 減少

中譯 科技，像是手機，常常促進平等並且幫助人們脫貧。

解析 poverty 貧窮、貧困；lift oneself out of poverty 脫貧。

52. In the story about belling the cat, the mice know that life would be much safer if the cat were stuck with a bell around its neck. The problem is, who will gamble his life to bell the cat?

(A) achieve 達成　(B) resolve 解析　(C) gamble 賭博　(D) persist 堅持

中譯 給貓掛鈴鐺的故事中，老鼠們知道如果貓的脖子掛上鈴鐺，自己的生活會比較安全，但問題是，誰要賭上自己的性命去給貓掛鈴鐺呢？

解析 gamble 賭博，此題的答案也可換成risk。

53. Master Sheng Yen devoted his entire life to spreading the Dharma, using simple and practical language to help bring people from all walks of life closer to Buddhism.

(A) saved 救援　(B) donated 捐贈　(C) devoted 奉獻　(D) savored 品嚐

中譯 聖嚴法師奉獻一生來宣揚佛教，用簡單且實用的語言來幫助人們的生活更接近佛祖。

解析 重點單字為devoted to 奉獻。

54. Simply put, no society can truly flourish if it smothers the dreams and productivity of half its population, women.

(A) deteriorate 惡化　(B) flourish 蓬勃發展

(C) ravage 毀滅　(D) smuggle 走私

中譯 簡單來說，沒有一個社會可以真正的蓬勃發展，如果它阻擋了一半的人口——性的夢想以及生產力。

解析 重點單字為flourish 蓬勃發展。

55. Increasing tourism infrastructure to meet domestic and international demands has raised concerns about the impact on Taiwan's natural environment.

(A) impact 影響　(B) input 投入　(C) itinerary 旅程　(D) identity 身分

中譯 增加旅遊業的公共建設來滿足國內外的需求，對於台灣的天然環境而言已經有所影響。

解析 infrastructure 公共建設；impact 影響。

56. Sweets aren't an intrinsic part of a meal, but their presence on the dining table is often a great source of happiness.

(A) link 連結　(B) source 來源　(C) pardon 原諒　(D) ordeal 考驗

中譯 甜點本來不是正餐中的一部分，但它的出現成為餐桌上快樂的來源。

解析 intrinsic 內部的、本體內的；source 來源。

57. Wushantou Reservoir began its construction in 1920 and was completed in 1930. It became the Wushantou Scenery Park in 1969.

(A) construction 建造　(B) congestion 壅塞
(C) contamination 污染　(D) confrontation 對抗

中譯 烏山頭水庫於1920年開始建造，並於1930年完工。於1969年成為烏山頭景觀公園。

解析 construction 建造。

58. I'll pay a visit to the Wolfsonian, an extraordinary museum in Miami. I love its collection of decorative artifacts and propaganda materials from 1885 to 1945.

(A) edible 可食的　(B) outrageous 無理的
(C) awful 糟糕的　(D) extraordinary 特別的

中譯 我會參觀沃爾夫索尼亞博物館，這間位於邁阿密的博物館很特別。我喜歡他的裝飾性藝術品以及1885年到1945年的宣傳資料收藏。

解析 重點單字為extraordinary 特別的。

59. The support for suspending death penalty has gained momentum, and it is very likely that someday the congress of the country will pass its suspension.

(A) monument 紀念碑　(B) motivation 動機
(C) module 組件　(D) momentum 勢力

中譯 支持廢死已越來越有勢力，某天很有可能國會通過廢死。

解析 congress 立法機關；momentum 勢力。

60. Thailand is a pleasure for the senses. Tourists come from around the world to visit the nation's gold-adorned temples and sample its delicious cuisine.

(A) sky diving 跳傘　(B) cuisine 美食
(C) bungee jumping 高空彈跳　(D) horseracing 賽馬

中譯 泰國是個讓人感官感到愉悅的地方。來自世界各地的觀光客來拜訪此國家以黃金裝飾的廟宇以及品嚐美食。

解析 重點單字為cuisine 美食。

61. The world is full of beautiful places, many with enchanting stories to tell.

(A) vast 廣闊的　(B) urgent 迫切的
(C) occasional 偶然的　(D) enchanting 使人著迷的

中譯 這個世界到處都是美麗的地方，有許多使人著迷的故事。

解析 enchanting 使人著迷的。

62. If you've ever seen a jazz band perform or tried your hand at playing a saxophone, there is a good chance that the instrument you've seen in action or handled yourself came straight from the township of Houli, Taiwan.

(A) perform 表演　(B) vanish 消失　(C) perish 死亡　(D) vomit 嘔吐

中譯 如果你有看過爵士樂團表演，或是試著薩克斯風，這個你曾經看過，或是摸過的樂器，很有可能是出自於台灣后里。

解析 perform 表演。

63. Music was one of the first industries that have been disrupted by the Internet because audio files are so easy to share, but it is found that when paying for songs is made easier than stealing them, people will pay.

(A) audio 聲音的 (B) visual 視覺的
(C) physical 身體的 (D) psychological 心理的

中譯 音樂界是第一批受網路打亂的產業之一，因為聲音檔案很容易分享，但發現當付錢買歌比偷容易時，人們會付錢。

解析 由music可知是audio 聲音的。

64. In a world that is ever more complex, turbulent and dangerous, Secretary Clinton has made a great contribution to strengthening the United States' relationships with allies, partners and friends.

(A) confirmation 確認 (B) ambition 志向
(C) contribution 貢獻 (D) satisfaction 滿意

中譯 在這個複雜、動盪且危險的世界，國務卿柯林頓對於加強美國與盟友、夥伴和朋友的關係有卓越的貢獻。

解析 turbulent 動盪的；contribution 貢獻；由strengthen 增強來推知答案為contribution 貢獻。

65. A bill to legalize gay marriage in Washington State has won final legislative approval and taken effect starting 2012.

(A) approval 贊同 (B) rejection 拒絕
(C) veto 否決 (D) admission 承認

中譯 華盛頓州同性婚姻合法的法案已經通過了最後立法同意，並於2012年生效。

解析 bill在此為法案。由taken effect可推知答案為approval。

66. One of the most painful things you may experience in life is that a friend you trust most betrays you.

(A) protects 保護 (B) bores 麻煩
(C) betrays 背叛 (D) persuades 說服

中譯 人生中你可能遇過最痛苦的事情之一就是你最相信的朋友背叛你。

解析 betray 背叛。

67. Out of ignorance and selfishness, many people discriminate against others based on their races, sexual orientation, age, or other reasons.

(A) falter 支吾、結巴 (B) discriminate 區別
(C) respect 尊重 (D) beam 光束

中譯 出於無知和自私，許多人基於他人的種族、性傾向、年紀和其他原因而歧視他人。

解析 discriminate against 歧視。

68. Dogs are said to be our most faithful friends because they enrich our life with their loyal company and never complain.

(A) faithful 忠誠的　(B) stink 惡臭的
(C) passive 被動的　(D) vulnerable 脆弱的

中譯 狗兒常被視為我們最忠誠的朋友，因為牠們用忠誠的陪伴，以及從不抱怨來豐富我們的生活。

解析 faithful 忠誠的；enrich 使豐富。

69. Be grateful to the people who make us happy because they are the charming gardeners who make our souls blossom.

(A) grateful 感激的　(B) resentful 不滿的
(C) shameful 可恥的　(D) mournful 悲慟的

中譯 對讓我們開心的人心懷感激，因為他們是讓我們的心靈開花的可愛農夫。

解析 grateful 感激的；blossom 開花。

70. Only love is powerful enough to overcome hatred, an often underestimated emotion that deprives us of our happiness.

(A) passion 熱情　(B) admiration 欽佩
(C) worship 尊敬　(D) hatred 憎恨

中譯 只有夠強大的愛可以克服憎恨，常常被低估的情緒剝奪了我們的快樂。

解析 hatred 憎恨；overcome 克服；deprive 剝奪、從……奪走。

71. Men often give excuses to justify their wrongdoings.

(A) justify 合理化　(B) reject 否決　(C) knit 針織　(D) irritate 刺激

中譯 男人總是合理化他們的錯事。

解析 justify 合理化。

72. Recovering from the depression of losing one's beloved, you need all the help you can get, so I very recommend much a meditation program.

(A) recruit 招募　(B) shrug 聳肩
(C) recommend 推薦　(D) shudder 發抖

中譯 因為你剛從失去摯愛中的憂鬱中走出來，你需要所有可得的幫助，所以我推薦冥想課程。

解析 副詞子句簡化的分詞構句，可以還原成 Since you have recovered from...。由help可推知答案為recommend 推薦。meditation 沈思、冥想。

73. When visiting Alishan, one of the most popular tourist destinations in Taiwan, it's worth spending a few days to learn about the indigenous people living in mountain villages and take in the marvelous scenery.

(A) prick on 刺上
(B) take in 欣賞、參觀
(C) put off 推遲
(D) pick up 撿起

中譯 當參觀最受歡迎的台灣景點——阿里山旅遊時，很值得花幾天去學習原住民的高山生活方式，和欣賞絕美風光。

解析 take in 欣賞、參觀；indigenous 本地的；marvelous scenery 絕美風光。

74. At 3,952 meters, Yushan is not only Taiwan's tallest peak; it is also the tallest mountain in Northeast Asia.

(A) peak 山峰
(B) dip 傾斜
(C) vale 山谷
(D) creek 小溪

中譯 高3,952公尺，玉山不只是台灣的最高峰，也是東北亞的最高峰。

解析 peak 山峰、高峰。

75. Having secured political and economic stability and overcome severe flooding, Thailand's ability to bounce back is to appealing investors.

(A) annoying 惱人
(B) enduring 持久
(C) appealing 吸引
(D) scaffolding 鷹架

中譯 既然泰國已經確保政治與經濟穩定度，且克服了嚴重水患，現在可以回到吸引投資客的能力了。

解析 副詞子句簡化的分詞構句Having secured...可以還原成Since Thailand has secured...。appealing 吸引；severe 嚴重的、劇烈的；flooding 洪水、水災。

76. There is no denying that much of the world is still mired in an economic slowdown, but some of the brightest examples of significant and lasting opportunity are right under our nose.

(A) All around the world 全世界
(B) There is no denying 不可否認的
(C) In the meantime 此時
(D) It is a turning point 轉折點

中譯 不可否認的是，世界大部分都深陷於經濟趨緩的狀況下，但其實有一些最棒以及持續的機會正在我們的眼前。

解析 deny 否認。由there is no denying 不可否認的來帶出雖然經濟狀況不好，但是「but」還是有許多不錯的機會。

Businesses often want to find out the level of service that is being provided by the employees in a particular store or place of business. In order to do this, they hire people who are known as mystery shoppers. These are people who shop at a store and secretly gather information about the store and the employees. They often also give their opinions about the overall experience they have while shopping.

中譯 公司總是想知道自己的員工在那些特定的商店或是地方，提供何種服務。為了想知道情形，他們會聘請所謂的祕密客。這些人會在商店消費，並且祕密地收集關於商店和員工的資訊。他們常會給予關於整體消費經驗的意見。

Any type of business that deals with the public may be visited by a mystery shopper. These businesses include but are not limited to hotels, restaurants, retail stores, gas stations, and banks. Practically any business whose management needs to learn what the end consumer sees and experiences can benefit from mystery shopping.

中譯 任何一種與大眾打交道的生意都可能會被祕密客拜訪。這些生意不限於飯店、餐廳、加油站和銀行。實際上其實任何需要了解消費者體驗的商家，在管理上都能從祕密客上受惠。

Mystery shopping has become a big industry in the U.S., with estimated value of this industry at over $600 million in 2004. However, most people who work as mystery shoppers are unable to make a living doing it. Rather, they simply do it for fun and get free meals, merchandise, and sometimes money. The industry has also been hit in recent years by criminals who try to get people to pay in order to become certified as mystery shoppers.

中譯 祕密客在美國已經成為一個很大的產業，2004年產值超過6億美金。但是大部分的祕密客卻不能以此為生。相反的，他們只是因為好玩，或是可以得到免費的餐食、商品，有時候有一些錢。這個產業近年來受到重創，因為罪犯為了騙錢而讓人付錢而成為祕密客。

單字 in order to 為了……
retail store 連鎖店
industry 工業、企業
retail 零售的
practically 幾乎、差不多
mystery shopper 祕密客

77. According to the passage, what does a mystery shopper do?

(A) Observe how customers behave. 觀察客戶的行為。

(B) Gather specific information about services. 收集服務的資訊。

(C) Visit some stores and talk with managers. 拜訪店家和經理們聊天。

(D) Exchange information in a mysterious way. 以神祕的方式交換訊息。

中譯 根據本文，祕密客主要做什麼？

解析 由第一段可知。

78. According to the passage, which of the following is true?

(A) Mystery shoppers wear special costumes at work.
祕密客在工作時穿特殊的服裝。

(B) Gas stations are among the potential places mystery shoppers will visit.
加油站是祕密客可能拜訪的地方。

(C) There are over 600 million mystery shoppers in the U.S.
在美國有超過6億人當祕密客。

(D) Mystery shoppers are in danger because they may be beaten by criminals.
祕密客很危險因為可能被罪犯打。

中譯 根據本文，何者為真？

解析 由These businesses include but are not limited to hotels, restaurants, retail stores, gas stations, and banks.可知。

79. Which of the following is implied in the passage?

(A) Mystery shopping began in 2004.
祕密客始於2004年。

(B) One has to look great in order to be a mystery shopper.
當祕密客必須看起來很稱頭。

(C) One earns a lot of money by working as a mystery shopper.
當祕密客可以因此賺很多錢。

(D) In reality, mystery shopping is just another market research tool.
實際上，祕密客可以算是另一種行銷研究的工具。

中譯 由本文可推論以下何者？

解析 由Practically any business whose management needs to learn what the end consumer sees and experiences can benefit from mystery shopping.可知。

80. Which of the following is closest in meaning to "certified" in the last line of this passage?

(A) qualified 合格的　　(B) talented 有天賦的

(C) instructed 受教育的　　(D) identified 分辨的

中譯 以下哪項最接近本文最後一句「certified」的意思？

解析 certified 認證的、合格的。

Part 4 精選必考 領隊導遊英文試題

(　　)1. Am I ______ to compensation if my ferry is canceled?
(A) asked　(B) entitled　(C) qualified　(D) requested

(　　)2. It is the high season, and I'm not sure whether the hotel could provide enough ______ for the whole group.
(A) vacation　(B) locations
(C) recommendation　(D) accommodations

(　　)3. This traveler's check is not good because it should require two ______ by the user.
(A) insurances　(B) accounts　(C) signatures　(D) examinations

(　　)4. We have seen a marked increase in the number of visitors to the theme park, but cannot understand why the total income indicates ______.
(A) a demand　(B) a decline　(C) a distinction　(D) a disruption

(　　)5. It took us no time to clear ______ at the border.
(A) costume　(B) costumes　(C) custom　(D) customs

(　　)6. When you stay in a hotel, what basic ______ do you think are necessary?
(A) activities　(B) capabilities　(C) facilities　(D) abilities

(　　)7. Airport limousine service, valet parking service, and concierge service are some of the most poplar items among our ______.
(A) car services　(B) guest services
(C) sales services　(D) retail services

(　　)8. I would like to ______ my American Express card, please.
(A) choose this to　(B) charge this to
(C) chain this to　(D) change this to

(　　)9. Wild Formosa Sika deer became ______ due to extensive hunting of the animal during the Dutch colonization period.
(A) extinct　(B) excite　(C) exact　(D) explicit

( )10. Your detailed ______ is as follows: leaving Taipei on the 14 of June and arriving at Tokyo on the same day at noon.

(A) item (B) identification (C) itinerary (D) inscription

( )11. Client: Are there any direct flights to Paris?
Clerk: No, you would have to ______ in Amsterdam.

(A) transfer (B) transport (C) translate (D) transform

( )12. The hotels in the resort areas are fully booked in the summer. It would be very difficult to find any ______ then.

(A) vacations (B) visitors (C) views (D) vacancies

( )13. If the tapes do not meet your satisfaction, you can return them within thirty days for a full ______.

(A) fund (B) refund (C) funding (D) fundraising

( )14. While many couples opt for a church wedding and wedding party, a Japanese groom and a Taiwanese bride ______ in a traditional Confucian wedding in Taipei.

(A) tied the knot (B) knocked off (C) wore on (D) stepped down

( )15. Passengers ______ to other airlines should report to the information desk on the second floor.

(A) have transferred (B) transfer
(C) are transferred (D) transferring

( )16. "We are approaching some turbulence. For your safety, please keep your belts ______ until the 'seat belt' sign goes off."

(A) fasten (B) fastened (C) fastening (D) be fastened

( )17. The flight will make a ______ in Paris for two hours.

(A) stopover (B) stepover (C) flyover (D) crossover

( )18. If you carry keys, knives, aerosol cans, etc., in your pocket when you pass through the security at the airport, you may ______ the alarm, and then the airport personnel will come to search you.

(A) let on (B) let off (C) set on (D) set off

(   )19. My father always asks everyone in the car to ______ for safety, no matter how short the ride is.

(A) tight up   (B) fast up   (C) buckle up   (D) stay up

(   )20. Client: What are this hotel's ______?

Agent: It includes a great restaurant, a fitness center, an outdoor pool, and much more, such as in-room Internet access, 24-hour room service, and trustworthy babysitting, etc.

(A) installations   (B) utilities   (C) amenities   (D) surroundings

(   )21. Tourist: What is the baggage allowance?

Airline clerk: ______.

(A) Please fill out this form.

(B) Sorry, cash is not suggested to be left in the baggage.

(C) It is very cheap.

(C) It is 20 kilograms per person.

(   )22. A bus used for public transportation runs a set route; however, a ______ bus travels at the direction of the person or organization that hires it.

(A) catering   (B) chatter   (C) charter   (D) cutter

(   )23. Palm Beach is a coastline ______ where thousands of tourists from all over the world spend their summer vacation.

(A) airport   (B) resort   (C) pavement   (D) passage

(   )24. After disembarking the flight, I went directly to the ______ to pick up my bags and trunks.

(A) airport lounge   (B) cockpit   (C) runway   (D) baggage claim

(   )25. Working as a hotel ______ means that your focus is to ensure that the needs and requests of hotel guests are met, and that each guest has a memorable stay.

(A) commander   (B) celebrity   (C) concierge   (D) candidate

(   )26. Mount Fuji is considered ______; therefore, many people pay special visits to it, wishing to bring good luck to themselves and their loved ones.

(A) horrifying   (B) scared   (C) sacred   (D) superficial

(   )27. ______ unemployed for almost one year,

Henry has little chance of getting a job.

(A) Having been   (B) Be   (C) Maybe   (D) Since having

(　　)28. If you have to extend your stay at the hotel room, you should inform the front desk at least one day ______ your original departure time.

(A) ahead to　(B) forward to　(C) prior to　(D) in front of

(　　)29. Prohibited items in carry-on bags will be confiscated at the checkpoints, and no ______ will be given for them.

(A) argument　(B) recruitment　(C) compensation　(D) decision

(　　)30. She can speak English and French with ______.

(A) faculty　(B) future　(C) facility　(D) frailty

(　　)31. The waiters will show you where to bed down.

(A) The waiters will tell you the place that you may put your beddings.
(B) The waiters will ask for your assistance later.
(C) The waiters will tell you where you may stay tonight.
(D) The waiters will provide everything you need.

(　　)32. Mr. Jones has got the hang of being a tour guide.

(A) Mr. Jones quit his job.
(B) Mr. Jones needs our help now.
(C) Mr. Jones met some strangers on his way home.
(D) Mr. Jones has learned the skills of being a tour guide.

(　　)33. Due to the impending disaster, we have to ______ our flight to Bangkok.

(A) provide　(B) cancel　(C) resume　(D) tailor

(　　)34. The tour guide ______ him into buying some expensive souvenirs.

(A) persuaded　(B) dissuaded　(C) suggested　(D) purified

(　　)35. The travel agent ______ the delay.

(A) astonished at　(B) astonished　(C) apologized　(D) apologized for

(　　)36. The wedding anniversary is worth ______.

(A) being celebrated　(B) celebrating
(C) of celebrating　(D) celebrated

(　　)37. Wulai (烏來) is a famous hot-spring ______.

(A) resort　(B) mansion　(C) pivot　(D) plaque

(　　)38. You must check the ______ date of your passport. You may need to apply for a new one.

(A) explanatory　(B) exploratory　(C) expiry　(D) expository

(　　)39. After the plane touches down, we have to remain in our seats until we ______ to the gate.

(A) pass by　(B) stop over　(C) take off　(D) taxi in

(　　)40. Is there any problem ______ my reservation?

(A) in　(B) of　(C) to　(D) with

(　　)41. I enjoyed the stay here. Thank you very much for the ______.

(A) hospital　(B) hospitality　(C) hostilities　(D) hostel

(　　)42. If I cancel the trip, will I ______ ?

(A) be refunded　(B) refund　(C) refunded　(D) refunding

Destinations can be cities, towns, natural regions, or even whole countries. The economies of all tourist destinations are (43) to a significant extent on the money produced by tourism. It is possible to (44) destinations as natural or built: Natural destinations (45) seas, lakes, rivers, coasts, mountain ranges, desert, and so on. Built destinations are cities, towns, and villages. A resort is a destination constructed mainly or completely to serve the needs of tourism, (46) Cancun in Mexico.

Successful destinations are seen to be unique in some way by those who visit them. Climate is one of the (47) that determines this uniqueness. Not surprisingly, temperate and tropical climates attract the greatest number of visitors.

(　　)43. (A) dependent　(B) disconnected　(C) repellent　(D) preferred

(　　)44. (A) amplify　(B) classify　(C) signify　(D) verify

(　　)45. (A) concern　(B) consist　(C) include　(D) involve

(　　)46. (A) so on　(B) so so　(C) such as　(D) so that

(　　)47. (A) conclusions　(B) specializations　(C) superstitions　(D) features

(　　)48. Our hotel provides free ______ service to the airport every day.

(A) accommodation　(B) communication

(C) transmission　(D) shuttle

(　　)49. Tourists enjoy visiting night markets around the island to taste ______ local snacks.
(A) authentic　(B) blend　(C) inclusive　(D) invisible

(　　)50. Expo 2010 ______ in Shanghai, China from May 1 to October 31, 2010.
(A) will hold　(B) will be holding　(C) will be held　(D) is holding

(　　)51. Millions of people are expected to ______ in the 2010 Taipei International Flora Expo.
(A) participate　(B) adjust　(C) emerge　(D) exist

(　　)52. ______ has become a very serious problem in the modern world. It's estimated that there are more than 1 billion overweight adults globally.
(A) Depression　(B) Obesity　(C) Malnutrition　(D) Starvation

(　　)53. John has to ______ the annual report to the manager before this Friday; otherwise, he will be in trouble.
(A) identify　(B) incline　(C) submit　(D) commemorate

(　　)54. Our company has been on a very tight ______ since 2008.
(A) deficit　(B) management　(C) budget　(D) debt

(　　)55. I need some ______ for taking buses around town.
(A) checks　(B) exchange　(C) change　(D) savings

(　　)56. The Department of Health urged the public to receive H1N1 flu shot as a ______ against potential outbreaks.
(A) prohibition　(B) preparation　(C) presumption　(D) precaution

(　　)57. Guest: What ______ do you have in your hotel?
Hotel clerk: We have a fitness center, a swimming pool, two restaurants, a beauty parlor, and a boutique.
(A) facilities　(B) benefits　(C) itineraries　(D) details

(　　)58. Go to the office at the Tourist Information Center and they will give you a ______ about sightseeing.
(A) destination　(B) deposit　(C) baggage　(D) brochure

( )59. It's difficult to find a hotel with a/an ______ room in high season.

(A) occupied (B) vacant (C) lank (D) unattended

( )60. Cathedrals, mosques, and temples are all ______ buildings.

(A) religious (B) natural (C) political (D) rural

( )61. Tourism has helped ______ the economy for many countries, and brought in considerable revenues.

(A) boast (B) boost (C) receive (D) recall

( )62. The caller: Can I speak to Ms. Taylor in room 612, please?
The operator: Please wait a minute. (pause) I'm sorry. There's no answer.
May I ______ a message?

(A) bring (B) take (C) leave (D) send

( )63. I'm afraid your credit card has already ______. Would you like to pay in cash instead?

(A) cancelled (B) booked (C) expired (D) exposed

( )64. You will have to pay extra ______ for overweight baggage.

(A) tags (B) badges (C) fees (D) credits

( )65. You will get a boarding ______ after completing the check-in.

(A) pass (B) post (C) plan (D) past

( )66. May I have two hundred U.S. dollars in small ______?

(A) accounts (B) balance (C) numbers (D) denominations

( )67. Many tourists are fascinated by the natural ______ of Taroko Gorge.

(A) sparkles (B) spectacles (C) spectators (D) sprinklers

( )68. All passengers shall go through ______ check before boarding.

(A) security (B) activity (C) insurance (D) deficiency

( )69. The time ______ is thirteen hours between Taipei and New York.

(A) decision (B) division (C) diligence (D) difference

( )70. You will pay a ______ of fifty dollars for your ferry ride.

(A) fan (B) fate (C) fair (D) fare

For those who travel on a __71__ , flying with a low-cost airline might be an option because you pay so much less than what you would be expected to pay with a traditional airline. Companies such as Ryanair, Southwest Airlines and Easyjet are some good examples. It's so easy to fly with these low-cost __72__ . From booking the tickets, checking in to boarding the plane, everything has become hassle-free. You only need to book online even if there are only two hours left before departure. You can also just __73__ the check-in desk and buy the tickets two hours before the plane takes off. Checking in is also easy and quick, and you're only required to arrive at the airport one hour before departure. But since traveling with these low-cost airlines has been so __74__ , you cannot expect to get free food, drinks or newspapers on board. There is also no classification regarding your seats and the flight attendants, who might be wearing casual clothing as their uniform, won't certainly serve you. As most of these low-cost airlines are __75__ , you might need to get ready for landing even after you have only gone on board for a few minutes.

( )71. (A) schedule (B) budget (C) routine (D) project

( )72. (A) forms (B) means (C) cruises (D) carriers

( )73. (A) pop in (B) break in (C) fill in (D) come in

( )74. (A) inexpensive (B) inconvenient (C) inefficient (D) inappropriate

( )75. (A) good-haul (B) huge-haul (C) short-haul (D) long-haul

Vacation rentals are fully private homes whose owners rent them out on a temporary basis to tourists as an alternative to hotels. They are available in all kinds of destinations, from a rustic cabin in the mountains to a downtown apartment in a major city. They can be townhouses, single-family-style homes, farms, beach houses, or even villas.

Vacation rentals are generally appealing for many reasons. They are, to name some on the top, cost-saving, spacious, great for large groups, separated from crowds, and no tips or service charges. Besides, they have kitchens for cooking, living rooms for gathering, outdoor spaces for parties or barbeques, and they offer the appeal of living like locals in a real community. They are usually equipped with facilities such as sports and beach accessories, games, books and DVD libraries, and in warmer locations, a swimming pool. Many vacation rentals are pet-friendly, so people can take their pets along with them when traveling.

Customers who choose hotels often enjoy the advantages of brand recognition, familiar reservation processes, and on-site service, while booking a vacation rental may mean stepping out of that comfort zone in order to get privacy, peace and quietness they offer -- things that are hard to obtain in a hotel room. For tourists, choosing a vacation rental over a hotel means more than short-term lodging -- vivid experiences and lifelong memories are what they value.

(　　)76. What is this reading mainly about?

(A) Planning leisure trips.

(B) The values of different vacation destinations.

(C) Alternative accommodations for tourists.

(D) Booking accommodations for fun trips.

(　　)77. What is the major concept of a vacation rental?

(A) Private houses rent out on weekdays only.

(B) Private homes rent out to tourists.

(C) Furnished homes for rent when owners are on vacations.

(D) Furnished rooms for short-term homestays.

(　　)78. Which of the following is NOT considered the reason that makes vacation rentals appealing?

(A) Familiar booking processes.

(B) Being economic.

(C) Being equipped with many useful facilities.

(D) Being pet-friendly.

(　　)79. What is the major advantage when tourists choose hotels rather than vacation rentals?

(A) Fame and wealth.　　(B) Living like locals.

(C) Fair prices.　　(D) On-site service.

(　　)80. Which of the following statements is a proper description of vacation rentals?

(A) They are shared by many owners.

(B) Tipping is not necessary at vacation rentals.

(C) They are built for business purpose.

(D) Daily cleaning is usually included in the rental contract.

★標準答案

1. (B)	2. (D)	3. (C)	4. (B)	5. (D)
6. (C)	7. (B)	8. (B)	9. (A)	10. (C)
11. (A)	12. (D)	13. (B)	14. (A)	15. (D)
16. (B)	17. (A)	18. (D)	19. (C)	20. (C)
21. (D)	22. (C)	23. (B)	24. (D)	25. (C)
26. (C)	27. (A)	28. (C)	29. (C)	30. (C)
31. (C)	32. (D)	33. (B)	34. (A)	35. (D)
36. (B)	37. (A)	38. (C)	39. (D)	40. (D)
41. (B)	42. (A)	43. (A)	44. (B)	45. (C)
46. (C)	47. (D)	48. (D)	49. (A)	50. (C)
51. (A)	52. (B)	53. (C)	54. (C)	55. (C)
56. (D)	57. (A)	58. (D)	59. (B)	60. (A)
61. (B)	62. (B)	63. (C)	64. (C)	65. (A)
66. (D)	67. (B)	68. (A)	69. (D)	70. (D)
71. (B)	72. (D)	73. (A)	74. (A)	75. (C)
76. (C)	77. (B)	78. (A)	79. (D)	80. (B)

精選必考外語領隊英文試題中譯與解析

1. Am I entitled to compensation if my ferry is canceled?

   (A) asked 要求　(B) entitled 有權享有

   (C) qualified 有資格　(D) requested 要求

   中譯 如果我的遊輪行程被取消了，我有權力要求補償嗎？ 102領隊

   解析 entitled to 有……資格的；compensation 補償、彌補。相關考題例句：Prohibited items in carry-on bags will be confiscated at the checkpoints, and no compensation will be given for them. 隨身行李中的違禁品將會於檢查站被沒收，且沒有任何的補償。 101領隊

2. It is the high season, and I'm not sure whether the hotel could provide enough accommodations for the whole group.

   (A) vacation 假期　(B) locations 位子

   (C) recommendation 推薦　(D) accommodations 住宿

   中譯 現在是旺季，我不確定飯店是否可以提供足夠的住宿給整個旅行團。 102領隊

   解析 high season是旺季，而It's high time則是時間剛好。

3. This traveler's check is not good because it should require two signatures by the user.

   (A) insurances 保險　(B) accounts 帳戶

   (C) signatures 簽名　(D) examinations 考試

   中譯 旅行支票不好用是因為它需要持有者的兩份簽名。 102領隊

   解析 sign 簽名，動詞；signatures 簽名，名詞。

4. We have seen a marked increase in the number of visitors to the theme park, but cannot understand why the total income indicates a decline.

   (A) a demand 需求　(B) a decline 下降

   (C) a distinction 區別　(D) a disruption 中斷

   中譯 我們看到主題樂園的遊客數已有顯著的增加，但卻不懂為何總收入卻下滑。 102領隊

   解析 decline、decrease都是下降、減少的意思。

5. It took us no time to clear customs at the border.

(A) costume 服裝 (B) custumes 服裝 (C) custom 風俗 (D) customs 海關

中譯 於邊界通關沒有花我們什麼時間。102領隊

解析 clear customs 結關、清關或者通關，指進口貨物、出口貨物和轉運貨物在進入一國海關關境或國境時，必須向海關申報，並辦理海關規定的各項手續。custom為風俗；customary為約定俗成的；customs為海關，考題常出現此三個單字。

6. When you stay in a hotel, what basic facilities do you think are necessary?

(A) activities 活動
(B) capabilities 能力
(C) facilities 設施
(D) abilities 能力

中譯 當你住在飯店時，你認為哪些基本的設備是必須的？102領隊

解析 facilities 設施，為重點單字。考題例句如：Guest: What facilities do you have in your hotel? 客人：你們飯店有什麼設施？ Hotel clerk: We have a fitness center, a swimming pool, two restaurants, a beauty parlor, and a boutique. 飯店服務員：我們有健身中心、游泳池、兩間餐廳、一間美容室和女裝店。99領隊

7. Airport limousine service, valet parking service, and concierge service are some of the most poplar items among our guest services.

(A) car services 汽車服務
(B) guest services 客戶服務
(C) sales services 銷售服務
(D) retail services 零售服務

中譯 機場接送服務、代客泊車、管家服務是我們最受歡迎的客戶服務項目之一。102領隊

解析 guest services 客戶服務；room service 客房服務。

8. I would like to charge this to my American Express card, please.

(A) choose this to 選擇
(B) charge this to 付費
(C) chain this to 鍊
(D) change this to 交換

中譯 我希望可以用我的美國運通卡付費，麻煩了。102領隊

解析 charge名詞為費用，動詞為收費、把帳掛在……，此題為動詞。charge為名詞的例句：All drinks served on the airplane are free of charge 所有在飛機上所供應的飲料都是免費的。動詞例句：The hospitals charge the patients for every aspirin. 醫院的每一片阿斯匹靈都要病人付錢。

9. Wild Formosa Sika deer became extinct due to extensive hunting of the animal during the Dutch colonization period.

(A) extinct 滅絕 (B) excite 使興奮 (C) exact 準確 (D) explicit 明確

中譯 因為荷蘭殖民時期的濫捕，台灣野鹿已經絕種。102領隊

解析 extinct 滅絕的、破滅的，也作熄滅的。

10. Your detailed itinerary is as follows: leaving Taipei on the 14th of June and arriving at Tokyo on the same day at noon.

(A) item 物件 (B) identification 識別

(C) itinerary 行程 (D) inscription 碑文

中譯 你詳細的行程如下：6月14日離開台北，當天中午抵達東京。102領隊

解析 itinerary 行程，例句：The manager gave a copy of his itinerary to his secretary and asked her to arrange some business meetings for him during his stay in Sydney. 經理交給他的祕書一份旅行計畫（行程），並且要求她幫他在雪梨安排一些業務會議。101領隊

11. Client: Are there any direct flights to Paris?
Clerk: No, you would have to transfer in Amsterdam.

(A) transfer 轉移 (B) transport 運輸 (C) translate 翻譯 (D) transform 轉變

中譯 客人：有到巴黎的直飛班機嗎？
服務員：沒有，你必須到阿姆斯特丹轉機。102領隊

解析 transfer flights 轉機。例句：Passengers transferring to other airlines should report to the information desk on the second floor. 要轉搭其他班機的旅客請到2樓的櫃台報到。101領隊

12. The hotels in the resort areas are fully booked in the summer. It would be very difficult to find any vacancies then.

(A) vacations 假期 (B) visitors 旅客 (C) views 觀點 (D) vacancies 空缺

中譯 度假勝地的飯店在夏天時被訂滿了。那時很難找到空房。102領隊

解析 經常考訂房相關議題，如：Reservations for hotel accommodation should be made in advance to make sure rooms are available. 旅館的訂房應提早訂，才能確保有房間。98領隊

13. If the tapes do not meet your satisfaction, you can return them within thirty days for a full refund.

(A) fund 資金　(B) refund 退款

(C) funding 提供資金　(D) fundraising 募款

中譯 如果這些膠帶不能讓你滿意，你可以在30天內退還並獲得全額退款。101領隊

解析 refund 退款，為常考單字，例句：We can refund the price difference. 我們可以退還差價。meet satisfaction 達到滿意的程度。

14. While many couples opt for a church wedding and wedding party, a Japanese groom and a Taiwanese bride tied the knot in a traditional Confucian wedding in Taipei.

(A) tied the knot 結婚　(B) knocked off 敲昏

(C) wore on 時間推移　(D) stepped down 降低

中譯 當許多情侶選擇教堂婚禮以及婚宴時，一對日本新郎以及台灣新娘在台北選擇傳統的儒家婚禮互訂終身。101領隊

解析 tie the knot為結婚的慣用說法，若不熟此片語，仍可由關鍵字wedding將其他選項剔除。groom 新郎；bride 新娘

15. Passengers transferring to other airlines should report to the information desk on the second floor.

(A) have transferred　(B) transfer

(C) are transferred　(D) transferring

中譯 要轉搭其他班機的旅客請到2樓的櫃台報到。101領隊

解析 簡化形容詞子句的步驟：

(1) 去關係代名詞

(2) 將形容詞子句中的動詞改為現在分詞Ving

(3) 如遇be動詞改為being，則將being省略

例句：Passengers transferring to other airlines should report to the information desk on the second floor.

= Passengers who transfer to other airlines should report to the information desk on the second floor.

16. "We are approaching some turbulence. For your safety, please keep your belts fastened until the 'seat belt' sign goes off."

(A) fasten （現在簡單式）

(B) fastened （過去分詞）

(C) fastening （現在分詞）

(D) be fastened （被動式）

中譯 「我們正接近某個亂流。為了你的安全，請繫緊安全帶直到座位安全帶的指示燈熄滅。」 101領隊

解析 fasten為繫緊之意。keep 維持（某事某物的狀態），接受詞以及受詞補語，故選fastened過去分詞。過去分詞當補語的例句：She had her photo taken. 她照了相。過去分詞taken當受詞her photo 的補語。

17. The flight will make a stopover in Paris for two hours.

(A) stopover 中途停留　　(B) stepover 跨距

(C) flyover 天橋　　(D) crossover 臨界

中譯 飛機將短暫停留巴黎兩個小時。 101領隊

解析 重點單字：stopover 中途停留，transit則是轉機。

18. If you carry keys, knives, aerosol cans, etc., in your pocket when you pass through the security at the airport, you may set off the alarm, and then the airport personnel will come to search you.

(A) let on 洩漏祕密 (B) let off 寬恕　　(C) set on 開啟　　(D) set off 引發

中譯 如果你帶著鑰匙、小刀、噴霧罐等東西在你的口袋，當你通過機場的安檢區時，你可能會引發警報器，接著機場的人員會來搜查你。 101領隊

解析 set off 引發。其他安檢例句為Please examine your luggage carefully before leaving. At the security counter, every item in the luggage has to go through inspection. 在出發前請仔細檢查你的行李。在安檢櫃台時，行李內的每一項物品都會被檢查。 99領隊

19. My father always asks everyone in the car to buckle up for safety, no matter how short the ride is.

(A) tight up 綳緊一點　　(B) fast up （無此片語）

(C) buckle up 繫好安全帶　　(D) stay up 熬夜

中譯 不管路程多短，為了安全著想，我爸爸總是要求車上每個人都繫好安全帶。 101領隊

解析 buckle up ＝ fasten seatbelt 繫好安全帶。Please keep your seat belt fastened during the flight for safety. 飛行途中請束緊安全帶，為了安全。

20. Client: What are this hotel's amenities?
Agent: It includes a great restaurant, a fitness center, an outdoor pool, and much more, such as in-room Internet access, 24-hour room service, and trustworthy babysitting, etc.

(A) installations 裝置
(B) utilities 實用
(C) amenities 設施
(D) surroundings 環境

中譯 客戶：這間飯店有什麼設施？
代理商：有一間很棒的餐廳、健身房、戶外游泳池、和其他設施，像是室內網路、24小時客房服務，和值得信賴的保母服務。 101領隊

解析 由a great restaurant、a fitness center、an outdoor pool可推知是amenities設施。

21. Tourist: What is the baggage allowance?
Airline clerk: It is 20 kilograms per person.

(A) Please fill out this form. 請填這表格。
(B) Sorry, cash is not suggested to be left in the baggage.
抱歉，不建議現金放在行李內。
(C) It is very cheap. 這很便宜。
(D) It is 20 kilograms per person. 每個人20公斤。

中譯 旅客：行李的限額是多少？
航空公司職員：每個人20公斤。 101領隊

解析 baggage allowance 行李的限額，故選It is 20 kilograms per person.。

22. A bus used for public transportation runs a set route; however, a charter bus travels at the direction of the person or organization that hires it.

(A) catering 餐飲 (B) chatter 閒聊 (C) charter 租賃 (D) cutter 切割機

中譯 用來當大眾運輸工具的巴士有固定的路線，然而，承租的巴士（遊覽車）依照租車的人或團體來行駛。 101領隊

解析 charter bus 遊覽車。set route 固定的路線。

23. Palm Beach is a coastline resort where thousands of tourists from all over the world spend their summer vacation.

(A) airport 機場 (B) resort 名勝 (C) pavement 人行道 (D) passage 通過

中譯 棕櫚灘是海岸度假勝地，來自世界各地的上千名遊客都到此來度過暑假。101領隊

解析 必考單字：resort 名勝。常見的retreat則是僻靜之地。

24. After disembarking the flight, I went directly to the baggage claim to pick up my bags and trunks.

(A) airport lounge 機場貴賓室 (B) cockpit 駕駛員座艙
(C) runway 逃亡 (D) baggage claim 行李認領處

中譯 下飛機後，我直接走向行李認領處拿我的包包和行李箱。101領隊

解析 常考單字：baggage claim 行李認領處。

25. Working as a hotel concierge means that your focus is to ensure that the needs and requests of hotel guests are met, and that each guest has a memorable stay.

(A) commander 指揮官 (B) celebrity 名人
(C) concierge 門房 (D) candidate 候選人

中譯 身為飯店的門房，表示你的重點是要確保客戶的需求與要求被滿足，讓每位房客有個難忘的停留回憶。101領隊

解析 concierge 門房；concierge service 管家服務，其他例句：The concierge at the information desk in a hotel provides traveling information to guests. 旅館服務台人員提供旅遊資訊給客人。99領隊

26. Mount Fuji is considered sacred; therefore, many people pay special visits to it, wishing to bring good luck to themselves and their loved ones.

(A) horrifying 恐懼的 (B) scared 害怕的
(C) sacred 神聖的 (D) superficial 膚淺的

中譯 富士山被視為神聖的，因此許多人會特別拜訪，希望可以替自己以及所愛的人帶來好運。101領隊

解析 sacred 神聖的，亦常用來形容廟宇。

27. Having been unemployed for almost one year, Henry has little chance of getting a job.

(A) Having been　(B) Be　(C) Maybe　(D) Since having

中譯 因為亨利已經幾乎一年沒有工作了，他找到工作的機會很小。101領隊

解析 在副詞子句的主詞與主要子句的主詞相同時（此題為Henry），我們可將副詞子句中的連接詞及主詞去掉，並將動詞改為Ving（動詞為主動語態，須為「現在分詞」（Ving）；被動語態，須變為「過去分詞」（PP）），即為簡單分詞構句。原句的副詞子句為Since he has been unemployed，簡化成Having unemployed。little chance 幾乎毫無機會。

28. If you have to extend your stay at the hotel room, you should inform the front desk at least one day prior to your original departure time.

(A) ahead to 提前　(B) forward to 期待

(C) prior to 在……之前　(D) in front of 正前方

中譯 如果你必須延長在飯店房間的時間，你至少應該在原定離開時間的前一天告知櫃台。101領隊

解析 prior to 在……之前。A is prior to B A在B之前。

29. Prohibited items in carry-on bags will be confiscated at the checkpoints, and no compensation will be given for them.

(A) argument 爭論　(B) recruitment 招聘

(C) compensation 補償　(D) decision 決定

中譯 隨身行李中的違禁品將會於檢查站被沒收，且沒有任何的補償。101領隊

解析 compensate 補償。安檢的延伸考題會有Please examine your luggage carefully before leaving. At the security counter, every item in the luggage has to go through inspection. 在出發前請仔細檢視你的行李。在安檢櫃台時，行李內的每一項物品都會被檢查。99領隊

30. She can speak English and French with facility.

(A) faculty 全體教員　(B) future 未來

(C) facility 流利　(D) frailty 弱點

中譯 她可以說很流利的英文和法語。100領隊

解析 with facility 流利，本句可替換成She can speak English and French fluently.。fluently 流利地。

31. The waiters will show you where to bed down.

(A) The waiters will tell you the place that you may put your beddings.

服務生將會告訴你哪裡可以放寢具。

(B) The waiters will ask for your assistance later.

服務生等會兒將要求你的援助。

(C) The waiters will tell you where you may stay tonight.

服務生將告訴你今晚你會下榻在哪裡。

(D) The waiters will provide everything you need.

服務生會提供你所需的每樣東西。

中譯 服務生將告訴你今晚你會下榻在哪裡。100領隊

解析 bed down 夜宿，也就是下榻之處。

32. Mr. Jones has got the hang of being a tour guide.

(A) Mr. Jones quit his job. 瓊斯先生辭職了。

(B) Mr. Jones needs our help now. 瓊斯先生現在需要我們的幫忙。

(C) Mr. Jones met some strangers on his way home.

瓊斯先生在回家途中遇到一些陌生人。

(D) Mr. Jones has learned the skills of being a tour guide.

瓊斯先生已經學習到當一位導遊的技巧。

中譯 瓊斯先生已經學習到當一位導遊的技巧。100領隊

解析 get the hang of sth. 掌握某事的訣竅。

33. Due to the impending disaster, we have to cancel our flight to Bangkok.

(A) provide 提供 (B) cancel 取消 (C) resume 重複 (D) tailor 裁縫

中譯 因為即將到來的災害，我們必須取消到曼谷的航班。100領隊

解析 impending 即將發生的、逼近的；disaster 災害、災難。due to 因為，例句：Due to the delay, we are not able to catch up with our connecting flight. 因為延遲，我們無法趕上我們的轉機班機。102領隊

34. The tour guide persuaded him into buying some expensive souvenirs.

(A) persuaded 說服 (B) dissuaded 勸阻

(C) suggested 建議 (D) purified 淨化

中譯 這名導遊說服他買昂貴的紀念品。100領隊

解析 persuade into Ving 說服；souvenir 紀念品。

35. The travel agent apologized for the delay.

(A) astonished at (B) astonished

(C) apologized (D) apologized for 道歉

中譯 旅行社因為行程延誤而道歉。100領隊

解析 apologize to 人 for 某事，意思是為某事向某人道歉，故選(D)。

36. The wedding anniversary is worth celebrating.

(A) being celebrated (B) celebrating 慶祝

(C) of celebrating (D) celebrated

中譯 結婚周年很值得慶祝。100領隊

解析 「worth of + 動名詞」與「worth + 動名詞」兩者形式不同，但意思相同。worth of + 動名詞－被動式的動名詞；而worth後面接主動式的動名詞，雖然在形式上是主動的，但其意義仍然是被動的。如 The wedding anniversary is worth of being celebrating. = The wedding anniversary is worth celebrating.。

37. Wulai (烏來) is a famous hot-spring resort.

(A) resort 名勝 (B) mansion 大廈 (C) pivot 中心點 (D) plaque 名牌

中譯 烏來是著名的溫泉度假勝地。100領隊

解析 hot-spring 溫泉；resort 休閒度假之處、名勝。

38. You must check the expiry date of your passport. You may need to apply for a new one.

(A) explanatory 解釋的 (B) exploratory 探險的

(C) expiry 到期、滿期 (D) expository 說明性

中譯 你必須檢查您的護照的到期日。你也許需要申請一本新的。100領隊

解析 expiry 到期的；expire 到期，例句:I am afraid your credit card has already expired. Would you like to pay in cash instead? 恐怕你的信用卡已經過期了。你希望改以付現代替嗎？99領隊

39. After the plane touches down, we have to remain in our seats until we taxi in to the gate.

(A) pass by 經過 (B) stop over 短暫停留

(C) take off 起飛 (D) taxi in 飛機在跑道上滑行

中譯 飛機降落後，我們必須待在座位上，直到滑入機坪入口。 100領隊

解析 touch down 著陸；taxi in 飛機在跑道上滑行。

40. Is there any problem with my reservation?

(A) in (B) of (C) to (D) with

中譯 我的預約有任何問題嗎？ 100領隊

解析 某事有問題，用with problem。

41. I enjoyed the stay here. Thank you very much for the hospitality.

(A) hospital 醫院 (B) hospitality 熱情好客

(C) hostilities 敵意 (D) hostel 宿舍

中譯 我喜歡住這裡。謝謝你的熱情好客。 100領隊

解析 hospitality 熱情好客。

42. If I cancel the trip, will I be refunded?

(A) be refunded (B) refund (C) refunded (D) refunding

中譯 如果我取消行程，我可以退費嗎？ 100領隊

解析 refund是退款，人之於refund 退費為被動，refund在此處為動詞，亦可為名詞，如：The guest is given a refund after he makes a complaint to the restaurant. 這名客人在他和餐廳抱怨之後拿到退款。 99領隊

Destinations can be cities, towns, natural regions, or even whole countries. The economies of all tourist destinations are dependent to a significant extent on the money produced by tourism. It is possible to classify destinations as natural or built: Natural *destinations* include seas, lakes, rivers, coasts, mountain ranges, desert, and so on. *Built destinations* are cities, towns, and villages. A *resort* is a destination constructed mainly or completely to serve the needs of tourism, such as Cancun in Mexico.

中譯 旅遊地點，可以是城市、小鎮、自然區域甚至整個國家。所有旅遊景點的經濟有很大一部分是依賴旅遊業所帶來的收益。旅遊景點可被區分為自然以及人為的：自然旅遊景點包含海洋、湖泊、河流、海岸、山脈和沙漠等等。人為的景點則是城市、小鎮以及鄉村。度假聖地就是大部分或是部分用來因應旅遊業的需求，像是墨西哥的坎昆。

Successful destinations are seen to be unique in some way by those who visit them. *Climate* is one of the features that determines this uniqueness. Not surprisingly, *temperate* and *tropical* climates attract the greatest number of visitors.

中譯 熱門的旅遊景點對於參訪的旅客來說是具有獨特性的。氣候就是決定獨特性的因素之一。無庸置疑地，溫帶以及熱帶氣候是最受青睞的。100領隊

單字 region 地區、地帶
and so on 等等
uniqueness 獨一無二、獨特性
extent 程度、限度
determine 決定

43. (A) dependent 依靠的 (B) disconnected 不相連的
(C) repellent 相斥的 (D) preferred 偏好的

44. (A) amplify 放大 (B) classify 分類
(C) signify 象徵 (D) verify 驗證

45. (A) concern 關心 (B) consist 組成
(C) include 包含 (D) involve 牽涉

46. (A) so on 等 (B) so so 還好
(C) such as 例如 (D) so that 以便

47. (A) conclusions 結論 (B) specializations 專業
(C) superstitions 迷信 (D) features 特色

48. Our hotel provides free shuttle service to the airport every day.
(A) accommodation 住宿 (B) communication 溝通
(C) transmission 傳輸 (D) shuttle接駁工具

中譯 我們飯店每天免費提供到機場的接駁巴士服務。99領隊

解析 THSR Shuttle Bus 台灣高鐵接駁巴士，如從車站至機場兩點固定來回的，即稱 shuttle bus。

49. Tourists enjoy visiting night markets around the island to taste authentic local snacks.

(A) authentic 真正的　(B) blend 融合
(C) inclusive 包含的　(D) invisible 無形的

中譯 遊客喜歡在島上到處參訪夜市，嚐嚐真正的道地小吃。99領隊

解析 local snacks 道地小吃。由local可推知為authentic 真正的。

★authentic 真正的，例句：This restaurant features authentic Northern Italian dishes that reflect the true flavors of Italy. 這間餐廳的特色為反映義大利口味的道地北義大利菜。101領隊

★其他關於夜市的考題

Night markets in Taiwan have become popular tourist destinations. They are great places to shop for bargains and eat typical Taiwanese food. 台灣的夜市已經成為受歡迎的觀光景點，他們是討價還價和吃傳統台灣料理的好地方。101領隊

50. Expo 2010 will be held in Shanghai, China from May 1 to October 31, 2010.

(A) will hold　(B) will be holding　(C) will be held　(D) is holding

中譯 2010年的世界博覽會將在5月1日到10月31日於中國上海舉行。99領隊

解析 hold是舉行，活動是「被」舉辦的，故選will be held。

★舉辦活動的兩個常見單字：

① host 主辦（帶有主辦人的意思）

- Rio will host the 2016 Summer Olympic Games. 里約將主辦2016年夏季奧運。
- An open-minded city, Taipei hosted Asia's first Gay Pride parade which has now become an annual autumn event. 身為一座心胸開放的都市，台北主辦亞洲第一屆同志遊行，並且成為每年於秋天所舉辦的活動。100領隊

② hold 舉行、舉辦

- The Olympic Games are held every four years. 奧運每4年（被）舉辦一次。
- The first Taipei Lantern Festival was held in 1990. Due to the event's huge popularity, the festival has been expanded every year. 第一屆的台北燈籠節於1990年舉行，而因為這場活動受到極大的歡迎，慶祝活動一年比一年盛大。98導遊

51. Millions of people are expected to participate in the 2010 Taipei International Flora Expo.

(A) participate 參加　(B) vadjust 調整

(C) emerge 浮現　(D) exist 存在

中譯 幾百萬人期待參加2010年的台北國際花卉博覽會。99領隊

解析 participate in 參加。

52. Obesity has become a very serious problem in the modern world. It's estimated that there are more than 1 billion overweight adults globally.

(A) Depression 沮喪　(B) Obesity 肥胖

(C) Malnutrition 營養失調　(D) Starvation 飢餓

中譯 肥胖已經成為現代世界很嚴重的問題。預估全球有超過10億成人過胖。99領隊

解析 由overweight可推知為obesity 肥胖。estimate 估計、估量；globally 全球地。

53. John has to submit the annual report to the manager before this Friday; otherwise, he will be in trouble.

(A) identify 識別　(B) incline 傾斜

(C) submit 提交　(D) commemorate 慶祝

中譯 約翰必須在這週五之前提交年度報告給經理，不然他就完蛋了。99領隊

解析 submit 提交；submit a plan 提出一項計畫；otherwise 否則、不然。

54. Our company has been on a very tight budget since 2008.

(A) deficit 虧損　(B) management 管理

(C) budget 預算　(D) debt 債務

中譯 自從2008年，我們公司的預算就很緊縮。99領隊

解析 budget 預算，為名詞，亦可當成動詞，為編列預算。例句：Parents should teach their children to budget their money at an early age. Otherwise, when they grow up, they will not know how to manage their money. 父母應該在孩子還小時就教導他們如何控制花費，否則當小孩長大時，將不知如何理財。98領隊 budget在此為動詞。我們俗稱的廉價航空公司即為budget airline或是low-cost airline。

55. I need some change for taking buses around town.

(A) checks 支票　(B) exchange 匯率

(C) change 零錢　(D) savings 儲蓄

中譯 我需要一些零錢搭公車到鎮上。99領隊

解析 change 零錢；bill 紙鈔。

56. The Department of Health urged the public to receive H1N1 flu shot as a precaution against potential outbreaks.

(A) prohibition 禁令　(B) preparation 藥劑

(C) presumption 推測　(D) precaution 預防

中譯 衛生處勸導公眾接受H1N1流感疫苗作為預防，以對抗潛在的爆發。99領隊

解析 urge 催促、力勸；outbreak 暴動；precaution 預防；caution 警告，例句：Motorists are strongly advised to take caution when they drive along windy mountainous roads to avoid plunging into a ravine. 強烈告誡摩托車騎士，當走風很大的深山時，要特別注意避免墜入深谷。100領隊

57. Guest: What facilities do you have in your hotel?
Hotel clerk: We have a fitness center, a swimming pool, two restaurants, a beauty parlor, and a boutique.

(A) facilities 設備　(B) benefits 利益　(C) itineraries 遊記　(D) details 細節

中譯 客人：你們飯店有什麼設施？
飯店服務員：我們有健身中心、游泳池、兩間餐廳、一間美容室和女裝店。99領隊

解析 parlor 休息室、接待室；boutique 流行女裝商店、精品店，例句：Sara bought a beautiful dress in a in a fashionable boutique district in Milan. 莎拉在米蘭的流行時尚區的一間精品店買了一件漂亮的洋裝。101領隊

58. Go to the office at the Tourist Information Center and they will give you a brochure about sightseeing.

(A) destination 目的地　(B) deposit 存款

(C) baggage 行李　(D) brochure 手冊

中譯 去旅遊中心他們會給你一本觀光手冊。99領隊

解析 Tourist Information Center通常會提供brochure 手冊以及map 地圖。

59. It's difficult to find a hotel with a/an vacant room in high season.

(A) occupied 已占滿的　(B) vacant 空著的

(C) lank 細長的　(D) unattended 沒人照顧的

中譯 在旺季時很難找到有空房的飯店。99領隊

解析 vacant 形容詞，空的；vacancy 名詞，空房、空位。

60. Cathedrals, mosques, and temples are all religious buildings.

(A) religious 宗教性的　(B) natural 自然的

(C) political 政治的　(D) rural 鄉村的

中譯 教堂、清真寺、寺廟都是宗教的建築。99領隊

解析 religion 宗教；religious 宗教性的。

61. Tourism has helped boost the economy for many countries, and brought in considerable revenues.

(A) boast 自誇　(B) boost 提振　(C) receive 收到　(D) recall 想起

中譯 旅遊業在許多國家已經幫忙振興經濟，且帶來許多可觀的收入。99領隊

解析 boost the economy 振興經濟；economic recession 經濟蕭條；revenue 稅收。

62. The caller: Can I speak to Ms. Taylor in room 612, please?
The operator: Please wait a minute. (pause) I'm sorry. There's no answer.
May I take a message?

(A) bring 帶　(B) take 拿　(C) leave 留下　(D) send 寄

中譯 來電者：我可以和612號房的泰勒女士說話嗎？99領隊
接線生：等一下。（停頓）我很抱歉。沒有人應答。我可以幫你留話嗎？

解析 leave a message 留話給某人；take a message 幫某人留話。

63. I'm afraid your credit card has already expired. Would you like to pay in cash instead?

(A) cancelled 取消　(B) booked 預定　(C) expired 屆期　(D) exposed 揭穿

中譯 恐怕你的信用卡已經過期了。你希望改以付現代替嗎？99領隊

解析 expired 屆期、過期的。

64. You will have to pay extra fees for overweight baggage.

(A) tags 標籤 (B) badges 徽章 (C) fees 手續費 (D) credits 信用

中譯 你必須替超重的行李支付額外的費用。98領隊

解析 由pay可以直接推知答案為fees。fee為通稱的費用，而tuition fees則是學費。charges為收取費用之意，No charge則為不需收費。fee的例句：The museum charges adults a small fee , but children can go in for free. 博物館向成人收取少許入場費，但小孩則可以免費參觀。98導遊

65. You will get a boarding pass after completing the check-in.

(A) pass 通行證 (B) post 郵件 (C) plan 計畫 (D) past 過去

中譯 在完成登機報到手續之後，你將會拿到一張登機證。98領隊

解析 ★boarding pass 登機證。

66. May I have two hundred U.S. dollars in small denominations?

(A) accounts 帳目 (B) balance 餘額

(C) numbers 號碼 (D) denominations 面額

中譯 我可以兌換200美元的小額鈔票嗎？98領隊

解析 denominations 面額，例句：In what denominations? 要什麼面額的？

67. Many tourists are fascinated by the natural spectacles of Taroko Gorge.

(A) sparkles 火花 (B) spectacles 奇觀

(C) spectators 觀眾 (D) sprinklers 灑水機

中譯 許多觀光客為太魯閣的自然奇觀所著迷。98領隊

解析 spectacles 奇觀；fascinate 迷住、強烈地吸引。fascinating用來形容某事，fastened則是人被迷住了的意思。

68. All passengers shall go through security check before boarding.

(A) security 安全 (B) activity 活動 (C) insurance 保險 (D) deficiency 缺乏

中譯 上機前所有旅客都應該通過安全檢查。98領隊

解析 security 安全；flight security 飛安。

69. The time difference is thirteen hours between Taipei and New York.

(A) decision 決定　(B) division 區分　(C) diligence 勤奮　(D) difference 差別

中譯 台北與紐約的時差為13個小時。98領隊

解析 time difference 時差。

70. You will pay a fare of fifty dollars for your ferry ride.

(A) fan 電風扇　(B) fate 命運　(C) fair 博覽會　(D) fare 費用

中譯 你要付50元的費用來搭乘渡輪。98領隊

解析 ★fees和fare的差別：

① fee 服務費
- pay the lawyer's fees 付律師費
- a bill for school fees 學費帳單

② fare （大眾運輸）票價：
- What is the bus fare to London? 到倫敦的公共汽車費是多少？
- travel at half / full / reduced fare 半價 / 全價 / 減價
- Most taxi drivers in Kinmen prefer to ask for a flat fare rather than use the meter. 大部分金門的計程車司機喜歡使用單一費率而非使用計程表。100導遊

For those who travel on a budget, flying with a low-cost airline might be an option because you pay so much less than what you would be expected to pay with a traditional airline. Companies such as Ryanair, Southwest Airlines and Easyjet are some good examples. It's so easy to fly with these low-cost carriers. From booking the tickets, checking in to boarding the plane, everything has become hassle-free. You only need to book online even if there are only two hours left before departure. You can also just pop in the check-in desk and buy the tickets two hours before the plane takes off. Checking in is also easy and quick, and you're only required to arrive at the airport one hour before departure. But since traveling with these low-cost airlines has been so inexpensive, you cannot expect to get free food, drinks or newspapers on board. There is also no classification regarding your seats and the flight attendants, who might be wearing casual clothing as their uniform, won't certainly serve you. As most of these low-cost airlines are short-haul, you might need to get ready for landing even after you have only gone on board for a few minutes.

中譯 對於想要低價旅行的人來說，搭廉價航空也許是個選擇，因為你所要付的比起你預期要付給傳統航空公司的錢少得多。像是瑞安航空、西南航空，以及易捷航空都是很好

的例子。搭乘廉價航空非常容易，從訂票、到機場登記登機，每一件事都是輕而易舉的。甚至你只需要在出發前2個小時之前在網路上訂票。你也可以直接在起飛前2個小時跑到簽到櫃台前買票。辦理登機手續也很容易以及快速，而且你可以在起飛前一個小時到機場即可。既然廉價航空是如此廉價，你不能期望在飛機上有免費的食物、飲料和報紙。而且對於你的座位也沒有艙等之分，空服員可能還穿休閒服當成制服，當然也不會服務你。多數的廉價航空航班都是短程的，甚至可能你登機後沒幾分鐘你就要準備降落了。99領隊

單字 low-cost airline 低成本航空公司 option 選擇
hassle-free 輕而易舉 classification 分級

71. (A) schedule 計畫 (B) budget 預算
(C) routine 慣例 (D) project 專案

72. (A) forms 格式 (B) means 方法
(C) cruises 航遊 (D) carriers 航空公司

73. (A) pop in 突然出現 (B) break in 闖入
(C) fill in 填寫 (D) come in 進來

74. (A) inexpensive 便宜的 (B) inconvenient 不方便的
(C) inefficient 無效率的 (D) inappropriate 不適當的

75. (A) good-haul 好的長途 (B) huge-haul 巨大的長途
(C) short-haul 短程運輸的 (D) long-haul 持久

Vacation rentals are fully private homes whose owners rent them out on a temporary basis to tourists as an alternative to hotels. They are available in all kinds of destinations, from a rustic cabin in the mountains to a downtown apartment in a major city. They can be townhouses, single-family-style homes, farms, beach houses, or even villas.

中譯 假期租屋是完全的私人住宅，其屋主短暫的將屋子出租給遊客當成是飯店以外的選擇。依目的地的不同也有不同的選擇，像是山中的小木屋，或是大城市中的市中心公寓。可以是連棟的住宅，也可以是獨棟透天屋、農場、海邊住宅甚至是別墅。

Vacation rentals are generally appealing for many reasons. They are, to name some on the top, cost-saving, spacious, great for large groups, separated from crowds, and no tips or service charges. Besides, they have kitchens for cooking, living rooms for gathering, outdoor spaces for parties or barbeques, and they offer the appeal of living like locals in a real community. They are usually equipped with facilities such as sports and beach accessories, games, books and DVD libraries, and in warmer locations, a swimming pool. Many vacation rentals are pet-friendly, so people can take their pets along with them when traveling.

中譯 假期租屋在很多方面都是很吸引人的，比如說，從最吸引人的來說，就是省錢、空間大、適合一大群人、和其他人群隔開，以及沒有小費和服務費。此外，還有廚房可以煮菜，客廳可以聚會，戶外空間可用來舉辦派對和烤肉，就像真實住在當地社區的居民一樣。這些租屋通常會有運動設施、海灘設備、遊戲、書本，和許多DVD，氣候溫暖的地方甚至會有游泳池。許多假期租屋是可以帶寵物入住的，所以很多人會帶著寵物一起旅行。

Customers who choose hotels often enjoy the advantages of brand recognition, familiar reservation processes, and on-site service, while booking a vacation rental may mean stepping out of that comfort zone in order to get privacy, peace and quietness they offer -- things that are hard to obtain in a hotel room. For tourists, choosing a vacation rental over a hotel means more than short-term lodging -- vivid experiences and lifelong memories are what they value.

中譯 客戶選擇飯店常是享受品牌知名度、熟悉的訂房流程和客房服務。然而假期租屋則意味著要走出舒適圈，以獲得隱私、平和與安靜，這些都很難從飯店住宿中獲得。對於遊客來說，選擇假期租屋而非飯店，表示比短期住宿更重要的是道地的生活體驗以及一輩子的記憶才是他們所重視的。101領隊

單字 rental 租賃
separate 區分
brand 商標、牌子
spacious 廣闊的
advantage 優勢
recognition 贊譽認可

76. What is this reading mainly about?

(A) Planning leisure trips. 計劃休閒旅遊。

(B) The values of different vacation destinations. 不同假期目的地的價值。

(C) Alternative accommodations for tourists. 觀光客另外的食宿選擇。

(D) Booking accommodations for fun trips. 預定有趣旅程的住宿。

中譯 本文的主旨為何？

解析 由第一段They are available in all kinds of destinations可知。

77. What is the major concept of a vacation rental?

(A) Private houses rent out on weekdays only. 私有的房屋只在平日出租。

(B) Private homes rent out to tourists. 私有的房屋出租給觀光客。

(C) Furnished homes for rent when owners are on vacations.
已布置好的房子在屋主度假時出租。

(D) Furnished rooms for short-term homestays.
已布置好的房間給短期的寄宿家庭。

中譯 短期租屋的主要概念是什麼？

解析 由Vacation rentals are fully private homes whose owners rent them out on a temporary basis to tourists as an alternative to hotels.可知。

78. Which of the following is NOT considered the reason that makes vacation rentals appealing?

(A) Familiar booking processes. 熟悉的訂房程序。

(B) Being economic. 便宜。

(C) Being equipped with many useful facilities. 備有許多有用的設施。

(D) Being pet-friendly. 對寵物友善。

中譯 哪一項不是短期租屋吸引人的地方？

解析 由Customers who choose hotels often enjoy the advantages of brand recognition, familiar reservation processes可知familiar reservation processes為飯店的優點，而非假期租屋的優點。

79. What is the major advantage when tourists choose hotels rather than vacation rentals?

(A) Fame and wealth. 名聲和財富。

(B) Living like locals. 像當地人一樣生活。

(C) Fair prices. 平價。

(D) On-site service. 現場服務。

中譯 當遊客選擇短期租屋而非飯店時，最大的優點是什麼？

解析 由最後一段第一句可知。

80. Which of the following statements is a proper description of vacation rentals?

(A) They are shared by many owners. 他們為很多主人所有。

(B) Tipping is not necessary at vacation rentals. 短期租屋不一定要付小費。

(C) They are built for business purpose. 短期租屋因商業用途而建。

(D) Daily cleaning is usually included in the rental contract. 每天的清掃通常包含於租賃合約內。

中譯 以下哪項對於短期租屋的敘述為正確的？

解析 由Vacation rentals are generally appealing for many reasons. They are, to name some on the top, cost-saving, spacious, great for large groups, separated from crowds, and no tips or service charges.可知。

( )1. A ______ is simply another name for a small specialty shop.

(A) boutique (B) body shop (C) bonus (D) beauty

( )2. When the table filled with some ______ refreshments was removed, the host announced that dinner would be served.

(A) strong (B) heavy (C) light (D) bright

( )3. Strictly speaking, Venice is now more of a ______ city than a maritime business city.

(A) waterfront (B) Italian (C) tourism (D) modern

( )4. I like Rome very much because it has many historic ______ and it is friendly to visitors.

(A) stories (B) glory (C) sites (D) giants

( )5. When traveling in a foreign country, we need to carry with us several important documents at all times. One of them is our passport together with the ______ permit if that has been so required.

(A) entering (B) entry (C) exit (D) ego

( )6. When answering questions of the immigration officer, it is advisable to be straight forward and not ______.

(A) historic (B) hesitating (C) hospitable (D) heroic

( )7. Customs officers usually have a ______ face and they have the right to ask us to open our baggage for searching.

(A) good-looking (B) funny-looking (C) stern-looking (D) silly-looking

( )8. Mingling with tourists from different backgrounds helps tour guides ______ and learn new things in answering curious visitors' various questions.

(A) blow their own horn (B) broke up

(C) broke in (D) broke down

( )9. If we remember our social ______, particularly in a big crowd, we shall win people's admiration though we may not feel it.

(A) ages (B) manners (C) news (D) recruits

(　　)10. Taiwan is the home of hot springs. Located along Wenshui River, the Taian Hot Springs were developed during the Japanese ______.

(A) oration　(B) operation　(C) orientation　(D) occupation

(　　)11. Taiwan government said yesterday it will not give up restrictions it imposes on imported beef, after a warning by U.S. lawmakers that the issue could ______ free trade talks.

(A) facilitate　(B) advance　(C) delight　(D) cripple

(　　)12. The financial ______ that started in the U.S. and swept the globe was further proof that—for better and for worse—we can't escape one another.

(A) data　(B) tadpole　(C) advent　(D) crisis

(　　)13. Increasing tourism infrastructure to meet domestic and international demands has raised concerns about the ______ on Taiwan's natural environment.

(A) impact　(B) input　(C) itinerary　(D) identity

(　　)14. A bill to legalize gay marriage in Washington State has won final legislative ______ and taken effect starting 2012.

(A) approval　(B) rejection　(C) veto　(D) admission

(　　)15. When visiting Alishan, one of the most popular tourist destinations in Taiwan, it's worth spending a few days to learn about the indigenous people living in mountain villages and ______ the marvelous scenery.

(A) prick on　(B) take in　(C) put off　(D) pick up

(　　)16. At the annual food festival, you can ______ a wide variety of delicacies.

(A) sample　(B) deliver　(C) cater　(D) reduce

(　　)17. On my flight to Tokyo, I asked a flight ______ to bring me an extra pillow.

(A) clerk　(B) employer　(C) chauffeur　(D) attendant

(　　)18. Cloud Gate, an internationally ______ dance group from Taiwan, demonstrated that the quality of modern dance inAsia could be comparable to that of modern dance in Europe and North America.

(A) refunded　(B) reflected　(C) retained　(D) renowned

( )19. The ______ of our trip to Southern Taiwan was A Taste of Tainan where we had a lot of delicious food.

(A) gourmet (B) highlight (C) monument (D) recognition

( )20. Bopiliao, ______ in Wanhua District, Taipei, and serving as the setting for the film, Monga, is a popular tourist spot.

(A) selected (B) featured (C) located (D) directed

( )21. The man at the passport ______ did not seem to like the photo in my passport, but in the end he let me through.

(A) station (B) custom (C) security (D) control

( )22. Thanks to India's economic ______ and the booming growth of its airline industry, more Indians are flying today than ever before.

(A) prosperity (B) souvenir (C) decline (D) evidence

( )23. The tour guide is a ______ man; he is very polite and always speaks in a kind manner.

(A) careless (B) persistent (C) courteous (D) environmental

( )24. This restaurant features ______ Northern Italian dishes that reflect the true flavors of Italy.

(A) disposable (B) confident (C) authentic (D) dimensional

( )25. With crystal clear water, emerald green mountains and various outdoor activities to offer, it's not ______ that Sun Moon Lake is one of the most visited spots in Taiwan.

(A) identified (B) apparent (C) grateful (D) surprising

( )26. Taiwan is well known for its mountain ______ spots and urban landmarks such as the National Palace Museum and the Taipei 101 skyscraper.

(A) scenic (B) neutral (C) vacant (D) feasible

( )27. Night markets in Taiwan have become ______ tourist destinations. They are great places to shop for bargains and eat typical Taiwanese food.

(A) tropical (B) popular (C) edible (D) responsible

( )28. Taroko National Park ______ high mountains and steep canyons. Many of its peaks tower above 3,000 meters in elevation.

(A) lacks (B) features (C) excludes (D) disregards

( )29. To ______ health and fitness, we need proper diet and exercise.

(A) maintain (B) apply (C) retire (D) contain

( )30. Jennifer is ______ in several languages other than her mother tongue English.

(A) fluent (B) quiet (C) universal (D) tall

( )31. With its palaces, sculptured parks, concert halls, and museums, Vienna is a city ______ in cultures.

(A) chronic (B) elite (C) provincial (D) steeped

( )32. The oldest of all the main Hawaiian islands, Kauai is ______ for its secluded beaches, scenic waterfalls, and jungle hikes.

(A) due (B) known (C) neutral (D) ripe

( )33. Please check your ticket and ______ that you are sitting in the correct seat.

(A) make sure (B) be aware of (C) find out (D) pay attention

( )34. When you arrive at the airport, the first thing you do is go to ______.

(A) the departure lounge (B) the check-in desk
(C) the arrival desk (D) the customs

( )35. His one ambition in life was to go on ______ to Kenya to photograph lions and tigers.

(A) safari (B) voyage (C) ferry (D) yacht

( )36. The hiking route of the Shitoushan Trail is not ______ and so is suitable for most people, including the elderly and young children.

(A) slick (B) smooth (C) steep (D) steady

( )37. As a general rule, checked baggage such as golf clubs in golf bags, serfboards, baby strollers, and child car seats are not placed on a baggage ______.

(A) carnival (B) carrier (C) claim (D) carousel

( )38. Demographers study population growth or decline and things like ______, which means the movement of populations into cities.

(A) classification (B) normalization (C) industrialization (D) urbanization

( )39. Most taxi drivers in Kinmen prefer to ask for a ______ fare rather than use the meter.

(A) flat (B) high (C) set (D) deal

( )40. An open-minded city, Taipei ______ Asia's first Gay Pride parade which has now become an annual autumn event.

(A) expanded (B) governed (C) hosted (D) portrayed

( )41. Middle-aged smokers are far more likely than nonsmokers to ______ dementia later in life, and heavy smokers are at more than double the risk, according to a new study.

(A) deflect (B) demote (C) deliberate (D) develop

( )42. Earth is unique in the universe for its ______ of water, amounting to 70 percent of its surface.

(A) benevolence (B) abundance (C) redundance (D) attendance

( )43. Unlike other springs locations, Taian Hot Springs is relatively serene, with no more than six large-scale resorts in the area, so the place is not as ______ as Wulai and Beitou.

(A) congested (B) displaced (C) isolated (D) populated

( )44. Many people consider Yangmingshan National Park a pleasant ______ from the bustle of the city.

(A) retreat (B) removal (C) departure (D) adventure

( )45. The temple was really colorful. It had blue and red tiles all over it and there were ______ of different gods on the walls and on the roof.

(A) states (B) status (C) statues (D) stature

( )46. Taiwan's premier said 2010 was a boom year for tourism in Taiwan and he ______ the success to the improvements in cross-strait relations.

(A) administered (B) advertised (C) acclaimed (D) attributed

( )47. Living near the airport, I am very much ______ by the noise of airplanes. I can not sleep well and often feel uneasy.

(A) marked (B) bothered (C) expected (D) confused

( )48. Claire loves to buy ______ foods: vegetables and herbs from China, spices from India, olives from Greece, and cheeses from France.

(A) sea (B) stingy (C) tranquil (D) exotic

( )49. As a result of the accident, Shirley was ______ for three weeks before gradually recovered.

(A) unconscious (B) prehistoric (C) gorgeous (D) fortunate

( )50. To ______ money, buy just what you need and refrain from buying unnecessary stuff.

(A) invent (B) discard (C) save (D) exhaust

( )51. With a ______ smile, Robert showed how happy he was when he won the swimming contest yesterday.

(A) fertile (B) historic (C) pollutant (D) complacent

( )52. Since our economy has been improving recently, I hope that my boss will give me a big ______ this year.

(A) conquest (B) consumption (C) rise (D) raise

( )53. Some soils are extremely rich in ______ and nutrients such as iron and copper.

(A) minerals (B) mermaids (C) miniatures (D) manuscripts

( )54. People who have a great sense of ______ are often very popular, because they are usually intelligent, open-minded, and witty.

(A) frustration (B) humor (C) betrayal (D) inferiority

( )55. A ______ person is usually welcomed by everyone, because he never irritates people.

(A) selfish (B) naughty (C) pessimistic (D) humble

( )56. For centuries, artists, historians, and tourists have been ______ by Mona Lisa's enigmatic smile.

(A) ignored (B) characterized (C) fascinated (D) embraced

( )57. Fireworks and firecrackers are often used in Chinese communities to ______ greeting good fortunes and scaring away evils.

(A) sign (B) symbolize (C) identify (D) underline

( )58. A ______ is a necessary document for the passenger to get on the airplane.

(A) boarding pass (B) passport (C) identification card (D) visa

(　　)59. Besides participating in local cultural activities, people who desire to explore the ecology of Kenting can ______ plenty of wildlife and plants.

(A) observe　(B) pick up　(C) object　(D) plan

(　　)60. When people travel to popular destinations during peak seasons, it is necessary to reserve ______ before the trip.

(A) generation　(B) accommodations
(C) identification　(D) confirmation

(　　)61. If you want to find the cheapest airplane ticket, ______ can usually be found through the Internet.

(A) bargains　(B) destinations　(C) reservations　(D) itinerary

(　　)62. Please examine your luggage carefully before leaving. At the security counter, every item in the luggage has to go through thorough ______.

(A) relation　(B) invention　(C) inspection　(D) observation

(　　)63. The flight is scheduled to ______ at eleven o'clock tomorrow. You will have to get to the airport two hours before the takeoff.

(A) land　(B) depart　(C) cancel　(D) examine

(　　)64. Formed in 1991 and having toured internationally in Europe and Asia, the Formosa Aboriginal Dance Troupe is a group that ______ Taiwanese folk music.

(A) performs　(B) results　(C) achieves　(D) occurs

"Good evening, ladies and gentlemen. This is the pre-boarding __65__ for flight 67B to Vancouver. We are now inviting those passengers with small children, and any passenger __66__ special assistance, to begin boarding at this time. Please have your boarding pass and identification ready. Regular boarding will begin in __67__ ten minutes. Thank you."

(　　)65. (A) forecast　(B) announcement　(C) denouncement　(D) definition

(　　)66. (A) depending　(B) digesting　(C) requiring　(D) including

(　　)67. (A) approximately　(B) separately　(C) indirectly　(D) indefinitely

Unlike bird watching, which is often most __68__ in the very early morning or just before dusk, butterfly watching is best done between around 10:00 a.m. and 4:00 p.m.. Moreover, butterflies are more __69__ than birds because they are less sensitive to sound. For these reasons, butterfly appreciation is perhaps a more __70__ hobby than bird watching.

( )68. (A) competent (B) extinct (C) successful (D) diplomatic

( )69. (A) approachable (B) edible (C) unbearable (D) affordable

( )70. (A) portable (B) curious (C) available (D) moral

What kind of job description would fit your idea of "the best job in the world"? Tourism Queensland (TQ) lately launched a talent hunt as a part of massive tourism campaign worldwide.

They are looking for a caretaker to live on Hamilton Island of the Great Barrier Reef, whose major responsibility is to be their spokesperson on the island. The contract starts from this July to January next year, and the salary for the six months is AU$150,000, around NT$3.38 million.

"The caretaker is required to do some basic chores, such as cleaning the pool, feeding over 1,500 species of fish, and sending out the mails by plane," said Kimberly Chien, Marketing Manager of TQ. "The major task is to explore islands in Barrier Reef and keep updating an online journal with photos to share a caretaker's life with the world." The position is open to anyone who is over 18, a good swimmer and communicator.

Applicants are required to make a one-minute video explaining why he or she is the best candidate for the job. Tourism Queensland will organize a group of referees to select 11 candidates, including one from an internet voting which will be held in March. The 11 candidates will then be invited to Hamilton Island for the final interview; only one of them will win the position to do "the best job in the world."

( )71. According to the passage, what is the purpose for the state government of Queensland, Australia, to offer people a job like this?

(A) To make money. (B) To seek foreign aid.
(C) To promote tourism. (D) To provide entertainment.

( )72. Which of the following job requirements is NOT mentioned in the passage?

(A) Over 18 years old (B) A good swimmer.
(C) A good communicator. (D) A native English speaker.

( )73. According to the passage, which of the following is on the job description for this position?

(A) To host a TV talk show.
(B) To meet with international leaders.
(C) To let people know what life is like on the island.
(D) To produce a formal documentary about the island.

(　　)74. According to the passage, what is the application procedure for this job?

(A) To provide an overseas passport.

(B) To make a self-introduction video.

(C) To call and make a reservation for an interview.

(D) To submit a completed application form by post.

(　　)75. According to the passage, which of the following is true?

(A) It is a permanent job.

(B) The job begins this coming July.

(C) Twelve candidates will be selected for the final interview.

(D) The winner will be decided by an internet voting.

While on vacation, not everyone likes staying at nice hotels, visiting museums, and shopping at department stores. Some would rather jump out of an airplane, speed down a river, or stay in a traditional village. They are part of a growing number of people who enjoy adventure tourism. It is a type of travel for people looking to get more out of their vacations.

With the Internet, it is easier than ever to set up an adventure tour. People can plan trips themselves, or they can find a suitable tour company online. Some popular countries to visit are Costa Rica, India, New Zealand, and Botswana. Their natural settings make them perfect for outdoor activities like hiking and diving. Rich in wildlife, they are also great for bird watching and safaris. Learning about the local history and culture is also popular with adventure travelers. In Peru, people love visiting the ruins of Machu Picchu. And, travelers in Tanzania enjoy meeting local tribes. In some countries, it is even possible to live and work in a village during a vacation. While building houses and helping research teams, travelers can enjoy local food and learn about the culture.

Besides being a lot of fun, these exiting trips mean big money for local economies. Tourism is already the world's largest industry, worth some $ 3 trillion. Of that, adventure tourism makes up about 20% of the market. That number is growing, as more people plan exciting vacations in their own countries and abroad.

(　　)76. What can we infer about adventure tourists from the passage?

(A) They like safe and comfortable vacations.

(B) They have little interest in culture.

(C) They enjoy trips that are exciting.

(D) They rarely play on sports teams.

(　　)77. Where would you go to visit Machu Picchu?

(A) Tanzania　　(B) Europe　　(C) Peru　　(D) The Himalayas

(　　)78. What is NOT a reason why people enjoy traveling to New Zealand?

(A) Tours there are cheaper than in other places.
(B) It is a great place for nature lovers.
(C) One could easily set up a bird watching trip.
(D) There are many outdoor activities.

(　　)79. What does the word rich in paragraph 2 mean?

(A) wealthy　(B) plentiful　(C) funny　(D) heavy

(　　)80. What does the passage suggest about the tourism industry?

(A) It may soon be worth $3 trillion.
(B) Adventure tourism brings in the most money.
(C) Most of the industry is facing hard times.
(D) It is important to local economies.

★標準答案

1. (A)	2. (C)	3. (C)	4. (C)	5. (B)
6. (B)	7. (C)	8. (D)	9. (B)	10. (D)
11. (D)	12. (D)	13. (A)	14. (A)	15. (B)
16. (A)	17. (D)	18. (D)	19. (B)	20. (C)
21. (D)	22. (A)	23. (C)	24. (C)	25. (D)
26. (A)	27. (B)	28. (B)	29. (A)	30. (A)
31. (D)	32. (B)	33. (A)	34. (B)	35. (A)
36. (C)	37. (D)	38. (D)	39. (A)	40. (C)
41. (D)	42. (B)	43. (A)	44. (A)	45. (C)
46. (D)	47. (B)	48. (D)	49. (A)	50. (C)
51. (D)	52. (D)	53. (A)	54. (B)	55. (D)
56. (C)	57. (B)	58. (A)	59. (A)	60. (B)
61. (A)	62. (C)	63. (B)	64. (A)	65. (B)
66. (C)	67. (A)	68. (C)	69. (A)	70. (C)
71. (C)	72. (D)	73. (C)	74. (B)	75. (B)
76. (C)	77. (C)	78. (A)	79. (B)	80. (D)

精選必考外語導遊英文試題中譯與解析

1. A boutique is simply another name for a small specialty shop.

(A) boutique 精品店　(B) body shop 車身修理廠
(C) bonus 獎金　(D) beauty parlor 美容院

中譯 精品店也表示是賣特殊紀念品的小商店。102導遊

解析 boutique 專賣流行衣服的小商店、精品店。

2. When the table filled with some light refreshments was removed, the host announced that dinner would be served.

(A) strong 強烈的　(B) heavy 巨大的　(C) light 輕的　(D) bright 明亮的

中譯 當整桌的輕食都被移走時，主人宣布晚餐準備開始了。102導遊

解析 light food 易消化的食物、輕食；refreshment 茶點。

3. Strictly speaking, Venice is now more of a tourism city than a maritime business city.

(A) waterfront 濱水地區　(B) Italian 義大利的
(C) tourism 觀光業　(D) modern 現代的

中譯 嚴格來說，威尼斯比較像觀光城市而不是海洋的商業城市。102導遊

解析 strictly speaking 嚴格地說；tourism 觀光業。

4. I like Rome very much because it has many historic sites and it is friendly to visitors.

(A) stories 故事　(B) glory 光榮　(C) sites 遺址　(D) giants 巨人

中譯 我非常喜歡羅馬，因為它有很多歷史遺跡，對遊客也很友善。102導遊

解析 historic sites 歷史遺址；site 地點、場所、網站、遺址。

5. When traveling in a foreign country, we need to carry with us several important documents at all times. One of them is our passport together with the entry permit if that has been so required.

(A) entering 進入　(B) entry 進入　(C) exit 出口　(D) ego 自我

中譯 當在外國旅遊，我們需要隨身攜帶幾份重要的文件。其中一項就是我們的護照和入境許可證，如果被要求的話。102導遊

解析 entry 進入（名詞）；enter 進入（動詞）；permit 允許、許可。

6. When answering questions of the immigration officer, it is advisable to be straight forward and not hesitating.

(A) historic 有歷史性的 (B) hesitating 猶豫的
(C) hospitable 好客的 (D) heroic 英勇的

中譯 當回答移民官的問題時，建議實話實說，並且不要猶豫。102導遊

解析 the immigration officer 移民局；hesitating 猶豫的。

7. Customs officers usually have a stern-looking face and they have the right to ask us to open our baggage for searching.

(A) good-looking 好看的 (B) funny-looking 看起來搞笑的
(C) stern-looking 看起來嚴厲的 (D) silly-looking 看起來傻傻的

中譯 海關官員通常看起來很嚴肅，而且他們有權利為了搜查的目的而要求我們打開行李。102導遊

解析 stern 嚴厲的、嚴格的。

8. Mingling with tourists from different backgrounds helps tour guides broaden their horizons and learn new things in answering curious visitors' various questions.

(A) blow their own horn 自吹自擂
(B) take their breath away 使他們大吃一驚
(C) fall from grace 失寵
(D) broaden their horizons 開拓視野

中譯 與不同背景的觀光客打交道讓導遊開拓視野，也學習回答好奇旅客不同的新問題。102導遊

解析 mingle 使混合、使相混；broaden their horizons 開拓視野。直譯為擴大海平面。

9. If we remember our social manners, particularly in a big crowd, we shall win people's admiration though we may not feel it.

(A) ages 年紀 (B) manners 禮貌 (C) news 新聞 (D) recruits 新成員

中譯 如果我們記得我們的社交禮儀，特別是在群眾中，我們應該會贏得人們的尊敬即便我們沒有感覺到。102導遊

解析 social manners 社交禮儀；table manners 餐桌禮儀。

10. Taiwan is the home of hot springs. Located along Wenshui River, the Taian Hot Springs were developed during the Japanese occupation.

(A) oration 演說 (B) operation 手術
(C) orientation 定方位 (D) occupation 佔領時期

中譯 台灣有許多溫泉。汶水溪旁的泰安溫泉於日本佔據時期所開發的。102導遊

解析 occupy 佔領；occupation 佔領時期。

11. Taiwan government said yesterday it will not give up restrictions it imposes on imported beef, after a warning by U.S. lawmakers that the issue could cripple free trade talks.

(A) facilitate 促進 (B) advance 提出 (C) delight 喜愛 (D) cripple 破壞

中譯 台灣政府昨天表示不會放棄對於進口牛肉課稅的限制，在經過美國立法單位警告這項議題會破壞自由貿易。102導遊

解析 impose 徵（稅）；cripple 嚴重毀壞（或損害）。

12. The financial crisis that started in the U.S. and swept the globe was further proof that — for better and for worse — we can't escape one another.

(A) data 數據 (B) tadpole 蝌蚪 (C) advent 來臨 (D) crisis 危機

中譯 金融危機始於美國，且橫掃全球，更佳證明了，我們誰都逃不過。102導遊

解析 financial crisis 金融危機。

13. Increasing tourism infrastructure to meet domestic and international demands has raised concerns about the impact on Taiwan's natural environment.

(A) impact 影響 (B) input 投入 (C) itinerary 旅程 (D) identity 身分

中譯 增加旅遊業的公共建設來滿足國內外的需求，對於台灣的天然環境而言已經有所影響。102導遊

解析 infrastructure 公共建設；impact 影響。

14. A bill to legalize gay marriage in Washington State has won final legislative approval and taken effect starting 2012.

(A) approval 贊同 (B) rejection 拒絕 (C) veto 否決 (D) admission 承認

中譯 華盛頓州同性婚姻合法的法案已經通過了最後立法同意，並於2012年生效。102導遊

解析 bill在此為法案。由taken effect可推知答案為approval。

15. When visiting Alishan, one of the most popular tourist destinations in Taiwan, it's worth spending a few days to learn about the indigenous people living in mountain villages and take in the marvelous scenery.

(A) prick on 刺上
(B) take in 欣賞、參觀
(C) put off 推遲
(D) pick up 撿起

中譯 當去最受歡迎的台灣景點——阿里山旅遊時，很值得花幾天去學習原住民的高山生活方式，和欣賞絕美風光。102導遊

解析 take in 欣賞、參觀；indigenous 本地的；marvelous scenery 絕美風光。

16. At the annual food festival, you can a sample wide variety of delicacies.

(A) sample 品嚐 (B) deliver 運送 (C) cater 承辦宴席 (D) reduce 減少

中譯 在一年一度的美食節，你可以品嚐各類佳餚。101導遊

解析 由food festival與delicacies得知，為sample 品嚐。此處的sample也可以用taste 品嚐來替換。delicacy 美味、佳餚。

17. On my flight to Tokyo, I asked a flight attendant to bring me an extra pillow.

(A) clerk 店員
(B) employer 雇主
(C) chauffeur 汽車司機
(D) attendant 空服員

中譯 在前往東京的班機，我要求空服員給我額外的枕頭。101導遊

解析 飛機上常見的人員為flight attendant 空服員；cabin crew 機組人員；captain 機長。另外，stewardess為空姐，steward則為空少。此處由flight to Tokyo可猜出答案為attendant 空服員。

18. Cloud Gate, an internationally renowned dance group from Taiwan, demonstrated that the quality of modern dance in Asia could be comparable to that of modern dance in Europe and North America.

(A) refunded 退還 (B) reflected 反映 (C) retained 保留 (D) renowned 有名

中譯 雲門，來自台灣的國際知名舞蹈團體，證明亞洲現代舞水準可和歐洲以及北美的現代舞媲美。101導遊

解析 renowned也可以用famous替換，此處由comparable to that of modern dance in Europe and North America可知為internationally renowned 國際上知名的。demonstrate 論證、證明。

19. The highlight of our trip to Southern Taiwan was A Taste of Tainan where we had a lot of delicious food.

(A) gourmet 美食家 (B) highlight 亮點
(C) monument 紀念碑 (D) recognition 承認

中譯 南台灣之旅的亮點就是台南小吃，我們在那裡吃了很多美食。101導遊

解析 由we had a lot of delicious food可推知，是此趟旅程的highlight 亮點。

20. Bopiliao, located in Wanhua District, Taipei, and serving as the setting for the film, Monga, is a popular tourist spot.

(A) selected 選擇 (B) featured 以……為特色
(C) located 位於 (D) directed 指揮

中譯 剝皮寮位於台北萬華區，曾是電影《艋舺》拍片的場景，是個受歡迎的觀光景點。101導遊

解析 由in Wanhua District即可推知為located 位於。tourist spots、tourist attractions為觀光景點。

21. The man at the passport control did not seem to like the photo in my passport, but in the end he let me through.

(A) station 車站 (B) custom 風俗 (C) security 安全 (D) control 管理

中譯 在護照審查管理處的人似乎不喜歡我的護照照片，但最後還是讓我通過了。101導遊

解析 此處可能誤選為custom 風俗，但海關為customs（有加s），故passport control才為正解。

22. Thanks to India's economic prosperity and the booming growth of its airline industry, more Indians are flying today than ever before.

(A) prosperity 繁榮 (B) souvenir 紀念品
(C) decline 衰退 (D) evidence 證據

中譯 歸功於印度的經濟繁榮，以及該國航空業的成長，如今有更多印度人搭飛機。 101導遊

解析 由the booming growth 蓬勃的成長，可推知prosperity 繁榮。I wish you all prosperity.則是「我祝你萬事如意」的意思。booming 景氣好的；growth 成長。

23. The tour guide is a courteous man; he is very polite and always speaks in a kind manner.

(A) careless 粗心的 (B) persistent 堅持不懈的

(C) courteous 禮貌的 (D) environmental 環境的

中譯 導遊是一個有教養的男生，他非常有禮貌，談吐也得宜。 101導遊

解析 courteous、well-mannered、polite都有「禮貌」的意思，而沒禮貌則為discourteous、ill-mannered、impolite。manner 態度、禮貌。

24. This restaurant features authentic Northern Italian dishes that reflect the true flavors of Italy.

(A) disposable 可丟棄的 (B) confident 有信心的

(C) authentic 道地的 (D) dimensional 尺寸的

中譯 這間餐廳的特色為反映義大利口味的道地北義大利菜。 101導遊

解析 由reflect the true flavors of Italy可知，是非常authentic 道地的。reflect 反射、反映，此作反映。

25. With crystal clear water, emerald green mountains and various outdoor activities to offer, it's not surprising that Sun Moon Lake is one of the most visited spots in Taiwan.

(A) identified 被識別的 (B) apparent 明顯的

(C) grateful 感恩的 (D) surprising 驚訝的

中譯 有著清澈的水、翠綠的山脈，以及多種戶外活動可選，日月潭是台灣遊客最多的景點之一並不讓人驚訝。 101導遊

解析 spot 場所、地點。

26. Taiwan is well known for its mountain scenic spots and urban landmarks such as the National Palace Museum and the Taipei 101 skyscraper.

(A) scenic 風景的 (B) neutral 中立的

(C) vacant 空的 (D) feasible 行得通的

中譯 台灣以其高山風景景點聞名，以及城市的地標，像是故宮博物院和台北101摩天大樓。101導遊

解析 scenic spots 風景景點，tourist spots、tourist attractions 觀光景點，此兩處景點經常出現於考題中。scenary則為風景（名詞）。well known、famous都是有名的意思，亦為常考單字。urban 城市的；rustic則是鄉下的。

27. Night markets in Taiwan have become popular tourist destinations. They are great places to shop for bargains and eat typical Taiwanese food.

(A) tropical 熱帶的　(B) popular 受歡迎的
(C) edible 可食用的　(D) responsible 負責任的

中譯 台灣的夜市已經成為受歡迎的觀光景點。他們是討價還價和吃傳統台灣料理的好地方。101導遊

解析 觀光景點的各類用法請務必牢記：tourist destinations、tourist spots、tourist attractions。destination 目的地。

28. Taroko National Park features high mountains and steep canyons. Many of its peaks tower above 3,000 meters in elevation.

(A) lacks 缺少　(B) features 以……為特色
(C) excludes 不包含　(D) disregards 不理會

中譯 太魯閣國家公園以高山和陡峭的峽谷為特色。許多高峰海拔超過3,000公尺。101導遊

解析 feature為重點單字，當動詞時，feature為「以……為特色」，如考題The zoo features more than 1,000 animals in their natural habitats.；當名詞時，feature為「特色」，如Her eyes are her best feature. 她的雙眼是她最大的特色。elevation 高度、海拔、提高，此作海拔。

29. To maintain health and fitness, we need proper diet and exercise.

(A) maintain 維持　(B) apply 申請　(C) retire 退休　(D) contain 包含

中譯 為了維持健康和體態，我們需要適量的節食和運動。101導遊

解析 此處的maintain 維持也可替換成keep 保持。

30. Jennifer is fluent in several languages other than her mother tongue English.

(A) fluent 流利的　(B) quiet 安靜的　(C) universal 宇宙的　(D) tall 高大的

中譯 珍妮佛除了自己的母語英文外，還精通數國語言。101導遊

解析 mother tongue = native language都為母語之意。

31. With its palaces, sculptured parks, concert halls, and museums, Vienna is a steeped city in cultures.

(A) chronic 長期的 (B) elite 精英

(C) provincial 省份的 (D) steeped 充滿的

中譯 有皇宮、用雕刻裝飾的公園、音樂廳和博物館，維也納是一座充滿文化的城市。101導遊

解析 be steeped in 充滿著、沉浸於，如The castle is steeped in history. 這座城堡充滿了歷史。

32. The oldest of all the main Hawaiian islands, Kauai is known for its secluded beaches, scenic waterfalls, and jungle hikes.

(A) due 由於 (B) known 知名的 (C) neutral 中立的 (D) ripe 成熟的

中譯 身為夏威夷群島最古老的島嶼，考艾島以隱密性的海灘、美景瀑布與叢林健走聞名。101導遊

解析 known for = famous for = well know for都為某事物「知名」之意。secluded 隱蔽的、僻靜的。

33. Please check your ticket and make sure that you are sitting in the correct seat.

(A) make sure 確定 (B) be aware of 意識到

(C) find out 發現 (D) pay attention 專心

中譯 請檢查你的票並確認你坐在正確的座位上。100導遊

解析 make sure 確定。

34. When you arrive at the airport, the first thing you do is go to the check-in desk.

(A) the departure lounge 候機室

(B) the check-in desk 辦理登機手續的櫃台

(C) the arrival desk 入境櫃台

(D) the customs 海關

中譯 當你到達機場時，你要做的第一件事就是要去辦理登機手續的櫃台。100導遊

解析 the check-in desk 辦理登機手續的櫃台。

35. His one ambition in life was to go on safari to Kenya to photograph lions and tigers.

(A) safari 狩獵遠征　(B) voyage 航程
(C) ferry 渡船　(D) yacht 遊艇

中譯 他畢生的雄心之一就是到非洲肯亞狩獵遠征，拍獅子和老虎。100導遊

解析 由lions and tigers可知為safari。ambition 雄心、抱負。

36. The hiking route of the Shitoushan Trail is not steep and so is suitable for most people, including the elderly and young children.

(A) slick 光滑的　(B) smooth 平坦的　(C) steep 陡峭的　(D) steady 穩定的

中譯 獅頭山步道的健行路線不太陡峭，所以適合大多數的人，包含老人和小孩。100導遊

解析 由so is suitable for most people, including the elderly and young children.可知是不steep。

37. As a general rule, checked baggage such as golf clubs in golf bags, serfboards, baby strollers, and child car seats are not placed on a baggage carousel.

(A) carnival 嘉年華會　(B) carrier 搬運者
(C) claim 認領　(D) carousel 轉盤

中譯 一般來說，登機行李像是高爾夫球俱樂部的高爾夫球袋、衝浪板、嬰兒推車以及兒童汽車安全座椅不會被放在行李轉盤上。100導遊

解析 baggage carousel 行李轉盤。

38. Demographers study population growth or decline and things like urbanization, which means the movement of populations into cities.

(A) classification 分類　(B) normalization 正常化
(C) industrialization 工業化　(D) urbanization 都市化

中譯 人口統計學家研究人口的成長或是削減，以及像是都市化表示人口往城市移動。100導遊

解析 由populations into cities即可猜出答案urbanization 都市化，字根urban為都市。demographers 人口統計學家；decline 下降、減少。

39. Most taxi drivers in Kinmen prefer to ask for a flat fare rather than use the meter.

(A) flat 平坦的 (B) high 高的 (C) set 設定的 (D) deal 買賣

中譯 大部分金門的計程車司機喜歡比較喜歡固定車資計價而非跳表。100導遊

解析 固定車資的用法為flat fare，因為車資固定，故使用flat 平坦的。

40. An open-minded city, Taipei hosted Asia's first Gay Pride parade which has now become an annual autumn event.

(A) expanded 使擴張 (B) governed 管理

(C) hosted 主辦 (D) portrayed 描寫

中譯 身為一座心胸開放的都市，台北主辦亞洲第一屆同志遊行，並且成為每年於秋天所舉辦的活動。100導遊

解析 舉辦活動有兩個常見單字：①host 主辦（帶有主辦人的意思），例句：Rio will host the 2016 Summer Olympic Games. 里約將主辦2016年夏季奧運。②hold 舉行、舉辦，例句1：The Olympic Games are held every four years. 奧運每四年（被）舉辦一次。例句2：The first Taipei Lantern Festival was held in 1990. Due to the event's huge popularity, the festival has been expanded every year. 第一屆的台北燈籠節於1990年舉行。而因為這場活動受到極大的歡迎，活動一年比一年盛大。98導遊

41. Middle-aged smokers are far more likely than nonsmokers to develop dementia later in life, and heavy smokers are at more than double the risk, according to a new study.

(A) deflect 偏斜 (B) demote 使降級

(C) deliberate 仔細考慮 (D) develop 發展

中譯 根據一項新的研究，中年吸菸的人比不吸菸的人在往後的日子裡更容易得到失智症，而有菸癮的人有超過2倍以上的風險。100導遊

解析 develop a new symptom 出現新症狀。Fresh air and exercise develop healthy bodies. 新鮮空氣和運動能使身體健康。

42. Earth is unique in the universe for its abundance of water, amounting to 70 percent of its surface.

(A) benevolence 善行 (B) abundance 充裕

(C) redundance 過多 (D) attendance 出席

中譯 地球在宇宙中很獨特因為有充沛的水，大約表面70%都是水。100導遊

解析 由70 percent of its surface可知為abundance 充裕，例句：The tree yields an abundance of fruit. 這樹結果甚多。unique 唯一的、獨一無二的。

43. Unlike other springs locations, Taian Hot Springs is relatively serene, with no more than six large-scale resorts in the area, so the place is not as congested as Wulai and Beitou.

(A) congested 擁擠的　(B) displaced 取代的
(C) isolated 孤立的　(D) populated 粒子數增加的

中譯 不像其他地區，泰安溫泉相對安靜，這區域的大型度假村不超過6個，所以不像烏來和北投一樣擁擠。100導遊

解析 由serene可知不擁擠。serene 寧靜的。

44. Many people consider Yangmingshan National Park a pleasant retreat from the bustle of the city.

(A) retreat 僻靜之處　(B) removal 遷居
(C) departure 出發　(D) adventure 冒險

中譯 許多人認為陽明山國家公園是個遠離城市喧囂的僻靜之處。100導遊

解析 由from the bustle of the city可知為retreat。bustle 鬧哄哄地忙亂。

45. The temple was really colorful. It had blue and red tiles all over it and there were statues of different gods on the walls and on the roof.

(A) states 說明　(B) status 身分　(C) statues 雕像　(D) stature 身高

中譯 寺廟非常的色彩繽紛。鋪滿藍色和紅色的磁磚，且在牆上以及屋頂上有許多不同的神明雕像。100導遊

解析 statues 雕像，如the statue of liberty 自由女神像。

46. Taiwan's premier said 2010 was a boom year for tourism in Taiwan and he attributed the success to the improvements in cross-strait relations.

(A) administered 管理　(B) advertised 做廣告
(C) acclaimed 喝彩　(D) attributed 歸因

中譯 台灣的行政院長說2010年是台灣旅遊業大幅成長的一年，他將此成功歸因於兩岸關係的改善。100導遊

解析 attribute sth. to 認為某事物是……的屬性、把某事物歸功於；cross-strait relations 兩岸關係。

47. Living near the airport, I am very much bothered by the noise of airplanes. I can not sleep well and often feel uneasy.

(A) marked 標記 (B) bothered 打擾

(C) expected 預期 (D) confused 困惑

中譯 住在機場附近，我深受噪音困擾。我不能睡好，而且常常感到不安。99導遊

解析 由I can not sleep well and often feel uneasy可知，深受bothered 打擾。Don't bother me! 別打擾我！uneasy 心神不安的、拘束的、不自在的。

48. Claire loves to buy exotic foods: vegetables and herbs from China, spices from India, olives from Greece, and cheeses from France.

(A) sea 海洋 (B) stingy 小氣的

(C) tranquil 鎮靜的 (D) exotic 異國風情的

中譯 克萊兒喜歡買異國風情的食物：來自中國的蔬菜和草藥、印度來的香料、希臘來的橄欖，以及法國來的起司。99導遊

解析 exotic 異國風情的；foreign則為國外的、陌生的；foreigner 外國人。由題目中提及的各個國家可知，答案為exotic 異國風情的。

49. As a result of the accident, Shirley was unconscious for three weeks before gradually recovered.

(A) unconscious 無意識的（不省人事的）

(B) prehistoric 史前的

(C) gorgeous 美麗的

(D) fortunate幸運的

中譯 這次意外的結果，雪麗在逐漸恢復之前昏迷了3個星期。99導遊

解析 相關單字有unconscious 無意識的；conscious 有意識的；subconscious 潛意識的。

50. To save money, buy just what you need and refrain from buying unnecessary stuff.

(A) invent 發明 (B) discard 拋棄 (C) save 節省 (D) exhaust 耗盡

中譯 為了省錢，只買你需要的東西，且克制不買不需要的東西。99導遊

解析 refrain from 避免，有忍住、抑制之意。unnecessary 不需要的；necessary 需要的。stuff 物品、東西。

51. With a complacent smile, Robert showed how happy he was when he won the swimming contest yesterday.

(A) fertile 富饒的　(B) historic 歷史的
(C) pollutant 汙染的　(D) complacent 滿足的

中譯 有著滿足的笑容，羅伯顯示出當他昨天贏了游泳比賽時有多開心。99導遊

解析 從題意可知是和開心有關的smile，故選complacent 滿足的，但若不懂第二句，光靠smile也能將其他選項刪除。

52. Since our economy has been improving recently, I hope that my boss will give me a big raise this year.

(A) conquest 克服　(B) consumption 消耗
(C) rise 上升　(D) raise 加薪

中譯 因為我們的經濟情況最近一直持續好轉，我希望我的老闆今年可以幫我大加薪。99導遊

解析 raise 加薪，例句： Since the economy is improving, many people are hoping for a raise in salary in the coming year. 既然經濟已經好轉，許多人希望明年能加薪。99領隊
salary 薪水；由economy has been improving 經濟情況持續好轉推知，是想要求a big raise 加薪。recently 最近。

53. Some soils are extremely rich in minerals and nutrients such as iron and copper.

(A) minerals 礦物質　(B) mermaids 美人魚
(C) miniatures 縮樣　(D) manuscripts 手稿

中譯 有些土壤富含礦物質以及營養素，像是鐵和銅。99導遊

解析 解題時若是不了解soils的意思，由iron 鐵可得知答案可能為minerals 礦物。

54. People who have a great sense of humor are often very popular, because they are usually intelligent, open-minded, and witty.

(A) frustration 挫折　(B) humor 幽默
(C) betrayal 背叛　(D) inferiority 劣質

中譯 非常有幽默感的人通常很受歡迎，因為他們通常是聰明、開放心胸以及機智的。99導遊

解析 有這樣特質的人are often very popular 通常很受歡迎，可得知是sense of humor 幽默感。open-minded 心胸寬的、無先入為主之見的。

55. A humble person is usually welcomed by everyone, because he never irritates people.

(A) selfish 自私的　(B) naughty 調皮的
(C) pessimistic 悲觀的　(D) humble 謙虛的

中譯 一個謙虛的人通常受到每個人的歡迎，因為這樣的人從不激怒其他人。99導遊

解析 humble 謙虛的；down-to-earth 樸實的；irritate 使惱怒、使煩躁。

56. For centuries, artists, historians, and tourists have been fascinated by Mona Lisa's enigmatic smile.

(A) ignored 忽視　(B) characterized 特徵
(C) fascinated 迷倒　(D) embraced 擁抱

中譯 數個世紀以來，藝術家、歷史學家，以及觀光客都對蒙娜麗莎謎樣般的微笑深深著迷。99導遊

解析 fascinate 使神魂顛倒；fascinated 被迷倒的；fascinating 令人目眩神迷的。enigmatic 謎樣的；enigma 謎。

57. Fireworks and firecrackers are often used in Chinese communities to symbolize greeting good fortunes and scaring away evils.

(A) sign 記號　(B) symbolize 象徵
(C) identify 確認　(D) underline 強調

中譯 煙火和鞭炮常用於華人社會中，來象徵迎接好運以及將晦氣嚇跑。99導遊

解析 symbol 符號；symbolize 象徵；greet 打招呼；scare away 將某事嚇跑。

58. A boarding pass is a necessary document for the passenger to get on the airplane.

(A) boarding pass 登機證　(B) passport 護照
(C) identification card 身分證　(D) visa 簽證

中譯 登機證是乘客登機的必要文件。99導遊

解析 get on / get off airplane 上 / 下飛機；take off / land 起飛 / 降落。

59. Besides participating in local cultural activities, people who desire to explore the ecology of Kenting can observe plenty of wildlife and plants.

(A) observe 觀察　(B) pick up 撿起　(C) object 反對　(D) plan 計畫

中譯 除了參與當地的文化活動外，想在墾丁探訪生態環境的人也可以觀察豐富的野生動物與植物。99導遊

解析 由desire to explore the ecology of Kenting 想探訪墾丁的生態環境，可得知observe plenty of wildlife and plants 觀察豐富的野生動物與植物。

60. When people travel to popular destinations during peak seasons, it is necessary to reserve accommodations before the trip.

(A) generation 世代　(B) accommodations 住宿
(C) identification 身分　(D) confirmation 確認

中譯 當人們於旺季到熱門觀光景點旅遊時，一定要在旅途前先預約住宿。99導遊

解析 reserve accommodations 預約住宿；peak seasons 旺季。

61. If you want to find the cheapest airplane ticket, bargains can usually be found through the Internet.

(A) bargains 特價商品、便宜貨　(B) destinations 目的地
(C) reservations 預定　(D) itinerary 旅程

中譯 如果你想要找最便宜的機票，通常可以在網路上找到特價商品。99導遊

解析 A bargain is a bargain. 說話要算話。bargain-hunting 四處覓購便宜貨。

62. Please examine your luggage carefully before leaving. At the security counter, every item in the luggage has to go through inspection.

(A) relation 關係　(B) invention 發明
(C) inspection 檢查　(D) observation 觀察

中譯 在出發前請仔細檢查你的行李。在安檢櫃台時，行李內的每一項物品都會被檢查。99導遊

解析 examine以及inspect都為檢查之意，但inspect更有「權力」，因此這裡的security counter使用 inspect。

63. The flight is scheduled to depart at eleven o'clock tomorrow. You will have to get to the airport two hours before the takeoff.

(A) land 著陸、抵達　(B) depart 起飛
(C) cancel 取消　(D) examine 檢驗

中譯 班機預定於明天11點起飛。你必須在出發前2個小時抵達機場。99導遊

解析 depart、take off 起飛；land 著陸、抵達。

64. Formed in 1991 and having toured internationally in Europe and Asia, the Formosa Aboriginal Dance Troupe is a group that performs Taiwanese folk music.

(A) performs 表演 (B) results 結果 (C) achieves 實現 (D) occurs 發生

中譯 成立於1991年，也曾於歐洲以及亞洲國際巡迴表演過，福爾摩沙原住民舞蹈團是演奏台灣民俗音樂的團體。98導遊

解析 Form當動詞時為成立，當名詞時為表格，常見fill out the form 填妥表格；此處的perform亦可替換為play。

"Good evening, ladies and gentlemen. This is the pre-boarding announcement for flight 67B to Vancouver. We are now inviting those passengers with small children, and any passenger requiring special assistance, to begin boarding at this time. Please have your boarding pass and identification ready. Regular boarding will begin in approximately ten minutes. Thank you."

中譯 「大家晚安，各位先生女士們。這是飛往溫哥華的67B班機的登機前廣播。我們現在先請帶小孩、或是需要特別協助的旅客，準備開始登機。請準備好您的登機證以及身分證件。一般旅客約將於10分鐘內開始登機。謝謝。」98導遊

65. (A) forecast 預報 (B) announcement 宣布
(C) denouncement 譴責 (D) definition 定義

解析 在機場候機的旅客，通常需要注意Pay attention to pre-boarding announcement。若某班機已開始登機，則會廣播flight 67B is boarding，意為已在登機中，請旅客盡速前往某號登機門（Gate No. X）。

66. (A) depending 根據 (B) digesting 消化
(C) requiring 需要 (D) including 包含

解析 航空公司所提供的special assistance，通常的服務對象為Passengers with visual impairment / hearing impairment / wheelchairs 視障 / 聽障 / 行動不便的旅客。此題中的require亦可替換為need。

67. (A) approximately 大約 (B) separately 分開
(C) indirectly 間接 (D) indefinitely 無限期

Unlike bird watching, which is often most successful in the very early morning or just before dusk, butterfly watching is best done between around 10：00 a.m. and 4：00 p.m.. Moreover, butterflies are more approachable than birds because they are less sensitive to sound. For these reasons, butterfly appreciation is perhaps a more available hobby than bird watching.

中譯 不同於賞鳥的時間通常最好為一大清早或是黃昏前，最好的賞蝶時間則是從早上十點到下午四點。此外，蝶類比鳥類更容易接近，因為他們對於聲音較不敏感。基於這些理由，賞蝶也許比賞鳥為更容易養成的習慣。98導遊

單字 before dusk 黃昏前　　appreciation 欣賞

68. (A) competent 能幹的　　(B) extinct 絕種的
(C) successful 成功的　　(D) diplomatic 外交的

解析 賞鳥的最佳時間，也就是最容易看到鳥群的時間，故選successful。

69. (A) approachable 接近的　　(B) edible 可食的
(C) unbearable 不可忍受的　　(D) affordable 可負擔的

解析 由題意可知less sensitive to sound 對於聲音較不敏感，因此比較好接近。

70. (A) portable 可攜帶的　　(B) curious 好奇的
(C) available 可行的　　(D) moral 道德的

解析 正因蝶類對聲音比較不敏感，故更容易賞蝶，更為available 可行。

What kind of job description would fit your idea of "the best job in the world"? Tourism Queensland (TQ) lately launched a talent hunt as a part of massive tourism campaign worldwide.

中譯 什麼樣的工作是你心目中「世界上最棒的工作」？昆士蘭旅遊局最近發起了一項大型的全世界旅遊徵才活動。

They are looking for a caretaker to live on Hamilton Island of the Great Barrier Reef, whose major responsibility is to be their spokesperson on the island. The contract starts from this July to January next year, and the salary for the six months is AU$150,000, around NT$3.38million.

中譯 他們尋找一位臨時島主，要住在大堡礁的漢彌敦島上，主要責任為擔任該島的代言人。合約始於今年7月到明年1月，這半年的薪水為15萬澳幣，相當於新台幣338萬元。

單字 spokesperson 代言人　　contract 合約

"The caretaker is required to do some basic chores, such as cleaning the pool, feeding over 1,500 species of fish, and sending out the mails by plane," said Kimberly Chien, Marketing Manager of TQ. "The major task is to explore islands in Barrier Reef and keep updating an online journal with photos to share a caretaker's life with the world." The position is open to anyone who is over 18, a good swimmer and communicator.

中譯 「島主必須做一些例行工作，好比清理游泳池、餵1500種以上的魚、利用飛機寄信等等」，昆士蘭旅遊局的行銷經理金柏莉．簡表示，「主要的工作是要探索大堡礁的島嶼，並用照片更新線上日誌，和全世界分享島主的日常生活」。只要年齡18歲以上、擅長游泳、善於溝通的人都可應徵這個工作。

單字 chores 家庭雜務
task 工作

Applicants are required to make a one-minute video explaining why he or she is the best candidate for the job. Tourism Queensland will organize a group of referees to select 11 candidates, including one from an internet voting which will be held in March. The 11 candidates will then be invited to Hamilton Island for the final interview; only one of them will win the position to do "the best job in the world."

中譯 應徵者必須拍攝一分鐘的影片，解釋為什麼自己是最合適的人選。昆士蘭旅遊局會成立裁判團，先選出11名參賽者，包含3月份從網路上票選的一位。11位參賽者將被邀請到漢彌敦島上參加複賽，只有其中的一位會贏得「這世界上最棒的工作」。98導遊

單字 candidate 候選人

71. According to the passage, what is the purpose for the state government of Queensland, Australia, to offer people a job like this?

(A) To make money. 為了賺錢。

(B) To seek foreign aid. 為了尋求國外協助。

(C) To promote tourism. 為了推廣旅遊。

(D) To provide entertainment. 為了提供娛樂。

中譯 根據本文，澳洲昆士蘭政府為何要提供像這樣的工作機會？

解析 "The major task is to explore islands in Barrier Reef and keep updating an online journal with photos to share a caretaker's life with the world." 由此段得知主要是為了推廣旅遊。

72. Which of the following job requirements is NOT mentioned in the passage?

(A) Over 18 years old. 超過十八歲。

(B) A good swimmer. 游泳好手。

(C) A good communicator. 好的溝通者。

(D) A native English speaker. 英語母語人士。

中譯 以下哪個工作的必要條件未於本文中提及??

解析 The position is open to anyone who is over 18, a good swimmer and communicator. 此段文章中不含A native English speaker。

73. According to the passage, which of the following is on the job description for this position?

(A) To host a TV talk show. 主持電視節目。

(B) To meet with international leaders. 與各國領袖見面。

(C) To let people know what life is like on the island. 讓大家知道島上的生活情形。

(D) To produce a formal documentary about the island. 拍攝島上的紀錄片。

中譯 根據本文,以下哪一項工作描述符合此職位?

解析 由此段"The major task is to explore islands in Barrier Reef and keep updating an online journal with photos to share a caretaker's life with the world.",可得知答案。

74. According to the passage, what is the application procedure for this job?

(A) To provide an overseas passport. 提供外國護照。

(B) To make a self-introduction video. 製作自我介紹的影片。

(C) To call and make a reservation for an interview. 打電話預約面試。

(D) To submit a completed application form by post. 郵寄出完整的申請表格。

中譯 根據本文,哪一項是此工作的申請流程?

解析 由此段Applicants are required to make a one-minute video explaining why he or she is the best candidate for the job.,可得知答案。

75. According to the passage, which of the following is true?

(A) It is a permanent job.

這是一份永久的工作。

(B) The job begins this coming July.

工作即將從七月開始。

(C) Twelve candidates will be selected for the final interview.

共有十二位候選人可能晉級到決賽。

(D) The winner will be decided by an internet voting.

由網路投票來選出優勝者。

中譯 根據本文，以下哪項屬實？

解析 由此段The contract starts from this July to January next year，可得知答案。

While on vacation, not everyone likes staying at nice hotels, visiting museums, and shopping at department stores. Some would rather jump out of an airplane, speed down a river, or stay in a traditional village. They are part of a growing number of people who enjoy adventure tourism. It is a type of travel for people looking to get more out of their vacations.

中譯 度假時，不是每個人都喜歡待在舒適的旅館、參觀博物館以及逛百貨公司。有些人寧願從飛機上跳傘、泛舟、或是待在傳統的部落中。他們是一群人數正在成長的生態探險旅遊愛好者。這是一種讓人可在假期中得到更多的旅遊模式。

With the Internet, it is easier than ever to set up an adventure tour. People can plan trips themselves, or they can find a suitable tour company online. Some popular countries to visit are Costa Rica, India, New Zealand, and Botswana. Their natural settings make them perfect for outdoor activities like hiking and diving. Rich in wildlife, they are also great for bird watching and safaris. Learning about the local history and culture is also popular with adventure travelers. In Peru, people love visiting the ruins of Machu Picchu. And, travelers in Tanzania enjoy meeting local tribes. In some countries, it is even possible to live and work in a village during a vacation. While building houses and helping research teams, travelers can enjoy local food and learn about the culture.

中譯 有了網路，比以前更容易安排一趟冒險旅程。人們可以自己安排旅程，或是他們可以在網路上找一間適合的旅行社。有些國家很受歡迎，像是哥斯大黎加、印度、紐西蘭，以及波札那。他們的自然環境非常適合戶外活動，像是健行和潛水。豐富的野生動物，也讓他們非常適合賞鳥和狩獵。學習當地的歷史以及文化也很受探險旅遊者的喜愛。在祕魯，人們喜歡去參觀馬丘比丘遺跡。在坦尚尼亞的旅行者喜歡拜訪當地部落。有些國家，甚至可以在村莊內生活或是打工度假。當建造房子和幫助研究團隊的時候，旅行者可以品嚐當地食物和學習當地文化。

Besides being a lot of fun, these exiting trips mean big money for local economies. Tourism is already the world's largest industry, worth some $ 3 trillion. Of that, adventure tourism makes up about 20% of the market. That number is growing, as more people plan exciting vacations in their own countries and abroad.

中譯 除了會有很多樂趣外，這些刺激的旅程對當地經濟也有不小助益。觀光業已經是世界上最大的產業，價值約三兆美元。其中探險旅遊占了市場的百分之二十。數字仍在成長中，越來越多人計劃在自己的國家或是國外來趟刺激的假期。 99導遊

76. What can we infer about adventure tourists from the passage?

(A) They like safe and comfortable vacations. 他們喜歡舒適安全的假期。

(B) They have little interest in culture. 他們對文化不感興趣。

(C) They enjoy trips that are exciting. 他們喜歡刺激的行程。

(D) They rarely play on sports teams. 他們很少玩團體運動。

中譯 我們可以從本文推論出關於探險旅遊者的哪項資訊？

解析 由Some would rather jump out of an airplane, speed down a river, or stay in a traditional village.可知。

77. Where would you go to visit Machu Picchu?

(A) Tanzania 坦尚尼亞 (B) Europe 歐洲

(C) Peru 祕魯 (D) The Himalayas 喜馬拉雅山

中譯 你會去哪裡參觀馬丘比丘？

解析 由In Peru, people love visiting the ruins of Machu Picchu.可知。

78. What is NOT a reason why people enjoy traveling to New Zealand?

(A) Tours there are cheaper than in other places.那裡的行程比其他地方便宜。

(B) It is a great place for nature lovers. 對愛好大自然的人來說是很棒的地方。

(C) One could easily set up a bird watching trip. 很容易安排賞鳥的行程。

(D) There are many outdoor activities. 有很多戶外活動。

中譯 以下哪項理由不是人們喜歡去紐西蘭旅遊的原因？

解析 由Their natural settings make them perfect for outdoor activities like hiking and diving. Rich in wildlife, they are also great for bird watching and safaris. Learning about the local history and culture is also popular with adventure travelers.可知。

79. What does the word rich in paragraph 2 mean?

(A) wealthy 有錢的

(B) plentiful 豐富的

(C) funny 好笑的

(D) heavy 沉重的

中譯 第二段的rich是什麼意思？

解析 由Rich in wildlife, they are also great for bird watching and safaris可知。

80. What does the passage suggest about the tourism industry?

(A) It may soon be worth $3 trillion. 很快會價值3兆美元。

(B) Adventure tourism brings in the most money. 探險旅遊業帶來最多收益。

(C) Most of the industry is facing hard times. 大部分的產業面臨危機。

(D) It is important to local economies.對當地的經濟很重要。

中譯 本文對於旅遊業有怎樣的建議？

解析 由These exiting trips mean big money for local economies.可知。

如何準備英文導遊口試

如何準備英文導遊口試？

一般考生聽到英文口試，第一個反應通常都會先冒冷汗、倒退三步，但若從近年的口試錄取率來説（102年導遊口試參加人數1470人，通過人數1233人，錄取率高達83%），其實不需太過擔心。如果英文筆試可以及格，口試只要稍加準備，及格絕對非難事！

口試資格

外語導遊人員以筆試成績滿60分為錄取標準，也就是説筆試的各科平均成績要先滿60分才會有口試的資格，而口試成績則以兩位口試委員評分總和之平均成績計算。筆試成績占總成績75%，口試成績占25%，合併計算後為考試總成績。

口試題數與時間

每年口試題目與應考時間略有不同，不過大約都是3-5題，時間約10分鐘左右（100年為3題，時間約8-10分；101年為4題，時間10-12分）。

評分標準

外語個別口試之評分項目及配分如下：

外語表達能力60分，語音與語調20分，才識、見解、氣度20分。

考題方向

每年主管機關所公布的考題範圍稍有差異，但準備方向都是一樣的，如102年口試問題範圍為「自我介紹」、「本國文化與國情」、「風景、節慶與美食」。英文導遊口試的出題範圍，其實可以簡單歸納成一句話，就是「用英文介紹自己、介紹台灣」。但該如何介紹台灣？網路上有非常多的資源，簡單介紹如下。

推薦網站

　　這裡先列了最相關的7個網站，但其實和台灣旅遊相關的英文網站，除了台灣官方的觀光網站（如觀光局、國家公園），也有外國人經常造訪的旅遊網站（在首頁上打上Taiwan就能搜尋出所有台灣相關的資料）、以及國內英文新聞網站，建議每一個網站都可以點進去瀏覽。除此之外，有沒有最簡單、最不費力的英文導遊口試的準備方法？那就是每天逛一個相關網站，把自己當成是外國遊客，用英文看看哪裡好玩，還可以順便規劃一下自己週休二日的旅遊景點，在不知不覺中，就能累積關於台灣的知識以及英文能力，真是一舉數得！

❁ 交通部觀光局（英文版）

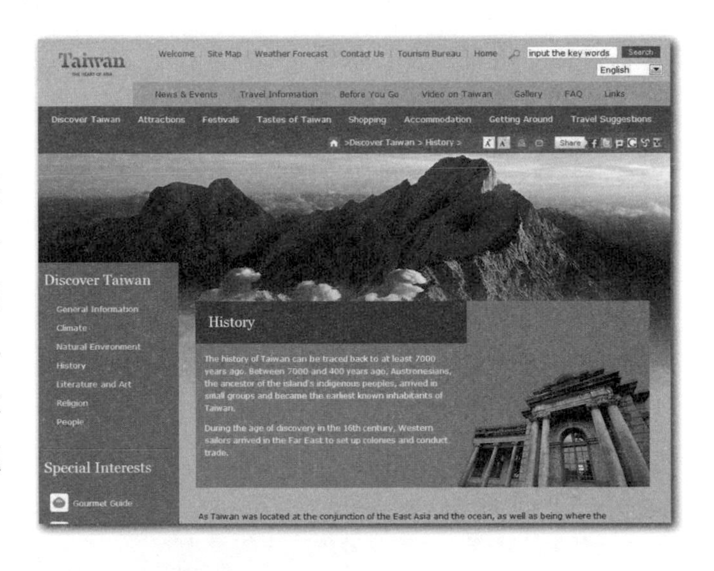

http://eng.taiwan.net.tw/

除了旅遊資訊之外，一定要看Discover Taiwan這個分類的資訊，裡頭包含General Information / Climate / History / People 等台灣的基本介紹，對於國情概況這類的題目，非常有幫助！

❁ 台北旅遊網

http://www.taipeitravel.net/en/

很用心製作的網站，特別推薦考生點Tourist Guide分類當中的Tourist Audio Guide（遊客導覽講解），這些導覽知名景點的英文解說，對於想要加強口說的考生而言，千萬不能錯過。

❁ 新北市觀光旅遊網

http://tour.ntpc.gov.tw/tom/lang_en/index.aspx

資訊雖然沒有台北旅遊網豐富，但比較特別的是分類中多了「Tour theme」（主題旅遊），可分成Old Street Tour（老街旅遊）、Rail Tour（鐵道旅遊）等。

★補充：除了台北旅遊之外，其他縣市的相關英文旅遊資源該怎麼找？最快的方法為到該縣市的文化局官網，只要點選English就能找到許多當地文化、旅遊等的英文資料。

❁ 台灣國家公園

http://np.cpami.gov.tw/english/index.php

這是最能詳細了解台灣自然風光的英文旅遊網站，若覺得自然資源等的英文太難，至少也要了解台灣北中南有哪些國家公園！特別推薦Photo Gallery裡國家公園的簡單解說以及圖說。

❋ 中國英文郵報

http://www.chinapost.com.tw/travel/

特別推薦Travel Topics，裡面分成Northern Taiwan / Central Taiwan / Southern Taiwan / Eastern Taiwan / Taiwan Offshore Islands，可以依照自己的所在地點選，用英文了解自己的家鄉。

❋ Lonely Planet 寂寞星球旅遊書出版社

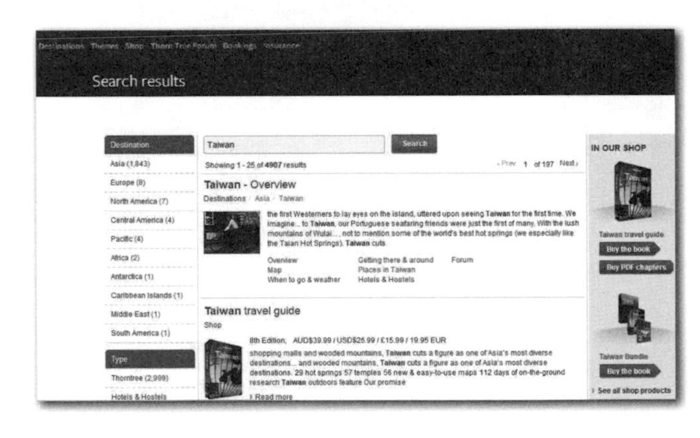

http://www.lonelyplanet.com

Lonely Planet為全球最大的旅遊書出版社，官網也有相當豐富的內容，只要在搜尋欄上打上Taiwan，即能看到許多國外作者撰寫介紹台灣的文章，相當生動有趣。

❋ 台灣光華雜誌

http://www.sinorama.com.tw/en/index.php

以英文報導台灣的本土萬象，正因為有各個面向的台灣報導，所以對於增進口試題目的廣度非常有幫助。此外，網站內的字彙通（Vocab notebook）還有英文發音，對要練習發音的考生而言，絕對不能錯過。

更多網站說明與連結，請上https://www.facebook.com/tourguideEnglish

MEMO

國家圖書館出版品預行編目資料

領隊導遊英文一本搞定！ / 陳若慈著
--初版--臺北市：瑞蘭國際, 2014.01
512面；19 x 26公分（專業證照系列；02）
ISBN：978-986-5953-59-1（平裝）
1.英語 2.讀本

805.18 102026647

專業證照系列 02

史上最強歸類整理

領隊導遊英文一本搞定！

作者｜陳若慈・責任編輯｜葉仲芸・校對｜陳若慈、葉仲芸、王愿琦

封面、版型設計｜余佳憓・內文排版｜余佳憓・印務｜王彥萍

董事長｜張暖彗・社長兼總編輯｜王愿琦・副總編輯｜呂依臻
主編｜王彥萍、葉仲芸・編輯｜陳秋汝・美術編輯｜余佳憓
業務部主任｜楊米琪・業務部助理｜林湲洵

出版社｜瑞蘭國際有限公司・地址｜台北市大安區安和路一段104號7樓之1
電話｜(02)2700-4625・傳真｜(02)2700-4622・訂購專線｜(02)2700-4625
劃撥帳號｜19914152 瑞蘭國際有限公司・瑞蘭網路書城｜www.genki-japan.com.tw

總經銷｜聯合發行股份有限公司・電話｜(02)2917-8022、2917-8042
傳真｜(02)2915-6275、2915-7212・印刷｜宗祐印刷有限公司
出版日期｜2014年01月初版1刷・定價｜580元・ISBN｜978-986-5953-59-1

瑞蘭國際

瑞蘭國際

瑞蘭國際

瑞蘭國際